Silver Apples of the Moon

REBECCA JAMES

First published in 2013 by Rebecca James

James, Rebecca.
Silver Apples of the Moon/Rebecca James
Library of Congress Cataloging-in-Publication Data
Registration Number: TXu 1-843-834

Library of Congress Control Number: 2013937888
Rebecca James
Charlottesville, VA

ISBN-13: 9780615795218 (Rebecca James)
ISBN-10: 0615795218

The Song of Wandering Aengus

I went out to the hazel wood, because a fire was in my head,
And cut and peeled a hazel wand, and hooked a berry to a thread;
And when white moths were on the wing, and moth-like stars were flickering out,
I dropped the berry in a stream and caught a little silver trout.

When I had laid it on the floor I went to blow the fire aflame,
But something rustled on the floor, and some one called me by my name:
It had become a glimmering girl with apple blossom in her hair
Who called me by my name and ran and faded through the brightening air.

Though I am old with wandering through hollow lands and hilly lands,
I will find out where she has gone, and kiss her lips and take her hands;
And walk among long dappled grass, and pluck till time and times are done
The silver apples of the moon, the golden apples of the sun.

W.B. YEATS

The End Makes All

PROLOGUE

Worthington, Pennsylvania,
Belvoir, 1997

*W*ho do we know in Australia, Mom?"

Angela Worthington had been so riveted to the package she held, she hadn't heard her daughter rustle over. Ever since Peyton's engagement had been announced, there'd been nearly daily deliveries of wedding gifts; but this was different. Worthington Steel documents Angela had assumed when she first glimpsed the DHL envelope tucked under the housekeeper's arm. "This just came for Peyton," Margaret Boyle said handing it to her. It was then that she saw the postmark and familiar handwriting.

Angela had been overjoyed by the prospect of her daughter's wedding. As soon as the engagement was announced, she flew to New York to help Peyton pick out her dress. They started out at Bergdorf's and Saks, but nothing caught their fancy. So Angela suggested they check out a couple of small boutiques on Madison Avenue. It was here at the end of a long day that Peyton tried on the dress both women instantly knew was The One. "Oh Mom," Peyton said, spinning around to embrace her mother, "I just love it!"

After the final fitting, the dress was sent to Belvoir where it was removed from an enormous tissue paper-lined box and hung in a guest room, with two chairs underneath to support the train.

This morning, when Angela had finally buttoned Peyton into the dress, she watched her daughter make her way over to the mirror, accompanied by the swishing of heavy satin. She saw Peyton's face light up at her reflection. A woman now, Peyton was beautiful to look at with regular features—oval face, full lips, large almond-shaped eyes—and character to match. Angela's heart swelled with pride. Meeting her mother's gaze in the mirror, Peyton cried out, "Now, I really feel like a bride," a rush of warmth coloring her cheeks.

"I can't wait to see Gus's face when he sees you coming down the aisle, Sweetie." Angela said, blinking back tears. She was crazy about

Gus, finding him everything she could want in a son-in-law: a Rhodes scholar finalist, he possessed intellect, but also charm and kindness in abundance. Most important, he adored Peyton.

It had been a tough few years and there was a lingering patina of sadness in spite of the joyousness of the occasion. Angela felt it acutely this morning with the photographer here to take the formal wedding portraits of Peyton dressed as the bride she would soon be: hair up-swept in a French twist, the Worthington rose-point veil crowning her head.

They began with pictures in the foyer where the photographer snapped Peyton standing on the gleaming black and white marble floor. He next positioned the bride-to-be on the graceful curving stair-case, first at the bottom, then a third of the way up and finally at the top poised to throw the bouquet.

With the interior shots completed, they moved onto the terrace. It was a glorious spring day resonating with the bright warble of bird-song. Mowers droned in the distance as a small army of landscapers worked on the estate, their labor evident in the air heavy with the smell of newly cut grass. Shortly into the session outside, a large cloud moved in and the photographer called for a break.

It was then that Peyton had crossed the terrace to join her mother, sitting motionless as a statue, a parcel in her hands.

"Mom—are you okay?" Peyton prodded, placing a hand on her mother's shoulder. Angela started. "I asked who we know in Australia."

Angela had been studying the package. What kind of salvo was it? A reproach of sorts, lobbed from the past to further roil emotions with the big day nearly here? She handed it to Peyton. "Why don't you go ahead and see what it is?" she suggested gravely, watching Peyton's pristine hem brush damp bricks. She'd been so careful earlier, making sure drop cloths were spread around the terrace to protect the dress. Now, it didn't seem to matter.

"Are you sure you're all right?" Peyton pressed.

"I'm fine, Sweetheart," Angela stammered. Peyton studied her mother a moment longer before she returned her attention to the pack-age. Ripping it open, she withdrew a rectangular object wrapped in cream-colored silk. She unwound the soft fabric to expose an inner cocoon of rice paper tied up with faded ribbon. Angela looked on in rapt silence as her daughter's fingers pulled away the paper.

And, there it was, an elaborately tooled book. Slowly, Peyton turned it over, a puzzled look on her face. Angela read the title she already knew embossed in gold on the spine: *The Collected Poems of W.B. Yeats*. She was overcome with sudden dizziness. To anyone else the book was merely a handsome gift, but to Angela it represented a valuable treasure and—dare she think—a missive meant expressly for her.

A musty aroma of worn leather and old paper emanated from the volume when Peyton opened it. She stared spellbound for some time at the engraved bookplate within. It was as if she had happened upon some ancient relic she must now decipher. Despite being yellowed and spotted with age, it remained exquisitely beautiful. Gilded, intertwining bamboo fronds framed the spidery inscription written in violet ink: Villa Indochine. Tears filled Angela's eyes as a fountain of regret welled within her and her mind turned to that impossible place, and impossible love of long ago. An envelope fluttered to the ground. Peyton reached for it, withdrawing a single sheet of paper to read:

Dearest Peyton,

I had intended to give this precious keepsake I have carried with me through the years to your mother, "my glimmering girl." However, it now strikes me as fitting that on the occasion of your marriage I pass it your way—a lone, yet priceless, legacy, my dear child. My wish for you is that you and your beloved may forever "walk among long dappled grass and pluck till time and times are done the silver apples of the moon, the golden apples of the sun."

Your Anamchara from afar...

PART ONE

Ten Years Earlier 1987

CHAPTER ONE

T he traffic light turned red just as Angela Worthington's car crested Main Street. From this vantage point she could see the town spreading out before her, its rain-washed streets and rusticated stone buildings presenting a bleak vista to the horizon. Here, at the summit, engaged in a monolithic face-off on either side of the intersection stood the town's two most commanding structures: the library and city hall. Their grandeur seemed so at odds with the drab streetscape that confronted her now, accentuating the sense of melancholy she always felt upon returning home from a trip.

To a stranger, Angela Worthington appeared to have it all. Possessed of beauty and wealth, her life seemed picture perfect. She had a devoted husband, a bright and pretty daughter, and a wide circle of friends. Yet, there was a quality about her that suggested she'd weathered a great sorrow—a cast of wistfulness to her lovely eyes a discerning visitor might observe that belied her gilded existence.

It had been a long drive from New York. Her thoughts kept returning to her daughter and their latest quarrel. It seemed they were always fighting these days. Angela sighed. It was hard to reconcile the strident young woman Peyton had become with the little girl Angela kept in her heart. The light turned green. Angela stepped on the gas and the powerful car glided down the hill.

On this chilly February afternoon, she was glad for its indulgent comfort—the soft leather, the sheen of bird's eye maple, the quiet of the airtight capsule. A birthday present from her husband, it cheered her recalling its presentation, how Henry, always one to make gift giving an occasion, had handed her a card attached to a string when she descended the stairs that morning. And how she had moved through Belvoir's rooms, winding the string around a spool to emerge into the garden with Henry at her heels and cross the south parterre where the shiny navy Jaguar was awaiting, a big, red bow on its hood. She remembered that first whiff of new leather, which remained to this day, the muffled click as she closed the door, and the purr of the engine as she turned the ignition key.

It was only when Angela visited the neighborhood where she grew up and passed houses that cost less that she felt twinges of guilt over the car's blatant luxury. Cars of this type were non-existent in Millmont, home to Worthington's working class where pickups mottled with blooms of rust, or sensible, American-made sedans were the vehicles of choice.

Angela drove past the tawdry strip malls on the outskirts of Worthington into open country. With the town behind her, her dark mood began to fade and she started to picture her arrival home. The dogs, Mollie and Jasper, would be tripping all over themselves in excitement at seeing her. There'd be a fire already roaring in the library as it did most winter nights and Margaret would be putting the finishing touches on a delicious dinner.

And, of course, Henry would be waiting for her. She steered the car through Belvoir's elegant gates and along the tree-lined drive, her headlights illuminating the brilliant strips of new grass glistening with rain beside the road and becoming snagged here and there in gauzy drifts of mist. Coming around a bend, she spotted the golden glow of the house through the gathering fog. She lifted her foot off the accelerator, allowing the car to roll to a stop. Observing the scene before her, she marveled once more at the combination of fate and luck that had brought her to this splendid place where all, or almost all, was as it should be. After a moment or two, she stepped on the gas once more.

As she pulled into the circle in front of Belvoir, the door was flung open and Henry's lanky figure was silhouetted in the doorway. Though she couldn't make out his face, she saw it clearly in her mind: its high, aristocratic forehead, which had become slightly broader with the passing years, thick brows and jocular blue eyes framed by crow's feet, the aquiline nose bracketed at its base by expressive lips. Beneath, a strong jaw, which embodied Henry's legendary determination, created a pleasing balance.

He stood there for a moment, his arm raised in salute as the two Labradors eagerly pushed past him, bounding ahead to greet her. Helping her out of the car, Henry embraced her as the dogs danced around at their feet. In his arms, Angela inhaled his scent—the familiar combination of laundry starch and vetiver, laced with the pungent aroma of wood smoke.

"Finally, you're here!" He kissed her temple then holding her at arm's length, he grinned, laugh lines crinkling his face. Angela was laughing now, feeling safe and protected, enveloped once again in Henry's world. She stooped to pat the two dogs, which were balanced on trembling haunches barely containing their urge to jump up. Straightening, she shrugged her shoulders against the cold. "B-r-r-r," she said taking hold of Henry's arm, "let's go inside."

"You go on in, I'll grab the bags," he said.

"All I need is my satchel, Honey—the rest can wait."

Popping the trunk, he paused for a minute surveying the interior. "Looks like you gals did some damage in the Big Apple." He whistled appreciatively, moving aside shopping bags to reach Angela's satchel.

"Oh, no you don't!" she exclaimed. "Don't forget, your birthday's just around the corner!" She shooed him away and closed the trunk. "I'll get them later."

He laughed heartily and wrapping an arm around her, guided her toward the steps. As they passed through the entrance hall on the way to the library, Angela observed how inviting it looked this evening, brightly lit and deliciously warm with a large vase of fresh flowers set upon the hall table.

The library was her favorite room in the house with its rich lacquered walls, deep sofa and comfy club chairs. She loved it most of all for the memories it held: stockings on Christmas morning, Scrabble and Monopoly on the window seat and the countless, intimate family evenings spent by the fire.

"Glass of wine?" Henry asked busying himself at the bar as Angela settled herself on the sofa. He removed a bottle of Château de Puligny-Montrachet from the fridge. There was a resounding pop followed by the gurgle of wine being poured out.

Henry refilled his own tumbler with whiskey and joined her by the fire. "So tell me about your trip. Did you have fun?"

"It was great, thoroughly enjoyable. We covered a lot of ground, including some birthday shopping for you—that's why you're not allowed to go poking around in my trunk!" She poked him in the ribs playfully.

He grinned, his face transformed into that of a little boy. "Aw, can't you give me a hint?" he wheedled.

Angela shook her head. "Nope, you'll just have to wait for the big day."

"Okay then, so what did you get yourself?"

She swirled the wine around in her glass admiring the glowing effect of firelight on the liquid. "Nada" she replied.

"Angela," he rolled his eyes. "You mean to tell me you went to the shopping capital of the world and you came home empty-handed? With all the credit cards you've got, I was expecting a foxy new dress."

"You and Peyton are driving me crazy," she exclaimed. "I mean I get it coming and going. Peyton, on the one hand, accuses me of putting on airs while you meanwhile don't even seem to understand me after all these years. Shopping's just not part of my blueprint."

"But Angela, it's important to me that you look good."

"Don't I?" she flared. "The way you talk, it's like I'm some sort of arm-piece for you."

"I'm sorry, Sweetheart of course you always look great," he soothed. "It's just that indulging you brings me pleasure."

"Well, if it makes you feel better, Henry, we didn't scrimp on our meals. We went to Le Cirque, in fact. Sirio made such a big to do; I was so flattered. And it gave us lots of time to talk—you know—over all those courses." Her expression darkened, a little furrow forming on her brow.

"What is it, Darling?" Henry pressed.

Angela sighed heavily before proceeding, a note of resignation in her voice. "I sense Peyton's not happy."

"Really?" Henry sounded concerned. "She seemed in perfectly good spirits in Sun Valley."

"Yes, I know, but don't forget, Darling, it was Christmas, and the pressures of college far away. Besides…you know how much she loves it there." She paused to study the flickering fire.

"I think she feels over her head at school." A log in the grate collapsed with a shower of sparks. Henry got up and reached for the fire tongs.

"I also suspect she's, well, a bit lonely." Angela sighed. "My impression is she'd be happier at a co-ed school."

"But we've been over this repeatedly," Henry interjected, returning to the sofa. His tone was mildly exasperated. "I thought Peyton decided the pros, namely Sweet Briar's terrific riding program, outweighed the cons. You and I agreed it was the right place for her." He shot his wife a knowing glance.

"Yes, but it's only natural being in a college environment has changed things, opened her mind to other possibilities. And, let's face it, ever since the fiasco last fall, her riding is less important." Angela looked at her husband to gauge his response. A passion for riding had been a bond shared by father and daughter. Henry had been so proud when Peyton had qualified for the prestigious Maclay finals at Madison Square Garden; but his hopes were dashed when she came down with Mono and couldn't compete. To add insult to injury, in Henry's mind Mono would always be "that God Damn kissing disease," even though Angela kept reminding him that was a myth.

Angela went on, "She told me she wants to transfer to the University of Virginia."

"I suppose there's a young man involved?" Henry suggested, an eyebrow arched.

"Well, as a matter of fact, yes, a Charlie somebody-or-other. But I think it's more than that. She doesn't like being 'squirreled away in an ivory tower' is how she put it."

Angela took a sip of wine. "In any event, she's invited this Charlie fellow to your party so we'll have a chance to meet him. Why don't you plan on having a heart-to-heart with her about all this then?"

In the dining room candlelight flickered off the antique Chinese wallpaper. Brought to Belvoir by Henry's grandmother, Arabella Peyton Worthington in its original sandalwood boxes, the wallpaper featured an extravagant pattern of flowers and birds. Opposite the Regency sideboard hung a full-length portrait of Arabella. It was a romantic work, depicting the young woman in a riding habit of cascading jet-black material, a crisp white stock pinned at her throat with a flashing diamond horseshoe. In one elegant gloved hand she grasped a whip with furled thong, her other, carelessly held a full-blown rose. She regarded the viewer with a challenging and supremely self-confident eye. There it was: beauty and youth, like the rose she held, at its prime. Lushly executed by the great society portraitist, John Singer Sargent with loose open brush strokes that perfectly matched young Arabella's winsome vitality, the painting was a tour de force. In the parapet behind her, Sargent had painted the inscription *El fin fa tutto: The End Makes All*—an apt motto for the fortune-favored Arabella.

During an age of legendary beauties, Arabella had been a standout. Raised in obscurity in a gracious, land rich, cash poor Virginia family; she burst onto the social scene unexpectedly and to great acclaim. Her parents, with ambitions for a good marriage, had scrimped and saved for her debut. They watched their daughter's triumph with pride and some measure of relief. When she captured the heart of the heir to Worthington Steel, surpassing all expectations, the Peytons were quick to overlook the fact he was a Yankee.

Following their marriage, the couple honeymooned in Europe. Though she had led a rather isolated life, Arabella was a social butterfly by nature, at ease and congenial. Dressed for the opera in her Worth gowns and Garrard jewels, Arabella enchanted all who saw her. And so it was that when she sailed for home, the girl from the James River left behind a legion of admirers including, Sargent himself, as evidenced by his radiant portrait that now presided over Belvoir dinner parties.

Once Angela and Henry had served themselves to the coq au vin Margaret had set on the sideboard, they returned to the library, plates in hand. Their conversation shifted from Peyton to other topics—Worthington Steel's proposed merger with a Swiss multinational conglomerate and the baseless lawsuit filed by a competitor with Henry gleefully parroting his lawyers as Angela listened with half an ear. She didn't have the heart to tell him how dull she found it all to be.

So it was a relief when he finally changed the subject. He described the practice he'd had with his jazz buddies Sunday. He hadn't picked up his trumpet in months, and it was great to get the juices flowing again.

"Oh, and Candace stopped by with the new Robert Ludlum for you," he reported. "And Millie called, something about a dinner party."

Presently, Margaret appeared with dessert and coffee. They lingered by the fire for a bit longer until at last Angela excused herself, "Darling I'm going to head up now, I'm bone tired."

Pausing at the top of the stairs, Angela cast a last look behind her—the gleaming marble floor, the graceful staircase, the chandelier prisms flashing spangled light around the room. After nearly twenty years, she'd grown accustomed to living at Belvoir. But at moments like these, after being away, she saw it again with fresh eyes and was dazzled anew.

She turned down the hall to her bedroom. Large and airy, the room faced east to receive the morning sunlight. The bed was turned down, a carafe of water and fragrant spray of freesias beside it. Angela went into the bathroom to draw a bath, sprinkling Dead Sea salts into the tub. She undressed, and lowering herself into the steamy water, closed her eyes, abandoning herself to the delicious warmth.

But her pleasure was short-lived as in a flash the ugly scene on the steps of the Metropolitan Museum came back to her. Her jaw tensed, as she felt again the sting of her daughter's words. It was the same old issue—why her D'Agnese grandparents weren't more a part of their lives. It had come up when Peyton asked if they'd been invited to Henry's birthday party. Angela tried to explain that they Poppa and Grandma didn't feel comfortable at Belvoir functions. She had stopped abruptly as they crossed the museum's Great Hall, just as if she'd run into a wall. In fact, that was exactly what it was, a wall of fragrance—the unmistakable scent of lilies. And standing there, she suddenly recalled being in that very place with her mother-in-law shortly after she and Henry had married, and Lucinda exclaiming— Angela could remember her words clearly: "What a magnificent gift!" She said, referring to the donation in perpetuity of fresh flowers—four huge urns of them—by the woman who founded *Readers Digest*.

It was when Angela and Peyton emerged from the museum's half-light into bright sunshine that Peyton lit into her. "The problem with you, Mom, is you're just so superficial! It was the same with Joey." At this particular recollection, Angela sighed and slid further down into the bath. She could hear Peyton ranting on. "Joey was born and raised in Millmont, same as you. His aunt even lived on your street! But you think you're better than him—the same way you think you're better than your own parents, just because now you live in a big house and wear Chanel. Face it Mom, after you married Daddy, you slammed the door on your past. Your own *family*! I mean, how could you?"

Joey was ancient history. A mere blip on the radar screen. She was troubled Peyton was still bringing him up. Sure, Angela had her qualms about him, but they had to do with habits and history. Joey was a dropout, dealing drugs. He had no future. The reality was she'd be accepting of any suitor of Peyton's, regardless of background, so long as he possessed integrity. But Angela knew this wasn't about Joey. Peyton had moved well beyond him. Whatever its origins, Peyton's outburst had struck a nerve.

Angela's gilt-edged life was not without sacrifice, despite outward appearances. Physically removed from her origins, she was, in essence, an alien—part refugee, part expatriate in the exotic realm of her marriage. Angela would catch herself reflecting upon how suddenly it had all happened—just as if she'd walked onto the set of her mother's favorite show, *Queen for a Day*—only to learn she'd been invited to take up permanent residence in fantasyland.

Certainly her interactions with her parents had suffered, but not because she was ashamed of them. It pained her that Peyton would think this. But, of course, Peyton couldn't know how hard it was straddling two such disparate worlds. Angela's struggles to knit them together had only met with her parents' resistance. How well she remembered her father's words: "Your mother and I appreciate what you're trying to do here, Angie. Truly we do. But the D'Agneses and the Worthington country-club-set just don't mix. There's no use forcing it, Honey." And though she couldn't really blame him, she was disappointed Henry hadn't taken more of an interest in her past. Once he had borne her away to his rarefied world, it was as if her former self had ceased to exist.

Angela's greatest regret was missing out on the cozy relationship she knew other women shared with their mothers—shopping for specials at the A&P, enjoying coffee and conversation over the kitchen table, reflecting on the pleasures of years gone by and dreams for the future—precious time that Angela and her mother rarely, if ever, enjoyed. Her family had naturally expected her to marry a regular Millmont guy, but joyfully embraced her union with Henry. How could they do otherwise? They were proud of their baby girl for she had accomplished the unimaginable, slipping seamlessly into the upper reaches of American society.

The bath water had grown cool. Angela grabbed a towel from the heated rack, and wrapping it around herself, padded into the bedroom to put on her nightgown. Picking up a brush from the dressing table, she stood before the full-length mirror brushing her hair. She regarded her face. Her mother had always stressed the importance of taking care of her skin and Angela was meticulous about this. So, her complexion glowed with merely a suggestion of delicate lines around her eyes, imperfections that served to temper her near perfect beauty. At nearly 40, her body was still girlish—the negligee hugged her slender figure accentuating the curves of her breasts and hips. Physically, Angela favored her mother; her fair hair and high Nordic cheekbones came from the Anderson family. But her olive skin and dark eyes were hallmarks of the Italian heritage on her father's side. A product of the world's greatest melting pot—brown-eyed and blonde-haired—she was a classic American Beauty.

She heard movement behind her and saw his reflection in the mirror. Their eyes met in the glass and she smiled. She watched him approach and felt his touch on her shoulders. He pressed his lips against her neck as he caressed the contours of her body. "Dearest, how I've missed you," he whispered, mouthing the words against her throat, his lips raising goose bumps on her skin. She arched her back and felt him harden in response. Gazing at their entwined reflections, she reached around to stroke his hair. She watched with growing excitement as his hand gently stroked her breast and then traversed the length of her torso to the swell of her hips. Her breathing quickened as waves of heat surged within her.

"My love," he breathed between kisses. He pulled the fabric up, slipping his hand underneath. Angela caught her breath as flesh touched flesh. Henry's hand trailed up her thigh until, almost tentatively, he touched the soft mound between her legs. She gasped softly and he gently pulled the nightgown over her head. It slid soundlessly to the floor into a glistening pool of silk. She turned to face him, whereupon, he stepped back, holding her at arms length to admire her naked body. She watched as his eyes rested on her breasts and then shifted to the dark, chiaroscuro blur below that evoked such ineffable sweetness.

Overcome with desire, he picked her up and carried her to the bed. "You're so beautiful," he murmured bending to kiss first one and then the other quivering nipple. She closed her eyes and her breathing deepened as all sense of time faded away.

Raw, sensual memory now engulfed her as she was transported, inevitably again to that meadowsweet moonlit glen deep in her subconscious. That precinct of long ago that remained sharply familiar in its appointments like a chamber in her own house—the clutch of pale buds overhead, the subtle aroma of orchard grass, the loamy smell of earth.

Finally, she heard a rushing in her ears signaling the approach of that sweetest of all pleasures. And, then, she was there, crying out as her body shook with exquisite rapture and she felt the fragrant earth underneath rising up to meet her.

CHAPTER TWO

As Henry pulled away from the house, he could hear the clamor of wild geese down by the pond. A molten shimmer, heralding the rising sun, was beating back the tremulous gray of fading night. Driving through the estate, he was filled with a renewed appreciation for the beauty of nature and for Belvoir itself. He wished Angela was beside him to share this moment. He felt supremely content thinking about her and how his life had unfolded. It could have turned out so differently. To think that after all the years he'd spent gallivanting around the globe, he had managed to find his precious Angela right there in his own backyard.

Those wild years of his youth seemed far away now: New Year's parties in St. Moritz, jetting to Paris for a weekend, sailing off Sardinia. And how about that crazy fixation Camilla had about Venice at Carnival? The house parties she organized with all those outrageous costumes and elaborate masks. He chuckled at the memory. His reveries always grew quiet, recalling that final over-the-top holiday, the safari in Kenya they'd taken mere months before the crash—and the evening he proposed to her on the Serengeti.

He could not help but ponder how entirely different his life would have been if Camilla and her sister had decided on New York instead of the Seychelles for their getaway. It had been a toss up, but in the end, the lure of exotic beaches in March had won out over a week in still wintry Manhattan. They hadn't even made it to the islands; their small plane plunged into the Indian Ocean during a thunderstorm while making its final approach to Mahé Island. One thing was certain, if he had ended up with Camilla, they wouldn't be living at Belvoir. She had made it abundantly clear she expected to make their home in her native South Africa.

As he passed by the pond, his gaze flickered over the water; so did his thoughts glide from Camilla to Angela and the serendipitous nature of their meeting; to stumble—and that was the word—upon Angela, in the aftermath of the tragedy, was nothing short of a miracle. He was a thoughtful man who invested time into his actions. His decision to marry her, such a weighty, life-altering choice, had been a departure from his general way of doing things—a sudden impulse coming to him in a flash in a parking lot. And though a snap decision, and despite their fundamental differences, it had been the best thing he'd ever done, this leap of faith. He had been right. Beyond her beauty, and despite her simple roots, he had recognized in her an immutable grace and goodness that ennobled her character and set her apart.

As he exited the gates, he sighed with satisfaction. Yes, Camilla's cruel death aside, he had to admit things had worked out for the best. For surely it was at Belvoir with Angela by his side that he belonged.

It was the gentle rattle of the breakfast tray that nudged Angela awake. She opened her eyes to see Margaret approaching the bed. "Master Henry requested you not be disturbed this morning," Margaret said, "but as it's going on ten o'clock, I thought you might like a cup of tea."

"Oh, my Gosh," Angela exclaimed. "It's Mama's birthday; I have to get up." Generally, Angela was awake before Henry left for work. An early riser, Henry would shower and shave shortly after six. Selecting a shirt and suit, he'd set aside the jacket, pull on the trousers and run a lizard belt through the belt loops. Then sinking into the Victorian slipper chair, he'd don socks and shoes. Once attired, he'd descend the back stairs to the kitchen where the dogs, upon seeing him, would rise sleepily from their beds to stretch their limbs and croon affectionately.

He'd turn on the kitchen radio and make coffee. Finishing his bran flakes and banana, he would ascend the stairs, with a steaming cup for Angela, to select a tie and go over the day's events with her before departing. Afterwards, supported by down pillows, Angela would hear Henry's tread upon the staircase, the staccato tap of his footsteps across the foyer, the click of the latch, and finally, the resonant thud of the heavy front door closing behind him. She, then, imagined him crunching across the gravel toward the toffee-colored Maserati parked beside the dressed granite curb.

Margaret set the tray on her lap. Prettily laid with Battenberg lace, it held a bud vase with a pink rose. Placing a silver tea strainer atop a delicately sprigged cup, the housekeeper poured out the tea. Angela took a sip; then noticing an envelope on the tray, set her cup down. She opened it to withdraw a note in Henry's boyish scrawl:

Darling—

You certainly know how to kindle the fire in the old boy. I leave you a sleeping princess this morning, my dearest one, and forever my temptress. I'm the luckiest man alive.

All my love,
Henry

Angela was touched. Though not in love with this man when they married, their day-to-day life together had sparked a profound affection and, today, Angela could truthfully say she loved Henry and enjoyed their lovemaking. Increasingly, however, she noticed Henry seemed content to simply hold her as they drifted off to sleep. So last night's passion came as a pleasant surprise.

It was a quarter to twelve when Angela's car pulled out of the Belvoir gates. Yesterday's rain had given way to a blustery, overcast day. Every now and then the sun would appear from behind low clouds throwing the countryside into a bright patchwork of duns and muted green. Happy at the prospect of seeing her mother, Angela relaxed into the drive and before long, she was at Old Orchard Estates. She rarely passed the subdivision without recalling the annual outings she and her mother made to Moorman's Apple

Orchard. Together they'd fill a bushel basket with ruddy-hued fruit. She remembered how she liked to polish the apples, and how the juice ran down her chin when she bit into the shiny skin. When she grew tired of picking, she and her mother would lie on their backs under a tree and watch the leaves dance against the sky. Even now, the scent of apples, at once sweet and tangy, epitomized a perfect fall day for her. From their harvest Angela's mother made apple butter. Delicious spread thickly on toast, it was a favorite treat of the D'Agnese children. Best of all, on the evening of the apple-picking expedition, Angela helped her mother make traditional Swedish apple cake. Nothing compared to the aroma that wafted through the house when the cake was baking.

Angela felt a vague twinge at the recollection of the old copse, the memories it held and the lost storyline it evoked; she had always meant to take Peyton there, to share with her daughter this place that held such fond memories for her. But now the orchard was gone, replaced by a plat of houses and a wide paved road bisecting the grid once planted with fruit trees.

In town, Angela turned onto Main Street and parked in front of Harris & Sons Fine Jewelry. As she opened the door, a bell jangled and Mr. Harris looked up from a stack of papers. "Good morning, Mrs. Worthington," he beamed. "I've polished the pin for you and it looks stunning." Disappearing behind a screen at the rear of the store, he returned a few moments later with a small velvet box. Here it is," he said, opening it with a flourish.

"Oh, it's beautiful!" She turned the box so that light flashed off the diamond and pearl brooch within. "My mother will love it."

With the gift stowed in her purse, Angela walked half a block to the Meadowbrook Pharmacy to pick out a birthday card, and then to the florist for her mother's birthday corsage, a tradition she had maintained year after year. Back in the car, she turned onto Lenape River Road and headed toward Millmont to pick up Anna D'Agnese.

Here, the streets were narrow and lined with the stark brick facades of industrial buildings. She cracked her window and could detect the acrid, yet curiously sweet smell of coal fire fumes tinged with an odor akin to burnt coffee and could hear the rhythmic throbbing of turbines at work. She passed the McRae Locomotive and Cunningham Silk Works across from which loomed the sprawling complex that comprised her husband's company. Always she noticed the Worthington Steel sign looming over the high hurricane fence. She grew up with this sign, never giving it a second thought; it was just part of the scenery. How surreal it appeared now to her, the privileged wife of the man whose empire it described, this potent emblem neatly delineating those who have power from those who do not.

Leaving the factories behind, she entered the oldest part of Millmont with its squat, asbestos-sided houses attached to rickety porches. Each lot boasted a distinguishing feature: a shade tree, a grape arbor at the rear for homemade wine, a rose bush, touching relics of former domestic husbandry. Seeing how bedraggled the neighborhood now seemed, she wistfully recalled how well kept it had been and before she realized it, she had come upon what had been her grandparents' house.

As she drove by, she saw once again her late grandfather, Poppa D'Agnese, in worn cardigan and corduroy slippers shuffling about his neat yard trimming his beloved fig tree, brought as a cutting all the way from Italy, or pinching off redundant squash blossoms. These, he would give to Nonna to batter and fry in olive oil. Angela salivated at the thought of her grandmother's cooking—the simple peasant fare of Salerno from which her grandparents had emigrated at the dawn of the Jazz Age.

She recalled the sepia photograph taken soon after their arrival in America that hung in pride of place over the gas fireplace. Though dirt poor and barely able to speak English, they still managed to have a picture taken to record this early step in a bold new life. That they had held on to their dignity and hope in the future despite their hardscrabble circumstances was something Angela had always found moving. Dressed in their Sunday best, they appeared so solemn in the picture—unsmiling and glum, and rather nervous, which no doubt they were. Her grandmother held Aunt Seraphina tightly wrapped in a blanket and standing on her grandfather's thigh, her two-year-old father stared out from the photo with enormous black eyes.

The car crossed the river and entered the part of Millmont where she grew up with its streets lined with cookie-cutter ranch houses centrally positioned on uniform lots. She hadn't gone far when up ahead she saw construction vehicles and a detour blocking the road. She realized with dismay she'd have to take Elm Street by Green Valley High School. She always made it a point not to drive by her old school even if it meant going several blocks out of her way. But today she had no other choice.

She'd never been back, had missed every reunion so the high school was barely recognizable as the institution she'd attended nearly two decades before. New wings now flanked the original school building, beyond which, she could just make out the football field. She felt a tightness in her chest as she passed by.

Turning onto the D'Agneses' tidy street, a wave of nostalgia swept over her. It was almost as if she'd never left.

She pulled into her parents' driveway and spotted her mother peering through lace curtains. A few moments later she emerged from the house and came down the path. At 60, Anna was girlishly slim and naturally elegant.

"Happy Birthday, Mama!" Angela exclaimed when the car door opened. She leaned over to kiss Anna as she got in.

"Thank you, Dear," Anna said, speaking her words precisely with a wisp of a Midwestern accent.

"Don't you look nice!" Angela beamed at her mother. "What a pretty jacket!' It goes so well with your scarf." Angela was pleased to see that Anna was wearing the scarf she and Peyton had picked out in Paris the previous spring.

"You don't want the knot so tight," she said, reaching over to rearrange the scarf. "The silk should pouf out, like this."

Angela enjoyed showering her mother with gifts. Though Anna was always appreciative, it wasn't clear to Angela if her mother ever used any of them. Indeed, once, when Anna was in bed with a bad cold, Angela, rummaging through the closet in search of a bed jacket, discovered an assortment of things she'd given her mother over the years neatly arrayed on the shelf in their original boxes.

"So, Ma," she demanded. "What's up with all this?" she gestured at the closet.

"Oh, you found my stash." Anna looked sheepish. "Well, Honey, I'm saving them for a special occasion." What Angela didn't know is how many hours Anna spent contemplating this treasure trove. When all her chores were done, Anna would routinely repair to her room to go through her inventory. She'd open each of the boxes, touching the silk, unfolding a cashmere sweater, modeling a hat. Over and over again, as if for the first time, she would try them on and, admiring herself in the mirror, invariably make plans to wear some article on Sunday at church. But when Sunday arrived, she would think better of it, leaving all the extravagant things safely behind in her closet.

Angela rolled her eyes. "Geez, Ma, I get you presents because I love you and want to make a fuss over you. So wear them, already!" she scolded, helping her mother into the bed jacket.

Her mother's scarf now adjusted to her satisfaction, Angela reached behind her seat for the corsage. "You know…our little tradition," she said handing the box to Anna. Within the folds of green tissue paper lay a fragile orchid, shell-shaped, shell-hued, shot through with pink.

"My birthday badge! How lovely, Darling!" Anna exclaimed pinning it to her lapel.

It was a short drive to Vinnie's restaurant. The lunchtime crowd had filled up the parking lot. "Oh, look, there's Tony's pickup," Angela gestured to the blue dualie parked near the entrance.

Heads turned casually in their direction when they stepped through the door and there was a lull in the conversation. Vinnie's nephew, Sal Lombardo hurried over from behind the bar to greet them.

"It's been a while since we've seen you here, Mrs. Worthington," he bowed. "Can I get you a table?"

Inwardly wincing, Angela managed to flash him a smile. "That would be great, Sal, but please call me Angela."

"Of course…Angela," he smiled apologetically. Grabbing two menus, Sal led them across the room. Angela recognized a number of faces and nearing their table felt a hand on her sleeve. It was Rose Rubio, eyes sparkling under a choppy fringe of platinum hair. As usual Rose was attired in pink, her signature gold rose pendant dangling from her neck. A few years older than Angela, Rose had the vivacious personality that complemented her looks. Angela's brother Tony had fallen hard for her. But she threw over the jock in favor of Mark Gleason, president of the high school debating club. Their marriage was a happy and prosperous one, with Mark proving himself an excellent businessman, expanding Rubio's Dry Cleaning into a multi-franchise operation. Though she had known the girl only vaguely, Angela had always liked Rose. When she heard the Gleasons had purchased property down the road from Belvoir and knowing how snooty the neighbors could be, it had occurred to her she should oversee the introductions. With this in mind, she paused momentarily at Rose's table to invite her over for coffee.

Angela scanned the familiar space, her eyes taking in the checked tablecloths, red Naugahyde banquettes and knotty pine paneling on which hung travel posters from Italy. She recalled the many family milestones that had taken place here: Her First Confirmation lunch, Poppa D'Agnese's eightieth birthday party, Tony and Pam's wedding reception. The waitress came over with water and a plastic basket of bread. Sal handed Angela the wine list and lit the candle in the net covered holder.

"So, Sal," Angela said. "I saw Tony's truck out front. Would you let him know we're here?"

She turned her attention to the menu. "Let's see...how about if we start with mussels marinara? I know you love the veal piccata, Mama. So let's order that and split an order of the gnocchi." She looked up at her mother. "As for wine, I think a Chianti would be nice. How about the Sonnino?"

No sooner had they ordered than Tony appeared at the table. "Well, well, if it isn't Mom and Sis having lunch in the old neighborhood!" His deep voice boomed. "So, what brings you to the other side of the tracks, Angelina?" He bent to kiss them both. Then, catching sight of Anna's corsage, he slapped his forehead.

"Awww, Ma—it's your birthday! How could I forget?" he cried. "Well in that case, can I join you for a few minutes?" He sat down and ran his fingers through his hair. When most men his age were losing theirs, Tony's head of hair remained as full as ever, its intense color and sheen recalling the midnight blue of a comic book character.

"Would you lay off with the 'other side of the tracks' malarkey." Angela glared at him. "Millmont's still my home."

Tony laughed heartily. "My, aren't we touchy today? Sorry Angie, it's just so much fun teasing you."

He turned to his mother. "So, I bet John's already called you from L.A. I guess I'm the only deadbeat in the family."

"Nonsense, Tonino. I don't play favorites with my children. But, yes I spoke with him this morning. He was on his way to San Francisco for some kind of legal convention."

Tony was only half listening absorbed as he was in perusing the room. Spotting his old flame, Rose, he chortled: "Well, well I see "Twin Peaks" Rubio's here." Angela kicked him under the table. He yelped.

Anna, bemused, shook her head. "It's the same old, same old with you two. No matter how old you get—you'll always be a couple of Bickersons."

Before they knew it, the main course had been cleared away and Sal was bringing a slice of cake with a candle in it over to the table. They began singing "Happy Birthday." Other voices picked up the tune until the whole room had joined in. Anna beamed with pleasure. Afterwards, several well-wishers came over to the table, including Gabriela Carbone, the mother of Angela's old school friend, Gina. It had been many years since Angela had seen Mrs. Carbone, but she would have recognized that mass of tight black curls anywhere.

"Gina will be thrilled to hear I saw you. You know she lives in New York now—in Great Neck. On the Island. Ernie's an agent at State Farm, and Gina's a homemaker there." She was fumbling in her purse for something and finally pulled out a small pink photo album. "My brag book," she explained proudly. She put it in front of Angela and began to flip through the pages. "Here they are—Christmas last year—aren't they adorable? "Kayla's a star gymnast, Lauren's our comedian and there's Morgan, the baby." Angela leafed through the album, interjecting polite comments as Mrs. Carbone chattered on. "Please give Gina my very best when you next talk," Angela said handing the book back to Mrs. Carbone.

Tony looked at his watch and rose. "I don't mean to interrupt, but I gotta run, Sis. We're on a tight deadline with the Albano job. But, listen, kiddo, keep in touch. And say hello to the big bosseroo for me." He winked at Angela, kissed his mother goodbye and ambled toward the door.

When mother and daughter were alone once more, Sal appeared at the table with two flutes of sparkling wine. "Compliments of the House," he chimed. "After all, it's not every day I get two such beautiful young ladies in here."

As they sipped their wine, Angela handed the neatly wrapped box to her mother. "Happy Birthday, Mama! From Henry and me."

Anna untied the ribbon, winding it into a small ball; then, slitting the Scotch Tape, she carefully removed and folded the wrapping paper. She opened the box. "Oh, Sweetheart," she cried. "What a lovely pin, but much too fancy for me! Where on earth would I wear such a thing?" By way of an answer, Angela took it out of the box and pinned it to her mother's lapel beneath the corsage.

Over coffee, Anna asked eagerly about Peyton. She treasured the times she spent with her granddaughter: all those sleepovers when she would set her hair and do her nails. Though a tomboy, Peyton was delighted with the attention, and afterwards would parade around the house delighting her grandparents with her play-acting. In the evenings, they made popcorn and took it with mugs of ginger ale to the den to watch *Bonanza*. When the show ended, Tony Sr., would head off to bed, leaving "the girls" to watch the Million Dollar Movie.

Anna pressed her daughter for more details about her recent trip. Though somewhat uncomfortable about discussing her chichi life with her mother, she knew how much Anna relished her accounts. Even an ordinary day sounded exotic. The subject of Henry's party came up and Angela, with Peyton in mind, reached over and squeezed her mother's hand, "Won't you and Pop reconsider and come this time?" By way of an answer, Anna looked down at her coffee cup and Angela withdrew her hand.

CHAPTER THREE

*I*t was just after 3:00 when Angela dropped her mother off and headed back to Belvoir. With only two hours of light left, she'd have to hurry. She was feeling slightly drowsy from the wine and a brisk ride would do her good.

Angela had taken riding up when Peyton was a child. She loved her horse, Ross, a handsome cob: small, sturdy and calm. She was eager to get back in the saddle after her trip to New York, relishing these excursions both for the exercise and for the pleasure of being on an adventure with her horse. These solitary rides had a trance-like effect; whole hours would elapse without an actual thought passing through her head. She would return home exhilarated, refreshed and renewed.

Once back at Belvoir, Angela dressed warmly, donning a heavy tweed hacking jacket. She headed to the mudroom by way of the kitchen where she found Margaret rolling out dough on the pine table. Angela loved the old-fashioned kitchen and, on Margaret's days off, enjoyed spending time here making a hearty Bolognese sauce or cookies with Peyton at Christmastime. Bidding Margaret goodbye, Angela collected her gloves and down vest. Seeing her, the two dogs jumped to their feet, knowing exactly what was up.

She jogged down the lane, the dogs at her side. When they entered the barn, Ross and Peyton's show horse, Salutation, whinnied impatiently and Henry's big hunter shifted noisily around in his stall. As usual classical music was playing on the radio for Paddy Donohue, Belvoir's barn manager believed, among other things, that music had a salubrious effect on animals. On one wall of the immaculate tack room, gleaming saddles were arranged on racks. Most of these belonged to Peyton and were used for competition. Paddy kept them cleaned and polished regardless of whether they'd been used, so the barn was permeated with the earthy smell of well-oiled leather. Personalized bridles hung on hooks below each horse's enamel nameplate. Tidily arranged around the room, was an assortment of trunks, storage boxes and buckets. A pile of plaid horse blankets sat neatly folded on a Victorian settee.

A shrine of sorts to Peyton, the room featured glass-fronted cabinets, filled with her trophies, spanning one wall. Colored ribbons, most of them blue, formed a multi-tiered fringe that ran around the entire room at ceiling height. The remaining wall space was plastered with photographs of Peyton astride Salutation, clearing what seemed to be impossibly high, or impossibly wide jumps. Angela remembered the many times she'd watched with her heart in her throat as Peyton competed. But Peyton never faltered and rarely fell off. She'd never been badly injured during the course of her lengthy and demanding riding career, which had begun with lead-line classes when she was six.

How Angela had enjoyed those occasions when she, or less frequently, Henry had walked Peyton's Shetland pony, Cookie, around the ring with little Peyton turned out in perfect show attire right down to her tiny paddock boots. She had been quite the picture, sitting tall in the saddle, stirrup leathers wrapped twice around the irons to accommodate her short legs, eyes shaded by the brim of a velvet helmet. Even then, she took competition seriously as her steely expression indicated.

Angela entered Ross's stall. "Good old soul," she cooed, stroking his neck. He nickered softly. She kissed his velvety muzzle, breathing in his warm equine scent then she led him out to the cross ties to groom and tack him up. She enjoyed caring for her horse and was glad Paddy wasn't around to take over.

After brushing the horse down, she took a hoof pick and worked on his hooves. Then placing pad and saddle on his back, she buckled the girth into place. Finally, she put Ross's bridle over his head. He immediately opened his mouth and took the bit. "Good boy!" she praised. Grabbing her hat and chaps, she led Ross to the mounting block just outside the barn. Once mounted, she whistled for the dogs, and they set off.

As they left Belvoir's manicured grounds and headed into open fields, Angela urged Ross into a trot. It felt wonderful plunging through the bracing air. They continued across the field maintaining their even pace. Every now and then, one of the dogs would shoot off in pursuit of some scent, returning after a few moments at top speed to rejoin them. Eventually, they came to a stream where heavy rains had washed away the bank. Angela looked around for the best place to cross. The dogs, meanwhile, were cavorting happily in the mud. "Baths for you two tonight," she declared, smiling indulgently.

She guided Ross toward the edge. He hesitated briefly before picking his way cautiously down the muddy bank and splashing into the stream. Once on the other side, Angela coaxed her horse into a canter. The dogs, temporarily distracted by the creek suddenly appeared bounding through the tall grass.

At the far side of the field, Angela pulled up her mount at the trailhead. They entered the woods, startling several deer that crashed away through the underbrush, white plume-like tails held erect in alarm. Mollie and Jasper bolted after them. Angela patted Ross on the neck, praising him for his composure.

Winding through the woods, the trail became steeper. At the summit, Angela paused to survey the view through bare branches. The valley floor stretched out before her; she could see beyond the gentle undulations of hills and Belvoir's slanted roofline poking above the trees. Here was the Worthington domain: land and structures commensurate to their wealth and standing, but also something more intangible and noble: beauty, family and tradition. She was seized by a momentary feeling of disorientation. Eager to escape this unsettling sensation, she nudged Ross forward in the direction of the gorge. A favorite picnic spot in summer, Henry and Peyton delighted in perching on the rocks beneath the sluiceway, allowing the water to rush over them. Angela, sunbathing on the rocks opposite, would watch contentedly as father and daughter frolicked in the water.

She shivered; the sun was sinking fast, and it was time to go home.

Paddy was waiting when she returned to the barn. Angela suspected he'd been perusing the racing form stretched out on the tack room sofa, a mug of milky tea on the floor beside him.

"Good afternoon, Mrs. W. did you have a pleasant stroll?" His soft brogue greeted her as he took Ross's reins, deftly replacing bridle with halter. Short and wiry, Paddy had been a jockey in his youth. His once flaming red hair had faded to a soft buff that matched his unruly eyebrows. These gave him a rather severe look, but his twinkling Irish eyes below were more accurate gauges of his character.

"Yes, Paddy, we did. It was brisk out there though. I think Ross is glad to get back to his stall." Angela unzipped her chaps and removed her hat.

Paddy smiled, giving Ross a proud once-over. "I can see you had a bit of a go from the sweat the laddie's worked up." He indicated the damp area with his brush. "I'll walk him for a bit before I put him up."

The sudden warmth of the house made Angela's cheeks tingle. She removed her boots sliding her feet into sheepskin slippers. She filled the electric kettle and found a tin of Margaret's homemade shortbread in the pantry. When she finished her tea, Angela went upstairs to shower before changing for dinner.

Once in the library, she glanced at her watch. Henry would be home soon. She settled herself on the sofa with her needlepoint, an intricate trompe l'oeil pattern featuring a ribbon that curved around on top of itself.

The phone rang. It was Millie Watson calling about the school fundraiser she and Angela had co-chaired for several years. "Remember, Dearheart, I won't get back from Scotland until the 17th. But I'll be all set to roll my sleeves up then, even though I know you're perfectly capable of running "Tea for Treasures" all by yourself!

"Oh, and by the way, did Henry pass along my message about Saturday?" she asked.

"Yes, and we'd love to join you." Dining at Beau Pre was always a treat Angela thought hanging up the phone. Though Millie was older than Angela by many years, the two were close. Their affinity had been immediate, "My mother always said, you don't meet friends, you recognize them," Millie had told Angela, when they first worked together on Lucinda's pet project, the Fresh Air Fund.

A bit of a renegade, with little patience for pretensions of any kind, unconventional Millie was known for her wicked sense of humor, and delighted in telling off color jokes to the most unlikely people. "Knocks the stuffing right out of 'em!"

Whether on the hunt field, at tony functions, or running errands in town, Millie was always well-turned out, sporting her trademark Lilac Champagne lipstick and looking sleek and elegant. Though her skin was deeply creased from a life spent outdoors, she was still a handsome woman. Tall and lean, Millie held herself like a queen. She alternated between wearing her blonde hair—"I was born with it—as God is my witness!"—twisted into a chignon, or in a flip held in place with a black velvet headband. She was known for well-tailored suits and flamboyant hats, and when she entertained casually, such as a brunch preceding a hunter pace, she'd invariably dress in jodhpurs, tattersall shirt, and handmade Italian walking shoes. On her wrists jangled colorful crystal bracelets featuring horses, hounds and foxes. A crackerjack bridge player, Millie had been Lucinda's partner for many years, and together they made a formidable team. It had been Millie who had volunteered to coach Angela so she could join their bridge group.

Then, there was Candace Hutchinson who lived just down the road. Closer in age and background to Angela, Candace, a former stewardess, had met her husband, Bob, on a flight to West Palm Beach. Men couldn't resist Candace with her mane of red hair and intense green eyes. With a failed marriage behind her and a string of unhappy affairs she was ready to settle down. Bob was a charmer, and they immediately hit it off. Through idle banter, she'd put together the pieces of his profile—Fortune 500 company CEO, wine connoisseur, golfer and, most important: clearly attracted to her. It turned out, he was a regular on her route and once she set her mind to it, it had been easy. Hiking up her skirt as she reached above him into the overhead compartment had led, a couple of flights later, to a tryst in the first class restroom whereupon she'd ushered him into the mile-high club.

In no time, she'd quit her job and was occupying a condo with wrap-around views of the Atlantic that was conveniently located a short drive from the fairway of the Everglades Club.

From there, it had been only a matter of time before Bob's wife, Pamela, became the "First Mrs. Hutchinson," and Candace and Bob were married in Acapulco. Through it all, Candace's conscience remained clear; she knew Bob's marriage had been over for some time and Pamela was well taken care of. She got to keep the sublime Casa Esmeralda, and Bob also threw in the duplex on Park Avenue. As for Candace, he showered her with jewels and built a lavish new house on North Ocean Boulevard, ensuring an effortless segue way into Palm Beach society.

My, how these two women added spice to her life, Angela mused. Millie the more polished of the two was all talk. Candace: action. On her first official date with Bob, so she said, she wore nothing but a mink coat and stilettos. Recalling her description of the wild sex that ensued made Angela laugh and blush all over again.

A sudden commotion by the dogs announced Henry's arrival home. Angela started. She stuck the needle in the border of the tapestry and rolling up the canvas together with her steamy thoughts, rose to greet him.

CHAPTER FOUR

*B*rilliant sunlight was flooding the morning room. A decidedly feminine space, it was appointed with delicate French furniture, pastoral paintings and Lucinda's prized collection of German porcelain. At her desk, Angela sorted through the mail. She separated bills to give to Henry's secretary and skimmed through her correspondence. Finishing this task, she glanced up and the photograph she kept on her desk caught her eye. Taken a dozen years before on a summer holiday in Switzerland, it showed Peyton in pink and blue dirndl perched on her father's lap squinting into the camera. Her crooked smile, displaying missing teeth, was disarming. Henry, in Tyrolean jacket, grinned broadly. He looked tanned and relaxed and, Angela noticed, so much younger. She thought of the sunny little child Peyton had been. And of the ordinary pleasures they'd shared. Bubble baths in Angela's big tub, Teddy bear tea parties followed by leisurely afternoon naps under the mohair throw Peyton dubbed the "magic blanket," for its unfailing power to induce sleep.

Undeniably, Henry and Angela had indulged their only child, with lavish, themed birthday parties and annual Christmas excursions to New York, including a ritual shopping spree at F.A.O. Schwartz. How could one say no when presented with a golden head of curls cocked beseechingly, or the winning smile that played across rosebud lips? Despite her own frugal upbringing, or maybe because of it, Angela found herself caving in against her better judgment. No wonder Peyton was spoiled. Of course, there had been attempts at discipline, but for the most part, these were unsuccessful. And as she grew, Peyton learned how to manipulate her doting parents.

Charming when it suited her, sullen if she didn't get her way, she regularly tested boundaries; and as a teenager, ignored curfews and broke rules. Joey Marino came to mind once more. Angela would never forget the day he came into their lives. She and Peyton had ridden over to the Watsons' farm. But instead of finding Millie mounted and ready to go, they were met by her new groom holding her favorite horse.

As they drew near, Millie's horse, known to be spirited, began to snort and prance about. The boy tightened his grip on the lead line. "Quit," he commanded. The horse immediately quieted. Then, turning to Angela, he said, "Mrs. Watson's on the phone and'll be right here." Angela had noted the boy's good looks right away— the seductive dark eyes, Roman nose and raven hair worn tossed back from the forehead—and the deliberate way in which he sauntered past her daughter in tight, low-slung Levis; it was a provocative swagger, a liquid, smooth gait with a touch of insolence. And the heat contained within the sidelong glance he gave Peyton was palpable. Angela recognized it and remembered.

She hadn't given him another thought until a month or so later, when Henry, coming out of the drug store, happened to glance toward the street just in time to see his daughter flash by on the back of a motorcycle, her arms wound tightly around an unfamiliar young man. When Henry called Angela a few moments later, she was beside herself: Peyton was supposed to be at Nina Cantwell's house working on a school project. Who was she with? Of course. The boy who worked for Millie rode a motorcycle. It was bad enough knowing that Peyton had lied to her; to discover she was secretly carrying on with this boy in a reckless fashion was intolerable.

Though Payton was grounded after this incident and placed under Margaret's watchful eye, she still found ways to see Joey. Unbeknownst to Angela, Peyton regularly began saddling up Salutation and riding over to the Watsons'. It was only when Millie, at their weekly bridge game, casually mentioned seeing Peyton disappear into the woods on horseback that she figured out what was going on.

Matters came to a head one night. With Henry away on business, Angela returned early from a dinner party. Not finding Peyton in the house, she walked down to the barn. As soon as she crossed the threshold, she heard muffled whispers and giggling coming from the other end of the barn. Following the sound, she came upon Peyton and Joey rolling about in an empty stall. Hearing her, the young couple abruptly pulled apart. Angela gasped: Joey's shirt was off, revealing a well-developed torso, her daughter's unbuttoned.

"What the hell's going on here?" She lunged at Peyton and grabbing her arm, pulled her to her feet as Peyton fumbled with her top.

Angela turned to Joey. "How dare you! Get off my property this minute!" she yelled, her cheeks flushed with anger. "And don't you dare show your face around here again!"

Peyton had begun to sob as Paddy, hearing the commotion from his apartment, appeared in the doorway carrying a pitchfork. "Is everything all right, Mrs. Worthington?" he asked, glaring at Joey. The boy picked his jacket up from the floor, brushed off bits of hay and taking his time, walked out of the barn, an impudent smirk on his face. They could hear his motorcycle roar to life and the spray of gravel as he took off down the drive.

Angela turned to Peyton, "I just don't know what to say."

Peyton glared at her mother, tears streaking her face. She turned and ran out of the barn.

"That boy's a bad lot." Paddy shook his head. "I tried warning Mrs. Watson about him."

"You know him?" Angela asked, surprised.

"Not personally, but I know who he is. He's worked different jobs. The Wawa over on Maple. For a while, at least. Landscaping. That kind of thing. He does have a way with the horses, I'll give him that. His uncle owns the Lazy D guest ranch out on Route 20."

First thing in the morning, Angela called Millie. Joey's position at the Watsons was terminated. And within a couple of weeks, after a flurry of phone calls and a hefty contribution to the annual fund, Peyton was packed off to boarding school.

Angela sighed, recalling this distressing period.

Returning her gaze to the photograph she thought wistfully of those carefree days when Peyton was small. She wondered for a moment if her nostalgia was misplaced. "No," she said out loud. "Things truly were different then." For one, thing they had lost their matriarch. The aneurysm, which struck Lucinda down without warning five years ago had been a terrific shock. Complaining of a slight headache Lucinda had retired early for the evening, never to wake up. It happened on the summer solstice just two weeks before she and Peyton were to depart for Switzerland. So, for Peyton who had spent a portion of each summer ever since she was small at Davos with her Grandmamma, the loss was immediate. She adored these excursions, staying at the grand hotel where she was treated like a princess by the old world staff.

As for Henry, Lucinda's death was a seismic shift. An only child, he was especially close to his mother who had polished and burnished him into the man he was. Angela could never really grasp how much Henry missed his mother, nor know how often he turned to her, even after her death, for comfort and direction when dealing with life's challenges. But as he would later admit, Lucinda went just as she would have wanted—suddenly and at the conclusion of the longest day of the year.

Angela pondered this bouquet garni of recollections and sentiments seasoned by the poignant reality of aging, not so much her own, but of those around her—her husband, about to be 50, her parents no longer the vital couple of her youth, and the bittersweet transformation of her rosy-cheeked little girl into a young woman, smart, good-looking and, at times, maddeningly difficult.

On impulse, she picked up the phone to call Peyton. The answering machine picked up. "Hi, Sweetie, just checking in to make sure you got back safely. What fun we had in New York! Daddy and I can't wait to see you and your friend, Charlie on the 14th. Call me when you have a chance. Big hug."

She replaced the receiver and turned her attention to the tally of acceptances compiled by Henry's secretary, Delores Graves. Angela smiled picturing her sitting at her neatly ordered desk in proper bouclé suit, bifocals perched on the end of her nose, lips pursed in concentration. Her perfectly manicured nails leafing through piles of documents or searching the Rolodex for a telephone number requested by Henry through the intercom.

She scanned the neatly typed page. At this point, there were 40 acceptances, but she knew it would end up being more. She went over the logistics in her head, deciding to count on six tables of eight set up in the front hall. That would leave just enough room to accommodate the combo she'd hired for dancing. Drinks would be served in the drawing room and after dinner coffee and brandy in the library.

From her desk, she withdrew the blue leather book used to record Belvoir's social occasions listing the menu, flowers and other relevant details. Earlier volumes were shelved in the butler's pantry to be consulted now and then for inspiration. She glanced over the menus to see if anything appealed to her. Next, she picked up the phone and dialed *L'Assiette d'Or* to finalize the menu.

For the starter, Chef Alain Ducasse suggested individual ramekins of smoked salmon and avocado mousse, "These will be magnifiques! Beautiful to look at with a little cilantro and de-li-cieux." He made a "mwha" sound and she knew he'd kissed his fingers in the classic gastronomic gesture of delight. She giggled at the image, putting her hand over the mouthpiece so he wouldn't hear. For the second course, he suggested wild mushroom bisque to be followed by a main course of filet of beef, braised vegetables and duchesse potatoes. Alain would choose the selection of cheeses to accompany the salad. "To top it off, a merveilleux chocolate almond layer cake. And, may I suggest, your très mignonne daughter present the cake? Now, that will bring a smile to your husband's face!"

"It all sounds perfect, Alain. Henry will love it."

She wrote the menu out so Henry could make the proper wine selections from the cellar and made a mental note to ask George, the gardener, what was available from the greenhouse. Whatever he had could be augmented with blooms ordered through the florist. Closing the party planner, she was startled to see Henry walk in. She looked at her watch and then, back at him. He smiled.

"Surprised to see me?" he asked stooping to kiss her. "I'm feeling a bit under the weather and thought a little 'flat work' would do me some good." Angela furrowed her brow, worried.

The subject of Henry's birthday party came up at Louise Samuels's the next day. After a couple of hands of bridge, the group broke for lunch, signaled by Althea parading into the dining room with a large soup tureen and platter of watercress sandwiches. Four places had been laid at one end of the long Sheraton dining table: lace place mats, festive green goblets surrounded a generous arrangement of pink tulips.

Once settled in their seats, Louise started right in. "So, Angela, Darling, is everything set for Henry's fête?" Angela assured them that excepting a few minor details, all was in order.

"And how many are you expecting?" asked Millie.

"Let's see, out of 50 invitations give or take, there are only two re-grets—Fred and Mary, who'll be in Vail then," Angela replied.

"The same old crowd, I see," Candace said. "What fun! I love our group," she gushed, lifting a spoonful of vichyssoise to her mouth. "Well," she continued, "I certainly hope you're not inviting those flashy nouveaus—the... what's-their-names?" She paused pressing a napkin to her lips, then let out a little giggle. "You know who I mean, the Sleaze-ons."

Louise and Millie looked at each other and exchanged superior smiles. But Angela squirmed inwardly and felt her face redden. Hearing good-hearted Rose thus maligned for being socially unworthy needled Angela. It always bothered her, such talk.

Angela thought how funny it was to hear Candace go on in such a superior manner. Angela knew Candace's roots were on a par with the Gleasons' and her own people in Millmont, not with Bob's upper tier family, or Millie's or Louise's for that matter. And her disdain seemed particularly insensitive, given she should know that Angela, a local girl, very likely knew Mark and Rose growing up.

She often wondered if her own failure to reach out to her old friends after her marriage was construed as a brush-off. How they might have thought she no longer had time for them. But the truth was when she first moved to Belvoir, she felt so much a guest in her new home, it never would have occurred to her to invite anybody over.

Briefly, her mind shifted to that last meeting with Suze and Gina, her best high school friends—a farewell lunch for Suze shortly after Angela was married. She shuddered at the memory. It had been a challenge picking out a gift. She had not wanted to appear ostentatious, yet imagined her friend might expect something expensive. In the end, she decided on plain gold hoop earrings that Suze seemed genuinely pleased with. She remembered the awkward silence when the check arrived after lunch as all eyes latched on to it. And how, after a moment's hesitation, she had reached across the table with forced casualness saying, "You know, why don't I get this?"

How she had fretted afterwards that this gesture was taken as a crass display of grandeur rather than a reflection of her own discomfiture about her change in fortune. Candace, on the other hand, was being deliberately snobby.

"If you mean Mark and Rose Gleason," Angela finally managed to say, her tone crisp. "I actually was thinking about it, but it being a birthday party with everybody knowing each other, I decided they'd feel left out."

"Well," Candace retorted, "I just don't think they're our sort. Particularly her. I mean she's so in your face with those clothes and that hair. She cornered me at Fiori's the other day and I could barely get away. Considering I really don't know her, it was really too much."

So what if Rose had sex appeal and liked to flaunt it? Angela reasoned. She and her mate had stuck by each other since high school. No infidelities there. At the very least, you had to admire their work ethic. Over two decades, they toiled tirelessly on building a successful business, amassing the resources that allowed them to buy into Worthington's gold coast. Whereas Candace had taken the escalator to the top, landing Bob Hutchinson on the aisles of a 727, thus dramatically changing her social echelon in a mere matter of months; a story, indeed, akin to Angela's own rapid passage into privilege. One thing for sure was certain. Having "arrived," Candace wanted to make sure the door was firmly shut behind her.

The dishes cleared, Althea set tiny pots-du-crème at each place. "Ah-h, chocolate," Millie declared, "the eighth wonder of the world!"

CHAPTER FIVE

ngela rose early the morning of Henry's party. As she dressed, she took inventory of what remained to be done. The Worthington style of entertaining was altogether different from what she'd grown up with. D'Agnese parties had been casual, boisterous affairs featuring copious amounts of hearty food—Italian antipasti with capicola and provolone, stuffed mushrooms, roasted peppers along with a selection of her mother's favorite Swedish delicacies, Janssen's Temptation, gravlax and mandeltorte. By contrast, at Belvoir the hors d'oeuvres were limited to two or three selections passed on silver salvers. Tonight's line-up would include "Devils on horseback" and cheese puffs, augmented by spiced pecans in silver Revere bowls. Sometimes Angela missed the hearty fare of her youth, which seemed to touch something deep within her for it expressed so much: love, family, heritage.

Angela spent the morning doing the flowers for the tables, using a combination of creamy-hued roses, lilies and blue bachelor buttons. She loved working with flowers, enjoying the quiet simplicity of selecting contrasting colors and shapes to create a striking effect. It was a hobby she'd picked up from Lucinda who had studied floral arranging as a young girl in Baltimore. Two large arrangements had been ordered from the florist for the hall and library. The final detail would be several dozen long-stemmed, yellow roses from the Belvoir greenhouse for Granny Peyton's ornate Tiffany vase.

In the kitchen, Alain and his staff were absorbed in preparations. Meanwhile in the front hall his wife, Leanne assisted by their young daughter Odette, filled balloons with helium. They had already blown up a number, attaching trailing ribbons to them. Nearby, bolts of silver lamé and blue tulle were stacked haphazardly.

Entering the hall, Angela greeted Leanne. "Oh, good, you're here. The centerpieces are all done and waiting for you in the pantry." She caught sight of Odette. "And look who's here!" she exclaimed. "My special pal!"

The girl's face lit up. Hastily, she tied the balloon she was holding to the handle of the helium tank and ran over to hug Angela. "Tante Ange!" she cried.

Angela stroked the girl's hair. "My, you've gotten tall, Sweetie-pie." She said glancing over to exchange a smile with Leanne. "I almost didn't recognize you!" Odette grinned, her eyes shining.

"Is Peyton here?" she asked shyly.

"Not yet, cricket. But she's coming this afternoon. Maybe you'll still be here. I know she'd love to see you." Angela patted the girl on the back. "Guess who else would love to see you?"

Odette's eyes danced. "Cookie?" she cried eagerly.

Angela nodded, smiling. "Tell you what, when your Mom can spare you, you ask Margaret for some carrots to take to the barn. Mr. Donohue will be there."

Odette clapped her hands in delight at the prospect of seeing Peyton's old pony. Angela turned to Leanne, "do you have everything you need?"

Leanne nodded. "I know it looks a bit chaotic, but everything's going to fall into place, I promise."

Angela smiled. "I know. It always does. Especially now that you have such a capable helper," she indicated Odette. "Which reminds me, how are the twins? They must be getting big."

Leanne beamed. "Yes, they just turned three. They're a handful. Let me tell you. I've got pictures." She trotted over to her purse returning with a photo, which she handed to Angela.

"Oh, my, they're adorable. Alain must be so proud."

Leanne blushed. "Yes, he is. He already has them in the kitchen."

Angela laughed. "I'm not surprised. I bet Odette's a wonderful big sister. You must bring them next time you come."

Angela had urged Peyton to book a flight rather than make the long drive home. Aside from wanting her daughter to arrive earlier rather than later, Angela knew she drove too fast. Peyton had always loved the sensation of speed. Whether on a roller coaster at the state fair with her father at her side, or later when she started riding lessons, she would always clamor to go faster. When Peyton moved on to cars, it didn't help that Henry, despite Angela's protests, bought his daughter a bright red Triumph TR-8 for her 18th birthday. Two speeding tickets and a warning later, she was at risk of having her license suspended, a turn of events Angela welcomed since it would take Peyton off the road.

But Angela's appeals fell on deaf ears: Peyton was bringing her boyfriend, so they decided to drive.

At noon, Angela left for her hair appointment. She'd invited Peyton to join her, but Peyton had other ideas. "You know me, Mom. When I get home, I'm heading straight to the barn. I want to see my babies."

"Well, Henry will just have to see she's on schedule," she sighed, then caught herself. Wasn't it time she faced up to things? Leaning on Henry where Peyton was concerned had become a regrettable pattern. She'd ceded parental power long ago in the face of their close bond. She envied their easy rapport, particularly these days when her own relationship with Peyton was strained.

When Angela returned from the hair salon, she found the hall transformed. "Wow," she breathed, thinking how glamorous and festive it looked. "Just like a chic supper club done up for New Year's Eve," she murmured. She stood there for several minutes admiring it before going into the morning room.

Angela was just finishing up the place cards, when Peyton burst in. Kissing her mother hurriedly, she turned to introduce the young man lagging behind her. "So, Mom, this is Charlie, Charlie Tazewell."

"Hello, Charlie." Angela rose from her desk, extending her hand. "Welcome to Belvoir."

"Very nice to meet you, Mrs. Worthington," he said, taking her hand. Angela could see he was quite handsome in a conventional sort of way. Tall with the broad shoulders of an athlete, he had closely cropped, red hair and abundant freckles, which gave him an appealingly boyish look.

She turned to her daughter. "I've put Charlie in the willow room. Can you take him up and get him settled?"

"There's plenty of time for that, Mom. First, we're going to check in with Paddy." Charlie shrugged sheepishly at Angela as if to say, she's in charge.

"Have you had anything to eat?" Angela asked.

Charlie's face brightened. "We're fine, Mom," Peyton insisted, grabbing his arm. She beamed up at him. "C'mon, it'll be fun. You'll like Paddy." She pulled him toward the door. To someone less familiar with Peyton, her breezy manner might have come across as indifference, but her mother saw immediately that the opposite was true—the girl was smitten.

"Okay, Sweetheart. I'm going to go ahead and take my bath, so, Charlie," she pointed at him, lightheartedly, "I'm counting on you to keep her on track."

Seated at the dressing table after her bath, the finishing touches of make-up applied, Angela took a sip of the champagne Henry had brought her only moments before. After slipping on rhinestone sandals, she rose and walked over to the bed where her evening gown was laid out. Shrugging off her peignoir, she slid the dress over her head, shimmying it into place. She pulled the zipper closed, and the grey charmeuse column embraced her form.

She reached for the bottle of Diorissimo, a Mother's Day present from Peyton. The scent, with its distinctive note of lily-of-the-valley, filled her with a rush of nostalgia, calling to mind the inexpensive version, Muguet, she'd worn as a young girl. Lucinda had stressed to her that perfume could deaden a pearl's luster, so she made sure it had dried before removing the magnificent necklace of Tahitian pearls from its velvet case and fastening it around her neck. She paused before the mirror and was pleased to see how much life the pearls gave to the dress's soft, gray hue. A final glance at her refection and she was off to inspect the house one last time before the guests arrived.

Downstairs, the flower-filled rooms emitted a fragrance made up of lilies and roses and the aroma of burning cedar. Blended together, these scents were transformed into a delicious and utterly distinct smell that evoked the yin and yang of the olfactory range. In the entrance hall, foil confetti glinted on every surface. It was as if a big blue and silver fairy had just passed through, sprinkling her magic dust behind her. Garlands of balloons formed a festive swag that wound up the staircase. Heavy Georgian candlesticks flanked Angela's centerpieces and festive skirts of colored silk shot with silver peeked out from beneath fine damask cloths.

The musicians were setting up in the corner. Angela went over to Chet Watkins, the bandleader to go over the program: unobtrusive background music, a mixture of show tunes and jazz until the drum roll heralded the arrival of the cake. Once dessert was served, the serious dance music could begin.

Always fastidious about wine, Henry was in the butler's pantry, assisting Floyd Munson in uncorking the Chateauneuf-du-Pape so it would have ample time to breathe. For as long as anyone could remember, Floyd had been tending bar at Belvoir and could be counted on to assemble a well-stocked array of spirits, mixers and garnishes which ensured that even as a party was winding down, Floyd's bar continued to hum along smoothly, never lacking for anything, abundant reserves still on hand.

"Darling," Angela urged with a touch of exasperation tingeing her voice, "our guests are due in less than 30 minutes. You need to get dressed!" Henry turned to his wife and let out an admiring whistle.

"Don't you look gorgeous, Honey!" He said giving her a kiss. "What do you think, Floyd? Isn't Mrs. Worthington a knock-out?"

"Please ignore him, Floyd," Angela said.

"What a stunning dress," Henry continued, lightly fingering the pearls at her throat. "I don't believe I've seen it before."

"You most certainly have!" she countered, "I wore it at the Junior Assembly in New York last year. Now, get a move on!"

He picked up a tumbler of sparkling water in which a wedge of lime danced among the bubbles, drained it in one gulp, and then set the empty glass on the soapstone counter.

"Okay, I'm done here." He clasped his hands deferentially. "But before I disappear, can I get you some more bubbly, Sweetheart?"

Angela shook her head. "Off you go, Henry. No more dawdling." she urged, giving him a gentle swat. "Everything's in perfect order—except *you*!" She wasn't really worried for her always impeccably attired husband didn't squander time in the dressing room.

Angela walked through the downstairs rooms, inspecting the lighting, and checking the placement of nuts and ashtrays, pausing to straighten a stray bloom, and plump up the odd down pillow. At the bar, Floyd busied himself cutting curls of lemon zest as Margaret pushed through the swinging door with George's yellow roses.

"Thought these needed a little more water and have re-cut the stems to keep them perky," she reported.

"Aren't they lovely? And Edgewood has done such a nice job with the other flowers. Now, is there anything else we should go over before the guests arrive?"

As Margaret led Angela through the busy kitchen, she greeted the party staff: Daisy Lombardo, Sal's sister, and May Shifflett, an old friend of her mother's. At Margaret's desk, Belvoir's command center, they reviewed the housekeeper's checklist. "It looks like everything's in order, Margaret. I can't begin to thank you for all you've done."

"You know I'd do anything for Master Henry—for the Worthingtons," Margaret replied.

The soft strains of Cole Porter's *Begin the Beguine* had just begun to play when the doorbell rang. As if on cue, Henry appeared on the up-stairs landing and began descending the staircase attired in a slim fitting tuxedo. Sapphire studs fastened his starched evening shirt, and he sport-ed a perfectly tied Turnbull and Asser "papillon." His hair, combed back from his brow, set off sparkling blue eyes. The door opened to reveal the Hutchinsons. Candace's fruity voice and rich laugh proclaimed that this was a party, and she intended to have fun.

"Bob! Candace! Welcome!" Henry called from the stairs. "Let Sims have that," he gestured to Candace's chinchilla wrap. Bob held out a telltale turquoise shopping bag to him.

"Here's a little something to mark the big day." He said, grinning.

"I thought Angela made it clear: presence, not presents." Henry de-clared jovially, leaning forward to kiss Candace on the cheek. "But, I'm not one to protest too loudly on my birthday." He added, taking the bag and handing it to Sims.

"A man only turns half a century once, Henry," declared Bob.

Henry laughed heartily, slapping his friend on the back "Now, how about a drink?"

In the drawing room, they were greeted by a maid bearing a tray of champagne flutes. Angela appeared in the doorway and seemed to float across the room in her silvery dress. Her entrance provoked delighted squeals from Candace. Henry beamed proudly at his beautiful wife as she approached. The attention then turned to Candace, stunning in black lace tonight. Her dress had a deep décolletage, which showed off her jewels and bosom to equal effect. She wore her red hair swept up into an elaborate arrangement of cascading ringlets.

"Angela, this is such fun!" Candace exclaimed, her green eyes widening with excitement.

"And don't you look divine! Valentino—right?" she remarked, appraising Angela's dress with an expert's eye. Well, it's to die for! And," she continued, gesturing with a sweep of her hand, "the place has never looked so gala!" She lifted her flute in Henry's direction. "To the birthday boy!" she called out coyly, forming lacquered lips into a kiss. "Your fortieth—right?" She winked as the group laughing heartily at her little joke. "Well, Happy Birthday, Mr. Pre-si-dent..." she purred in a whispery Marilyn Monroe voice.

"Candace, you're too much," laughed Henry as he raised his glass to her. Candace turned to Angela and whispered, "Hey, Girl, I'm dying for a cig."

"By all means, Candace. Go right ahead." Angela offered, gesturing at the ashtrays.

"No, I'd better not; I promised Bob I wouldn't," she moaned. Then, brightening, she added, "he told me if I was good and quit for real this time, he'd make it worth my while. I can't wait to find out what he's got up his sleeve! I just love surprises—especially his!" She giggled throatily and looked over at her husband. Catching his eye, she winked suggestively.

Other guests were arriving. Sims and two maids were kept busy answering the door and transporting coats upstairs. The drawing room rapidly filled with guests and the noise level rose accordingly. Gay chatter, laughter and tinkling glasses created a festive hubbub. The usual pleasantries were exchanged between old friends, how well the other person looked, what they'd been up to, before moving on to more serious matters—politics, steel industry profits, the recent acquisition of American Motors by Chrysler, stock market returns—eventually broaching the full gamut of ever popular personal themes—a recent quail-hunting trip, a must-read bestseller, children's prep schools, sports or college news, summer plans.

Presiding over the lively gathering from its position of honor over the fireplace was a portrait of Angela and little Peyton. The fine brushstrokes used by the artist to capture their likenesses—porcelain skin, luminous eyes, golden hair—and aspects of the detailing—the intricacy of Peyton's tightly smocked bodice, the opalescence of the pearls at Angela's throat, gave way to the broader brushstrokes describing the creamy silk sheath Angela wore, the pale blue folds of Peyton's dress, and the voluptuously rendered backdrop of Belvoir's gardens spreading off to the temple folly in the distance. There was a sweetness in Angela's eyes, and yet, a striking maturity. Her hand was draped tenderly around the little girl who leaned against her knee gazing adoringly up at her. It was a painting that commanded attention and guests at Belvoir would invariably find their eyes drifting to it. A single detail drew Angela's eye—not for the first time—the vein on the back of her hand—rendered with such veracity—not bluish, simply there, a rise and fall with a hint of shadow. Masterfully, the artist had caught the undeniable evidence of humanity, pulsing—it was something Angela was sure only she noticed. A buried clue to her essence, it breathed life into the portrait, and testified to her corporeality. Yes, she was Angela Worthington, now, even if her biological ties lay elsewhere. Seeing this vein reminded her of this.

Angela took a sip of champagne, savoring the delectable bubbles prickling her tongue. She surveyed the room. Her eyes rested fleetingly on the petit point upholstery, coral silk brocade, and roses in the vase on the fruitwood commode all bathed in soft light. It gave her a warm feeling, this rich pastiche of color and texture that now evoked home.

Who was still missing, she wondered? Governor Woolsey and his charming wife, Betsy, were in view and evidently in high spirits. And she noticed that Henry's Aunt Clay had arrived and was engaged in an animated discussion with Tootie Bishop. The room reverberated with laughter. She was pleased. Everyone was having a good time.

Just then, she caught a glimpse of Peyton chatting with the Hutchinsons, in the adjoining room, no doubt about Whit, Bob's son from his first marriage. Angela was disappointed that Peyton had chosen to wear a rather shapeless velvet dress. While in New York, she'd tried without success to get her to buy something more stylish for the occasion. Well, at least she'd thought to put on Granny Peyton's diamond and sapphire pin.

Millie Watson, bejeweled and wearing a red taffeta gown, had attached herself to Charlie and was chattering away. Poor Charlie must be getting an earful, Angela thought. At one point, she heard Millie's voice above the others. "Shoot, if I'd known this shindig was going to be *this* fancy, I'd have worn underwear!" She cackled heartily. Charlie looked stricken. Angela smiled at Millie being Millie and wondered if strait-laced Charlie had the slightest inkling he was being teased. Angela hadn't yet had a chance to form an opinion of him, though he seemed nice enough. She could tell he was somewhat intimidated by Belvoir. She could relate, having once been in his shoes.

Dinner was announced and the guests spilled out into the hall, milling around the tables looking for their place cards. As always, Henry had been consulted on the seating plan. It was something he felt strongly about—guests should be mixed up in such a manner to ensure diversity and conviviality. And, of course, there were certain basic rules: spouses were never seated next to one another, and the lady and gentleman deemed the most important of the evening, either by virtue of social rank, or seniority, were placed respectively at Henry's and Angela's right hand. The next most important guest would get the hosts' left hand, with the balance of the seating falling into place thereafter. This meant that tonight Angela was flanked on her right by Governor Woolsey with Ambassador Milliken to her left, while Betsy Woolsey and Henry's Auntie Clay sat on either side of him.

"Hey, Mom, you look totally glam." Peyton remarked, brushing past Angela on the way to her table. "I sure hope Daddy put me next to someone interesting for a change. This could be totally bor-ING," she added, mouthing the last word.

"Actually, you're between Bob Hutchinson and Charlie." Angela placed her hand on her daughter's arm. "I'm sure it won't be as tedious as you think, and I hope you will try and enjoy yourself, Honey. It means so much to your father." She tried to keep her tone light, finding Peyton's complaints on this night of all nights particularly trying.

All through the first course, Angela listened to Scofield Woolsey expound at length on his enthusiasm for golf. Alas, his duties as governor had limited the amount of time he could devote to the sport. While he managed to play with some regularity at Gleneagles on getaway weekends and occasionally at the Rolling Rock when in Pittsburgh, his playing had been significantly curtailed since taking office. A real coup had been playing the St. Andrew's course two years ago, and he had subsequently secured honorary membership in the Royal Dornach Golf Club in Scotland. Over New Year's, he'd been able to take a break from gubernatorial duties and whisk Betsy away to Tryall. Now that was a nice course—and what a view! But he wasn't entirely comfortable in Jamaica, particularly after that sniper incident on the golf course in St. Croix a few years back. While he knew Henry played—they'd been on the golf team together at St. Paul's so many eons ago—did Angela swing a club?

Angela could hear Auntie Clay's voice, rising over the din as she described a favorite Puccini aria, and Beebee Haskins waxing eloquent on the subject of bee-keeping. Had her childhood nickname played a subliminal role in Henry's cousin, Beatrice, pursuing this unusual hobby, Angela wondered. As the soup course was served, the Governor became wrapped up in a good-natured sparring match with Chauncey Wilkens, an elderly neighbor seated across the table about the state's social service programs, and Angela seized the opportunity to focus her attention on her other dinner partner. Asa Milliken's great passion was roses. George's spectacular specimens—their exquisite purity of form and hue—had captured his attention before dinner. How does he do it? Angela flashed him a smile. Had he not visited the Belvoir greenhouse? Well, he must. George would love to talk roses with him.

Angela had always found Asa exceedingly charming. He'd enjoyed a successful career as an investment banker, working in both New York and London. Rewarded with the plum position of ambassador to Spain after a large contribution to the presidential campaign, he took early retirement. Though a political appointee, he was no slouch; fluent in four languages and possessing an astute understanding of the various forces at play, he was a natural for the diplomatic corps.

It was curious such an attractive man had remained single, and Angela wondered if he was perhaps gay. She immediately thought about AIDS—it was so much in the news these days. If that was indeed his preference, she hoped he was careful; she liked Asa and didn't want anything to happen to him.

The soup, served piping hot with an accompanying glass of sherry, was delicious. Angela savored the woodsy broth, a nice counterpoint to the rich salmon and avocado mousse starter. Then the main course arrived, eliciting high praise all around. Angela was pleased at how it had all turned out. Everything tasted delicious and looked almost too perfect to eat. When she saw that everyone had finished, she gave the signal and the dinner plates were cleared and champagne poured out. Conversation slowed in anticipation of the birthday cake. There was a dramatic drum roll, joined by a trumpet playing the opening notes of "Happy Birthday." Everyone began to sing as Peyton appeared pushing a cart, bearing a tiered birthday cake. Her face, lit by candlelight, possessed an uncomplicated sweetness.

Watching his daughter approach, a look of sheer delight spread across Henry's face. Though part boyish response to being the center of attention,

Angela knew it was mostly pure adoration for his cherished offspring. Cheers and rousing applause ensued. Henry rose from his chair with glass in hand. "Thank you all for making the effort to be here. It is I who should be toasting you!" He raised his glass in salute. "I can't think of anything better than being surrounded by my dearest friends on the occasion marking my ascendancy to the big 5-0." He paused for effect. "The good news is that after the Middle Ages comes the Renaissance!" The room reverberated with laughter. Henry beamed, clearly enjoying the response.

The room quieted. "I must say I do feel rather like a Renaissance man at this moment," he raised his glass in Angela's direction. "I want to toast my beautiful wife. She's behind this bash. Thank you, Darling—what an evening!"

He turned to face Peyton. "And to have our wonderful daughter, here tonight…well, that's the best present of all! We had to do some serious arm-twisting to get her here, let me tell you," Peyton pouted playfully, and he blew her a kiss.

There followed a series of toasts starting with his old school mate, Governor Woolsey. Auntie Clay recounted several amusing stories from Henry's childhood, such as when he commandeered an elevator at the Grand Hotel in Rome at the age of ten. It was one of those old-fashioned cage elevators inside a circular stairwell, she explained, and it became almost an international incident with all the hotel staff running up and down the stairs in hot pursuit as a gleeful Henry eluded them. "It took them a surprisingly long time to divide and conquer, and so Henry retained control of the elevator for quite awhile. It was priceless." Everybody laughed.

Geordie Jennet-Smith spoke of Henry's resilience and sportsmanship on their fishing trip to Montana the previous summer after their guide discovered that a tent and a portion of the provisions had been left behind. "Well, that didn't stop Henry; his response was: 'a tent short, it may be loud, but at least we'll stay warm, and as for the food, I don't knows about you boys, but I'm goin' fishin'!'"

Finally, it was Peyton's turn. She was brief. "Happy Birthday, Daddy. Even if you're old-fashioned and I don't always agree with you, I love you. You're the best." Angela studied her daughter as she spoke. Despite some pudginess, Peyton was a very pretty girl with the fine bone structure of her mother. Her distinctive dimples and flashing eyes, an enduring gift from her father.

With dessert over, Henry rose from his seat and, catching Angela's eye, gestured to the dance floor. Excusing herself from her dinner companions, Angela made her way around the tables. A hush fell on the room as the guests turned their attention to the handsome couple. Henry tall and regal, Angela a vision in shimmering satin, the candlelight-infused pearls at her throat glowed like drops of moonbeam. As they began dancing, an appreciative buzz moved from table to table.

After a few minutes Peyton and Charlie joined them. Watching their graceful waltz, Angela pondered the bare canvas their lives presented. What lay ahead was for each to embellish. She wondered how it would turn out—if they would choose to undertake this masterwork together, or go their separate ways. The music swelled luring others to the floor. The tempo picked up and the young couple sidled up to Angela and Henry, nudging them into a double cut. Peyton grabbed her father's hands and urged him into an elaborate swing dance crossover, tossing her head back and laughing gaily. Henry's eyes shone.

Charlie was an able partner, a product, no doubt, of a proper dancing school. He guided Angela deftly through the now crowded dance floor. Well-versed at making polite conversation, he chatted with ease, telling her about his family in Richmond and his interests in lacrosse and political science.

When the music paused, Geordie called out, "How about a tune, Henry?" The other guests began clapping and stamping their feet. Geordie grabbed Henry's arm and pulled him toward the stage where Chet was waiting with Henry's trumpet in hand. Henry laughed into the microphone. "I see you have an accomplice in my wife." He winked at Angela. "Okay folks, here's a little something I've been working on. It's by my idol, the great Miles Davis." He lifted the trumpet to his lips and began to play, lingering over the notes, filling the space with the soulful melody of *Blue in Green.* The guests listened enthralled, some with glistening eyes. There was a moment of total silence when he finished, before wild clapping and cheering erupted.

The band took over once again and dancing resumed. Those guests not on the dance floor filtered back into the drawing room, or headed toward the library where coffee and cognac were being served. Several ladies repaired to the downstairs powder room while Angela led a contingent upstairs. She checked her hair in the mirror and reapplied lipstick, chatting lightly all the while with Betsy Woolsey and Louise Samuels. "Well, Henry seems to be having a ball." Louise observed.

"Yes, I'm so glad Scotty cleared the decks so we could come." Betsy chirped in. "Really, Angela, you've outdone yourself. It's the party of the decade!"

"Why, thank you! Having you all here means the world to Henry." Angela replied.

Back downstairs, she was glad to see Peyton and Charlie still dancing. "She sure doesn't look bored now," she exalted.

Before joining the guests in the library, Angela decided to check in on the kitchen crew, which was still hard at work. She clapped her hands to get everyone's attention. "I want to take a minute to thank everyone for helping make tonight such a success. The birthday boy's having the time of his life."

Pleased, they all turned back to their tasks, resuming their chit-chat, with Margaret scraping leftovers into the dog dishes. "My, aren't the doggies going to have a good breakfast, bless their little hearts."

Feeling parched after champagne and dancing, Angela lingered in the kitchen, to get a glass of water. Though not focusing on the conversation around her, she overheard random snippets. Suddenly, two words strung together—a proper name—reached her ears. It was a run-of-the-mill sort of name: Steve Ryle. But the effect was electric. Angela's mind whirled. Steve Ryle. Steve Ryle. The name drummed in her head. She concentrated intently, the glass held to her lips. Had she heard correctly?

Daisy was speaking. "Yes, poor Johnny. He had a hard life, he did—what with Kathleen dying so young and him raising those two kids all on his own. And, then, young Stevie—his father's pride and joy, mind you—going off to Vietnam and all." She clicked her tongue sympathetically. "Well, that whole ordeal nearly killed him." She sighed heavily, then, continued matter-of-factly.

"I understand from May, they've set the ceremony for next Thursday. At the gravesite. Both kids'll be there—Imagine, Stevie Ryle coming all that way!"

Angela's heart pounded. She grabbed hold of the counter to steady herself. The kitchen noise seemed suddenly muted, the surroundings a-blur. It was as if she was catapulted inward to a faraway place, a sanctuary unvisited these many years, where memories, priceless as jewels—some thrilling, some poignant and some unbearably sad—were reposited.

Steve Ryle. The name echoed in her head, the key to a rich storehouse of ancient sensations and longings that had been shelved for so long in some back annex of her mind. Now they were suddenly transported, cobweb-strewn, to the glaring forefront of consciousness. "So, you've come back after all these years?" she thought and slowly, in trance-like fashion she made her way to the breakfast nook and sank onto one of the banquettes.

Margaret bustled over and Henry was summoned. After several minutes, Angela was revived and strong enough to take her husband's arm and join the guests in the library. "I suppose it's the champagne," she murmured as they crossed the hall.

"You're just over-tired. And, no wonder, Dearest; you've knocked yourself out on this party." He kissed her forehead. "Everyone's had a grand time. Now, *you* need to put your feet up."

He guided her to the sofa and pressed a dram of single malt into her hand. The guests ignorant of their hostess's distress, drifted in and out of the library helping themselves to coffee or a nightcap and engaging in lighthearted conversation. Angela did her best to play the gracious host, making a valiant attempt to pepper conversations with light remarks, but inwardly, she was in tumult, the once vibrant evening ruined. What had been a joyous affair—one of Belvoir's best soirees—would be, in the end, forever eclipsed by an offhand remark overheard in the kitchen.

The carriage clock on the mantle struck one. The chimes and ensuing observations about the lateness of the hour spread through the room and, slowly, guests prepared to depart. Finally, Henry escorted the last group out. Angela, now alone, sank deeper into the sofa, transfixed by the fire. The heat and the down-filled cushions were the only aspects of the situation that were comforting. The library had always been a pleasant haven for reflection. But tonight, tormented by recollections, an old wound opened. She felt her heart ache as she spooled through images from the past and grasped for answers. The warmth of the fire and its hypnotic effect finally overtook her troubled mind. She drew her legs up, curling her body into a fetal position and slept.

Presently, Henry returned to escort his wife upstairs and was so struck, moved even by her grave beauty and the deep slumber that enveloped her—the slumber of one almost under enchantment, he mused—that instead, he reached for a nearby cashmere throw tucking it gently around her sleeping form. Then, after banking the fire, he retreated, quietly shutting the door behind him leaving his wife amidst the volumes of stormy tales and ethereal poems that filled the space in which she slept—an uneasy, fitful sleep—to confront the past of Angela D'Agnese.

PART TWO

Worthington, Pennsylvania, 1965

CHAPTER ONE

"*H*ey, beautiful. Are you deaf or something? I asked if this seat was taken." Startled, Angela looked up to meet a pair of laughing blue eyes. It was Steve Ryle. She recognized him right away. Everybody knew who he was. Now, here he was in living color emerging as it were, from the one-dimensional black and white pages of *The Worthington Clarion's* sports section.

"Oh, sorry," she stammered, blushing. His hand, clutching his books against his thigh caught her eye—the manly fingers bronzed by sun and the glint of golden hair on taut forearm. She shifted her gaze to his face, the pleasing nose, the generous lips, the smile framed by dimples. And, then, wanting to know more, she allowed her eyes to alight briefly on his hair. Most boys she knew wore their hair cropped short or slicked back; Steve Ryle's fell in loose, soft waves, the color of honey.

"So, is it okay if I sit here?" he persisted.

"Yes, of course," she replied.

He sat down extending his hand to her. "Say, I'm Steve, by the way." Before she could answer, the bell rang, and Mr. Tolles strode into the class-room wearing one of the colorful plaid sports coats he was known for.

"Okay, class, settle down. I know you're excited to be back at GVH, but it's time to put a lid on it," he rubbed his hands together briskly. His eyes scanned the room to assess the new batch of students. On spotting Steve, he looked momentarily perplexed, then, irritated. "Er—Excuse me, Mr. Ryle," he said in his nasal voice. "I seem to recall you took this class last year. For your information, Fourth Year Spanish finished ten minutes ago." Giggles erupted in the back of the room.

Steve stood up. "Sorry, Mr. Tolles, I was just leaving, sir."

"Well, then, let's make it snappy. I've got a class to teach."

There were more giggles as Steve collected his books and, winking at Angela, sauntered out of the classroom. His wink set a tremor of butterflies loose within her. Was he flirting with her? She couldn't believe it! The captain of the football team had lingered to chat with her, even risking Mr. Tolles's ire. She blushed at the recollection of his voice. "Beautiful," he'd called her.

If she'd been told when she set off for school with her brother John that bright September morning that she would be encountering Steve Ryle, she would never have believed it.

Transferring to Green Valley High for junior year had been a huge milestone for Angela. After a campaign waged over many months, she had finally been able to persuade her parents to let her leave St. Hilda's where she'd been since fifth grade. If it had been up to her father, he would have kept her cloistered within the walls of a convent until marriage. And, St. Hilda's was the next best thing. Angela's mother, however, had supported the switch, recognizing how important it was for a young girl to be out in the world going to parties, dances and football games with kids her own age. In the end, the prospect of not having to pay tuition tipped the scales for Tony D'Agnese, and Angela got her way.

Green Valley High was a typical, one-level brick school. To one side, Worthington's skyline, such as it was, stretched into the distance beyond the Lenape River. To the other, the land sloped gently upward through woods. The football fields, where epic battles with rival schools were waged each fall, were immediately behind the school, bordered by tiers of battle-ship gray bleachers partitioning off the track beyond. To these, someone had tacked a hand-painted, banner, which read "God Bless our Boys in Vietnam."

After years of wearing St. Hilda's maroon tunic and gray flannel blazer, Angela was delighted to be attending a school, which didn't have a uniform. A major project of the summer had been going through the pages of *Seventeen* looking for a suitable outfit to wear the first day of school—she knew how important initial impressions were. Finally, she settled on a turquoise and beige hounds-tooth skirt and matching vest, inspired by a "Back-to-School" feature she'd seen in the magazine. Though they couldn't get the exact fabric, her mother was a talented seamstress, and she managed to recreate the design and achieve a similar effect. They'd gone to the outlet store on Lenape Street for the material and to Woolworth's for the Simplicity pattern. While there, she picked out a close-fitting, ribbed "poor boy" sweater to complete the look.

To fill out the rest of Angela's new school wardrobe, her mother had bought her a couple of skirts and four tops. Using the check she'd gotten for her birthday, Angela purchased a pair of brown T-straps at Kinney's, and two pretty eyelet bras on the sly at the Five and Dime while her mother was at the next cashier buying undershirts for Tony.

On the way home, she convinced her mother to stop at The Emporium, which sold trendy clothing. Angela had often strolled past the store with her St. Hilda's pals, stopping to admire the merchandise in the window. On one of these occasions, she'd seen a shoulder bag she liked. As she now placed the leather purse on the counter, Angela tried to assume an off-hand, casual air. Her mother reached over to examine the price tag and gave Angela a look as much to say "No."

Angela reddened and glanced at the proprietor, a thin man with pock-marked skin and stringy hair, who was observing mother and daughter with a bemused expression.

"I'll take it, thank you," she said firmly, pushing the bag toward him.

"That'll be $16.80 with tax," he said. Angela carefully counted out the bills from her wallet. Placing the purchase in a shopping bag, the man winked at Angela as he handed her the change. "Come on back any time, baby."

Back on the street, Anna declared: "I didn't like that place one bit—and that man, my goodness, what an unattractive specimen."

"Oh, Mom," Angela retorted. "He wasn't that bad. You're just *so* old-fashioned. Anyway, *you* don't ever have to go there again!"

The night before the first day of school, Angela washed her hair with Breck shampoo and brushed it 100 times, just like the ad said. The next morning, she donned a grosgrain headband centering the bow just above her bangs. With Jean Shrimpton of the pouting Yardley ads on her mind, she grabbed the contraband lipstick and mascara her parents so disapproved of and stashed them deep within her book bag.

Green Valley was a completely different world from St. Hilda's where girls conversed in hushed tones under the watchful eyes of the Sisters. Everything at this new school was bigger and louder beginning with the P.A. system, which crackled to life first thing in the morning in a burst of static followed by Principal Barlow reciting the Pledge of Allegiance.

In the beginning, Angela kept to herself, studying the other students to determine potential allies and whom to avoid. There were several distinct groups, with the jocks and cheerleaders, the *de facto* aristocracy of the school, topping the list. It didn't matter what your father did, or what side of the tracks you were from, if you could throw a ball, tackle an opponent, score a touchdown, or make it onto the cheerleading squad, you were part of this elite group.

At gym, Angela felt like she'd been thrown into the deep end of the pool. "Look out!" a voice yelled as a ball whizzed by her ear. Before she could absorb what was happening, another ball slammed into her side. She winced. Recovering from the blow, she looked in the direction the ball had come to see a pretty blonde staring at her, a satisfied little smile on her face. Angela reached for the ball to hit her back. "You're out," the girl next to her informed her brusquely. "When you get hit by the ball, you're out." She pointed to a group of girls on the sidelines.

"So how do you like this game?" A friendly voice asked Angela when she joined them.

"It's awful," Angela replied. "That ball really hurt." She rubbed her side.

"I guess that's why they call it Blitzkrieg: because the balls rain down on you like Nazi bombs."

"We never played anything like this at St. Hilda's."

"No, I wouldn't expect so. By the way, I'm Gina, Gina Carbone. You go to Mass at St. Boniface right? Weren't we in the same Catechism class?"

"Oh, that's right, I thought you looked familiar. I'm Angela D'Agnese."

A petite girl, everything else about Gina was large—almost to the point of exaggeration: the pouf of raven hair that hovered over her shoulders, her full lips, and wide hazel eyes balanced a larger-than-life personality that included an infectious laugh. Growing up with five older brothers, she could more than hold her own when teased and was popular with the boys in a chummy sort of way.

Just then another girl ran up. "Geez–Louise, I almost made it to the end this time," she panted, out of breath.

"Hey, Suze, this is Angela. Remember? From St. Boniface?"

Suze studied Angela's face, "Yeah, yeah I do." She grinned. "I'm Suzanne Wilson; everybody calls me Suze."

Suze was more reserved than the extroverted Gina, but she had a quick smile and ready laugh. Her kind eyes and slightly bucked teeth gave her an endearing look.

"You're the girl from St. Hilda's right?" Suze asked. Angela nodded.

"So what kind of sports did you do there?"

"Kickball and volleyball mostly. The school was divided into two teams: The Violets and the Blues."

"That's weird, to pick such close colors." Gina said.

"Well, the Violets represent the Sacrament of Reconciliation, and the Blues, symbolize expectation and hope—the blue of a new day." Angela explained.

"Wow, that's a riot, those nuns don't give it a rest do they?"

The worst part about gym class was the girls' locker room afterwards. Here, her path would cross with the snooty girls on the cheerleading squad. She felt particularly vulnerable in the communal shower, stripped bare while the cheerleaders pranced about, casting disparaging looks at the other girls and making loud, pointed remarks about the "new elements" invading their space. Angela recognized the ringleader, Marcia Kincaid as the girl who'd hit her so hard with the ball that first day. Marcia's father owned the big funeral home in town. Spoiled and indulged, she was used to getting her way. For her 16th birthday, Marcia's father handed over the keys to a candy apple Mustang that was the envy of the school. Bossy and loud, it was her voice that could be heard above everyone else's, taking over whatever space she inhabited.

Marcia wore her white blonde hair gathered into a ponytail high atop her head. With her pretty eyes, snub nose and small perfect teeth; Marcia was an attractive girl who knew how to strut her stuff. When not in her cheerleading outfit, Marcia favored tight fitting clothes that accentuated her curves. Marcia was always the first to disrobe in the locker room, taking evident pleasure in releasing her perky breasts from the confines of their Maidenform bra to shudder and bounce as she paraded about.

She mostly ignored Angela, but Angela sensed she was on Marcia's radar screen. First there was the ball incident, and then one day Marcia accidentally-on-purpose knocked over Angela's bottle of lotion as she brushed past the bench. "Ooh, did I do that?" she asked innocently, though Angela could see the steely glint in her eyes.

The cafeteria was another challenge. The first few days of school, Angela sat with a bunch of quiet, bookish kids in back. It was a relief when toward the end of the week Suze and Gina called her over to their table. "So, what do you think of Green Valley so far?" asked Gina as she mixed her creamed chicken, rice and peas into a pile in the middle of her plate.

During that first lunch together Suze and Gina gave Angela pointers about her new school and chatted about what the year had in store for them. From school topics, their conversation shifted to future plans. Gina was adamant. "My old man wants me to do community college—says I'll get a better job." She set down her fork and began examining a lock of hair for split ends. "But I don't want to work. I just want to find me a nice guy, settle down and start a family."

"Right off the bat? You gotta be kidding!" Suze slapped the table edge with her hand. "That's not for me. I'm hightailing it out of here to New York City first chance I get. To one of those secretary schools…Katherine Gibbs maybe. I hear that's real high class. You wait, in no time, I'll be sitting pretty working for some hot shot."

"I can see you now—just like *That Girl*. Gee, I hope you get her wardrobe," teased Gina. "Maybe, the hot shot will look like Steve McQueen!"

The girls turned their attention to Angela. "So, what are your plans? Ever thought about being a model? You're sure pretty enough."

Angela blushed. "Actually, I want to be a nurse, like my Mom." She hesitated, looking from one expectant face to the other. "Of course, I also want to get married and have kids someday," she added quickly.

Gina surveyed the room. "There're some cute boys here, don't you think? Anybody special you'd like to spend Seven Minutes in Heaven with?" she asked breezily. Angela shook her head and looked away.

"Oh, come on, don't tell me you haven't checked out the merchandise," Gina protested. "Seriously, you must have a fave."

Angela was not sure what Suze was talking about, but answered anyway, "well, actually, Steve Ryle's cute."

"Steve Ryle," Suze and Gina exclaimed in unison, eyes wide, mouths agape. "You gotta be kidding."

"Shhh, you guys. Keep your voices down." Angela's eyes darted about the room. Suze and Gina looked around furtively. Neither of them had any direct contact with Steve Ryle, but they knew he was off-limits. He was Marcia Kincaid's boyfriend.

"It's heavy," Gina said. "And you know what *that* means," Suze raised an eyebrow and, leaning across the table, mouthed, "going all the way." Angela felt a wave of jealously at the thought of Steve with another girl.

"You don't want to mess with Marcia." Gina warned. "Any of the cheerleaders, in fact. They're trouble, the whole bunch. Right, Suze?"

Though Angela heard what her friends were saying, an inner voice told her something quite different. The electricity she felt that day in Mr. Tolles's class was real. The magnitude of her attraction to this boy was intoxicating, filling her with a potent sense of destiny. It didn't matter that Steve was with Marcia for now. He of all people would have a girlfriend. She understood that. But relationships end and people move on. She was sure Marcia was a mere dalliance and that Steve was destined for a more profound bond. "We'll just see about Mr. Ryle," she told herself.

CHAPTER TWO

While Angela caught glimpses of Steve in the distance, days passed without a repeat encounter. Looking through an open window during study hall one balmy afternoon, she watched as pumpkin-hued leaves danced against the sky and thought how pleasant it would be to be *in* that tree with the rustling of leaves all about her—to be *outside* with her books on this gorgeous day.

She became aware of the distant, muffled sounds of football practice. It suddenly occurred to her that if she were to take her books to the football field...well, she could knock off her studies in the fresh air, and she just might run into Steve. Emboldened, she hastily gathered up her books and set off.

Settling herself in the bleachers, she opened her chemistry book. She raised her eyes, now and again, to watch the skirmishes. Just as she had become absorbed in a particularly challenging problem, a football landed with a terrific crash on the bench beside her. She jumped and looking up, saw him grinning at her from the field. It was just as she had hoped.

He sprinted up the bleachers, two steps at a time. "Sorry about that, Angela D'Agnese," he said, grasping the ball. A film of sweat glistened on his cheekbones. She felt the heat of his azure gaze.

"That's okay," she stammered, coloring at the sight of his broad smile and irresistible dimples.

"You're Tony D's kid sister—I just realized." She nodded.

"What an athlete." Steve remarked. He looked over at the field, "oh, Geez, I gotta go," he exclaimed, flashing her another smile. "Well, see ya," he winked and was gone.

It wasn't until the night game against longtime rival, George Washington High School from nearby Salem that she saw him again. All day long the Green Valley Spirit Boosters had been broadcasting reminders about the season kick-off over the school's loudspeakers. Emotions were running high, and a large, boisterous crowd had assembled. It had turned warm again and felt more like August than mid-September.

By the time Angela arrived with Suze and Gina, the cheerleaders were already on the field in their saucy little uniforms performing an elaborately choreographed routine.

Everyone rose for *The Star Spangled Banner,* then the teams were announced and the individual players introduced. Finally the game began. Angela's attention was immediately trained on player number 22. She kept thinking about their last meeting, replaying all the details: the dazzling smile, his charming manner and the warmth that had filled her. It was a delicious, almost proprietary connection she now felt. Her eyes followed Steve for the entire game as he passed and received the ball and, in one glorious play, sprinted three-quarters down the field, football in hand, neatly eluding the opposing team to secure what was the most dramatic touchdown of the evening.

The cheerleaders darted out as Steve's teammates hoisted him on their shoulders. "Green Valley Falcons: Fight, Fight, Fight!" pealed the girls' voices. "'Cause you're the team that's right, right, right!" Right after, when Steve approached the bench, Marcia Kincaid grabbed his arm and pulled him to her. Angela fumed as she watched Marcia plant a lengthy kiss on his lips. Steve broke away, grinning and let his hand slide down Marcia's back, lingering, so it seemed, over the flare of her skirt. Angela was consumed with hot jealously. Her earlier feelings of confidence faded in an instant, and she wondered if she'd misread Steve.

Banishing these doubts from her mind she returned to the bleachers the following Monday. The musky scent of autumn leaves wafted over the empty playing fields. Football practice had not yet begun as Angela picked up a book. No sooner had she begun to read than she felt his presence.

"You're back." he said grinning. "What you working on?"

"Oh, Hi," she replied, trying to sound casual. "My English." She held up the book of poems for him to see.

"Cool," he laughed.

"Say, I noticed you at the game Saturday." She felt herself flush— *he'd noticed her?* "So, did you have fun?" She was tongue-tied—still trying to process the fact he'd spotted her in the crowd.

"Yeah. I had a great time." She said, running her fingers through her hair. "That was some touchdown."

"Gee thanks." He looked down at his feet, smiling. She was charmed by his modesty. There was a pause. He looked up. "So, you like football?" She nodded, meeting his eyes briefly before shifting her gaze to the safety of the distant hills.

"Well, I guess you'd have to, with two older brothers." Clearing his throat, he began speaking slowly, feeling his way through the words. "So, Angela, I was wondering if you're doing anything Saturday night? I was thinking we could maybe catch a movie together."

Angela couldn't believe her ears. Was Steve Ryle asking her out on a date?

"So, Angela, how 'bout it?" he persisted, an impish smile playing across his face—his laughing eyes daring her...to do what? She didn't know.

"But what about Marcia?" she blurted.

"What about her?" Steve demanded.

"I don't know," she stammered. "I thought you two were going steady."

"You did, did you? Well, that's finished," he said. He sat down beside her and there was an awkward silence. "So, Angela," he pressed, "you'll go out with me?"

Before she could answer, Coach McIntire bellowed from the field, "Hey, Ryle! Get yer butt over here. NOW. Flirt with the girls on your own time. Between three and five: you're on my clock!"

"Er—sorry, Coach, I'll be right there," he called. He glanced back at Angela raising his eyebrows to reiterate the question that remained unanswered.

He turned to the field, and Angela feeling the moment slip away, reached out to touch his arm. "Yes," she said.

On the way home, Angela could barely contain her excitement, but her elation soon evaporated as she began to think of her father's reaction. In the excitement of the moment, she'd completely forgotten about him—the dragon at the gates. Old school, Tony D'Agnese would never in a million years let his 17 year-old daughter—his innocent girl—go on a date unchaperoned. Her heart sank; her father's strict ways would surely put an end to a relationship with Steve before it even began. "Well," she said to herself defiantly, "I'll just sneak out behind his back if I have to."

Gina and Suze, sensing something was up, probed their friend relentlessly, but Angela didn't breathe a word, determined to keep the date a secret.

As the weekend approached, she began to lose her nerve and realized she couldn't disobey her parents. Passing her in the hall on Friday, Steve slipped her a note that read, "Can't wait 'til tomorrow."

After supper that evening, Angela was in the kitchen helping her mother with the washing up, her father situated in his La-Z-Boy watching the Huntley-Brinkley Report in the family room when the phone rang.

"It's a boy named Steve Ryle for you, Honey." Angela froze. Her mother's eyes twinkled—it was the first such call her daughter had received. Angela put down the dishtowel. She felt sick to her stomach.

"Hello?" she said into the mouthpiece as she dragged the receiver into the hall for privacy.

"How you doing Angela?" His voice was cheerful. "I was just checking what time I should pick you up tomorrow."

"Oh, Steve, I'm glad you called because... it turns out I can't go." Catching sight of her reflection in the mirror, she watched guiltily as her mouth formed the lie. "I don't feel so good. I think I must be coming down with the 'flu or something."

There was a silence at the other end of the line. Finally, Steve spoke, his words were measured, his tone suspicious, "Well, Gee, Angie, that's a shame. I was really excited about tomorrow."

"Yeah, me too," she said dully, nervously twisting the phone cord around her finger.

"Well, maybe we can do it another time," his voice was cool. But she suspected with a sinking heart there wouldn't be a next time.

"Yeah, sure," she replied.

Their conversation over, she was filled with overwhelming self-pity, but mostly she was ashamed of lying to Steve. Just then, Anna breezed into the hallway from the kitchen, drying her hands on her apron as she headed for the stairs. She paused fleetingly behind her daughter, lightly pressing a hand on her shoulder.

"Everything okay, Honey?" she asked, concerned.

Angela blinked back tears and nodded. Her mother moved away and started up the stairs. "Don't forget, Angelina," she called out, "Nonna's birthday's tomorrow. I just started on the cake."

Angela sighed heavily. Now, instead of spending time with the boy she had a crush on, all she had to look forward to was another boring weekend with her family. Yet, she was cheered by Anna's compassion. Though a mere filament of expression, the underlying message felt powerful: she could count on her mother.

As she replaced the receiver in the cradle, she could hear the TV in the den. A young pacifist at an anti-war demonstration had been arrested for burning his draft card. "The guy's a coward, plain and simple," she heard her father bellow.

Angela was relieved when the final bell rang on Monday. She had made it through the whole day without running into Steve. But this sentiment was short-lived: he was waiting for her outside. "So Angela," he challenged. "You feeling better? You look A-okay to me."

"Oh, Hi, Steve," she answered, clasping her books tightly to her chest, "Yes, much better, thanks."

"That's good. I'm glad you made such a *speedy* recovery." His sarcastic tone stung. "Actually, I know you lied to me. Jack Meeker said he *saw* you Saturday night, out with some guy when you were supposedly so sick." He glared at her.

Angela stared at him mutely.

"I don't know what kind of game you're playin', Sweetheart," he continued, "but you could have been straight with me from the get go and told me there was someone else in the picture."

Angela's cheeks burned "*No*," she cried. "That's not it. There's nobody else. I swear," she insisted. "I was at my grandmother's house Saturday afternoon." Then it dawned on her. "I know; Jack must have seen me with my cousin, Bobby. He walked me home from Nonna's."

"Okay, so why did you lie to me about being sick and break our date?" Steve asked.

She avoided his eyes, "You wouldn't understand."

"Try me," he said evenly.

"It's my father. He's very strict." She hesitated. Their eyes met. "I did want to go out with you, Steve, honest I did, it's just that my Dad…he won't let me." There, I've said it, she thought. He'll probably laugh in my face and take off.

Instead, he reached over and gently brushed a lock of hair from her cheek. "Angie…" he began, "is it okay if I call you that?" She nodded. "Why didn't you tell me this from the start?"

"I guess I was embarrassed," she mumbled. "I thought you'd think it was, well, weird or something."

"Well, it *is* old-fashioned," he said. "But, I understand. You're something special, Angie, and you should be treated special." He paused. "I'd still like to go out with you though—even if your entire family comes along."

"You would?" she asked, incredulous.

Steve grinned, "Uh-huh, I sure would."

"Well, I suppose my father might go for your coming to dinner at the house," Angela suggested.

"That'd be great. I bet your Mom's a good cook."

"Well, how about Saturday? I'll check with my parents and see if it's okay."

They lingered for a few moments longer. Then, Steve raised an index finger to his lips, kissed it and, reaching over, placed it tenderly on Angela's cheek. "I'll call you tonight after you've talked to your folks."

Saturday evening Steve arrived at the D'Agneses' house promptly at 6:00 p.m. Angela's father greeted him at the front door with a perfunctory hello and led him into the living room. They sat together for what seemed like an eternity, with Steve trying gamely to engage Mr. D'Agnese in conversation.

Finally, Angela's brothers joined them. "Well, well," Tony Junior grinned, crossing the room to shake Steve's hand. "I'd no idea my sister started dating. But you know what? She's got good taste—I've seen you in action on the field, and I have to say, I'm a big fan."

REBECCA JAMES

"Hey there, Ryle," John nodded, smiling warmly at his classmate. "Good to see you."

"Your playing's been great so far," Tony Junior continued, as he sat down on the sofa grabbing a handful of peanuts from a bowl on the coffee table, and popping them into his mouth one by one. "'Course the season's still young—I got sidelined pretty early on, senior year. Tore my meniscus." He reached down to rub his knee. "That was it for me."

"Yeah, I remember. That was my first year on the team," Steve said. "It was a real blow losing you. I don't think we won a single game after that." Tony grinned, pleased by Steve's compliment.

"So what're you up to these days?" he asked.

"I work construction. Grassi Brothers." Steve nodded in recognition. "Can't complain, keeps me off the streets," Tony Junior chuckled. "Pay's good and the work keeps me in shape." He flexed his arm. "See that?" he gestured with his chin at the bulging bicep. "Not bad, eh?"

Steve grinned. "Not bad at all.' He then turned to John. "So John, I never see you. How's your year been panning out?"

John talked about the tri-county debate he'd be attending with Green Valley's forensics team; qualifying for the nationals looked promising.

"Sheez, my brother, the brain," Tony groaned as he grabbed his head, shaking it back and forth in mock exasperation.

"Hey, I think it's cool," Steve protested.

John shot him a grateful look and then addressing his brother, said, "We all know you played football without a helmet, so we'll let your wisecracks slide."

Angela appeared in the doorway, before Tony Junior could reply. Seeing her, Steve jumped to his feet. "Hey, Angela," he beamed. "You look nice."

"Thanks." Her eyes shone.

"So, Angie," called out Tony Junior from the plastic-covered couch. "It's your first date, where you gonna go—the playground?" He guffawed, elbowing his brother.

Angela ignored him. "Supper's almost ready if any of you care to wash up," she offered. Steve leapt at the excuse to leave the room. Angela showed him to the half bath under the stairs.

"How'm I doing?" he whispered to her in the hall.

She smiled. "I heard laughter—that's always a good sign."

"Hope so," he grinned, ducking into the bathroom.

He emerged as the others were filing into the kitchen. Angela's mother was standing at the sink pouring a steaming pot of spaghetti into a colander. Upon seeing Steve she set the pot down and, smiling warmly, took his outstretched hand in hers. She had a pleasant face; it was clear she'd been a beauty, and he could see Angela in her features.

"Pleased to meet you, Steve. Glad you could join us." She turned back and began transferring the spaghetti to a large platter, ladling thick tomato sauce and meatballs over it. The family took their places around the table. Anna placed the steaming dish in front of her husband and then took her seat herself.

"Gee, Ma, this smells good," Tony Junior exclaimed appreciatively.

"Mmm-hmm," agreed John passing the garlic bread.

They bowed their heads while Angela's father said grace, before digging into the meal. For a while, the only sounds were of people chewing and cutlery scraping against china.

Angela's father broke the silence, "Anna you outdid yourself tonight. Steve here's going to think I married you for your cooking."

"Yeah, Ma, the gravy's sure good," added Tony Junior, leaning back in his chair and patting his stomach with satisfaction. "I think I've got to get more."

"Better watchit, Tony," teased John. "Now you're not playing ball, you're going to get fat if you don't cut back." His older brother shot him a baleful look.

"Oh, hush, Johnny," said Anna, "Tonino's fine." She flashed Steve a smile, "So, Steve, tell us a little about yourself."

"Well, Mrs. D'Agnese, let's see. I'm a senior at Green Valley with John. And, I'm on the football team, like Tony was," he gestured to her older son, "and I work part-time for my Dad fixing cars. He's a mechanic." He took a bite of spaghetti.

"Oh, yes, I pass by Ryle's Garage all the time. Over on Montrose—right?" Steve nodded.

"And where do your folks live?" Anna continued.

"We live on Locust, just off Drummond Avenue. But it's just me and my Dad. My Mom died a long time ago—when I was six. My older sister's a nurse in Pittsburgh."

"Oh, that's right. I remember hearing about your mother's passing. I'm sorry." Anna said. "It must be hard for your father, not having your sister nearby. But I imagine there's a lot more nursing opportunity in a big city like Pittsburgh."

"She's got a great job at Mercy Hospital. But, these days she's having a tough time. You see, Carmel's husband's over in Vietnam. He's an army medic. So she's basically a single mother these days."

"Well, God bless him. Every day I say a prayer for those brave boys." Anna crossed herself.

"I wish *I* could go over there and kick some gook butt," snarled Tony Junior.

"Oh, Tony, don't talk like that!" Anna glared at her son. Then turning back to Steve, she explained, "Tony hurt his knee playing football you know, and flunked his physical. So, thankfully," she raised a hand to her breast to finger the cross on its chain, "he's exempt from serving."

"Ironic, ain't it?" Tony Junior piped in. "Here's I want nothing more than to go teach those Commie dinks not to mess with the good Ol' 'U-S-of-A. Meanwhile, there's plenty of faggot cowards out there—you, know, spoiled college boys, who've always had somebody to wipe their noses—who are shitting bricks—excuse me, Ma," he looked over at his mother nervously, "wondering how to stay out of it. Ha! That's a laugh."

"Tonino!" exclaimed Anna sharply. "Enough, already."

"Listen to your mother, Tony, and put a lid on it," added Mr. D'Agnese sternly. "There's ladies present."

"I don't know if Angela's told you, Steve," Anna said, changing the subject. "But, like your sister, I trained as a nurse. In fact, that's how I met Angela's father," she added brightly, glancing at her husband. "He was wounded in the South Pacific and shipped to the V.A. hospital where I was working in Chicago."

"I thought I'd died and gone to heaven when I came to and saw this angel bending over me." Mr. D'Agnese smiled for the first time that evening.

"It always struck me as downright cruel—I mean here I was flat on my back, weak as a kitten, and there's this gorgeous woman taking care of me," he winked at his wife. "There were some real good-looking nurses in that hospital, though believe me, no one could hold a candle to Anna Anderson—I think it was some sadistic army muckety-muck's idea of a joke. Instead of old crones for nurses, we got bombshells. On the plus side, they kept our hearts beating along at a good clip and gave us a reason to get better!" He shook his head. "From the moment I laid eyes on her," he continued to no one in particular, gesturing with his chin in Anna's direction, "I knew she was the one." Anna blushed and the room fell quiet for a few moments.

"Well, that's enough about us," she finally said. "I hope everybody got enough to eat. Steve? How about some more?"

"Oh, no thank you, Mrs. D'Agnese. I'm fine," he answered. "But it sure was good."

She smiled at him. "I'm so glad you liked it. Now, if you'll excuse me for a minute, I'll see about dessert. Angie, could you give me a hand?"

The dinner dishes cleared, a stack of lusterware dessert plates, and a cake dusted with powdered sugar were set before Mr. D'Agnese. The cake was cut and passed around.

"This is delicious," Steve declared.

"Why, thank you. An old family recipe—Swedish Apple Cake."

After supper, Steve offered to help with the dishes. "Oh, no thank you, Dear. Tony and John will help me," she replied coyly, looking at her sons.

"Oh, Ma!" the boys groaned in unison.

She shushed them. "Now, now, your sister has a guest tonight." She turned to her daughter, "Angie, why don't you take Steve out on the porch?"

It was cool outside; Angela pulled her cardigan around her. She smiled shyly at Steve before looking away. They'd only exchanged a few words since he arrived and now, finding themselves alone, there was a momentary awkwardness. Angela walked over, sat down on the swing and began pushing it back and forth with her feet.

Self-conscious within the D'Agnese walls, Steve had been hesitant to even look at Angela. Now they were alone, his eyes drank her in, resting on her lovely face and softly gleaming hair, which fell in a loose cascade. He found himself momentarily caught off guard; she appeared so innocent, yet he sensed a smoldering inner core beneath that demure façade.

How those beautiful eyes beckoned, igniting in him the thrill of anticipation. He longed to put his arm around her, draw her to him and kiss her. He wondered wildly for a moment whether if he began, he'd be able to stop. But he dared not make the slightest advance; he might have a toe in the D'Agneses' door now, but one false move could bring it slamming shut. Being with Angela on the darkened porch, Steve, then and there, resolved to do everything he could to gain her parents' trust. Even at this early stage, he was convinced that she was everything he ever wanted in a girl. If this meant he had to take things slow, well, so be it. She was worth it.

"Mind if I join you?' he asked, taking a seat beside her. They swung in silence for a few minutes until it suddenly occurred to Steve that Mr. D'Agnese was right on the other side of the wall, his attention likely focused on the porch, and lengthy silences probably weren't a good idea. "So, Angie, I really enjoyed meeting your family."

"I'm glad you had a good time," Angela smiled. Her face turned pensive. "I'm sorry about your Mom, Steve," she added gently.

"Thanks, Angela. Like I said, it was a long time ago—I was just a little kid."

"What was she like?" she asked.

Steve hesitated, not accustomed to talking about his mother to anyone. He was surprised how easy it was to open up to Angela, unlocking such private memories. Angela studied him as he talked. His collared shirt was open and she found her eyes wandering to his throat, where she noticed a slight pulsing. Her gaze moved to his chin and along his jaw settling on his lips. How she yearned to reach out and touch him, to trace her fingers across his face, but knew she must not. Not here. Not yet. She had to concentrate to make out his words and calm the fluttering within.

"Well, she was very pretty," he began, "dark hair and blue eyes. I still remember the way she smelled. Like roses, from the soap she always used. Every now and then, I get a whiff of something that reminds me of her, and the memories come flooding back. And then there was her voice. She came over from Ireland when she was 18 so she had an accent." His voice trailed off. "She loved to sing. I remember sitting on her lap, wrapped up in a shawl as she sang about drownings and betrayals—great kids' stuff," he laughed." They sat silently for a few minutes listening to the night sounds.

"So, how did they meet? Isn't your father American?" Angela asked.

"Well, it was kind of like an arranged marriage. I know that sounds funny, but it was pretty common back then. Dad had cousins in the same village as my Ma in Donegal. He went over to Ireland to meet her, they married and he brought her back here."

"How romantic!" Angela said.

"Well, I guess it was, at least in the beginning. But, it was hard. My mother was homesick. Most Irish immigrants pine for the old country, in spite of all the hardships they leave behind. In fact, did you know when people left Ireland in the old days, their families would throw them a fare-well party, called an American Wake? They knew they'd never see them again, which was certainly true in Ma's case. But, as it happened, most of her family ended up leaving anyway," he continued. "A couple of uncles stayed behind, but my aunts all emigrated. Aunt Maureen and Aunt Maire settled in the Boston area, and Aunt Deirdre, in Australia."

"It must have been so very sad for you and your family, losing your mother. What happened?" Angela asked. "Or, maybe you'd rather not talk about it."

"No, that's okay. I don't mind telling you. She had rheumatic fever as a child, which weakened her heart. The strain of having children was too much. She died giving birth to my brother. Poor little Paddy only lived a couple of days himself. They're buried together over in Woodvale Cemetery."

"Oh, Steve," she reached over impulsively to press his hand; he caught her fingers in his and Angela felt a current of warmth run through her.

He studied their entwined hands. "Well, I guess we all have our crosses to bear, right? I just hope I've already borne my share. Life's unpredictable. If things had worked out differently, we would have been a happy family of five, Dad, Ma and three kids. Like yours, I guess. But, as it turned out, we were down two—my Dad suddenly a widower with a couple of little ones to raise by himself. Strange how fate works."

Steve brightened. "But, you know, I feel my mother's presence with me every day. I know that may sound strange. But just before she died she promised she would always be with me, not in body—in spirit. To watch over me. My *anamchara* is what she called herself, literally soul-friend in Irish, but it also means guardian angel. I was only a little boy at the time, but I've never forgotten that—leaning against my parents' bed and Ma, looking up at me, an angelic smile on her face." Angela squeezed his hand tenderly.

"So, not only is Ma's anamchara with me, one day I'll get to meet Aunt Dee, her twin who lives in Australia. I'm looking forward to that; it'll give me a sense of what Ma would have been like."

They chatted a while longer before Steve stood up. Looking down at her, he thought how easy—what heaven it would be—to draw her into his arms. He thought of pressing his lips into her hair and feeling her body

74

against his... He glanced at his watch and cleared his throat. "I think I better be going now."

She looked up at him, wondering to herself what it would be like to kiss those lips—how they'd feel against hers. She stood up.

"Before I leave, I want to thank your Mom for dinner." He opened the screen door and followed Angela into the living room. Anna was darning a sock while her husband divided his attention between the news broadcast and the issue of *Life* lying open on his lap. Combat images from Vietnam. Bleak footage sharply contrasted to the cozy domestic scene flickered across the screen accompanied by Roger Mudd's familiar voice.

Back on the porch again, Angela leaned against the screen door, her heart racing, in anticipation of her first kiss. But to her surprise, Steve merely extended his hand. "Goodnight, Angela," he said. "I'll see you Monday." He winked at her, then, turned and disappeared into the night.

Angela barely slept; visions of Steve kept her tossing and turning all night. But the possibility of seeing him at Mass the next morning roused her, and she shot out of bed when the alarm went off.

"Good morning Sweetheart," Anna greeted her in the kitchen. "Well, your friend seemed to be having a nice time last night. What a polite boy he is. And so handsome!" She smiled seeing her daughter's cheeks redden.

A few minutes later Angela's father came in from the garage. "Okay, okay, let's get the show on the road," he said, clapping his hands. "I'm glad to see you two gals are ready. Now, where're the boys? It's 8:35 already!" He strode into the hall and yelled up the stairs, "Tony! John! Get a move on. You're gonna make your mother late."

His sons hurried down the stairs. "Haven't you two heard of that new-fangled invention? You know, the alarm clock?" Tony swatted his oldest boy playfully across the back of the head. "Ouch!" Tony Junior cried, flinching, though it really didn't hurt.

They piled into the car, John and Tony Junior baiting each other relentlessly. "Now, now," admonished Anna from the front seat. "I want none of that. If you can't be civil, keep your traps shut. I mean it now!"

"That's right kids," added their father. "Show some respect. It's Sunday."

They drove through the quiet streets to St. Boniface, where the bells were tolling loudly. Tony dropped his family off in front before parking the car. With Anna in the lead, they joined other latecomers entering the crowded church. It was a large Byzantine-style structure. Inside, muted light glinted off gold mosaics. The air was thick with incense.

Finding seats in a pew near the back, they left a space for Tony at the end. He arrived just as the service was beginning, hurrying to take his seat before the procession started up the aisle. As the priest led the congregation through the service, Angela scanned the crowd for Steve. Even as she searched, she continued to go through the motions of the service, genuflecting as required, repeating the liturgy by rote, proceeding to the communion rail for the Holy Eucharist. This gave her a chance to check out the other parishioners and that's when she realized Steve was not in church.

The remainder of the day dragged on. In the afternoon, the D'Agnese men folk watched a Steelers game with Tony's buddies from work. Angela was trying to study in her room, but the play-by-play interrupted by spontaneous cheering, was distracting. Realizing she was making no headway, she closed her notebook and went downstairs. She found her mother in the kitchen starting supper. Anna put Angela to work on the meatloaf while she peeled potatoes and made a chocolate pudding. As she worked at her tasks, Angela reflected on what a momentous weekend it had been.

She felt poised on the threshold of a bright new future and, though she couldn't discuss this with her mother—couldn't even put the words together to express it to herself—she felt reassured by her mother's loving presence as she contemplated these first steps toward her destiny.

CHAPTER THREE

*S*teve wanted to keep his romance with Angela to himself. His going with Marcia, the head cheerleader had been the expected thing to do, so he knew his friends would give him flak when they found out it was over. Steve would be the first to admit Marcia had been exciting—he was a virile young man, and Marcia, more than willing to accommodate him—but there was a shallowness there that bothered him. And having met Angela, he now knew he wanted more out of a relationship.

"Hey, what's up with you and Kincaid?" Chuck Wright finally asked. "I hear things been cooling down between you two. I mean I know she can be a pain in the ass and all, but man, she's hot!"

Steve met Chuck's prying with stony silence. But Chuck was not one to be put off. "You two were quite the item there for awhile and, if I recall correctly, Marcia Sugar Britches put out for you."

"Again and again," chortled Sy.

Generally, Steve didn't let people get to him, but this time his friends' teasing sent him over the edge. "That's going too far," he flared, snapping a damp towel at Sy.

"Ow!" hollered Sy, protecting his head with his arms. "Hey, cut it out, Ryle!"

"Sor-ree, didn't realize you were so sensitive," Chuck continued. "But seriously, you two make a great couple—not to mention, her father's loaded. He owns the friggin' Kincaid Funeral Home for cryin' out loud. You got any idea how much that place brings in a year? It's a fuckin' gold mine. You play your cards right, you could be working there."

"Gee, thanks, but I don't think so," replied Steve. "No way, I'm working in a funeral home. Gives me the creeps, just thinking about it."

"Hey, don't knock it. It's a good living, man, with a boatload of opportunity. Shit, people're always dyin'. And just think, ballin' Marcia all night"—he whooped at the thought of this, "that'd sure make up for dealing with the stiffs all day. Speaking of stiffs, man, just watching' her do those splits gives me a major boner."

Steve couldn't stand it anymore and finally blurted out: "It's over between Marcia and me." His friends looked at him, shocked.

"Man, you're crazy, all's I can say." Chuck shook his head.

"So, what's up? You're not going queer on us are you?" Sy grinned slyly. "Cuz there's one thing we won't put up with around here and that's a fuckin' faggot," he guffawed loudly.

"So, who you doin', lover boy? That snot-nosed Donny Knudsen?" goaded Chuck, as Sy collapsed in helpless laughter holding his sides.

"No, no," Sy squealed between gasps. "It must be Johnnie Ferraro. He's so damn pretty!" His voice rose to a simpering falsetto as he slid down the wall.

"Come on guys," Steve said wearily. "You know I'm no faggot—it's just that Marcia's not for me, besides I got other things on my mind."

"Oh yeah?" demanded Chuck. "Like what?"

"Well, school and plans for the future," Steve said.

"School-schmool. School's just for playing' ball and scorin' chicks. Forget about the rest. You'll never need any of that other stuff—except for, math, maybe, that's important," Sy allowed, "'cuz you gotta know how to add—in most jobs anyway."

Steve shook his head. "You just don't understand. I want a better life. My Pop, he's a great guy and all, but all he is and all he's ever gonna be is a mechanic. I just want more."

"Since when you get so ambitious?" Chuck asked suspiciously.

"Yeah, man, since when?" Sy chimed in.

Steve shrugged his shoulders. "I don't know, I've just been thinking is all."

Later that day, Steve was hanging around outside school when he spotted Angela leaving the building. He ran over to catch her. "So, did I make the cut with your folks?" he asked eagerly. Angela nodded, her eyes shining.

"Well, in that case, how about lunch Saturday? You think your parents would go for that?"

Angela smiled broadly. "I'll ask," she said.

She had not yet had a chance to broach the subject with her parents when the phone rang. They'd just finished supper. Anna and Tony were watching *Bewitched*; Angela was dawdling in the doorway, putting off homework until the first commercial break. John was already upstairs studying for a physics test, and Tony Junior had taken off to shoot pool with friends. "I'll get it," Angela volunteered.

"Say, about Saturday," Steve started right in. Angela hurried into the hall, stretching the phone line around the corner.

"I've been thinking. You know, Marcia and me were er—kinda dating. But that's all changed now. He paused. "Anyway, I don't want Marcia hearing about us through the grapevine. She's a nice girl underneath it all, and the least I can do is tell her myself." He took a big breath. "So I've asked her out for burgers Saturday—I hope you're okay with that."

Angela was grateful Steve couldn't see her dejected expression. It took a minute for her to reply. "You're right, Steve. That's what you need to do." Though she didn't like the idea of the two of them together, his desire to end things honorably with Marcia impressed her.

"I'm not looking forward to it, believe me, but thinking about you will get me through it. *You're* my girl now." The significance of this statement made him pause. "I'm sorry about our date, Angie. I'll make it up to you, I promise."

"*You're my girl now.*" The phrase echoed in her ears. Through the wall, she could hear Darrin and Samantha Stephens bickering. Angela crept back into the kitchen, to hang up the phone, grateful for the cover her mother's favorite show provided.

****

News of Steve and Marcia's break-up spread quickly. Steve took pains to make it look like he was the one who'd been dumped. At first, Chuck and Sy figured Marcia had finally gotten fed up with how boring Steve had become, but, not long afterwards, they spotted him holding hands with the pretty new girl, Angela D'Agnese, and they realized the truth.

From the beginning, Steve made it clear Angela was off-limits as far as their locker room banter was concerned. Doug Whitehead found out the hard way, asking Steve if he'd nabbed her cherry, only to receive a punch in the nose as an answer. Coach McIntire had to pull Steve off Doug, who staggered to the nurse's office clutching his bloody nose. Steve was suspended from the big game against Altoona. But he won the respect of the guys.

Meanwhile, Angela dreaded the inevitable encounter with Marcia. "She's gonna scratch your eyes out," Gina proclaimed melodramatically.

"Gee, thanks a lot," Angela scowled.

"Don't worry, me and Suze, won't let you out of our sight. Right, Suze?"

Suze nodded vigorously, adding, "If that bitch comes near you, we'll knock her lights out."

They didn't have to wait long. Sitting at the picnic tables the next day with Suze and Gina, Angela saw Marcia and two of her girlfriends coming their way.

"Okay, you little bitch," Marcia hissed when she reached Angela's side. "I've got a bone to pick with you."

"Pardon?" Angela responded.

"Don't act coy with me. You know exactly what I'm talking about," Marcia folded her arms across her chest. Her friends, Denise Miller and Kathy Monroe, followed suit.

Gina jumped up and laying her hand on Marcia's sleeve implored, "c'mon, Marcia, leave her alone."

Marcia yanked her arm away. "I'm not talking to you," she glared at Gina who'd been joined by Suze. "You two losers can take a hike!"

She turned back to Angela. "A little birdie told me my boyfriend, Steve Ryle, has been two-timing me," she glared. "I find that rather hard to believe, because quite frankly," she paused, looking Angela up and down derisively, "you're not his type. The idea that he'd throw me over for—for this! I mean, look at her." She turned to her friends. "And then look at me?" As she said this, she ran her hands suggestively along her body, accentuating her curves. Then, putting her hands on her hips, she continued.

"Maybe you fixed him with some weird 'eye-talian' love potion?" she said, her eyes flashing. "Well guess what? I intend to get him back. I know what he likes and how to serve it up. Nice and hot," she declared triumphantly. Angela's felt tears prick her eyes.

"Whasamatter, girlie?" Marcia sneered. "Ooh, did I hit a nerve? I guess it's a no-brainer that in that department you're no match for the likes of me!"

"Few are," Kathy guffawed.

"That's right," said Marcia, smiling at her friends. Returning her attention to Angela, she wagged her finger at her.

"You might not know this, because you're a new girl, but I happen to be somebody in this school, and I have no intention of letting a little nobody like you, a Junior no less, horn in on what's mine. And Steve Ryle is most definitely mine. Got it?"

None of the girls saw Steve until he was beside them. "Excuse me, Marcia?" he demanded. "What did you say?"

Marcia whirled around. "Steve!" Her tone had become suddenly girlish. "What are you doing here? I thought you were with Sy."

He wrapped a protective arm around Angela. "You okay?" he asked gently, before turning to confront Marcia. "How did you know I was with Sy?" She looked uncomfortable. His eyes narrowed as the realization sunk in. "Oh, I get it now. It was a set-up."

He took a step toward Marcia. "Let's get one thing straight. It's over between you and me. I thought I made that clear on Saturday." He paused. "I'm with Angela now. And I don't ever, and I mean ever, want you, or your little flunkies," he glared in the direction of Denise and Kathy, who averted their eyes, "bothering her again—you understand?" Marcia nodded mutely, her lips trembling.

Gina and Suze who'd been watching the scene unfold in shocked silence, looked at each other and grinned. "And now I want you to apologize to Angela," Steve demanded. He felt Angela squeeze his arm in protest but stood his ground.

"I'm waiting, Marcia," he prodded.

"I'm sorry, Angela," Marcia murmured finally, eyes downcast.

Once the girls had moved away and they were alone, Steve drew Angela into his arms. "Sorry about that, babe," he said.

"C'mon, I'll walk you home."

CHAPTER FOUR

*T*he following afternoon, as Angela was leaving Study Hall she was surprised to find Steve waiting outside in the corridor. "Hi Steve, what are you doing here? I thought you had football practice."

"It was cancelled, and I have a great idea."

She looked at him, puzzled.

"C'mon, it's a surprise," he replied, grabbing her hand. "Don't look so worried." They walked across the campus to where a path led up into the woods. After climbing for some time, they reached a clearing.

"I know where we are—Moorman's!" she exclaimed with delight. "I didn't know you could walk here from school."

The orchard was deserted; they made their way through the rows of apple trees, inhaling the spicy smell of ripening fruit. Finally, Steve stopped beside a venerable tree with gnarled bark and crooked branches. "Here we are," he declared triumphantly. They sat down under the old tree.

"Isn't the view great from up here?" Steve asked. Angela nodded and leaned back against the trunk. She looked at the gentle slope articulated by neat lines of fruit trees falling away toward a still-verdant valley floor.

"Oh, I have something I want to share with you." She reached in her book bag. "A poem we read in English Class today. It's called *The Song of*

Wandering Aengus, by William Butler Yeats —do you remember it from last year?"

Steve's expression went blank, and he shook his head. "We didn't study poetry in Mrs. Carter's class, just essays and short stories," he answered.

"That's a shame," Angela replied. "You really missed out. I love poetry—the way it distills thoughts, stories and emotions. I think this may be my favorite poem of all." Steve reached for the book and opened it. He paused at the beginning, his eyes resting on the poet's photograph.

"He sure looks glum," he observed.

"Well, he lived a pretty sad life. He was Irish, by the way," she grinned at him. "In fact, he was an Irish Nationalist, or revolutionary, or whatever you call it—I forget exactly. Anyway, he was in love with this woman, Maud Gonne, who was also a famous Irish patriot. But the sad thing is, she married some other guy. It nearly killed Yeats. I think this poem is about her—how she slipped through his fingers. You can really feel his pain. Mr. Benson says his suffering made him a better poet."

"An Irish Patriot you say? Sounds like my kind a guy," Steve replied. "So he never got over his lady friend?" he asked.

"Well, no actually. It gets even sadder. Years later, he falls for her daughter. But she's not interested in him either."

"No wonder, geez—that's gross. The dirty old man."

"I think it's sad. He probably didn't actually love the daughter, not really. But something in her reminded him of her mother, his true love. Don't you see? It was the mother he wanted, not the daughter."

"So, this poem's really got to you, huh?" He looked at Angela sitting beside him, an earnest expression on her face.

She nodded, "just wait'll you hear it." She began to read:

"I went out to the hazel wood because a fire was in my head..."

"Okay, Angie," he interrupted, a mischievous grin spreading across his face. "I'll listen to this, I promise. But, it's only fair that if you're going to fill my head with liter-a-ture," he affected a phony British accent, "I need to get a little more comfortable." He crawled over and laid his head in her lap. "There," he sighed, "that's better."

"So, is everything hunky-dory now?" she smiled, looking down at him.

He furrowed his brow quizzically, then answered, "yes, I can state with complete assurance that I am now officially comforta—er—in heaven." He squinted up at her framed by a filigree of leaves against the sky. A sudden

84

breeze sent a shudder through the sparse foliage and lifted her hair momentarily into a golden halo framing her face. He was dazzled by her loveliness.

Angela, in turn, was overcome by how handsome he was. How lucky she was to have this boy interested in her. She reached down and tenderly stroked his cheek. As she did so, he caught her hand, pressing her fingers to his lips.

"You are so gorgeous!" he whispered, his voice catching. "You take my breath away!" She blushed, her eyes taking refuge in the pages of the book. "Steve! You're distracting me. I want you to hear this." She cleared her throat and began to read:

"I went out to the hazel wood, because a fire was in my head,
And cut and peeled a hazel wand, and hooked a berry to a thread;
And when white moths were on the wing, and moth-like stars were flickering out,
I dropped the berry in a stream and caught a little silver trout.

When I had laid it on the floor I went to blow the fire aflame,
But something rustled on the floor and some one called me by my name:
It had become a glimmering girl with apple blossom in her hair
Who called me by my name and ran and faded through the brightening air.

Though I am old with wandering through hollow lands and hilly lands,
I will find out where she has gone, and kiss her lips and take her hands;
And walk among long dappled grass, and pluck till time and times are done
The silver apples of the moon, the golden apples of the sun."

When she finished, Steve's eyes were closed. She nudged him. "Well?" she asked. "You better not be asleep."

He opened his eyes. "No, no of course not," he protested. "That *was* beautiful. I never realized poetry could be so...so powerful. Makes me wish we'd studied it." He closed his eyes and said, "read me another."

"Don't fall asleep on me now," she reached down and poked him playfully in the ribs. In response, he twisted around and wrestled her to the ground.

"All right, sister," he said jokingly. "You're in trouble now." He began tickling her, and they tussled for a few minutes. Despite years of roughhousing with older brothers, Angela was no match for Steve, and he soon had her pinned by both wrists.

"Fair's fair. I listened to your poem. Now it's payback time," he teased, lowering himself to kiss her, pulling away momentarily to hold her eyes in his. He kissed her again deeply, their mouths becoming the center of the world. Presently, the urgency of their kisses slowed and they lay there gazing at each other. "Wow. What you do to me," he murmured.

Finally, Steve rolled over onto his back and Angela sat up, brushing the leaves from her hair. "We should be going," she said, gathering up her belongings.

"You were right, Angela, that poem's amazing." He reached over to brush a leaf off her shoulder. "I'd love to borrow the book when you're finished."

As Thanksgiving approached, Worthington was gripped with Homecoming fever. In shop windows along Main Street, Green Valley pennants and pompoms kept company with paper turkeys and pilgrims. Now that Angela was officially going steady with the captain of the football team, the big game took on special significance for her. She was attending it with her brothers, but her father had put his foot down about the after party. "I wasn't born yesterday, I know what kind of a freak show that'll be," he exclaimed.

Searching for Angela in the crowd following the game, Steve quickly picked her out. She seemed illuminated with everyone else in shadow. When she reached his side, he took her in his arms and kissed her. It was thrilling to be kissed in public like that. Angela felt so alive: the excitement of the game, the brazen kiss, basking in the adulation surrounding Steve. Her cheeks were flushed; her eyes sparkled.

Later, on the way to Norma's Diner, they passed a number of cars decked out in Green Valley colors, horns blaring, pompoms waving and passengers cheering. "Steve, you should be with them," Angela said, eyeing the spectacle.

"Nah," he replied, squeezing her hand, "My place's with you." Truth be told, there was a small part of him that missed the camaraderie of the post-game gatherings. Always fun, they were the ultimate ego trip, especially when your team won. But he'd been to plenty of those parties and his priorities had changed.

Known for its home-style meals, *"with a Greek accent,"* so the menu said, Norma's was open from 5:00 am until midnight, six days a week. The chrome-sided diner was presided over by Norma Leonides, a flamboyant woman in her late 50's whose candy-floss hair was arranged in a dramatic upsweep that added several inches to her height. To ensure that her eyes stood out from behind her diamante cat's eye glasses, she applied generous amounts of eyeliner and peacock blue eye shadow, topping everything off with thick false eyelashes. Somewhat of a beauty maverick, Norma favored shocking pink lipstick, but applied fire engine red polish to her nails. As she sat on her perch behind the cash register, in her bright colors and abundant gold jewelry, Norma resembled nothing so much as a large, tropical bird.

This evening, she greeted them warmly. She knew both the Ryle and D'Agnese families, and she loved to flirt with men, especially young and handsome ones. "Well, well what are you boys doing here? Shouldn't you be out celebrating with the other kids?" she asked. "Not that I mind! Believe-you-me," she added quickly. "I'm honored to have Worthingtons' finest at Norma's on Game Night!"

"Can you blame us? We wanted some good food!" Steve replied.

"Well, you've come to the right place then!" Norma chortled. Turning to Angela, she continued, "You know, Angela D'Agnese, you're one lucky girl! Out on the town with three such handsome young men! My lands! So what if two of them's your brothers." She beamed "I reckon Steve Ryle more than makes up for that!" She winked at Angela and, then, seeing a blush spread across the girl's face, she reached over and patted her hand, "Norma's only kidding, Doll. Don't pay me any mind. Now, let's get you seated."

A low counter with attached swivel stools ran the length of the diner. Opposite this a series of booths, each boasting a mini jukebox, stretched along the wall. As they walked to the back, several people called out to Steve and a spontaneous burst of applause spread from table to table. He smiled broadly. Angela was filled with pride and John and Tony grinned. They slid into the booth, Angela and Steve on one side opposite Tony and John. "Man," Tony said, "that was some reception."

The waitress arrived with menus and ice water.

"Hey, Charlene, I didn't expect to see you here tonight." Tony greeted her.

"It's so busy on account of the game," she gestured around the room. "I told Norma I could come in."

"Well, you missed a good one," Tony continued. "Our boy here," he pointed at Steve, "sewed it up—two touchdowns under his belt, he threaded a 30-yard pass through coverage for another with just seconds to go! You should have seen him." He reached over and cuffed Steve playfully on the arm.

"Gee whiz, Honey, that's great! Well, you must have worked up quite an appetite with all that running around." She took an order pad from her apron pocket and a pencil from behind her ear, holding it poised over the pad. "So what'll it be?"

"What do know, there's Rose and Mark over there," Tony mumbled. "I heard they're getting hitched." Tony had gone on a few dates with Rose Rubio and was smitten. He was wounded when she didn't return his phone calls.

With one eye on her brothers, Angela reached for Steve's hand under the table. His hand was warm and responsive. Lacing her fingers in his filled her with delicious warmth. She marveled at the power of this innocent joining and squeezed his hand affectionately. He pulsed back a response. Every now and then, she would untwine her hand and place it in full view on the table, so her brothers wouldn't catch on. She'd fiddle with her fork briefly, or brush away a strand of hair, and after a few moments return her hand to Steve's waiting grasp.

Charlene returned with their orders, and passed the plates around. As she turned to go, she hesitated, "say, any of you know someone who'd be interested in taking over my regular shift? I'm asking all my tables just in case. Ernie's schedule's changed. Now, I gotta stay home mornings with the kids."

Before she realized it, Angela piped up, "I'd be interested." She felt three pairs of eyes turn and stare at her.

"Wait a minute, Angie," Tony interjected. "You got any idea what Pop would say? I bet he'd have a canary."

Charlene ignored him. "How old are you Honey?" she asked. "You got to be at least 16, and you got to be dependable. The shift starts at 5:30 a.m., Monday through Friday, rain or shine. Norma doesn't take "no, ifs, ands, or buts." If she can't count on you, you'll be out on your kiester in no time."

Angela nodded. "I don't mind getting up early, and I'm reliable. Only thing is I'd have to leave at 8:45 in order to get to school on time. You think that'd be okay?"

"Well, most of the crowd's left by then. We'll have to ask Norma, though. I'm sure Bev can probably cover for you. She'll be glad of the extra tips." Charlene answered.

"Whoa, now. Hold the phone," exclaimed Tony, putting down his cheeseburger. "Angie, don't go making any promises you can't keep. You got to clear this with the big guy first."

Charlene turned to him. "Lookit, Mister Know-it-all, your Dad'll be okay with this. He's in here most mornings himself for coffee." Tony reddened. "And you want to know something else, I think it's real admirable that your kid sister here wants to get a job and earn a little spending money. Maybe she wants to put a little something away for the future. Maybe college, even, who knows? I hear you got a smart girl here." She winked at Angela and gesturing with a jerk of her head said, "Come on, Hon, let's see what Norma's got to say."

Angela followed Charlene to the front. Norma liked the idea. She even offered to speak to Angela's father herself. "I'll put it to him so he'll go for it—you know, dress it up a bit, put a cherry on top. No offense to Charlene, but business is going to pick up with a pretty young girl like you on deck," Norma grinned.

Angela returned to the table. "Guess what? I got the job! Norma's going to talk to Dad."

Steve winked at her. "You know what? I bet he'll say yes."

CHAPTER FIVE

*S*teve was right. Angela began the following week. The first couple of days she shadowed the other waitress until Bev finally said, "Okay, Angie, it's time," handing her a pad and pushing her toward the counter. Angela was nervous at first, taking orders and keeping everything straight as she delivered food from the kitchen. But she was a quick study and soon felt on a par with Bev.

Each morning Angela rose before five to hastily shower and dress, grabbed her school things and a quick glass of Tang, and joined her father in the idling car. As she got in, the cloying aroma of the pine tree air freshener, hanging from the rear view mirror, greeted her. Her father kept his car spotless, with only a box of Kleenex in the middle of the front seat. As usual, he had the radio on low, tuned to his favorite easy listening station.

At the diner, Tony took a seat at the counter and ordered coffee and a donut. When the 6:00 whistle blew, he rose and left with a terse, "Bye, Angie." Soon after, the place filled with workers coming off the graveyard shift. Bleary-eyed and grimy, some sat quietly eating their ham and eggs, lingering over steaming cups of coffee before heading home to bed. Others behaved as if it was an evening out, ordering beers to wash down their breakfast.

By eight o'clock, the crowd had dispersed, with most, returning to empty houses to sleep through the day; the less fortunate, going on to second jobs. As Angela's shift wound down, other, mostly white-collar, patrons began to filter in.

In no time, Norma declared that business had indeed picked up with Angela on the payroll. The observation hit a little too close to home; for Angela had been struggling with unwanted male attention, made more uncomfortable because she'd known some of these men since childhood. One morning, when Norma had gone to her trailer out back to fetch something, a customer, emboldened by beer, started pestering Angela. Noticing this, a buddy of Tony's interceded, "Frank, you probably don't recognize her all grown up, but that's Tony D'Agnese's girl." That's all it took; the word was out, and no one bothered her again.

Each week, she took her earnings to the Keystone Savings and Loan, passing her paycheck and tip money with her account book through the teller window. Walking away from the counter, she'd open up the book and note with pride the latest deposit. Looking at the neat columns of steadily increasing numbers was immensely rewarding. Charlene was right. Angela had plans. She was saving up for nursing school.

Steve had plans too. There was Angela to take out and a car to buy. So, on Saturdays, he worked at his father's garage. Hearing his father directing someone into the adjoining bay one afternoon, Steve looked up from an oil change. "Hey, Mr. Benson," he hailed him. "It's Steve Ryle. I'm a senior at GVH."

"Of course," Mr. Benson brightened. "I know who you are. I should have picked up the connection right away," he said, gesturing to the sign.

"My girlfriend, Angela D'Agnese, is always talking about what a great teacher you are. She's read some pretty amazing poems you've assigned."

"Angela? She's one of my best students," he declared. "So you like poetry?"

"To tell you the truth, it's new to me, except for the kiddie stuff we read in middle school. For some reason, we didn't have it last year. But, yes, I do—I'd like to read more. Though I guess I won't have another chance to study it, seeing as I graduate in May."

"That's a pity," Mr. Benson said.

"Which tire did you say it was?" Steve's father called out. Mr. Benson excused himself to join Mr. Ryle by the car.

A half an hour later, the oil job done, Steve slammed the hood shut, grabbed a paper towel, and wiping his hands, headed into the office where Mr. Benson was settling his bill.

"Say, I was just thinking, Steve," he said, tucking the receipt into his billfold. "You should consider taking my creative writing elective next semester. I always include some poetry in the mix. I kick it off with an overview of what, in my opinion, are some of the greatest poems ever written. Gets the creative juices flowing."

"That sounds great," Steve grinned.

"You might try your hand at writing; you never know...." He extended his hand.

Steve shook his head. "Oh, sir, you don't want to shake my mitt—I've been up to my elbows in engine grease," he laughed. "I'll definitely look into your class, though. Thanks for the tip."

The first week of December, lighted tinsel garlands appeared along Main Street, and Christmas carols filled the shops. Angela helped Norma ice the windows with spray snow, and hang colored lights above the counter. While Angela did the lunch set up, Norma washed out a large pickle jar making a slit in its lid with a knife. Using a red marker, she wrote, "Merry Christmas to Our Servicemen" on an index card, which she Scotch-taped to the front. She stood back to admire her handiwork.

That afternoon, Angela came home to a house filled with the delicious yeasty smells of baked bread. It was the Feast of St. Lucy, the patron saint of Sweden, and Anna had spent the morning making traditional saffron buns in her honor. Angela helped herself to a bun from the cooling rack and sat at the kitchen table while she waited for her mother changing upstairs. In a few minutes they were heading over to the St. Boniface Christmas bazaar to man the baked goods booth.

There was a sudden rapping at the back door. Angela looked up to see her mother's friend, Betty Perkins, through the window.

"Mrs. Perkins..." Angela began, opening the door, noting with alarm their neighbor was coatless on this frigid day and her ashen face was streaked with tears.

"It's Ricky..." Mrs. Perkins's voice trailed off, catching in a sob.

Angela gasped, "I'll get Mama." She helped the distraught woman to the living room couch.

"Mama, come quick," she called as she ran up the stairs. "It's Mrs. Perkins."

Anna met her on the upper landing. "Something's happened to Ricky," Angela whispered.

"Oh, my God!" Anna cried, dropping her cardigan and rushing down stairs.

As soon as she saw Anna, Betty Perkins cried out, "Ricky's been killed."

Anna hurried to the sofa and took her friend in her arms, "Oh, my poor Betty," she said gently. "I'm so terribly sorry."

"He only had two more months left," Betty sobbed, her face pressed against Anna's breast.

"Sh-h-h," said Anna holding her tighter. "There, there. Sh-h-h. Where's Dick?"

"He's on the road, I'm expecting a call tonight. I'll have to tell him then."

Anna turned to her daughter. "Angie, Honey, go put the kettle on. And, then, call the church office and tell them what's happened."

Once Betty Perkins had calmed down enough to have some tea, she started talking dully. "I had a premonition this morning. I can't really describe it, just this feeling of dread...and, then, when I saw the car and the uniform, I knew. I didn't want to answer the door. I thought that if I didn't answer it, I could stop it from happening." Her voice drifted off. "But, then, I realized, there was nothing I could do and so, I opened the door."

Angela was stunned. Only minutes before, she'd been so happy, anticipating the coming Christmas season. Now, in an instant everything had changed. Tragedy and grief, two unwelcome visitors, had come knocking at Millmont's door. She thought of the Perkins family, how alone and betrayed they must feel. For the rest of their lives, they would dread this season of joy, be reminded with every Christmas card and bit of tinsel of their immeasurable loss.

Shot down on a lonely road in a distant land with peach fuzz still on his face, the death of this Millmont son was a cruel blow. A mere boy really, Ricky was a good-natured free spirit. Known throughout the neighborhood as a go-getter, he never did anything half-heartedly, from his very first lemonade stand to his rock n' roll band that rehearsed every Saturday in the Perkins' garage. His death brought the Vietnam War home in a profound way, casting a shadow that darkened the long weeks of winter.

Though enveloped in sadness for the Perkins family, Angela counted her blessings: Steve was hers and safe at home.

CHAPTER SIX

After Christmas, Charlene approached Angela about getting her old shift back. "You can have my afternoons," she said. Angela leapt at the idea, happy to sleep later in the mornings. It tended to be slower so she took a hit on the tips, but she could often do her homework, which was a plus. She liked the other waitress, Paula, who looked like Joan Baez and was fun to be around.

"Just coffee, please," the well-dressed man smiled at Angela. Norma's was unusually busy, so she filled his cup hurriedly before moving onto her other customers. When he rose to leave, Angela was at the cash register. He handed her the check with some bills.

"Don't stop," he said.

"Stop what?" she asked, confused.

"Stop that beautiful smile," he answered with a grin. Angela, momentarily flustered, blushed as she made change.

A couple of days later, the stranger came in again. This time, the diner wasn't crowded. Angela was cramming for a history test when she glanced up to see him hesitating by the door, looking around for a place to park his dripping umbrella.

"Just put it over there," she said, indicating the corner behind the coat rack.

"Do you want to sit at the counter, or would you prefer a booth?" she asked.

"A booth would be great."

"You can sit anywhere you like."

"How 'bout here?" he gestured to a booth by the window.

"That's fine. Would you like to see a menu or just coffee again?"

"You've got a good memory," he sounded pleased. "Actually, I think I'll have a tuna on rye and a cup of your vegetable soup."

She brought his order, setting it before him. "Anything else?" she asked.

"No thanks."

Angela tallied up his bill and ripped it off her pad. "I'll leave this here then. Anytime you're ready."

She poured herself some ice tea and returned to her studying. After the man paid for his meal and left, Norma hurried over, "you know who that was?" she asked excitedly. Angela shook her head.

"None other than Henry Got Rocks Worthington!" she exclaimed. "His family *owns* this town." While, Norma was beside herself at having someone of his distinction in her establishment, Angela had only vaguely focused on the concept of the Worthingtons as a real-life family. She'd heard about them, of course. Everybody in Worthington knew who they were. But the pleasant man whom she'd waited on didn't correspond with the image of the snooty family people talked about.

The following week, Angela was clearing a table when Norma listed towards her as she passed by. Jerking her head toward the front of the diner her husky voice rumbled in Angela's ear, "so, I see we've got ourselves an admirer." Angela looked over to see that Henry Worthington had just come in.

"I daresay we'll be able to set our clocks by him soon," Norma chuckled.

Later, Norma buttonholed Angela. "It's plain as the nose on your face, Angela D'Agnese—somethin's drawing him to good ole Norma's all of a sudden, and it ain't the chow! The man's sweet on you."

"That's ridiculous!" Angela protested. "He's old. Besides, I'm a townie—not nearly fancy enough for him. And who says he's not after Paula, anyways."

"Nah. He never came in before during all the time she's worked here. I'm telling you, I been around the block a few times, and I know what I'm talking about. I'd bet my last dollar he's got his eye on a certain Mam'selle D'Agnese," she twinkled.

"You're crazy, Norma. He's probably married, or engaged or something." At this, Norma shook her head vigorously.

"Nope, that one's not married, though, Lord knows, he's ripe for the pickin'. I know the family." She lowered her voice, addressing Angela in a conspiratorial tone, "My cousin, Mamie's a friend of the housekeeper and says they live in a mansion. As big as The White House. I also follow their doings in *The Clarion*." Using the mock clipped accent of a society reporter, she began to recite loudly: "Mr. and Mrs. Andrew Carnegie and her Majesty, the Queen of England are weekend guests of Lucinda Worthington at Belvoir. The family will be hosting an intimate dinner party on Saturday night," she paused, "which the elegant and genteel Mrs. Norma Leonides will be attending." Angela laughed, entertained by the silly banter. Norma beamed broadly before continuing.

"Anyhoo, Mamie tells me that Henry Worthington was supposed to marry some foreign lady awhile back, but then there was this accident— I'm not sure what happened—but she died." She looked at Angela. "I know, terrible. After that, he moved back here, and now it's just him and his Mom rattling around in that big place. The father died when Mr. Henry was a kid and she raised him. Lucinda Worthington. Now, there's a grand dame for you. We used to call her "the duchess. They're very close, the duchess and her son. Maybe not so good for his future wife, but then on the plus side, he's gonna inherit quite a bundle, not to mention that showplace," she winked.

"Well, I don't care how rich he is," Angela exclaimed, "I have a boyfriend."

"I know, I know, Sugar, I'm only playing with you," Norma acknowledged. "But, I also have a feeling about this guy, and I'm pretty sure I got his number." She peered seriously at Angela through her cat's eye glasses and then her face broke into a smile. "I declare, Angela," she chuckled. "I'm amazed at how one can fill in the blanks about people with just a few clues. I see my customers maybe a few minutes a day, but I know more about them than their own families."

Norma wasn't the only one who noticed Henry's new-found interest in the diner. Paula commented on it, and walking into the diner one day, Steve felt a stab of jealousy seeing Angela in conversation with a strange man. He waited for what seemed like several minutes trying to catch her eye. When she saw him, she hurried over.

"What was that all about?" he demanded.

She looked at him mystified, not grasping what he was getting at. "You mean that guy? He's just someone who comes in here." Then, recognizing his clouded look for what it was, she laughed merrily. "Oh, please, you're not jealous are you, silly? Steve, can't you see, he's like 30 or something?"

"Are you sure it's nothing more?"

"Of course." She gave him a quick peck on the lips. "I'm in love with you, Steve. You know that."

She sensed Henry Worthington was watching them from his booth and couldn't help but wonder if all the speculation had been right.

CHAPTER SEVEN

"Guess what I just heard?" Gina plopped herself down at the Woolworth's lunch counter. "Marcia and Denise went dress shopping in Pittsburgh last weekend. Can you believe it? She's dressing to impress, so you better watch your back Angela!"

"Who's her date?" inquired Angela.

"Beats me." Gina pulled off her jacket. "You guys getting something?" She reached for the menu. "I know I probably shouldn't, but I could sure go for some fries." She scanned the menu. "I better not, otherwise no way will I fit into a size six." The waitress came over and Gina ordered a vanilla Coke.

"Mom and I are going to Jacob's on Saturday to check out their dresses. Either of you want to come?" Suze asked.

"I wish Mama would go for that. But she keeps insisting she's going to make my dress," Angela sighed.

"That stinks," Gina said, fiddling with her straw.

"I don't want to hurt her feelings, but I'm a little freaked out, even though she's really good," Angela continued. "I just don't want it looking homemade or like it's for a 12 year-old." She twisted a lock of hair nervously. "I want to look amazing for Steve."

"Sounds like you'll need it, seeing what Marcia's been up to," Suze remarked drily.

"You think you got problems?" Gina interrupted. "What a dimwit I am! I should've waited 'til after prom to break up with Greg! Now, who'll take me? I don't know any other available seniors."

Suze, who was going with her boyfriend, Tommy Sammataro piped up, "relax, Gina, we'll think of somebody." Her eyes lit up and she exclaimed, "how about Barry Friedman?"

"Barry Friedman? Barry Friedman's a total geek," retorted Gina grumpily taking a sip of her soda.

"He's not a geek. I think he's cute. And, besides, he's such a nice guy. Plus, his Dad's a dentist, so there's a lot of do-re-mi there. He might even lend Barry his Cadillac. Bet you wouldn't mind driving up to the gym in a baby blue Caddy." Suze looked at Gina to gauge her reaction.

"Angie. Jeez, you're in outer space!" Gina shook her arm.

Angela started. "Sorry—what were you saying?"

"Well," Gina said slyly, "We're just wondering if you and Steve have any special plans for prom night," she giggled.

"What she means," explained Suze, "is, are you two—you know—gonna go all the way?"

Angela colored. "I don't know. I mean," she faltered, "I haven't really thought about it."

But she had been thinking about it ever since the first time Steve touched her breasts, a tentative caress through her sweater. She was secretly thrilled about venturing further into this unchartered territory together.

After the last bell on Thursday, Angela and Steve returned to their special spot in the apple orchard. Though, with the football season now over for Steve, they were both free afternoons, they had not been back since fall. Worthington had been in the grip of a severe winter that continued through March and this was the first mild afternoon they'd had.

"Oh, by the way, Mr. Benson really liked my poem," Steve reported. "You know, the one I was working on last week," he said. "I scored an A," he beamed. "Mr. Benson says I show real promise—here, let me recite it for you. It's short, but to the point." He cleared his throat and began:

"A wanderer, I
Not seeking love,
Ignorant of its truth,
And scornful of its sway.

Spoiled boy, prideful and sated
Trammeled by ease, free of care.
But you, innocent and lovely,
Stripped me of such callow follies
And in your innocence, lifted me up
To touch the stars"

"Why, Steve, that's beautiful!" she exclaimed, blushing.

"I can see you can tell who it's about." He laughed, leaning over to kiss her. "Yeats lent me the inspiration of course. I guess you could say it's a kind of improvisation on his theme.

"I had no clue, Angie, that I could write a poem," he confessed, sounding pleased. "It's opened up a whole new world for me. I could actually imagine becoming an English teacher, like Mr. Benson." He leaned back against the tree. "Not a bad life, really." He turned and looked at Angela. "I mean helping kids find their way; you know, inspiring them. And of course, there's all that vacation time!" His eyes began to dance mischievously. "I hear college professors have lots of perks. How'd you like being a professor's wife one day?"

It was past midnight. Everyone was asleep, except Angela who remained bent over her dress, determined to finish it before she went to bed. With delicate stitches, she sewed the hem, as her mother had shown her, careful not to let the needle pierce the top layer of fabric. Finally, after what seemed hours, she reached the end and broke off the thread, sticking the needle into her mother's tomato pincushion. She stood up and held the dress out to admire.

In the end, Angela couldn't bring herself to spend money on something as frivolous as a dress. She'd worked so hard toward the goal of nursing school. There would be store bought dresses later; now was the time to save.

So, she turned to her mother for help. To her surprise, she ended up liking Anna's ideas. It was her mother who had suggested white, the perfect shade to showcase Angela's beauty. The dress was a ballerina style with a bodice of crepe de chine they found at the outlet shop. Clouds of white tulle formed the skirt, a pink satin ribbon at the waist the only embellishment.

She put the dress on and carefully opening her door, tiptoed across the hall to the bathroom. She had to stand on the toilet to see the dress in the mirror and even then she could only see parts of it. Still, she could tell it looked beautiful. She felt like a princess.

Hurrying to the Wilsons' house to pick up Suze and Gina the morning of the prom, Angela felt like the entire neighborhood had put on its Sunday best to match her mood. Daffodils and multicolored tulips bobbed in the breeze, and nearly every house boasted one or two showy azalea bushes. Ready to go, their coats on, the girls squealed with delight when they opened the door to greet Angela.

At the gym, Jimmy Reston, chairman of the prom committee, was on a ladder directing a crew attaching foil stars to the ceiling with fishing line. *Help Me Rhonda* was blaring from a radio. Making a beeline to Jimmy, the girls asked him what to do.

"Let's see...we still need help on star detail—the crepe paper's gotta be hung—and, oh yeah, the front of the bleachers needs to be faced with aluminum foil." Suze volunteered to do the crepe paper; Angela and Gina grabbed the foil and set to work, finishing up just as the pizza arrived. After a short break, they moved to the next task on Jimmy's "to-do" list, munching on the last of their slices. At three o'clock, Jimmy switched on the microphone, which screeched with feedback. "Let the prom begin!" He yelled.

The space was unrecognizable. The basketball hoops, swathed in tulle, had been transformed into fountains spouting cascading stars. Purple and lavender crepe paper streamers crisscrossed the space. Hundreds of stars dangled from the ceiling. "But wait, it gets better!" Jimmy cried, hoarse with excitement. He gave the signal: the overhead lights dimmed and on came the spots. There was a collective gasp as the room sprang to life. Silver foil winked from various points, and the giant mirror ball suspended over the dance floor slowly revolved, fracturing beams of light into a million dazzling shards.

"Gee whiz, it's magical," Suze whispered.

"Breathtaking," Angela sighed. She felt at the crest of a wave, so filled with happiness; she didn't want the moment to end, knowing things might not always be so perfect.

Suze broke the spell. "Well, I don't know about you two, but I gotta hightail it—I have a 4:00 hair appointment."

Gina consulted her watch. "I better scoot also."

"Me too," Angela said, running over to collect her sweater and purse from the bleachers.

Steve pulled up to the D'Agneses' house at seven on the dot. He got out of his father's sedan, a florist box, under his arm. Walking up the front steps, he smoothed his hair one last time and rang the bell. Anna opened the door.

"Why, Steve, don't you look handsome in your tuxedo!" she exclaimed. "Tony, doesn't Steve look nice?" She turned to address her husband just behind her.

"I have to record this for posterity," she said excitedly, indicating the Instamatic camera she was holding. Just then, Angela's brother, Tony Junior, came out of the kitchen.

"Well, well. If it isn't Captain Ryle in his monkey suit." He slapped Steve on the back.

He put his arm around Steve and pulling him close, whispered, "Hey man, I'm just yankin' your chain."

But he continued to tease. "Remember: just because you're wearing a monkey suit, don't mean you can pull any monkey business!" He chortled at his own joke.

"Anthony!" his mother protested. Mr. D'Agnese cleared his throat and looked uncomfortable; Steve felt himself turning red with embarrassment, thinking how quickly the situation was deteriorating. Changing the subject, he cleared his throat, "So, is John here?" he asked.

"Oh, no," replied Anna. "He left awhile ago to pick up Brenda. Why don't we wait for Angela in the living room? I'm sure she won't be much longer."

She ushered Steve into the front room where an elderly couple were sitting on the couch.

"Steve, I'd like you to meet Angela's grandparents, Mr. and Mrs. D'Agnese."

Anna turned to the couple, speaking loudly and slowly for the couple's benefit. "Nonna, Poppa, this is Steve Ryle, Angelina's date for the prom."

The woman was knitting, her arthritic hands moved dexterously as she manipulated flashing needles through rainbow colored wool. She grinned broadly, exposing pink gums. Her husband sitting close beside her, hands clasped over his expansive belly, nodded a terse hello.

"Please," Anna gestured to an armchair. "Can I get you anything, Steve? A Coke maybe?" she offered.

"No, thanks, I'm fine," he smiled.

"Here's the corsage?" He handed the box to Anna.

"Oh, my. A gardenia. Why, I haven't seen one of those for years." She paused turning the box this way and that to better examine the blossom. "They're very expensive. Where on earth did you find it?" Without waiting for his answer, she walked the box over to the couch.

"Nonna, guarda questo fioro. É bello, non?" Anna said, as she handed the box to her mother-in-law, who examined it, nodding appreciatively before passing it to her husband.

"Edgewood Florists. They had to order it," Steve said.

"Well, I guess all we're waiting for now is Cinderella," Tony Junior observed, getting up from the sofa and heading into the hall. "Yo, Angie!" he yelled up the stairs, adding in a falsetto sing-song: "Mr. Wonderful's here!"

"I'm coming, Tonino," she called down, the hem of her dress appearing through the balustrades at the top of the stairs. Tony Junior whistled.

"Keep your shirt on!" she whispered to her brother as she passed him reaching over to pinch his cheek before entering the living room. He howled in protest.

"Ah-h-h, Bellisima!" exclaimed Angela's grandmother, clasping her hands together appreciatively. "Tu es una princepessa, Angelina!" she beamed.

The others all rose. "Oh, Angie, Honey, you look so grown up!" Anna's eyes were misty. It was true. Angela's updo and the rhinestone drops at her ears, made her look much older than 17.

Steve had risen to his feet with the others, at a loss for words. "Hi, Steve," Angela said, glancing in his direction and waving shyly.

"Hi, Angie." His voice was soft. "You look beautiful."

"C'mon, I need to take some pictures of you two kids," Anna prodded. Steve and Angela stood together awkwardly, feeling self-conscious in their unaccustomed finery surrounded by Angela's family. "But wait," Anna lowered the camera, "the corsage! We need the corsage in the picture."

"Oh, that's right," Steve said. "I forgot." He picked up the box from the coffee table and handed it to Angela.

She removed the plastic top and the sweet smell of gardenia rose from within. "Oh, it's beautiful Steve," she breathed, looking up at him, her eyes shining.

"Be careful, Honey," Anna cautioned. "Don't touch the petals, otherwise, they'll turn brown."

Angela slipped the corsage on her wrist. "Steve, put your arm around Angela," Anna directed. Stiffly, Steve complied.

"Now, stand a little closer, yes, a little closer still." She lowered the camera. "You both look so tense," she exclaimed in mock exasperation. "Relax, this is supposed to be fun." There, that's better." She snapped a photo.

"I hope the Ridgeways are taking pictures," she remarked when she finally put the camera down. "I did take one of John, but it's just not the same without the dress."

"We should probably get going," Steve announced. When Angela went to get her wrap, Mr. D'Agnese turned to him and grasped his hand firmly. Their eyes met and a tacit agreement reached. All would be well.

They drove in silence for several blocks until without warning Steve pulled the car over to the curb. He sat with his hands grasping the wheel, looking straight ahead. Then he reached over and pulled Angela to him, saying, "I've been wanting to do this ever since I saw you." He kissed her. When they pulled apart, they smiled at each other. The spell had been broken. Everything was back to normal between them in spite of their fancy clothes.

"That was God-awful back there with your father glaring at me and your mother taking all those damn pictures!" He exhaled loudly.

"It was pretty funny when you think about it," she said, her eyes dancing.

"Yeah, right," he replied, laughing with her.

When they arrived, the parking lot was nearly full. Floodlights bathed the school in festive blue and green, and the excitement was palpable. Here and there, groups of tuxedo-attired boys stood together shadowed by girls in brightly colored net or sequins. Steve circled the lot looking for a place to park, finding a spot near a group who were passing a flask between them.

"Those guys are gonna be trashed before the fun even begins," Steve said, shaking his head. "Let's just hope one of the chaperones doesn't catch them."

"Hey, Ryle," yelled one of the boys, wiping the back of a hand across his mouth while raising the flask in salute with his other.

"What's shakin'? Come join us." It was Billy Emerson in a midnight blue brocade jacket. His drinking companions included Sy Caputo, the McGuire twins, Jimbo Murphy and Jack Meeker. Their dates, flushed with alcohol, huddled on the periphery, tittering.

"No, thanks, we're gonna go on in and check out the scene."

"Whatever floats your boat, man," Billy shrugged, turning back to his friends.

Steve took Angela's hand. As they crossed the parking lot, they could hear the throb of music from the gym. They entered the lobby. Mr. Tolles in a pin striped suit and Miss Griscom, the Spanish teacher, in a pink satin dress, were greeting students warmly; the formal clothes and special occasion had transformed everyone temporarily into peers. The band was playing *Baby Love,* and a few couples were dancing. "C'mon, Baby Love," Steve said, taking Angela's arm. "What do you say we warm up the dance floor?"

He spun her around twice and then pulled her close for a slow dance. As the song ended, the Diana Ross look-a-like moved out of the spotlight, replaced by a male vocalist, and the band segued into *My Girl.* Angela and Steve broke apart and continued dancing for a couple more songs after which, Angela suggested they take a break and get something to drink.

They made their way over to the punch bowl where Suze and Tommy and Chuck Wright and his date, Melinda Brown, were standing. Suze was in powder blue chiffon accented with feathers, the color a perfect foil for her auburn hair, which was arranged in cascading curls. Tommy's ruffled shirt matched her dress. Melinda was in pale peach satin. Chuck wore a dove grey tuxedo. After a few minutes, Gina and her date, Barry Friedman, joined them. Gina, in lavender lace, resembled a life-sized kewpie doll. Barry had done his best to coordinate. His shirt had lavender-edged frills and he'd bought her a matching orchid that was proudly displayed on her wrist.

"I saw you on the dance floor. You two looked so cute out there," squealed Suze.

"The band's cool," said Steve. "Where they from?"

"Beats me," replied Chuck. "Probably Pittsburgh. Jimmy found 'em." He turned to Melinda to see if she wanted some punch. She nodded and he refilled her cup.

"Jimmy did a dynamite job with everything," remarked Steve, looking around the room. "I can't believe it's the gym—it looks like a high-class hotel or something."

"Yeah, you know you're right. Jimmy boy delivered the goods, even if he *was* a major pain in the ass," agreed Tommy.

"Hey, it wasn't just Jimmy. We helped too," interjected Suze, looking from Gina to Angela for support.

"That's right," agreed Steve. "I'm sorry, I know you girls worked hard on this. Well, it looks terrific."

Angela spotted John and Brenda on the other side of the room talking with Mr. Tolles. "I should go over and say hi. I'll be right back." Angela excused herself and went over to them.

Steve followed her with his eyes. Every now and then the colored spotlights would catch her dress, changing it from white to a brilliant hue.

"So, I *said*, what do you think about the new line up?" asked Tommy loudly, jolting Steve back to reality.

"Coach McIntire's new line-up. What do you think?" Tommy persisted.

"Fergetaboutit, Tommy!" exclaimed Suze, "Stevie's in another world." She gestured with her chin toward Angela. "Somebody's in love!" she teased.

Steve looked at her sheepishly. "I guess it's no secret how I feel about her," he said.

"What are you guys talking about?" Angela was back. She slipped her hand into Steve's.

He turned, flashing a smile at her. "Hey, princess," he said. "I missed you. C'mon, dance with me."

Later, on their way to the apple orchard, they laughed, recalling how completely dorky Mr. Tolles looked doing the Frug with Miss Griscom.

Brilliant moonlight highlighted the surrounding landscape, silvering the branches and dappling the ground. Above, high, puffy clouds moved slowly against the blue-black sky. "It's so bright tonight," remarked Angela.

"Just look, there are shadows!" she exclaimed pointing to the ground. She inhaled deeply. "And it smells so good. Fresh. I love spring."

"I love how you see the world," he said, squeezing her hand. "You point out things I'd never notice...it's like nobody else I've ever met."

She smiled at him as they passed between the rows of trees that led to their special spot beneath the twisted old tree at the summit. The lights of Worthington twinkled below. Steve took off his jacket and spread it on the ground. "Madam?" he said gesturing to it.

"Won't you be cold?" she asked.

"Nope," he said helping her onto it. "Because," he continued, taking her into his arms, "I've got you to keep me warm." He leaned back against the tree; she put her head on his chest and sighed contentedly.

"Angie?" he questioned.

"M-mm?" she murmured.

"I was just remembering the first time we were here when you read me that poem."

"Un-huh."

He adjusted his position so they were facing each other. "I was just thinking..." he paused and, then, said slowly, "tonight in that dress in the moonlight you're that glimmering girl." Then he found his words, "you're *my* glimmering girl!"

She smiled at him, and then touched by the grave tone in Steve's voice, replied lightly, "well, I hope that doesn't make you Wandering Aengus. I don't want you to wander away from me."

Slipping his arms around her he pulled her close and they sank to the ground. Thrilled by her responsive mouth, he caressed her skin, drawing his hand across her bodice, his fingertips exploring the curve of her breasts. His mouth was on her throat, languishing in the little hollow at its base. With an unsteady hand, he unzipped her dress and slipped it down to expose her breasts. She shivered as the cool night air touched her bare skin. He leaned back to look at her in the silver light. She reached up and pulled the pins out of her hair. It fell loose onto her shoulders. Steve sighed with pleasure and then he began to kiss her breasts, inhaling her scent—a faint smell of lily of the valley, mixed with a sultry undertone all her own.

He was as an acolyte at the feet of a goddess, worshipful, adoring. He wanted to lose himself completely in her. She ran her hands through his hair, gently ruffling the curls, and he began to kiss her on the mouth again.

It felt so natural to be with him like this. She realized in a flash, that IT was happening. Tonight was the night.

"Oh, Steve," she moaned softly. "I want you."

He stopped suddenly and reached over to pull up her dress. He felt like a drowning man dragging himself from the vortex. "We can't do this," he said firmly.

"What?" she asked, surprised. "I don't understand…" she hesitated, suddenly shy. "I want to give myself to you tonight. Don't you want me?"

"Of course, I want you, baby! More than anything. But not like this, not here. Don't you see? I've never felt like this before." He looked deep into her eyes. "I see myself spending the rest of my life with you. So when we do make love, it has to be special. Not on prom night, tussling on the ground like everybody else. Okay?" She nodded and he kissed her forehead.

"So now, it's time I take you home."

CHAPTER EIGHT

A couple of Saturdays later, Angela was sitting on the floor of her bedroom gluing mementos into her scrapbook. She did this periodically when she had accumulated enough snap shots, ticket stubs, coasters and the like, to make the job worthwhile. She loved reliving each memory as she pressed the keepsakes firmly onto the page. She was trying to figure out how best to put the ribbon from her prom corsage into the book when she heard her mother's voice calling her from the lower hall, "Angie, Dear, Steve's here."

Surprised, she jumped up, ran to the mirror to smooth her hair then hurried down the stairs. "Don't you look nice," she exclaimed, eying his madras sports shirt and khaki slacks.

He smiled and took her hand. "There's something I want to talk to you about."

He seemed unusually serious, and she felt a flicker of apprehension. "Okay. Why don't you go out on the porch and I'll get us something to drink."

She grabbed a pitcher of iced tea from the fridge and a couple of glasses from the dish drainer. Handing Steve a glass, she poured one for herself and then sat down on the porch swing, expecting him to join her.

But he didn't sit down. He seemed nervous and held his glass as if he didn't know what to do with it. Angela patted the seat beside her and urged, "Come sit with me." He hesitated a moment before sitting down.

"Angie," he began, "I'm going to come straight to the point. I've been doing some thinking, what with graduation and all," he paused. "We've got a great thing going here, you and me." He looked at her intently. "I believe we belong together—I hope you do too." He took a gulp of tea.

She nodded encouragingly. He continued, "As I see it, the quickest way to make this happen, is for me to go into the army."

Angela nearly dropped her glass. "No!" she cried.

He placed his hand on her arm. "Now, hear me out, Angie. I want a better life for us. I can't afford college, and I don't want to work at Worthington Steel, no offense to your Dad, or be a mechanic like mine, even." He got to his feet and began to pace in front of her.

"I figure: I do my two years. Maybe I do go to Vietnam...but, more than likely," he added, noting her anguished expression, "I'll get posted to Germany, or some podunk town Stateside. When I'm done, I'll be eligible for the GI Bill. I can go to college, we can get married." He crouched before her, his hands in hers and continued confidently, "we'll have a bunch of kids, a nice big house and, long-story-short: we'll live happily ever after."

Angela felt a churning in the pit of her stomach. "But, there's no guarantee you'd go to Germany," she protested. "What if you are sent to Vietnam?" Her eyes clouded over, "think of Ricky Perkins."

"I'm not going to get killed," he scoffed, cupping her chin in his hand. "I promise," he said, kissing her.

"Things are escalating; they're drafting more and more people," he continued, getting to his feet. "I can only imagine it'll heat up further over the next year. I might as well get a jump-start before you graduate so I can get out and we can be together that much sooner. I'll be out, the end of '68. No time at all!" He grinned.

"Anyways it's not like I really have a choice. I'm not some rich kid with connections that'll keep me out of the draft. And right now, I can't afford college." He paused to examine the porch swing's chain. "Plus, if I play the waiting game with Uncle Sam and get drafted, then, my ass will be grass.

"From what I hear, there's a chance, a pretty good one too, that I'll be sent somewhere else. Sure Vietnam's on everybody's minds, but you have no idea, Angie, we've got military deployed all over the place." He looked down at the floor. "And if I do get sent to Vietnam, well, it's just a chance I've got to take, I guess. But babe, it'll be worth the risk. Two years and then I'm done—two years—it's nothing," he exclaimed. "I mean I know it sounds like a long time, but it'll go by like this." He snapped his fingers. "And then, when it's over, we can be together. Forever—end of story."

"But what about a scholarship? Couldn't you get one of those? Like John at Pittsburgh? Aren't there any football scholarships?"

"I didn't get my ducks in a row in time. College wasn't that important to me before I met you, but now I want to make something of my life." He paused. "You know, I had never hung out with a smart girl before." He grinned. "You've inspired me—turned me on to a part of myself I didn't know existed. I'm only just realizing how much life has to offer. And it's because of you, Angela." He took her hand and lifted it to his lips.

"Besides," he continued, "I've been playing football since middle school and I'm tired of it. If truth be told, football was always my Dad's thing. After Ma died he was so sad, I wanted to do things that brought him some joy. Well, it's about my joy now. Far as I can tell, the army's the quickest route to reach our goal."

"It scares me," she said, scanning his face to see if her words were having any impact. But his determination was apparent in the set of his jaw and she knew his mind was made up.

He promised Angela he'd delay enlisting until September. That way, they'd have the entire summer to spend together.

As Steve walked to the podium to receive his diploma from Principal Barlow on graduation day, Angela observed with a shiver of pride how handsome he was—his ready smile, the loose curls under the mortarboard, and the sincere warmth and enthusiasm of the audience, the whistles and wild applause that erupted on his behalf. As expected, he walked off with the Braddock Award for athletic excellence. But a murmur ran through the audience when he also nabbed the creative writing prize. Angela was so happy for him; she knew how much this particular honor meant.

She was doubly proud, cheering on not only Steve, but her brother, John who won the history and forensics prizes. The D'Agneses planned a graduation dinner for him, so at Steve's behest Mr. Ryle settled on hosting a celebratory lunch at Vinnie's with the Wrights and Caputos. This had also worked out better for Steve's sister, who had to get back to Pittsburgh. "So you're Stevie's Angela, it's so nice to meet you," Carmel said grasping Angela's hand warmly outside the auditorium. She looked forward to talking to Carmel about nursing.

Vinnie's was crowded. The place had a holiday atmosphere: graduates and their family members table-hopped. Steve ordered spumante, passing a foaming glass to Angela on the sly. Sweet and effervescent, it tickled her throat. She traced her lips with her tongue to taste the residual sweetness there. She felt a flush of warmth in her cheeks and a fluttery feeling in her stomach, partly from the wine, but mostly from happiness. Nothing could spoil this day—not even those twinges of apprehension that had dogged her ever since Steve revealed his plans to join the army.

From time to time, she could feel his gaze drift her way from across the table, where he sat talking to Chuck.

She knew she looked fetching with her hair pulled back from her face. Her confirmation crucifix, presented to her in this very room a decade before, winked at her throat as she breathed. In front of Steve, crumpled wrapping paper littered the table; his hand rested on the gift box containing the Sheaffer fountain pen and writing tablet she'd given him.

Working at his father's garage was hot and dirty, but Steve enjoyed it. Father and son had a good relationship, and Steve got along well with the other hired man, Sam Euell. Steve had been around cars all his life and the job was second nature. Occasionally, he asked his father or Sam for help, but most of the time he could handle the repairs himself. He relished his independence, losing himself in his work and his thoughts to pleasant daydreams. Lying on a trolley under some car, lug wrench and oil can in hand, his mind inevitably wandered to Angela, the home they'd make together, the successful career he'd forge and the children they'd have. He tried not to think about the army, telling himself it was a long way off—a whole summer away. He knew he'd painted a sunnier picture of his prospects to Angela. Deep down he was scared.

His father woke him every morning at quarter to seven. Stumbling down the hall to the bathroom, Steve splashed cold water on his face, brushed his teeth, pulled on clean jeans and a t-shirt and went down to the kitchen. Still groggy, he helped himself to a bowl of cornflakes as his father prepared the large thermos of sweetened coffee they shared at work. Ten minutes later, they were in the car, on schedule to open the shop at 7:30.

Most lunch breaks he took at the shop, with him or his father taking turns packing the lunch boxes the night before. But, a couple of times a week, he cleaned himself up and walked over to Norma's to visit Angela. She could usually only take a fifteen-minute break to sit with him at the counter, or on the bench out back. But when business was especially slow, Norma waved them away. "Come back in forty-five," she'd say. On those occasions, there was time to cross the street and traverse the back alley running beside the Essex Mill to a small swatch of grassy riverbank hidden by willow and honeysuckle thicket. Angela returned to work flushed those days. Seeing her come in, Norma and Paula would exchange a smile.

At five o'clock, Steve laid off work for the day.

Back home, he took a long, hot shower, scrubbing off the dirt and grease. Stepping from the tub to towel off, he wiped the fog from the mirror. He lathered up his face, shaving it clean of stubble, then slapped on a bracing splash of Aqua Velva.

Spick and span, he headed over to the D'Agneses' where Angela was waiting for him on the porch, her nose in a book. Sometimes, they ate with her family; other times, they'd go out for pizza, or a burger before catching a movie. Once, they sneaked off to the drive-in in Steve's refurbished Impala, a graduation present from his Dad where they made out freely in the flickering light of the big screen.

On weekends, they'd meet friends at the old granite quarry to swim. Fed by underground springs, the water was cold and crystal clear. No one knew for sure how deep it was, but popular lore put it at over 50 feet. A magnet for Millmont kids, they arrived armed with inner tubes and coolers of soda. Depositing their belongings in the shade of tall pine trees they'd labor up the steep path that ran behind the rock face. From the top, it was a heart-stopping thirty feet to the water. First, they'd drop their tubes into the still pool below; then, the daredevils would dive. The other kids took longer, but eventually everyone jumped accompanied by shrieks and whoops to cavort in the icy water until their lips turned blue and their teeth chattered. Then, shivering and laughing, they retreated to the water's edge to loll on the grassy bank until the heat drove them back into the water.

Toward the end of August, Angela and Steve went to the county fair over in Dunbar with a group of friends. They wandered through the booths looking at prize 4-H livestock; then, watched a sheep-shearing contest and, finally, stopped at the lumberjack competition. Steve and Chuck entered the two-man saw contest while their girlfriends cheered them on, beating out the other amateurs, to come away with fourth place.

A country western band was playing under a tent where cloggers performed onstage. Steve grabbed Angela, spinning her around the dance floor for a few minutes until it became clear they didn't have a clue how to dance to this kind of music and retreated to the sidelines laughing. Outside, they found Chuck and Melinda looking for them.

"Where are the others?" Steve asked.

"Who knows?" Chuck shrugged. "I told them we'd meet up at the concession stand at nine if we didn't run into them before. So, you want to check out the rides?"

"Sure," Steve answered.

"I can only do the baby ones," Angela protested. "I get too scared."

"Aww, but that's the point," moaned Steve. "You're supposed to get scared and reach for your honey." He grabbed her and pulled her to him as she squealed. "Like this." He kissed her, and the other two hooted.

"Okay, okay you two, keep it clean—it's a family show," Chuck scolded jokingly.

Steve compromised, taking Angela on the Ferris wheel. Each time it reached the top he kissed her. From up there, the fairground looked magical, a doll-sized version of itself, full of movement and color and twinkling lights. After the ride ended, the boys went on the Loop-the-Loop and the Tornado. Steve won a stuffed animal for Angela, a plush leopard, with a big red bow around its neck. At nine, they met up with the others as arranged. They sat at a picnic table exchanging stories about the evening between bites of their hotdogs and curly fries. A breeze picked up and Steve looked at his watch," Geez, it's getting late."

Polishing off the last of their sodas, the young people collected their trash and headed to the parking lot.

It had been a perfect August night—a happy memory to be looked back on during the months ahead.

Before Steve and Angela knew it, summer was drawing to a close. The day after Labor Day, Steve, fired up the Impala and headed to the recruiting office. He was to report to Fort Benning in two weeks. He was elated when he saw Angela. "The recruiter said with my qualities I'm just about guaranteed special training with a choice pick of assignments. Isn't that great, baby?" It did sound great, but Angela still worried.

His friends threw him a farewell party, the night before he left for basic training. Angela would have rather spent Steve's last hours alone with him, but she was determined to be a good sport about the party. They took over a large table at the back of the Lenape Tavern, which in no time became crowded with Rolling Rock long necks, overflowing ashtrays and peanut shells. A fog of cigarette smoke hung over the group and everyone had gotten very loud. No one noticed at first when Steve's father got up. He was tapping on his glass with a key trying vainly to get everyone's attention. Seeing him, Chuck put his fingers in his mouth and whistled loudly. The group fell silent, turning its attention to the slight man with the thick glasses that magnified pale, sad eyes. He cleared his throat and turned toward Steve.

"Son," he said, "you've made me very proud. I've watched you lead the Falcons to victory year after year. Now, it's time to do the same for this great country." He paused.

"But, before you go Son, I want to share this little prayer from the old country." He lifted his glass and everyone followed suit. In a quavering voice he began to recite the familiar lines:

"May the road rise to meet you
May the wind be always at your back
May the sun shine warm upon your face,
The rains fall soft upon your fields
And, until we meet again,
May God hold you in the palm of His hand."

When he finished, everyone clapped and cheered. Steve sprang to his feet, and made his way over to his father to embrace him.

Then, Chuck stood up, "I just want to say a few words of tribute to my buddy, Steve Ryle... the best friggin' quarterback Green Valley's ever had, and one helluva good guy: I love you, man!" His voice caught and he grabbed Steve in a bear hug.

As soon as they sat back down, Chuck pushed a tumbler of beer in front of Steve. Then with a sly smile he picked up a shot glass of whiskey and dropped it into the beer. The foam rose up instantly and began to overflow the rim. "Aww, man." Steve protested.

"C'mon, don't be a wuss," Chuck challenged. Steve shrugged and then picked up the drink. He winked at Angela before raising it to his lips, then tipped back his head and drank.

"Chug! Chug! Chug!" his friends shouted at him, hooting and whistling. The spirit downed, he dropped the glass with a resounding clink into a glass on the table. Sy grabbed the bottle of Jim Beam and started to retrieve the shot glass.

Steve threw his hands up in protest as another was urged on him. "Guys, guys—I can't," he pleaded. "I don't want to get completely shit-faced." Angela was surprised when he—the fitness freak—accepted a cigarette instead. Steve put his arm around her, pulled her to him, planting a wet, sloppy kiss on her cheek. With his other hand he picked up his Rolling Rock and, his speech slightly slurred, said:

"I wanna propose a toast to my girl....To Angela!"

"To Angela!" was echoed around the table. Steve regarded her and continued, "I want all yous guys to keep an eye on her while I'm gone. Make sure she's okay."

Another round of long necks was ordered and passed around. Feeling suddenly queasy, whether from the glass of beer she'd drunk, the smoky room, or the emotions welling inside her, Angela felt a sudden urge to be alone. She turned to Steve, "I'm not feeling so good. I need to go home."

"What's wrong?" he asked anxiously.

"It's no big deal. I just feel a little woozy.

"Lemme take you," he said.

"No, no. You stay here with your friends. I'm sure I can find a ride."

Mr. Ryle offered to give Angela a lift. Steve walked them out. He helped her into his father's car, squeezing her hand and mouthing the words "I love you" before closing the door.

Angela was restless and couldn't sleep. She finally dropped off into a deep slumber shortly before dawn. Too soon, she was awoken by her mother's gentle shaking, "Angie, honey? Steve's come to say goodbye."

She jumped out of bed. "Oh, Jeepers. What time is it?" Grabbing her wrapper, she threw it over her nightgown and ran downstairs. Steve was waiting on the porch. It was only fitting that this spot—where they'd spent so many hours together perched under the tendrils of the wisteria vine, or swaying on the swing—their courting seat—should be the setting of their goodbye. In the coming months, she would often think back to how he looked that morning—tanned and handsome—even after the bender of the night before—clad in a vivid blue shirt that brought out the color of his eyes.

"Oh, Steve," she ran to him. He held her close. After a few moments, she stepped away, "Gosh, I'm sorry I overslept. I meant to get up early."

"That's okay. It's better this way. No long drawn-out good byes—kinda like when you get a shot and the doctor distracts you somehow, and it ends up not hurting so much." He grinned at her. "Say, are you feeling better this morning?" His tone suddenly serious.

"Yes, I'm fine," she replied. "I don't know what came over me. Mostly, I guess I'm just upset you're leaving."

"Oh, baby," he murmured, putting his arms around her again.

"So, how do you feel after all those—'whatchamacallits?' she asked.

"Boiler makers," he laughed looking sheepish. "I only had one, but I've got to admit, I've felt better. At least, all I've got to do right now is sit on a bus and hopefully grab some shuteye."

A car horn honked.

"Well, I guess I have to go." He looked at her wistfully. "I'll be back, hopefully, for Thanksgiving, and at Christmas for sure. And I'll write just as soon as I know my address. You'll write back, right?"

"Yes, of course, I will. Every day. I promise."

He kissed her, breaking away at the next blast of the horn. She waved to him from the porch as the car drove away and disappeared down the street. She stood there rooted to the porch steps staring after the car. Her eyes filled with tears and the scene blurred before her.

CHAPTER NINE

*S*teve's letters were absorbing, informative and sometimes even funny. He enjoyed the physical challenges of boot camp, but on the whole, he found basic training "eight weeks of intimidation, fear and boredom." He described a brutal Sergeant with a hair-trigger temper whom all the recruits were afraid of. You could never be sure what would set him off. No one was safe, but he saved his special ire for the "weak links in the chain." His attacks could be merciless, reducing some men to tears. Steve disliked his methods, but came to realize his approach was a necessary evil if inexperienced "grunts" were to be turned into highly trained fighting machines. In one letter, Steve delivered the news that the special training promised by the recruiter back in Worthington wasn't going to pan out after all. He was stuck with everyone else in the infantry.

Angela sent him chatty, news-filled letters, keeping her tone upbeat and light. She included things she knew would make him laugh: a dime store photo strip of herself, a gumball compass, a snow globe with a mermaid, tucked in with packages of homemade cookies.

Several weeks elapsed before he could call her. He wrote in advance telling her what time to wait by the phone. She staked out her territory on Sunday afternoon, shooing away Tony Junior when he tried to make a call. Finally, the phone rang. Steve couldn't talk long because there was a line of soldiers behind him waiting their turn. She heard them in the background, raucous and impatient. It made it somewhat difficult to focus on the conversation. But just hearing his voice is what mattered. She could barely remember what they'd said, after she hung up, but she felt a lingering warmth. He said he'd changed ten dollars into quarters, which seemed like a lot, but the telephone quickly ate them up. Finally, he didn't have any more left. He told her he loved her and then the line went dead.

As it turned out, he didn't get Thanksgiving leave. Angela had been crossing the days off on her calendar and was bitterly disappointed. Then, a couple of weeks later a short note arrived wielding a far greater blow: he was to ship out for Vietnam in January. Angela fell on the bed sobbing.

When he finally got home for his Christmas leave, Angela was taken aback by his altered appearance. He looked older and more serious than the Steve she remembered.

During their time together they didn't discuss Steve's impending departure, filling their days with Christmas shopping and hanging out with friends. One afternoon, they went skating. Soon an impromptu ice hockey game took hold, and a sizeable bonfire was burning at the edge of the frozen pond.

The next day, Steve helped Angela deliver Christmas baskets to housebound St. Boniface parishioners. And on Christmas Eve, he stopped by after dinner to accompany the D'Agneses to midnight Mass. A light snow, like sifted sugar, had begun to fall, transforming Millmont into a storybook vision. "Just what I wanted," she whispered in his ear, "a white Christmas."

The next afternoon he came over and they exchanged gifts. Angela gave Steve a ribbed sweater of navy blue wool, and he gave her a Jean Naté gift box and some stationery—"so you won't forget to write!"

"It's not much," he said as she unwrapped the packages.

"Oh, c'mon Sweetie, you know you're the only present I want," she laughed as she playfully pressed a shiny red bow against his forehead.

"No, seriously," he said, grabbing her wrist. "I have something else, something special picked out for later. Let's call it a New Year's gift." His eyes twinkled mysteriously.

They came to the mutual decision—orchestrated by spare words—that the time had come to consummate their relationship. With Steve headed for Vietnam, it became imperative for Angela to express her commitment. And on some basic, atavistic level, she viewed their union as a rite that would protect Steve from harm and sustain them both through the long months that lay ahead.

The tryst—an entire, undisturbed night together—at the Twin Oaks Motor Inn in Dunbar, would take place a couple of nights before Steve's departure. Suze would provide Angela's alibi: a slumber party at her house. With Mr. and Mrs. Wilson away at a wedding in Ohio that weekend, Suze and her older brother, Jim, were on their own, poised to cover for Angela if an unexpected call came in from her parents.

In the days leading up to the big night Angela was filled with a mixture of apprehension and excitement. From her Health and Hygiene class she knew the basics—her mother had been hopeless on this front, presenting her, well after her first period, with a package of bulky sanitary napkins, elastic belt and a booklet describing menstruation in a series of chirpy drawings.

Along the way, Angela had picked up information about sex from her girlfriends. She knew the first time was supposed to be painful. But, the timing was good, she had just finished her period and Steve planned to use protection, he'd said as much. But sex remained a mystery, and she was self-conscious about her own inexperience and the magnitude of the passage ahead.

Suze and Gina insisted on helping her get ready, spending all afternoon with her. After a hot bath, they rubbed lotion on her skin, applied a facial masque whipped up from egg white and cucumbers, and painted her toenails and fingernails pink. Though the attention made her feel a bit like a prize show dog, the easy chatter of her girlfriends was reassuring.

Steve picked her up at 6:00 p.m. sharp. When she climbed into the car beside him, he stared at her quizzically. Her hand followed his gaze to the aqua chiffon scarf that covered her head. "The scarf was Suze's idea," she laughed nervously. "She also gave me these." She held up a pair of sunglasses. "But they make me look a little suspicious," she put them on. "Don't you think? I mean who'd be going around wearing these at night?"

He smiled at her. "I dunno, but I think you look nice. Real classy. Kinda like Jackie Kennedy."

They drove in silence. She sat close to him on the seat and Steve held her hand. "You okay?" he asked, when they pulled up to the motel.

She nodded and he kissed her. Then, sitting back, he regarded her gravely. "Tonight's our night and for now, I want to pretend we're man and wife." He paused, then, blurted out: "Goddamnit, Angela, I don't want to pretend! When I finish my tour, will you marry me?"

She flung her arms around his neck. "Oh yes, yes! With all my heart!" she exclaimed, her lips against his neck, little puffs of breath tickling his skin. They held each other, the distant rush of the river merging with the pulse of their hearts.

He groped in his jacket pocket and pulled out a velvet box. Flipping it open, he withdrew a ring, and slipped it on Angela's ring finger. She raised her hand to gaze upon a single, luminous pearl.

"Oh, Steve, it's absolutely beautiful," she gasped. "I love it." She shot him an adoring look. Then rotating her hand to better admire the pearl, she suddenly exclaimed, "I just realized what it reminds me of. It's a little silver apple of the moon!"

"That's exactly what I had in mind." He said, pleased.

She looked at him solemnly. "I will treasure it always, Steve."

Check in was a breeze—the ring on Angela's finger perhaps easing the way. The clerk was a funny looking man with an obvious toupee and tinted glasses. He'd cut himself shaving and was sporting a couple of toilet paper scraps on his chin. He put down his magazine. "Newlyweds?" he asked, studying the neatly attired couple. Steve, avoiding Angela's eyes gave the name: Mr. and Mrs. Stephen Rogers. Handing over the key, the clerk told them where the ice machine was and then returned to his reading. They burst out laughing when they got back outside. "What was wrong with his hair?" Angela finally managed to blurt out.

"It was a rug," Steve answered. "A bad one."

Their room was at the end of the wing. Steve moved the car to the parking space out front and retrieved Angela's small overnight bag from the back. He fumbled with the key in the lock. Observing this display of nerves, Angela felt a swell of warmth. He finally got the door open, and switching on the light, closed it behind them saying, "Well, here we are."

Setting down the bag, Steve drew Angela into his arms and kissed her. After a few moments, she pulled away. "I'll be right back," she said, grabbing her bag and hurrying into the bathroom. Steve fiddled with the thermostat and turned on the radio. He found a station playing soft rock music. He saw the blinds were open and went over to close them. He was standing there when Angela emerged wearing a clingy nightgown.

"You like it?" she asked shyly. "Suze helped pick it out."

"Like it?" he said crossing the room. "Why, Angie, you're the most beautiful thing I've ever seen." He kissed her. He was gentle, almost tentative at first, and then, he became more eager, his tongue probing hers, his hands sliding from her shoulders to linger on her breasts. She shivered as he shifted his mouth to her neck raising a trail of gooseflesh.

He slipped the straps off her shoulders, and the filmy garment fell away exposing her naked form. He paused momentarily to admire her— her round breasts, the curve of her waist and below, that mythic stronghold of undiscovered pleasure—a virgin peninsula cultivated in tawny curls. He embraced her again and Angela feeling emboldened, let her hand drift down to his crotch, tentatively resting there. Steve moaned softly and she pressed her fingers into the corduroy, feeling the fabric tighten as the flesh began to stir and rise. The power she possessed over this part of his anatomy excited her. Slowly, she undid his fly and slid her hand through the slit of his briefs to meet responsive flesh.

With passion mounting, a mysterious alchemy began taking place. As if by magic, their separate identities fused. It was no longer Steve and Angela's sensations, but had become one heat, one urgent yearning. He lifted her up and carried her to the bed, and bending over her, began the slow exploration of her topography.

She had not known what to expect, coming to this rendezvous armed only with love. Now, in bed with Steve she felt as if her whole life had been leading inevitably to this moment. Never before had she known such bliss. He and she were all there was. As the world, slipped away, she realized in a flash that it was this—this man, this moment, this melding of themselves—that was all she would ever desire or need from life.

"Oh, Steve," she moaned, arching her back to meet him. He began tearing at his clothes. She helped him pull off his shirt and watched him in the half-light as he undid his belt. He was beautiful, his muscles and sinews articulated by the play of shadows and light. She glimpsed the dark nest between his legs and forced herself to look at it. Instinct took over and she felt desire seize her gut.

His flesh was warm and soft against hers. As they embraced, he whispered hoarsely, "Oh, baby, I've dreamed about this moment for so long." She reached tentatively for him awed by the velvet softness and pulsing force.

He groaned with pleasure and rolled over to a kneeling position. "I wanna be inside you," he murmured, ripping open a small packet with his teeth, spitting out bits of foil onto the floor. She watched through half closed eyes as he rolled the condom over his engorged penis and then straddled her. He moved slowly at first nudging against her, seeking entrance. Feeling her tense, he stopped.

As if in response, she bit her lip and reaching around to grasp his buttocks in both hands, she pulled him toward her. He moaned with pleasure. Quite soon, she felt the first twinges of the earlier pleasure returning—then, growing and expanding as Steve moved within her. Sensing this, he increased the intensity of his thrusts. Through closed eyes, she saw as much as felt a molten orb of energy smoldering at her core from which, ever increasing waves of pure pleasure emanated. Suddenly, the orb exploded and she cried out in ecstasy as Steve's thrusting shook the bed noisily against the wall. A spasm racked his body, and he collapsed onto Angela.

In the early morning hours, Angela wiggled out of Steve's embrace and rose to open the blinds a crack so she could study her lover's sleeping form in the moonlight. She felt drained and sore and supremely happy, despite the knowledge Steve was leaving her and would very soon be in danger. She crawled back into bed, and as she lay beside him, she began to commit to memory the intricacies of his face—the mole above his lip, the hair-line scar on his chin, the thick lashes.

Quite suddenly, the tears began to well up and Angela began to sob. As if in response, Steve opened his eyes.

"How can I let you go?" she cried.

He consoled her with kisses and eventually had her laughing before they drifted off to sleep again. Later, she woke to find Steve staring at her. "I could look at you forever," he said. "You're just about the prettiest thing ever." He traced his finger along the outline of her lips. "Just like an angel." Then, very slowly, he lowered himself on top of her to plant a wisp of a kiss on her lips. His legs were astride her now and she felt him root against her for entry anew into that refuge of blissful oblivion; the center of her being, and was thrilled.

Steve's flight to Chicago left from the tiny Altoona Regional Airport. From Chicago he'd catch an army transport to Fort Travis in California for processing and final training prior to deployment. Then, he'd fly to Vietnam with stops in Hawaii, Guam and The Philippines.

Tony Junior drove Angela and Steve to the airport. They sat in the back seat holding hands. "I feel like a friggin' chauffeur, up here all by myself with you two lovebirds in back," he groused glaring at them in the rear view mirror.

In the airport lounge, Angela and Steve waited wordlessly. There was so much Angela wanted to say, but she couldn't find the words. She was trying not to cry, but this only made the lump in her throat thicken. She felt utterly helpless as time and events moved inexorably forward. When the plane was announced, Angela and Steve lingered at the gate until all the other passengers had boarded.

"Don't cry, Angie," he urged, laughing softly, "I'll be fine."

She leaned into him, pressing her cheek against the rough fabric of his coat. "I meant to be strong for you. I'm so sorry," she sobbed.

"Shhh," he said, smoothing her hair. He took her face in his hands and kissed her.

"I have to go," he said softly. "Good-bye Angela—my angel," he squeezed her hand one final time. Then he turned and walked swiftly through the gate.

From the observation deck, Angela watched him as he moved across the tarmac toward the waiting plane. Without hesitation, he ascended the stairway, pausing briefly at the top to turn toward the terminal where he knew she'd be watching. He raised his hand in a final farewell, and then, in a flash, he was gone.

CHAPTER TEN

*A*ngela woke to a gray February morning. Walking to school, she felt the raw air biting her cheeks. It was going to snow, she was sure of it. That afternoon, during bio lab she noticed the first lazy swirl of white flakes outside the window. By the time she left for work, it was coming down hard.

Angela was disappointed when Henry Worthington didn't appear at his accustomed hour. Norma's was deserted and she'd have welcomed the diversion. Despite their many differences, she had come to look forward to seeing Henry—as he insisted she call him. He was like nobody she knew: charming without being flirtatious, he made her laugh with his self-depre-cating humor. Most important, he left generous tips.

Of course, Angela was aware of the glances that shifted from one patron to the other when he was around. The atmosphere too, seemed notably sub-dued: "like the Pope dropped by or something," observed Norma.

On this snowy afternoon, Angela spent most of her shift sitting at a booth in back. She'd done her homework and was putting the finishing touches on a letter to Steve when, quite unexpectedly Henry burst through the door, stomping his feet and brushing snow from his jacket. Taking his regular seat, he flashed Angela a smile.

"Coffee?" she asked automatically.

"Nope. I'm going for a bite tonight. I've been on the road since 2:00 and am famished. What do you recommend? "

"Norma sent the cook home early so there's a limited selection. Beef goulash and Norma's moussaka—that's always good."

"Okay, I'll go with that then," he replied, rubbing his hands together. "When in Rome…" he grinned.

She handed Norma the order and returned with a pitcher of water. "So where you coming from? Were you out of town?"

"Oh no, I've been chauffeuring stranded employees around."

"That's nice of you." Angela was impressed. After she brought the food, she sponged off the counter and checked the condiment supplies.

The snow continued to fall steadily. There was a foot or so of accumulation on the ground already with no sign of letting up. The radio buzzed with bulletins concerning the Blizzard of '67. Aside from Henry, there was just one other table where a threesome was finishing up and preparing to go. Norma rang up the check and made change. "You drive safe, you hear?" she called out as they left. Angela looked out the window and shivered. She was glad she'd be leaving soon.

Henry gestured to her from across the room. "Say, I wouldn't mind another cup of coffee, if you'd join me."

Angela felt her face redden. "Oh, I'm afraid that's against the rules, but I'd be glad to get you a fresh cup." When she returned, Norma was talking to Henry. She looked up at Angela as she approached coffee pot in hand.

"Go ahead, sugar," she winked, "and get yourself a cup. We're all done for the night." Angela hesitated. She reluctantly slipped into the booth opposite Henry.

"Wouldn't you like something?" he asked.

"I'm fine. I just had a Coke on my break." She turned to look out the window at the empty parking lot where the snow swirled around sizable drifts.

"It's beautiful. Isn't it?" Henry observed following her gaze. She nodded in agreement.

"Reminds me of when I was in school in New Hampshire. Of course, it snowed a lot more there…'Où sont les neiges d'antan?'" He laughed and took a sip of coffee

"What does that mean?" she asked.

"It's a famous saying: 'Where are the snows of yesteryear;' it's about the passage of time and how our memories are imperfect."

"Oh, I get it. You always remember things as being bigger when you were little."

"Precisely. But in this case, I think it's safe to say that I'm right about the snows of my New England youth." He smiled at her. "I remember one time at school we got hold of a toboggan. We took it to the top of this big hill and all six of us piled onto that thing. We went hurtling down the slope right smack into this huge snowdrift at the bottom. I can tell you it was pretty funny when we emerged: we looked like a bunch of abominable snowmen!" He chuckled.

"Did you ever make maple candy?" Angela asked.

"Can't say that I did," Henry replied.

"I used to love doing that when I was a kid. It's easy: you heat up some maple syrup and pour it over snow and like magic it hardens into a kind of taffy."

"I'll have to try that sometime," he said. "So, it looks like I'm the last person here." He cast his eyes around the diner. "I hope I haven't been keeping you." He reached in his pocket for his billfold to take out a twenty, which he handed her with the check.

"No, not at all," she said, sliding out of the booth.

"Can I give you a lift home?" he offered.

"No thanks. I'll be okay," she answered, thinking of Steve.

"You sure?" he pressed.

She nodded. "I love walking in the snow."

"Well, I enjoyed our chat," he said, smiling.

Angela collected her things and they left the diner together. "Okay, then, see ya," she said before trudging off into the white night. Henry watched from his pick-up as she proceeded cautiously along through the deep snow obscuring the sidewalk. After about 50 yards, he started, seeing her slip and fall suddenly into a snowdrift. He put the idling truck in gear.

Pulling alongside her, he rolled down his window. "How about that lift now, huh?"

Angela was covered with snow. She brushed herself off and climbed in.

"You okay?" he asked. She nodded sheepishly. He steered his vehicle back onto the road, an unbroken carpet of plush white.

"Sorry about the truck, it's not the most comfortable thing in the world," he said apologetically. "But in this kind of weather, it does the job, getting me where I need to go—and the heater works well." He reached over to turn it up.

The truck maneuvered smoothly through the snowy streets, tire chains clinking. The houses, all frosted with a heavy coating of snow, were cozy and picturesque. Angela thought how they looked just like the advent calendar in the kitchen at home.

"You said 310 Laburnum, right?" he asked. They drove on in silence until, nearing the D'Agneses', Henry abruptly spoke up. "Forgive me for being bold, Angela, but I was wondering if you might join me for dinner some evening."

Angela was caught completely off guard. His words seemed distant and implausible, as if directed at somebody else. It wasn't until he pulled to a stop in front of her parents' house that she was able to answer.

"Oh, Mr. Worthington—Henry, I mean, I'm afraid that's not possible. You see, I have a boyfriend. He's in Vietnam." She opened the door. "Thank you, though, for the ride. I really appreciate it." She planted her feet in the drift outside, rose to her feet and trudged hurriedly through the snow to the front door.

Before she could reach for the knob, the door was swung open by Tony Junior.

"Just my luck!" exclaimed Tony. "It's snowing when you get a lift from Mr. Moneybags." He shook his head in disgust. "I would have loved seeing you drive up in that Aston Martin of his. Su-weet!"

"How did you know who it was?" she demanded.

"Pop called Norma's to check on you. Maybe next time he drops you off, he'll be driving that car," he added.

"There's not going to be a next time. He gave me a lift because of the snow. Period. He's not the least bit interested in me," she lied, pushing past him. Pausing at the newel post, she continued. "And, why don't you mind your own bee's wax for a change?"

She felt sure the exchange in the truck would put an end to Henry's diner visits, but she was wrong. The following Thursday, he appeared at the regular time and, smiling warmly at Angela, said, "ham and Swiss on rye, please."

CHAPTER ELEVEN

*A*ngela opened her window and breathed in the soft air. It smelled sweet and rich with possibility. She could hear the faint trill of spring peepers from the marsh behind the house. Could it be just a year ago that she was working on her prom dress? So much had happened in the intervening months, it seemed so much longer. She turned and picked up the textbook she'd been reading, stacking it with the others in a neat pile on her desk. She sighed wearily. She could not recall ever feeling so tired.

Each night before bed, she studied her changing body in the mirror. At first, her eyes would settle on her ripening breasts. Then, they would travel down to the barely perceptible swelling of her abdomen, a sight that both thrilled and frightened her. Resting her hand on her belly, she wondered how much longer she'd be able to hide her condition. The pregnancy had been a shock. She wasn't particularly worried when she missed her first period—they'd used condoms after all. But when it still hadn't come after two months and she began feeling sick in the morning, she knew something was up.

She'd have to tell her mother soon. Anna would be shocked at first but she would eventually come around. It was Angela's father who worried her.

The one thing she didn't worry about was Steve's reaction. She knew he'd be ecstatic about the new life they'd created together. Awed by her body and the miracle growing within it, she pictured him stroking her belly and cupping his hands around her full breasts. The thought excited her, and she sighed happily thinking of how, once married, they'd be free to love each other openly—to spend whole weekends in bed—replicating that magical night at the Twin Oaks. She thought again with a shiver of pleasure of her lover's form as he lowered himself onto her. Then the enormity of the distance separating them hit her and she began to weep.

This was how it was for her these days: a captive on a storm-tossed sea of emotion. An almost euphoric sense of wellbeing would suddenly give way to deep feelings of vulnerability and loneliness. She struggled to remain positive, trusting that her love would keep Steve safe. But there were times when her mood would darken, thinking of him fighting in a deadly war half a world away.

In a recent letter, he had seemed overcome by the loss of a member of his squadron, a guy he'd mentioned several times before. Forged in the cauldron of war, their bond, though recent had been intense, so much stronger, in fact, than any he shared with friends back home. This boy Marty's death upset Angela, reminding her yet again of Steve's own peril. Carried away by the urgent need to comfort him, she wrote back right away telling him all about the baby. But superstition overcame her: she wanted to see a doctor first to ensure all was well. She tore the letter up and wrote a new one with only a veiled reference in a postscript.

As it turned out, she had gotten the name of a doctor that very day from Paula. With her last customer paid up, Angela had disappeared into the restroom. Her back ached and she'd felt sick all day. The door safely closed behind her, she burst into tears at the sight of her forlorn reflection in the mirror, feeling so terribly alone. How was she going to cope? But she knew she had to compose herself. Norma, of all people, could never be trusted to keep a matter like this private. Though good-hearted, her boss was a chatterbox.

Paula unexpectedly pushed open the door. Angela moved to close it, but it was too late. "Are you alright, Hon?" she asked, worried. "No, I guess not," she answered her own question, a cue for more tears. "What's wrong?" She asked kindly. Angela shook her head, unable to speak. "I can-can't talk about it," she finally managed to say, tears glistening on her cheeks whereupon, Paula drew Angela into her arms. "Aww, Honey, it can't be that bad. Why don't you tell Paula what's wrong?"

Angela then proceeded to pour open her heart. Paula knew just the discreet physician. "Dr. Gorham will take good care of you, I promise."

"I saw you two together. That Steve Ryle's a good guy." Paula reached for the doorknob. "Now, why don't you wash your face and I'll get you that number." She opened the door then turned again to face Angela, "and, you know me, I'm no blabbermouth—your secret's safe." She winked and left.

Thanks to Paula, Angela would sleep well tonight. She'd call Dr. Gorham tomorrow. Unlocking the drawer to her vanity, she took out Steve's most recent letter:

My Dearest Angela,

It's early morning as I write this. For the time being at least, we're settled on the second floor of a dilapidated building. It was quiet last night. After dinner—freeze-dried beef—how's that for appetizing? I was finally able to snag some sleep. I'm the only one awake at the moment (other than Vernon who's on watch); the others are still passed out. Not a pretty sight, I can tell you. Someone's sawing logs big time.

Just now, looking out the window, I saw the sun rise. I can tell from looking at it, it's going to be another scorcher. I was woken up by the most beautiful trilling and went to the window to see what it was. I couldn't see anything at first—the foliage is so thick here, but then two large birds (storks, I think? You know, the kind that deliver babies) crossed in front of the sun. How ironic to be in the middle of war and yet witness such a sight. How surreal it all is—beauty and peacefulness continually juxtaposed with the ugliness of war.

My dreams—the sweetest ones (starring you!) are such a welcomed distraction from reality. My thoughts are always with you, my angel, and the bright future lying just ahead of us.

In closing, I send all my love to you, my Angela, my glimmering girl.

Your devoted,
Steve

Angela brought the paper to her lips and kissed it before refolding it. He'd mentioned storks. She caught sight of her reflection in the mirror and smiled. It was a sign. It had to be. Maybe he didn't consciously know about the baby, but its existence was being acknowledged by the universe.

She was sure of it. She placed the letter back in the drawer and reached for the jar of Ponds. Unscrewing the cap, she dipped her fingers into the cold cream and smeared it across her face. On Tuesday, she had made a record amount in tips—nearly thirty dollars. Wouldn't Steve be proud? Since starting the job, she'd been able to put aside close to $2,000. Her plan all along was to use the money she made toward nursing school tuition, but now with a baby on the way, she'd have to put that aside for the time being.

The waitressing was beginning to take its toll. These days she took a hot bath every night, waiting until after her brother, Tony, was finished with the bathroom so she could soak in the tub undisturbed. She liked to add baby oil to the water and a splash of the Jean Naté Steve had given her for Christmas.

She wiped the cold cream off with tissues and shuddered as she contemplated all the challenges ahead of her. There were only a few short months before the end of school, and day-by-day the baby was growing. How long could she continue with the semblance of a normal life? The prospect of facing childbirth and the first year of parenthood alone, without Steve was very scary.

She heard the phone ring. "That's funny," she thought. She wondered who'd be calling this late.

Several minutes passed. There was a soft rap on the door. She jumped. "Come in," she called, setting the brush down. As the door opened, Angela felt a chill. Her mind was already knitting together ominous strands of information: the late-night telephone call and, now, her mother's appearance at her bedroom door. Immediately, upon seeing Anna's face she knew something was terribly wrong.

Angela rose slowly from her chair as Anna reached for her with palms outstretched: an ancient choreography of tragic gestures. "Steve?" Angela posed his name as a question. Anna remained silent, struggling to form the words.

"Something's happened to Steve?"

By now, her mother had taken her hands, and holding them tightly in her own, she began:

"Mr. Ryle just called, Darling, to say that Steve's platoon..." she paused, trying to select words that would be as gentle as possible as she delivered such a devastating blow. "They were ambushed...I'm so sorry,

Sweetheart...." Anna broke off as Angela snatched her hands away and teetered backward onto the bed.

"No! No—it can't be," she wailed; her body convulsed with sobs.

Anna hovered over her daughter. "Sh-h-h, sh-h-h. There, there, Sweetheart," she cooed, stroking her daughter's brow. Angela's dressing gown had slipped open as she fell and Anna's eyes now drifted to her daughter's belly. "Oh, Mother of God, no," she whispered.

Angela's grief would dull all recollection of that long and torturous night. But Anna would never forget it—how her daughter tossed about inconsolable for hours, her eyes on fire. As if in a trance, she would recite her lover's name over and over like a mantra as she traced her fingertips across her abdomen.

Finally, toward dawn, Angela slept, clutching to her breast the stuffed leopard Steve had won for her the summer before. At peace now, her face was serene, angelic even, framed by a cloud of tangled curls, her eyes sealed tight beneath dark lashes. Anna gently pulled the comforter over her daughter, switched off the light and, like a sleepwalker, moved to the window to open the sheers. The moon was just dipping behind the snarl of paradise trees and TV aerials across the street. Anna sighed. It was comforting to behold the timeless passage of this celestial body on this sad night. "This too shall pass," she murmured to herself.

She slipped into bed beside her daughter, remembering how as a little girl, Angela would patter into her room in the middle of the night sobbing over a bad dream, and how she would hold wide the covers and scoop the small child into the warm maternal nest. They'd snuggle together and soon Angela, secure in her mother's embrace would slip soundly off to sleep. Now, some ten years later, it was a deep, agonizing wound Anna must dress. She quaked at the thought.

Crushed by grief, Angela would not leave her room. The house, which generally reverberated with commotion, was quiet. Her family spoke in low tones. Tony Junior found excuses to stay away—working overtime or hanging out at the Lenape Tavern. Angela's father also made himself scarce. When at home, he buried his head in the newspaper and watched TV with the volume turned way down.

At first, Angela refused to eat. Finally after several days, Anna took matters into her own hands. Armed with a tray of steaming chamomile tea, a soft-boiled egg and toast, she arrived at her daughter's bedside. "Angela, Sweetheart," she announced, "I've brought you some breakfast."

Met with silence, she began again. "Darling, you have to eat, even if you don't want to. Please, Honey...." Angela moaned softly and her eyes fluttered opened. "You know it's what Steve would want," Anna persisted. "For the baby's sake."

These last words had the desired effect. Angela looked at her mother for a minute and then nodded.

Sitting with Angela as she ate, Anna noticed with alarm how gaunt her daughter's face had become. She rose and opened the curtains.

Angela pushed the tray away. "Mama, what am I going to do? I don't know how I can go on without Steve." Her eyes filled with tears. Anna sat down on the bed and took her in her arms.

It was several days before Angela could bring herself to read Steve's obituary, having retrieved the paper from the stack in the utility room. Once in her bedroom, she unfolded it and stared in disbelief at the front page headline: *"Millmont Son, Stephen Brendan Ryle: Vietnam Casualty."* In smaller type it read: *"Confirmed Dead."* Her Steve. Dead. There it was in black and white. Now, there could be no denying it. He was gone.

She read on, picking out the facts of his life, hollow and insufficient descriptions of the man she loved. Seeing he'd been awarded a Bronze Star for valor was too much for her; the words swam before her eyes. Of course he would win such an honor! His character would demand that he behave in the bravest way possible.

Lying on her bed the next day, Angela heard the squeal of a truck pulling up outside, and then the doorbell. A few minutes later, her door opened and an enormous arrangement of flowers entered the room. The array of calla lilies, delphinium, lilac and fat-budded, long stemmed roses totally obscured her mother who was holding the vase. Immediately, the room was filled with the fragrance of the shimmering, sun-dappled tapestry of blooms.

"Just look at these gorgeous flowers! I've never smelled anything so sweet," her mother said peering around them.

Angela looked at them dully. "Who are they from?" she asked, wondering if her friends had chipped in to buy them for her.

"There's a note, Sweetheart," her mother responded, clearing off the bedside table and setting the vase down. She bent to kiss the crown of her daughter's head before leaving the room. Angela spied the plastic florist's trident poking out of the blossoms. She pulled out the card to read:

Dear Angela,

My thoughts are with you during this very sad time. I know what it is to lose someone you love.

With kindest regards,
Henry Worthington

She could only see the flowers as being a gesture from an admirer and so an affront to her beloved Steve. She lunged at the vase pushing it off the table. It landed on the floor with a great crash.

The church was jammed for Steve's service with all the people whose lives he'd touched: Dr. Hedges, the dentist, Mrs. Mason, the town librarian, Captain Mitchell, Chief of Police, Principal Barlow, Mr. Benson and many other faces from school.

As Angela made her way down the aisle flanked by her parents with all eyes on her, she felt oddly detached. It was as if she was outside her body, watching someone else. Initially, she'd worried she wouldn't be strong enough to attend the ceremony. But here she was, feeling surprisingly at peace—even as she recalled all those times she'd imagined walking down this very aisle to meet Steve, her groom, waiting at the altar.

The D'Agneses found space in a pew in the second row, just behind the one reserved for family. Vases of white flowers adorned the altar and several wreaths were on stands by the communion rail. Angela found her eyes resting on these during the service. Several people spoke movingly about Steve, including Chuck Wright, who became so choked up he couldn't finish his eulogy. Through it all, Angela remained like stone, staring dully ahead, her eyes dry.

Following the service, friends came over to her to express their condolences including Marcia Kincaid, her face streaked with tears and Norma, almost unrecognizable in somber black, sporting a felt hat and tent-like melton coat. She drew Angela to her ample bosom, "Oh, Sweetie, I'm so sorry," she whispered.

As Angela was turning to go, Mr. Ryle called to her. His face was ashen, his eyes watery behind his glasses. "I know my Stevie cared for you deeply." He reached into his pocket. "I want you to have something of his—something special to remember him by." His voice broke. "He was a good boy—no father could ask for a better son." He held Steve's high school ring out to her. "He left this behind when he went in the army. It's not much, I know, but he would have wanted you to have it."

"Thank you, Mr. Ryle. I will treasure it always." Angela said, kissing him on the cheek.

She rolled the ring around in her hand, running her fingers across the cold metal, feeling the hard facets of the stone and the decorative detail incised on it. Even if she hadn't known what it looked like, she could make it out by touch alone. She saw the ring so clearly on Steve's finger. He'd been so proud of it that day he'd picked it up and rushed to show it to her. She thought about the countless times she must have touched it when her hand was clasped securely within his. This could have made her weep, but instead, the feeling of metal in her palm filled her with strength.

That night she placed the ring, Steve's letters and his obituary in the flowered candy tin that she'd used since girlhood to store her treasures. She lay back on her bed and began to contemplate the many nights ahead—indeed, the long and lonely future stretching before her and her tears flowed freely at last.

She dreaded going to bed now; ever since Steve's death she'd had a recurring nightmare. It began pleasantly enough. She was in a meadow, at once familiar and exotic. Clad in an opulent silver robe, she made her way through the tall grass. Mist veiled the surrounding countryside. Presently, she became aware of a figure in the distance, just visible through the haze that she immediately knew was Steve. Instead of joy she felt apprehension. As she got closer, she could see he was in combat gear, though on his back was emblazoned the number 22. He was on the other side of the field, walking away from her. She called his name, but he did not respond and kept moving. She ran toward him, but her feet kept sinking in the soft earth and the silver robe, now heavy and cumbersome, weighed her down. Before she could reach him, he faded into the air like a mirage. Angela's eyes would snap open. And with each awakening, she experienced anew the realization that Steve was dead.

It took another week before Angela felt strong enough to return to school. She was relieved that the other kids left her alone. Once or twice, when she walked into a room, it fell quiet and she felt everyone looking at her. She worried, then, that they could tell she was pregnant.

Suze and Gina ate with her outside every day to avoid the cafeteria. Angela was grateful for this. And when the final bell rang, she hastily gathered up her books and headed straight for home. Life as a carefree high school student was over. Now she was simply there to do the work and try to rebuild her life. For herself, for the child she carried and for Steve.

One afternoon, thinking about him, she found herself drawn to the Yeats poem. When Steve was alive, the poet's words, and the love he described had meant so much to them together; but with Steve now dead, the poem was almost more than she could bear. She closed her eyes as she recited the final verse with a trembling voice:

Though I am old with wandering through hollow lands and hilly lands
I will find out where she has gone and kiss her lips and take her hands;
And walk among long dappled grass, and pluck till time and times are done
The silver apples of the moon, the golden apples of the sun.

.

PART THREE

Vietnam, 1967

CHAPTER ONE

*H*e drew her sleeping form to him, wrapping his arms around her. She was lying in a fetal position facing away from him and he mimicked her shape, nestling his legs within the curve of hers. He nuzzled her ear, tracing the lobe with his tongue and, then, moving his lips along the nape of her neck was thrilled by the sensation of sweet-scented hair brushing across his face. It was a humid night, pulsing with crickets, the air laden with the curious smell of the tropics. Even as he slept, he sensed the humidity coating their bodies and felt the dampness of the tangled sheets. He was aroused feeling her against him and moved his hand down her body.

Suddenly, nearby mortar fire shattered the night. Ripped abruptly from deep slumber, Steve sprang to his feet, weapon in hand, instantly transformed into a soldier on high alert. The sweet sensations of the dream vanished all at once. And she had seemed so real this time…he had thought for sure he was home at last.

Another explosion sounded, closer this time, and a plume of chit burst forth into the air. The men all dove for cover behind a ridge of rubble. First lieutenant and platoon leader, Bucky Campbell and Travis Boone, the company RTO, crouched over the PRC-25.

"Shells being fired—a thousand, maybe fifteen hundred yards due north," Bucky barked into the mike. "Looks like they're coming from the building cited earlier." The radio crackled back at him. More shells thundered this time on their flanks as the staccato of automatic rifle fire joined in. A band of Viet Cong perhaps, or possibly a lone sniper. Dangerous business in any case. Bucky again consulted command. Additional back up was on the way. They were to lie low until reinforcements reached them.

Steve ran a hand across his brow. All in a day's work, he thought. He'd been with the unit maybe six weeks or so, he'd lost count. It had been a so-called promotion, plucked up from the ranks, the carrot, a reduced tour of duty. Maybe cut in half—if you survived. But the engagements had been grueling. Even if you managed to get out in one piece, with all your limbs and your manhood intact, who was to say if your mind would ever recover?

All Steve's senses were affected. He'd seen things in 'Nam he'd never imagined possible: horrific things, surrealistic in their gore and excess, enduring images branded on his brain.

Then there was the noise, the constant barrage of rocket and mortar fire, the incessant ominous patter of automatic weapons; the screams of dying men. And the smells: acrid smoke, gasoline and worst of all the sweet, noxious odor of rotting bodies, human and animal, that lingered on and on in memory.

The reconnaissance team was on a mission to secure the way for the advancing front line, tracking and exterminating pockets of guerrilla resistance along the way. Day after day, they marched through a dense miasma of tedium and fear that settled over rain forest and rice paddy alike and penetrated the farthest reaches of their minds. This latest engagement found them at the periphery of a village where Viet Cong activity had been reported.

The unit had rapid turnover as its component parts were wounded or killed off as a matter of course. And then a replacement "part," like Steve, would be brought in with the promise of a shortened tour to join the "patsies," as they called themselves, and the cycle would begin all over again. To be quickly killed off or shattered for life maybe, but at least the whole fucking chapter in hell would be over and done with.

"Even if I survive, they'll probably have to haul me off to the loony bin," he mused bitterly.

That's why dreams of Angela offered such solace. His glimmering girl, his angel would appear to guide him away, if only briefly, from this hell-hole. Even now, in the midst of a deadly skirmish—not knowing if this was destined to be his last hour—a residual erotic heat warmed his loins.

"What I'd give to be in your arms, if only for one last time, Sweetheart," Steve whispered. Then, in compartmentalized fashion, typical of the soldier he had become, he closed the file on his girl and turned his attention to the perils at hand.

The firing had ceased and the night was now ominously quiet. The men were intensely alert. The humidity was oppressive, intensified by racing bloodstreams and skin coated with sweat. No one spoke, waiting for Bucky's signal. The silence was eerie. Though physically pressed together, the men were isolated by inner thoughts, each imagining the sudden burst of life-extinguishing shell overhead.

The minutes ticked by slowly, and in this way they would inexorably accumulate into hours. Hours that tallied up into a string of days and nights, indistinguishable from one another, demarcating survival from one day to the next, from yesterday to tomorrow, past to present. Timelessness and eternity all at once.

Finally, maybe forty-five minutes later, Bucky got on the radio to report that firing had ceased. Reinforcements would be recalled for now. Bucky's unit was to stay put and provide updates on any further activity. "Roger. Over and out." The radio crackled briefly, then clicked off. Still, none of the men spoke.

"I wonder what the other guys are thinking about. Their girls? Mothers? Dying?" Steve thought, hesitating as he always did before using the "D-word." Perhaps, it was just a foolish superstition on his part, but it was a feeling he couldn't shake: that merely invoking the dreaded word would tempt fate. They all had their superstitions, their lucky charms. He thought of Reggie with his girlfriend's garter hitched to his belt loop, or the fortune cookie fortune Kevin kept folded accordion-style in his package of Marlboros, careful always to transfer it to a new pack first thing after pulling off the cellophane. More noteworthy than the golden future it foretold—wealth and fame—was that it suggested a future at all.

Steve himself chose to carry a photo of particular significance—an early snapshot—perhaps even the first one—taken of him with Angela just a few short weeks after meeting each other. He remembered the day vividly, crystal clear, a bracing nip in the air. Green Valley had just won the Homecoming game against the Penn Hills Indians and Steve was on cloud nine.

He recalled seeing Angela squeezing her way through the swell of players, cheerleaders and fans pressing upon him, the look of supreme happiness on her face as their eyes met and how suddenly it was as if the crowd had vanished and they were all alone. He had moved slowly toward her, taking her in his arms as he buried his face in her hair.

Afterwards, he had kissed her. It had been their first real kiss. Then, somebody—it must have been Chuck—had taken the picture. It was a jubilant photograph, that post-first-kiss shot, capturing a certain knowing look on their faces, a sort of omniscient, fait accompli look as to the inevitability of their entwined lives; a moment frozen in time when Steve and Angela stood perched at the very edge of a sparkling future.

He examined her luminous face framed by a cloud of hair, looking squarely into the camera, a hint of a smile across her lovely mouth. Angela. Angel. All she lacked were wings. He felt a fleeting sense of well being just looking at her. "So, yeah, I guess we're all superstitious in our own way," he thought filing the treasured memento in his breast pocket close to his heart.

Then, his mind turned again to Marty. Marty, who had kept a supply of New York City subway tokens jangling in his pocket as if to ensure he'd make it home after all—through the subway turnstile at 59th and Lex and onto the R Train bound for Forest Hills and his stop, Woodhaven Boulevard.

Steve couldn't stop thinking about his friend. Good old Marty O'Connor from Elmhurst, Queens. They'd had their share of laughs as well as terror-stricken moments together. Though Steve had only met Marty six weeks ago when he joined the unit, they'd become like brothers over that short span of time, profoundly bonded through extraordinary experience. Marty was also planning to go to college on the GI Bill. The same college, the two conspired, somewhere back in Pennsylvania. Marty liked the idea of moving out of the city, "out West" as he put it. He liked the way it sounded—wholesome and friendly, a good place to put down roots and raise a family. The two had it all figured out. Eventually, they'd settle down the street from one another in Millmont. Steve had told Marty all about Angela and promised to fix him up with one of the cute girls back home. It was as good as done. That is, until last week when Marty, the point man on one particular mission, was killed. Steve had watched helplessly from the covert as the whole thing unfolded.

It had looked like a scene straight out of *Combat!* Certainly, not real. Marty running in a crouched position across an open space fringed with bamboo and yucca toward a dilapidated structure, his machine gun cocked. Then, only a few yards from safety, he was hit in the legs. Desperately, he'd tried to slither toward cover on his stomach—just as they'd been taught in boot camp—but out in the open like that, exposed to snipers, his body was struck again and again, twitching grotesquely with each bullet's impact until finally he lay motionless.

Steve, at first frozen in place, started to get up, yelling to the others, "We gotta go in after him. That's Marty out there!" Tommy pushed him down. "Are you crazy, man? You wanna die too? "

"We can't just sit here and let the fuckers waste him before our eyes!" Steve yelled, struggling violently as Moose and Tommy restrained him.

It had started to rain—a teeming downpour. Marty's body was still out in the open, an amorphous mass of blood-drenched flesh. Through tears, Steve stared at the blurry image of his friend and pleaded, "you can't die now, Marty. That's not part of the deal. We got a future together, man." How he wanted to run to him. But Marty was dangerous bait right now; they'd have to wait until nightfall to collect his body and prepare Marty for the dust-off.

Once they retrieved Marty, they laid him out under the protective cover of a ramshackle shed next to the remains of a pigsty from which the faint stink of swine emanated. Moose Billman, the company medic, did a routine inspection of the body before signaling to the RTO to radio in the report: one U.S. KIA. As a final gesture of friendship, Steve insisted on emptying his comrade's pockets, collecting his personal effects and putting them in a plastic bag along with his dog tags. There wasn't much. Marty had a jack knife, a packet of letters from his grandmother in Queens, a leather-bound New Testament and his subway tokens. Finally, Steve took the St. Christopher medallion from around Marty's neck. He looked at it for a moment, "A lot of good you did Marty, you asshole saint." He was tempted to toss the medallion as far as he could throw it, but thought better of it and placed it with the other things.

The medallion along with his mother's New Testament, a dainty volume of creased red leather had been Marty's prized possessions, relics of parents he had never known. Hunkering down in a foxhole one night, Steve was moved by Marty's account of his parents' young lives extinguished in a fiery car wreck one slick January night on the Long Island Expressway. Mere teenagers, they left behind one tenuous stab at eternal life—a robust baby boy. And now, he too was gone. Steve shook his head and looked at his fallen buddy.

Marty's left shoulder and a chunk of his side were missing. The mangled pulp that remained was ragged and lush with blood. His legs, too, had sustained repeated fire, and his fatigues were tattered and stiff with dried blood. But his face—a tribute to the impenetrable five pound steel helmet he was wearing—was unscathed, so that now, with his final battle over, Martin Seamus O'Connor, appeared from the neck up to be peacefully asleep; just as he'd looked catnapping on a quiet afternoon in the trenches of central Vietnam. A handsome face, dark hair and finely chiseled nose, full lips and, behind closed lids, sparkling sea green eyes whose fire was now snuffed out forever.

Once Marty's canteens and ammo were stripped off, his body was wrapped in his poncho. Steve had seen to this, gently, tenderly. When the helicopter landed, the medics zipped Marty into a body bag and solemnly placed him in the cabin. And so did he commence his final journey from Quang Tri Province to Cedar Grove Cemetery in Queens, New York on the other side of the world.

Huddling in his foxhole in the drizzle, Steve thought of Marty's grandmother, Rose, sitting in her tidy kitchen with its birdcage wallpaper. Marty had told Steve how once as a kid he had counted the number of cages. He'd never forget: 409. Steve imagined Grandma Rose lingering over a second cup of coffee in her cozy kitchen, as the morning's project, a lamb stew perhaps, bubbled on the stove. And how when the knock came at the front door, she would instantaneously know—the unexpected hour and general absence of callers—and would rise slowly from her chair, a sinking feeling in her chest, and shuffle toward the door.

Steve not only mourned the loss of his friend, but Marty's death spooked him badly. Marty had always been so optimistic about everything, never doubting that he and Steve would survive the war to go on to great things. So confident was he, Steve had begun to believe it, and their oft-discussed bright future had come to represent a kind of insurance policy, guaranteeing them each a ticket home. With Marty now gone, Steve was filled with the sickening realization that he, too, might very well die.

It had been four, maybe five, days since Marty was killed, but it seemed much longer. Steve even began to wonder if Marty was just a figment of his imagination. Such delusions were common to soldiers fueled by the brutality and peculiar time warped quality of the world they inhabited. No past. No future. Just a miserable present stretching from horizon to horizon. Down one since last week, they were a group of 14 now.

Finally, he must have dozed off, slumped in a heap. Bucky had first watch followed by Ricardo. They'd do hour-long shifts, carrying them through the night, picking up the sequence the following evening where they left off. Toward morning, Bucky would file a report and they'd receive their orders. Either they'd stay put, or move forward before daybreak, that is, if it was determined that the guerrilla forces had retreated and it was safe to advance.

Two hours or so before dawn during Tommy's watch, command headquarters ordered the unit to move out and secure the building. It had been five hours since the last incidence of enemy fire.

Psychologically, it was always hard pushing farther into uncharted territory. Staying put seemed so much safer. But who was to say? It was a crapshoot. Their present turf could erupt in a hail of mortars at any time. But with luck, and that's what it boiled down to, they'd have moved on and be concealed in another gully somewhere else when that happened. Of course, it could work the other way too.

Perhaps this attachment to the foxholes they dug along the way and into which they furiously burrowed like panicked animals when fired upon reflected a basic human impulse to homestead, even if only temporarily in a hole in the ground. Somehow, it recalled the games children play, like being on base in a game of tag. *Nah-nah-nah-nah-nah. You can't get me.* Steve found it darkly amusing that this whole dangerous business of dashing from one cover to the next recalled the game he'd played at his elementary school Christmas party. *Going to Jerusalem* it was called. Two-by-two, children marched in a circle, crossing brightly colored bath mats spaced at intervals around the gym's floor. If the music stopped and you weren't on a mat, you were out. Your time was up. Like when a footfall alighted on an unlucky swatch of ground detonating a land mine.

The plan was settled. Ricardo would lead, followed by Moose, Tommy, Steve, Ray, Vernon, Peewee and so on. As usual, Travis Boone, the unit RTO, would take up the rear, humping along 20-odd pounds of radio equipment through which he'd issue a final progress report to headquarters before following the others.

They would reassemble in a thicket of bamboo and viney undergrowth 100 yards or so ahead before resuming a diagonal course to the ravaged building, the site of the previous night's activity. After Travis joined them, the men would again split up to case the structure and the surrounding remains of a village and confirm they were abandoned. Then they'd re-group at a designated area, submit a status report and cool their heels to await further instructions. Most likely they'd set up camp there for the night.

The first part of the mission went according to plan as each man, covered by the remaining soldiers, their eyes straining to track their comrade's progress, made a dash into the inky night. As the men advanced, they were covered from both directions. Until, finally, it was Bucky's turn. Protected by his men in front, but exposed at the rear, he scuttled sideways like a hermit crab maneuvering across the stark expanse of a tidal pool ever on the lookout for danger—gun poised, body swiveling regularly in the direction from which he'd come. Once reunited, the men rested a few moments in the thicket before repeating the maneuver. The same sequence followed: Ricky, Moose, Tommy, Steve, Ray, Vernon, Peewee and so on down the line. No big deal.

Ricardo crouched at the edge of the bushes nervously waiting for Bucky's signal. Nobody liked to be the lead man. It was a rotating honor. Bucky nodded and Ricky sprang into the darkness. Fifteen seconds later, there was a crashing sound coming from the direction toward which he'd run, the heart-stopping sound of rocks and dirt tumbling and breaking up. This peculiar sound, terrifying in its unexpectedness in the midst of the still night, subsided and was replaced instead by a curious, almost inaudible, whirring sound. Then, all was quiet once more. The minutes dragged by slowly as the men tried to identify the cause of the disturbance, thinking all the while of Ricky, alone on what now seemed like the other side of an enormous chasm. And, then, at last, the welcome warble, like the soft call of a dove, penetrated the darkness signaling that all was well.

The balance of their progress toward the building took place without incident. Soon, the men were united again in a corner room of the bombed-out structure. Ricky related the cause of the crashing sound: he had apparently alarmed a large, roosting bird into flight. In the process, several large chunks of masonry had come unlodged from the roof, just missing him as he scurried for cover below. The men laughed at this—at themselves for the fear such a benign occurrence had provoked. Bucky then set about submitting a progress report. Word came back: they were to split up and fully investigate the target location. Once they established that the VC had moved on and the building was secured, the men could take a break, catch up on some Zs, and grab a bite while they awaited further orders.

CHAPTER TWO

*T*hey prowled about the building, dodging past blown-out windows, on the lookout for booby-traps. Though largely a ruin, the *beaux arts* detailing that remained suggested it had once been a French colonial outpost. The task completed, they congregated at one end of the second floor. Bucky handed around some freeze-dried beef and the men talked quietly until one by one they dozed off.

Vernon Matthews took the first watch, patrolling the space at intervals, an M-16 gas-operated assault rifle slung over his shoulder. He also carried several fragmentation and colored-smoke grenades. Dog-tired to begin with and laden down like a warship, steel-centered flak jacket, combat boots and helmet, he felt at any moment he might fall dead asleep, keel right over— Kaboom!—mid-stride. He whistled softly to keep awake—Sam Cooke's *Another Saturday Night*, as he circled the loft-like space, following a monotonous, counter-clockwise course his right shoulder brushing against the wall. He paused, at each window opening to peer cautiously out, scanning the view in both directions. Round and round he walked, maybe fifty circuits all-told, while everyone else slept.

The men were huddled about; several lay curled on their sides, heads propped on gear. One reclined against a broken chair, legs flat out in front of him, while others leaned against the wall. Despite the hard, unforgiving surface, all were sound asleep. Vernon marveled that not even Henshaw's loud snoring seemed to disturb them. It was a harmless, nonthreatening white noise, this constant rumbling—a welcome change from all the other menacing sounds they were exposed to. Set on the ground alongside Ray Jenkins, the sleeping machine gunner, was the fully loaded M-60 machine gun, along with fifteen pounds of ammunition secured in the belts that Jenkins routinely carried draped across his chest and shoulders, bandito-style. Matthews felt a warm glow of macho American pride as he regarded the no-nonsense, "don't-fuck-with-me" weapon.

At one point, passing before a window, Vernon heard an eerie wail that stopped him in his tracks. Then, recognizing it as a monkey, he chuckled taking a moment to unwrap and pop a piece of bubble gum in his mouth, enjoying the cloying sweetness spreading over his tongue. Bummer his Bazooka stash was nearly gone; he worried he'd run out before the next delivery of supplies.

Steve first saw the rising sun as a series of glinting rays through a tangle of lush vegetation. When it broke free at last, it was a fiery sphere rising above the horizon, signaling the insufferable heat that would bedevil them until it sank behind the opposing horizon some 12 hours later. He'd been awakened by the ripple of songbird, at once disorienting and enchanting, and had crept to the window to see two saru cranes, perhaps kin to the creature Ricky had flushed the night before, passing into view. Steve watched as they crossed before the sun, their great wings flapping lazily, aquiline beaks in front, legs folded neatly beneath them, their feet, sticking out behind like a delicate ironwork tail pipe. He was struck once again with the paradox of his present existence: to be in the midst of war, yet witness to scenes of such beauty. He pondered the cyclical nature of his ordeal. Mornings, waking under a flame tree in full bloom, or witnessing the meanderings of a delicate butterfly after strings of brutal engagements were precious and restorative. Steve luxuriated in the silence—a truly golden silence, broken only by Vernon's regular footfall. He returned to his spot on the floor to compose a letter to Angela.

The sun climbed higher in the sky, piercing the cracked and rutted roof and creating a cubist pattern of light on the walls and rubble-strewn floor. Moose stirred and stretched. He opened his eyes and yawned loudly. Then, he labored to his feet, picked up his M-16 and stumbled past Vernon toward the stair. "Gotta take a leak," he said. "Can you cover me?"

Vernon watched Moose as he darted from the building into surrounding underbrush. The medic's movements were smooth and fluid. Now that it was light, Vernon was able to study the surrounding area and the mean little ville in detail: a series of sagging, thatched huts, each invariably set off by a line of primitive pickets marking the family pigsty. In fact, the only movement in the abandoned settlement Vernon could detect was that of a lone weanling pig, snuffling about for something to eat. On the edge of the village, Vernon could make out the expanse of the communal paddy stretching to the banks of a muddy river and, then, more paddies in the distance extending toward the jagged Truong San Mountains.

Moose emerged from the undergrowth and darted back across the opening into the building. "Guess what I just spied with my little eye?" he asked, his tone jocular.

"Are you talking about that mighty nice set of spareribs running around on the hoof out there?" Vernon grinned.

"So, you saw it too? My mouth's watering at the thought of roast pork." There had been a few occasions of extended quiet when an errant chicken had been caught and cooked by daylight over a hastily laid fire. The freshly killed, roasted meat was like manna after an unbroken diet of C-rations. "You up for a pig safari?" Moose chuckled fiddling with a roll of lifesavers.

The others began to stir. Steve scanned the room, casually completing a silent roll call until all 14 men of Company Equinox were accounted for. Moose Billman, Reggie MacDonald, Tommy Christensen, Ricardo Valdez, First Lieutenant Campbell, Harrison Henshaw, Kevin Joyce, Travis Boone, Aldo Stern, Vernon Matthews, Ray Jenkins, Peewee Sprouse, Hal Bishop.

"Man alive, I'm starving," Tommy uttered in a voice made vibrato by a yawn.

"You got that right! I swear to God, I'd even consider eating roast dog at this point. Or, dog lo mein, or sweet and sour dog," Ricardo broke off, laughing. It wasn't even funny, this babble of his. Just silly. This is how they got at times, punch-drunk from lack of sleep.

"Hey, you feel like some roasted carne this a.m., Ricky? Cuz, I'm telling you there's a pig running around outside. How 'bout it guys?" Moose was as eager as a Boy Scout.

Kevin Joyce took a swig of water from his canteen, screwing the cap back on tightly. Then, he reached for a can of C-rations, opening it with his P-38. "Peaches is about all I can stomach at the moment," he said lazily.

"You and your damn peaches," retorted Moose. "Peaches with pound cake, peaches and peanut butter, peaches and Spam. Who needs roast pig? Let's roast us some peaches instead. Peaches Flambé Khe Sanh. We'll just sear the suckers with the flame thrower." He guffawed. "Really, Bud, to hear you go on about peaches, you'd think you came from Georgia or something. Tell the truth man, you ain't from Montana like you said, you're a honky from Atlanta, right?"

"I just like peaches. That's all." Kevin mumbled glumly. "If you ask me, sounds like you're the one that's fixated."

All this food talk was making them hungry, and they began rooting around in their packs. The pickings were getting slim. Twice a week the re-supply chopper would come, bringing a hot meal in green hermite cans and several large canvas cooler bags of beer. Nothing like some brews and hot chow to lift a soldier's spirits. The chopper was due any day now. In the nick of time. As always.

This morning, inertia had set in. Not one soldier had jumped to his feet at the mention of an impromptu barbecue. They were content to remain put for now and eat their meager provisions in silence. For several minutes, chewing sounds, of peaches, jerky, or baked beans, and the slurping of Kool-Aid, was all that could be heard. Then, there was the snap and flare of matches being lit and the rhythmic, soughing sound of smoking.

Steve popped one last Vienna sausage in his mouth and tossed the empty can to the side. Still hungry, he wistfully considered breakfasts back home. What he'd give for one of Norma's specials: two eggs over-easy with hash browns and bacon, buttered toast and a bottomless cup of coffee. He thought of the many times he and Angela had sat crammed together on one side of the booth. He remembered the last time they were there, the day they went Christmas shopping. Counting on his fingers, he was amazed it had only been three months ago. It felt like a lifetime. He rested his head against the wall behind him, shut his eyes and surrendered himself to his memories. Thus lost in reverie, he traced his tongue slowly across his lips

"All right, Ryle, let us in on your five-alarm wet dream," demanded Tommy Christiansen. "Describe her to us. Her thighs, her butt. Most important, her tits. We want to know all about her tits. For openers: her cup size. 36-double D—am I right?

Steve opened his eyes and glared at Tommy. "Cut it out, Christensen," he snarled. "It's none of your damn business what I'm thinking about."

"Your hard-on's making it our business, pal," jeered Tommy.

"Fuck you, asshole." Steve could feel his face turn hot. It wasn't this reference to his sexuality that irked him. In the locker room at Green Valley High, the guys would boast and tease each other about their sexual prowess. And it had been Steve, captain of the football team, who got the brunt of the friendly fire. Fact of the matter was he didn't want to share Angela with the other guys, as if exposure to them, to this war, would somehow sully her. She was his cherished secret and he was determined to keep it that way.

Over the weeks, life had been breathed into their various girlfriends. There was Dolly, Moose's girl, "flat-chested, but a good lay," and Crystal. "Right before I shipped out to Fort Bragg, I finally got the blow job I'd been hankering for. It was some going-away present, believe-you-me," Reggie had chortled in the telling. And Ricardo Valdez's, Lupe, raven-haired and virginal. "I had to get my rocks off with a working girl. What can I say? It's part of our tradition: no hanky-panky before the wedding night." Peewee's Melody was back home with three kids squeezed into her parents' trailer; Hal's wife Emily, a hardworking teacher in Boston.

Throughout it all, Steve had kept quiet about Angela. Only Marty knew anything about her, a confidence imparted one night in a foxhole that he'd taken to his grave. Occasionally, the group observed Steve pouring over a letter executed in careful script, or caught him studying a photograph. No doubt about it, Steve's girl was in their midst, but a mystery she would remain.

"Hey, man, don't get so touchy." Tommy replied, focusing intently on the task of scraping the last of the applesauce out of a tin, and thus avoiding Steve's eyes.

The conversation turned to the question of the re-supply chopper's arrival, always a bright topic. Bucky hoped it could be arranged for that afternoon, once they completed reconnaissance of the ville.

"Finish up your chow, guys, and let's roll. With luck, there'll be ice cold beer once we're done searching this here garden spot." He stubbed out his cigarette and nodded to Travis. "Radio, all set? Let's put in that call now."

The men readied their assault rifles, checked their grenades. Sniper fire was always a concern, so they moved with caution, heads swiveling, eyes working. As decided by lot, Steve and Aldo were the frontrunners this time. They emerged from the building and dashed for shelter alongside the nearest hut covered by the legs in the rear. The rest would follow, two at a time, as soon as Bucky gave the signal.

Today, they had the added advantage of a secured two-story home base from which three men could provide cover from above. Prior to the start of any mission, they would all fall quiet as they faced their fears and uttered silent prayers. Steve saw Marty again lying there in the mud. Only this time, it wouldn't be Marty lying there, but maybe himself. He felt the fear rising in his chest, "holy shit," he cursed silently. Of course, he'd never let on to the others how scared he was.

To calm himself he'd think of hours spent in the warmth of the D'Agneses' kitchen with its blue and white crockery displayed on open shelves and the delicious aroma-filled air. With only his father at home, and neither one of them particularly skilled in the kitchen, supper at the D'Agneses' had always been a treat.

Then he'd say his farewells. First, he'd take leave of his father, his aunts Maureen and Maire in Boston and Deirdre in Australia whom he'd never met, his best friend, Chuck. Sweetly and briefly, he'd address them all. Routinely, he'd ask forgiveness from Carmel for all the pranks he'd played on her.

He saved his good-bye to Angela for last. Today, as he stood on the threshold in the seconds before cocking his assault rifle and sprinting into the open, he took a deep breath and launched into his prayer to Angela.

However varied the content of the central entreaty might be, the ending was always the same. It's what he'd whispered in her ear their final night together: "May God bless us and keep us together." Steve always derived a sense of comfort and protection—relief, really—when he invoked these words. Having said them, he felt he'd done everything he could to stay alive. He finished up by pressing his hand against his breast pocket wherein lay her photo. So far, this superstitious ritual had worked. He was still alive.

No sooner had Bucky given the signal, than Steve sprang from the shadow of the doorway into bright sunlight, darting across the naked expanse that stretched toward a heap of decrepit dwellings, arranged haphazardly like so many children's blocks. He leapt into the foliage surrounding the first structure, turned and crouched in one sleek movement, rifle at the ready, to look back at his starting point and to cover Aldo.

And so, alternating their positions, in this manner, the two soldiers worked their way through the village, hut by hut, until every hootch was searched, peering cautiously around corners, slinking along walls. "Slow as treacle in February," Steve, thought, invoking a phrase he vaguely remembered his mother using when he dawdled as a child.

After they entered each shack, and their eyes adjusted to the gloom, they would proceed around the space, toppling jars of rice, kicking over stacks of baskets, and tearing down the bamboo screens dividing the space into compartments, never knowing exactly what they'd find. In one dwelling, they started at the flutter and cackle of a frightened chicken and Aldo, acting on reflex, fired his gun toward the direction of the sound to see a startled bird disappearing through the slats of the wall. Breathing a sigh of relief, they glanced at each other and grinned.

"Moose'll be pissed you let that sucker get away," Steve remarked.

They moved to a second series of adjacent huts, covering each other as they crossed the open space dividing the structures. Over here, their senses were assaulted by a nauseating stench, and they knew what lay ahead. The first three huts they entered were empty except for some household clutter. Such peasant abodes were sparsely furnished to begin with, containing only sleeping mats and cooking utensils, rarely any furniture save an occasional rickety stool. And when a raid made it necessary for villagers to flee their homes, they would pack up what belongings they could and like a band of gypsies, children lugging the valuable laying hen or a baby brother, they'd head into the hills. The soldiers often saw long lines of these refugees, in distinctive conical hats moving through warm drizzle. They walked slowly and with purpose across the patchwork landscape of red and mantis.

The corpse was in the last hut. A middle-aged man sprawled on his back, limbs akimbo, rubber sandals knocked off. His head was thrust backwards, so that the neck curved upwards in a graceful arc, his face toward the wall. Scattered around him were several overturned baskets and earthenware vessels.

Clapping hands over their noses, they approached him. Flies buzzed around the body. The hit, presumably from an automatic rifle, was close range and half the man's skull was blown away. All that remained was a gaping crater, penetrating shattered cranium and a mass of vascular pudding on which flies feasted and maggots writhed.

"Poor slob, never knew what hit him," remarked Aldo solemnly. Steve shook his head. From the looks of it, the man was mowed down as he fled. Thoughts of his impending doom hadn't even begun to enter his head, when, boom, he was blasted to eternity.

He looked to be about thirty-five, with spare frame and shiny black hair. No doubt, a hard-working farmer, with a wife and children, a baby maybe, that he'd helped hoist onto the shoulder of a bigger child just minutes before he was killed. Perhaps the poor fool had remembered something he'd forgotten, some rice, or maybe a jug of homemade wine, run back for it and paid with his life. Blown to bits in an instant by a zealous VC guerrilla, likely a teenager, whose ideology—to defend the land and uphold the age-old cultural tradition of the Dong Son Civilization—was not so dissimilar from the poor farmer's. Culturally speaking, if not for the war, the two might have been friends.

Aldo and Steve quickly retreated. They completed the final rounds in near silence. All continued quiet. No snipers, nothing suspicious. The pack of guerrillas whose fire had crackled through the air last night, had evidently fled into the surrounding countryside to terrorize and empty out other settlements. By midday, the ville had been thoroughly searched. The sun was high in the sky and burning hot. Aldo and Steve took shelter under a frangipani tree, lit a couple of cigarettes and waited for the others.

On the way back to the building, Moose got himself his pig. It was actually Vernon who shot it as it ran across their path. Moose immediately set about cleaning the animal, making an incision running the length of its belly, being careful not to pierce the internal organs, so as not to taint the meat. He then splayed the carcass open, reaching into the body cavity to remove the visceral membrane, a translucent bag that held all the organs. Meanwhile, the others built a fire and fashioned a spit from a stout bamboo rod. Soon the aroma of seared pork was wafting through the air. Everyone was in a good mood at the prospect of fresh meat. To top things off, it was confirmed: the re-supply chopper was coming the next day.

The men talked loudly while they ate, cheered by the tasty fare. It could have been a down-home country barbecue, save for the absence of beer and horseshoes. Gazing at the horizon, Steve watched the sun sink behind the mountains to the west, turning the sky a gaudy pink. The day that began peacefully was closing thus, much like an ordinary day back home. It was amazing to think that the same sun he now saw setting over a distant mountain range near Laos, would, in a matter of hours, be casting its rays over the rooftops of Millmont and filtering through Angela's bedroom window.

CHAPTER THREE

*T*he re-supply chopper arrived mid-afternoon. The crew doled out chili and beer, additional ammo and supplies. Steve stood with the others as the mail was distributed, starting slightly when his name was called. He retrieved his correspondence and handed the crewmember his letter to Angela. There were two letters, one, with colorful stamps and a Queensland postmark from his Aunt Deirdre, the other from Angela. He felt like he'd hit the jackpot. Looking around the circle of men, he noticed some—Peewee, Moose and Harrison—were empty-handed. So he carefully folded the envelopes in half and slipped them into his pocket to read later. He reveled in the anticipation.

The men devoured the chili. But the beer, as always, was the high point of re-supply day. Soon they were tipsy, their tongues loosened. "Shows what you gringos know about chili," Ricardo complained. "Now, if you could taste the chili of my mam , you'd see the difference right away. Chili, I mean, the real Mexican kind is made with carne secca—strips of meat, never hamburger," he said disdainfully, "chopped onion and jalapenos and a whole slew of different spices. But definitely, no beans." He made a dismissive gesture in the air. "This dog food's straight from the can!"

"Well, that didn't seem to slow you down none!" Tommy pointed at Ricardo's clean plate. "I mean whaddya expect out here in the paddies?

Cordon Blue? I can't complain. The food's hot and my stomach's happy."
He belched emphatically.

"You can say what you like about the chili," Vernon added. "But, this
beer sure hits the spot."

"You done with that, sport?" Harrison asked pointing to the ketchup.

"Look, Harrison, cut the 'sport' shit. You understand?" growled Tommy

"Sor-ree!" replied Harrison, waving his hands in mock distress. In a
flash, Tommy had him on the ground in a stranglehold.

"If you bait me again, you lily-livered fuck, I'm gonna rip your tongue
out—you hear?" Harrison, bug-eyed, nodded as best he could, his head
pinned under Tommy's massive arm.

"C'mon, let him go, Tom. He didn't mean any harm. You know how
these frat boys are—they act obnoxious to make up for their little dicks,"
quipped Bucky. Tommy released Harrison who rubbed his neck as he scurried over to the far side of the group, grabbing another can of beer as he
passed by the cooler.

Vernon began rolling a joint.

"Say, where did you get that?" Harrison demanded. "I thought you said
you were out."

Vernon smiled and waved a baggie full of marijuana at him. "They
don't call it the resupply chopper for nothing," he chortled, lighting the
joint and sucking in a big toke before passing it on to Reggie.

"That's one good thing about this war, weed's never in short supply."
Holding his breath, Reggie spoke in a clenched voice. He exhaled and
passed the joint to Bucky, while Vernon rolled another.

"It's times like these that you can almost forget you're in a friggin' war
zone," the first lieutenant drawled, taking a hit. "I mean I feel like we could
almost be on a fishing trip or something." He lazily stretched his arm over
his eyes.

"You mean like fly fishing?" Harrison asked brightly. "Now that's my
kinda thing. My Dad's a big fly fisherman. He belongs to a private club in
upstate New York where he and I and a bunch of guys go all the time. We
take along a couple cases of beer and some scotch and we have us a good
old time, getting lit, telling dirty jokes and just reeling in those trout,"
Harrison continued, trying to regain some face with the group. Travis
handed the joint to Harrison, who sucked greedily on it. He tried to hold

in the smoke as the others had taught him, but was overtaken by a violent coughing fit.

Bucky regarded Harrison's bent double form coolly. "Actually, I was referring to bass fishing, and it was on a <u>public</u> lake in the Sierra Nevadas. Private club crap ain't for me." He paused before continuing.

"As I was saying, it's times like these, you forget you're in the middle of this ass wipe war and you think, hey, this scene ain't so bad. Shit, I'm seein' the world, getting' some real experience under my belt, learnin' some skills that I can take to the bank. Bam!" He pumped the air with his fist. "The down side is," he paused for effect, "<u>all</u> the other times!" The men laughed. Everything seemed funny all of a sudden.

"You know what we need right about now is some tunes. Hey, Peewee, can't you break out your harmonica and accommodate us here?" Travis began singing a Rolling Stones tune, snapping his fingers in accompaniment.

"'I can't get no saah-tis-fac-tion,' "Stern sang in unison with Travis. "That's what I miss most about being in this hole, <u>good</u> music, with the volume turned way the fuck up so it rattles your bones. None of this crackling, rinky-dink shit we get over the army airwaves."

"How 'bout girls? You miss the tunes more than your Raquel Welch baby doll?" Tommy teased.

"You and your one-track mind! Sure I miss girls. Who doesn't? But, what do you suggest I do about it?" retorted Stern. "I gotta wait 'til my next leave to get some pussy. Tell you the truth, though, this whole business: the fighting, the marching, catchin' 40 winks in fox holes, all the filth we have to wallow through like a pack of pigs, has a way of putting the kibosh on the old sex drive. Look at me, look at all of us." He gestured at the group. "What woman would want to jump in the sack with any of us? We're a sorry group: flea-bitten, lice-infested, covered from head to toe in muck and stinking to high heaven. Right now, a foxhole is exactly where we belong." Aldo paused, before continuing in a slow, syrupy voice.

"Now, of course, if I were to find myself in a bedroom with a beautiful blonde lying naked under the sheets, just waiting for me to jump her bones, then sure, I could get into it, but only after a nice, hot shower."

"I like it—I like it," chortled Tommy exhaling a plume of blue smoke. "The Aldo-baiting was worth the description you just gave us. Close second to a Saturday afternoon matinee. Thank you. Private Stern. Who's next?"

"Not to rain on your parade, but don't any of you ever worry about whether there'll be a next time?" Hal asked slowly.

Reggie chimed in "Aw, c'mon. This man needs another hit." He leaned over to hand Hal the joint. "I don't want to think it might never happen again. The night my baby went down on me, I felt like I'd been to the moon and back."

"Hey, the conversation's sure heating up. What was her name Reg? Crystal was it? Sounds like quite a gal. I hear those black sisters are totally uninhibited. Say, Reggie-my man, perhaps we can work out some kind of trade when we get outta here. Whadya say?" quipped Tommy.

Reggie ignored the remark and Hal continued. "I just get so bummed out thinking about all we have to lose if we die out here."

"Shit, that's just screwy. If you're dead, you're dead. You don't find dead men hankering after blow jobs. Nothing'll matter anymore at that point. You won't know what you're missing," insisted Travis. "Instead, of focusing on that shit, you should be praying that if you do die, the end's quick. An instantaneous, lift-off to the hereafter. Me, I worry about getting blown to pieces and *not* dying, being shipped home a quad to God knows what kind of shit life."

"Guys, guys lighten up, okay?" pleaded Tommy. "This is bumming me out. Can't we go back to discussing pussy?"

"Hey, I can relate to what Hal's saying—sure I can," exclaimed Steve, picking up a stick and hitting it against the ground idly. "We're forced to face our mortality every day out here. Fact is, we might not make it home."

"It sucks." Ricardo exclaimed.

"All I can say," Vernon interjected, "is Uncle Sam came knocking on my door, and here I am."

"It's a job to me," added Reggie. "Just counting the days."

"I mean, I signed up and all, but now being here, it just seems really pointless," Steve continued. "We're thousands of miles from home fighting another country's fight. And for what? What the hell are we doing here anyway?"

"I hear you, man," said Aldo. "A buncha lowly grunts we are too. No rich kids here. 'Cept Harrison," he said jutting his chin in Harrison's direction. "So, Henshaw how come you're here? Didn't your Daddy make a big enough political donation?"

Harrison reddened. "I-I decided to take some time off from college and wanted to serve my country." He declared sanctimoniously.

"Oh come off it Henshaw," cried Bucky. "That's bull shit. You must have flunked out." Harrison looked stricken. "So what happened? Were you caught with a girl in your room? Did you get somebody pregnant? Come on now, spill the beans."

"It doesn't matter what I say, you guys never listen to me." Harrison said, his voice cracking.

"C'mon, guys" Steve urged. "Let's not turn this into a beat up on Harrison session. I'm just really questioning what's happening here. The country's certainly not behind us, look at all those protests back home and meanwhile we're over here stuck in this hare-brained, cluster fuck of a war. I just don't see a way out. Guess all we can do is pray."

"Amen. Say, that was profound," Christensen said sarcastically. Steve looked at him darkly and bit his tongue. He didn't want to engage in another round of pointless sparring with Christensen.

"I don't know what's worse," Bucky was speaking. "The fighting, or not knowing what's next. I don't have to tell you—Christ, we're all in the same boat. And right now we're the lucky ones—God knows we've lost some really great guys." His voice caught.

"But let's not focus on that. I just wanna tell all you Equinox guys that you're a helluva bunch. None of us is exactly thrilled being here, fighting our asses off in this god-forsaken jungle, but we sure can't complain about the company!"

"Let's hear it. Three cheers for Company Equinox!" The men whooped.

Company Equinox's "helluva of a bunch" were still boys, really, representing a broad cross-section of American youth, the majority in their late teens and early 20s, with the platoon leader, the oldest at 28. Young enough that most had left mothers behind who were still young themselves, and who still regarded their warrior sons as their little boys. Fused by universal maternal fears, burning devotion and abiding faith, these women were as one entity, the archetypal mother figure. Each of these women remembered vividly, the day her son was born, how it was like Christmas one hundred times over. And, of course, could recall exactly what her boy had been for Halloween when he was three, six or nine. She'd kept every one of the doily Valentines he'd proudly presented her—his one and only sweetheart, taping them to the refrigerator where they remained for untold time, some perhaps to this day. Each caught herself shuddering on occasion at the recollection of any number of memories—a dangerously high fever, a bad case of croup, or nasty gash that required stitches.

None of those circumstances, however, compared to the situation her son was in now. On the one hand, the anxious mothers waiting at home understood the danger their boys faced. But on the other—and for this the sons were grateful—they had no concept.

Steve looked around at the individual members of Company Equinox who together constituted a sort of "universal American boy" unified by kindred dreams, hope and despair. He thought how diverse they were from such different backgrounds across the nation. Several hailed from the western states, including, Kevin Joyce, from Missoula, Montana, and First Lieutenant Campbell, born and bred in the Los Angeles suburb of Temple City and Travis Boone from Sacramento. Ricardo Valdez was from Laredo, Texas, just north of the Mexican border, which his parents had illegally crossed twenty years before shortly after little Ricky was conceived in the hope of a better future.

Three were from the Central States, including, Tommy Christensen, a farm boy from the cornfields of Iowa; Moose Billman a proud Chicagoan and Reggie MacDonald from inner city Detroit. The rest were from the east, Steve Ryle from western Pennsylvania; Peewee Sprouse, Southside Virginia; Vernon Matthews and Aldo Stern, from Harlem and Brooklyn respectively; Ray Jenkins, Bridgeport, Connecticut; Hal Bishop, Boston; and Harrison Henshaw, III, a product of the affluent New Jersey suburbs.

Steve stood up. It was time to seek out a private corner and read his letters.

He began with his aunt's. The loosely scrawled script conveyed the haste with which it had been written. She wrote with such conversational immediacy; Steve could imagine her reciting the news about his cousin, Declan's forthcoming graduation from college, the stockman's wedding, for which she'd made the cake, and the litter of eight pups born on Easter Day to their border collie, Flash. "Dearest Stevie," the letter ended, "we hold you fast in our hearts and pray for you every day. Auntie Dee." He thought of the wide-open spaces, all those pictures and maps of Australia he'd pored over in National Geographic. How he longed to visit this exotic place with Angela one day.

At last, he turned his attention to Angela's letter, feeling a surge of pleasure. It was thrilling knowing the envelope he held in his hands had not so long ago been touched by her. Gently teasing it open, he drew the folded paper out with care, momentarily bewildered by the bits of what he thought was confetti falling onto his lap. He laughed softly, realizing they were petals she must have collected from their apple tree. Lifting them to his nose to see if he could detect any fragrance, he began to read:

Dearest Steve,

I got your letter a couple of days ago. I am very sorry it's taken me TWO whole days to write you back, but this is the first chance I've had. It's been a REALLY busy week both at school (two tests!) and at Norma's as Paula was sick.

I was distressed to hear about your friend Marty. It makes me terribly scared for you. That's why your letters mean so much—when I read them it's almost like you're talking to me and I know you're okay.

When I'm down, I think about the night we spent together and I feel much better. It all seems like such a dream now, lying in your arms all night. It just felt so right. All I want is to be with you forever. I can't wait 'til you get back. Your little "silver apple of the moon" fills me with such strength and makes me think about being with you again that way. (Blushing!) How I long to see you!

Everything's fine here. I've saved over $2,000 so far! Isn't that great? Not much else to report except I heard that Chuck and Marcia are seeing each other—can you believe it? They got together over spring break when she was home.

It's late, so I'm going to sign off now. I'll write again tomorrow.

I send you all my love, my Dearest Wanderer!

Angela,

P.S. I have a surprise for you that will change our lives in the most wonderful way. I promise to tell you more about it very soon! xoxo

His spirits lifted, Steve carefully collected all the apple blossoms and sprinkled them into the letter's crease before placing it in his breast pocket. Then, lying back beneath an acacia tree, he closed his eyes. A shadow of a smile flickered across his face as he dropped off, soothed as he was by musings of what his Angela had in store for him.

CHAPTER FOUR

For several days now, they'd been moving across broad expanses of rice paddy, beside a ruddy-hued river. They marched for hours on end until the blisters on their feet burned and they were utterly exhausted. Only then did they pull out entrenching tools and dig holes in the earth where they could collapse. Some hours later, they'd emerge, faces, fatigues and boots coated with a dusty red powder to re-fuel from a can of C-rations, swallow some pep pills and begin the process all over again.

Their route led them through small settlements, where they roused frightened peasants from tumbledown hootches or startled mama-sans spreading rice on mats to dry. They were observed as they moved past by thin, lactating curs, their recent litters of pups soon to be simmering in village stew pots, adding meat to spare human frames. Looking into the gentle, flustered faces of the villagers, the GIs could not help but feel sorry for these humble folk caught in the crossfire of a war they didn't understand.

And so they marched on, passing the occasional water buffalo under harness held securely by its owner, a formerly prosperous farmer, maybe, whose erect stance and handsome countenance reflected enduring dignity despite the cruel change in fortune war had wrought upon him and his country.

Company Equinox was on a search mission to find a Long Range Reconnaissance Patrol that had disappeared while collecting vital intelligence. All radio contact with the LLRP unit had been lost and an ambush was suspected.

The land here was heavily mined so they took turns carrying the thirty-pound mine detector. Each soldier wore a flak jacket, weighing close to seven pounds, which as they trudged through the humid air, became soaked with sweat, growing almost unbearably heavy.

By day, they continued to take sniper fire—a deadly tattoo that rattled the underbrush. They moved in silence, crouching between cautious footfalls. The tension was oppressive, as they tried to ascertain the position of the shooters. Shortly into the campaign, Kevin Joyce was hit in the side. Moose patched him up as best he could, injecting him with morphine and running plasma into a vein. The men carried him to a protected stand of jackfruit trees to wait out the hours until it was safe for a chopper to Medevac him away. It was a terrible night, the sky alive with mortar fire: brilliant starbursts with tails of trailing light. A ghastly son et lumière that was accompanied by Kevin's moans, an agonizing symphony of war. Finally, the shelling ceased and Kevin passed out. At first, they thought he was dead. But Moose said it was just the pain—a side wound was generally no big deal—and he thought he'd make it as long as he got to the hospital triage unit in Da Nang ASAP. Word was received that a helicopter had been dispatched. Now all they could do was hunker down and wait.

Just before sunrise, they heard the thup-thup-thup of approaching rotors and set off a flare to indicate their position. The chopper landed, flattening the tall grass with a great rush of warm air. There was an expediency to the task of loading the casualty aboard; a few, succinct words shouted between medics and soldiers over the noise, followed by the revving of engines and whirring of blades before the helicopter lifted off like some giant, prehistoric dragonfly.

As it disappeared, Steve couldn't help wondering whether the fortune Kevin kept folded up in his pack of cigarettes would pay off, wielding its power and sending the boy from Missoula home. To be discharged with honor and bound perhaps for a destiny filled with the riches it foretold? Or, would the paper strip let him down in the end and he'd succumb to his wounds? In either case, from this moment on, Kevin Joyce, ceased to exist for Company Equinox.

The soldiers kept on moving across the sepia-hued landscape through an incessant soft rain. At times, a dense shroud of mist enfolded them so they could barely see the way ahead. All sense of dimension was lost. Steve felt his heart beating like a metronome in his chest, tapping away the seconds. How much time did he have left anyway in this wretched platoon in Southeast Asia? Could death be lurking just around the corner? What was the status of the hourglass signifying his life? Had the sand now all but sifted through the narrow passage, or were there ample stores of the precious substance still remaining?

Eventually, the mist receded and it stopped raining. Just when things were looking up, without warning, they were attacked by a small band of Viet Cong. It was a sudden, furious fight, the men scattering and running for cover. No time to be scared. Miracle of miracles, nobody was hit—and they'd been such sitting ducks this time. It was the colored smoke grenades that Moose threw into the enemy that saved their skins. Fast. Three or four in sequence. Backed up by formidable American fire and a solid line of defense. Two or three dinks had escaped into the scrub. But five of the assholes were dead. Sprawled in the muck, bloody and mud-flecked, their motley inventory of black market weaponry scattered about them.

The men were giddy—it was like the high at the end of the Super Bowl. They'd fought admirably. Nuked five and sustained zero losses on the home team. Nobody killed. Not even a scratch. Tommy kicked one of the bodies, disdainfully.

"Hey, that's nothing," scoffed Harrison. He walked over to one of the dead men and undid his fly. A stream of urine splattered onto the upper chest of the corpse, splashing into the gaping mouth and coursing onto cheeks where it mixed with mud and blood, forming brown rivulets that ran down the neck and torso. A smirk played across Harrison's face as he urinated.

Steve turned away nauseated.

"Restrain yourself, Private!" Bucky's bark sliced the air.

Harrison looked around at the others for approval. No one met his gaze. Vernon pensively unwrapped some bubble gum, Tommy examined the radio equipment, Aldo and Steve walked away.

They continued now through deep forest toward the point of last radio contact with the LRRP, picking their way through dusky shadows interrupted here and there by pale shafts of daylight penetrating holes in the thick canopy. The vulnerability of the moment, etched clearly across each unblinking countenance, fingers stroking machine gun clips. Who knew what enemy was lurking there in the gloom beneath areca palm and vine?

The air was pungent with eucalyptus, a detail forever cemented in Steve's mind by what came next: the overwhelming sweet stench of the slaughterhouse that stopped the men abruptly in their tracks.

The destroyed radio was all they could make out at first in the failing light. Then, they noticed the ground strewn with ammunition casings. But it was the needling whine and tulle-like cloud of insects that led them to the bodies—three LRRPs blown to Kingdom Come. "Jesus, fucking Christ," Bucky cursed, off-loading the radio to fire it up, as Moose continued on to the bodies.

CHAPTER FIVE

*S*teve opened his eyes, but it seemed they were still shut, so complete was the darkness. His head throbbed with razor-sharp, driving pain that felt as if his skull would burst. Slowly, he moved his head forward and raised a hand to undo his chinstrap and then with great effort, he managed to pull his helmet off and cast it to one side. He placed his hand on his brow and ran it gingerly over the top of his head through the bristle of cropped hair until his fingertips touched the ground beneath him. Shifting to a horizontal direction, he traced the circumference of his head and concluded his skull wasn't breached.

Yet, as his fingers continued their scrutiny, sweeping across his forehead and along the hairline downward toward his ear, he flinched in pain as they bumped over an uneven area the texture of dried mud, rising to a lump at the crest of his left cheekbone. The center of the small crater was warm and wet. Evidently, the wound had bled profusely, for now he became aware of the veneer of dried blood covering his left cheek, his chin and the side and back of his neck.

Slowly, he assessed his surroundings. Why was the dark so complete? For a sudden moment, he thought he must be dead after all, just like Marty. He felt his chest convulse as a sob began to form.

It was the moisture of the tears coating his cheeks that roused him briefly to his senses. They were, after all, real, wet tears. I'm not dead, he thought in a fleeting, joyful moment. Then, what was he? And where? Squeezing his eyes shut, deepening the effects of darkness, he remembered. And then he let out a wail that slashed the velvet depths of the tropical night.

It came back to him: part nightmare, part cinematic spectacle. A collage of lurid images that began with a soldier's form against the descending night, who knows which, just prior to annihilation by a fleeting strobe of descending fire—a direct hit. In the instant before the man's body exploded, Steve thought he recognized Travis's familiar grin. Laughing at his own mortality. That's how it all began, Steve thought. The first hit.

Pressing his hands to his face, Steve tried desperately to reconstruct the deadly sequence of events that had occurred 15, maybe 20 yards from where he now lay. God-fucking damn, what the hell happened? I gotta think back, gotta remember, he gasped to himself, choking on another wave of tears, as he rubbed his injured head. The silence and darkness were oppressive, weighing down on him with palpable force. He felt like he was deep within some subterranean cave.

It took some effort to put the pieces together. Could it be the entire company was obliterated in a matter of seconds? He felt sick to his stomach. And why, goddamn it, had he been spared? He wanted the earth to swallow him up right then and there.

The sequence of events played out in his mind. Yes, it had been Travis, who was the first to go. And, then, Reggie and, he thought, Tommy were hit together. He could see Reggie's eyes gleaming like bright gemstones and thought he could recall a fragment of a curse from Tommy as he was hit.

Steve had been standing next to Harrison, close enough so that the impact of the explosion had knocked him over and bits of shrapnel tore at his clothes and pelleted his helmet, cutting into his flesh. He recalled looking up from where he lay on the ground and seeing swatches of the sky above him, alive with the pulse of light, and hearing the accompanying syncopation of bullets, grotesquely embellished by the screams of his dying comrades. It was a fireworks display from hell.

As he lay motionless on the ground, he was sure he could feel the nighttime damp rising from beneath the plaid blanket, and he was again a little boy, head upon his mother's lap, watching the spectacle of rockets on the Fourth of July. Then he felt the irresistible pull of unconsciousness descend over him, gently luffing like a sail as it fell. Just before he sank into oblivion, he saw the Grand Finale, extravagant, glorious—only this time the display rose from the earth in a great plume of fire into the night, fierce and illuminating, so that for an instant or two, the surrounding landscape was thrown into brilliant relief.

After several attempts, Steve was finally able to pull himself up on his elbow. Waves of nausea surged through his body and his saliva tasted metallic. He vomited, continuing to gag for several minutes more, producing only a trickle of yellow bile; his stomach was empty, squeezed tight like a fist.

When he lay back, Steve noticed a soft whimpering nearby. With animal impulse, he staggered to his feet and stumbled toward the sound, tripping and falling suddenly in a heap onto the lumpy form of Harrison who was just coming to. Steve grabbed onto him as he would a life raft on the open sea, hugging him fiercely as tears spilled onto his mud-caked fatigues.

Shrapnel had sliced through Harrison's uniform, cutting him in several places. Most of the wounds were cursory, mere scratches to the outer fatty tissue; the most serious was on his upper arm as evidenced by the profusion of blood soaking his shirt. Steve reassured Harrison as he tore his shirt open along the seam. "It's okay, I only want to take a look, that's all." Though deep, it was a clean puncture, just missing the major artery running through the limb. Nothing could be done for it. It would just have to mend on its own from the inside out. "See, it's not so bad." Steve said looking at Harrison's tear-streaked face. "It will heal up fine. Shouldn't affect your golf swing one bit." He smiled wanly. "We just gotta keep it nice and clean." He ripped off a strip from the edge of his own shirt and carefully bound up the wounded arm.

Steve scanned the destruction around them, forcing himself to approach a group of mangled bodies. Harrison stood silently by, shielding his useless arm protectively with his good one, as Steve numbly composed their dead comrades as best he could, so that at the very least, they might be left peacefully arranged upon the troubled land. Before retreating, he spotted with sickening realization a human torso off to the side. He stopped and said a silent prayer before backing away.

Forever after, Steve would be grateful that the grim ritual of laying the platoon members to rest occurred in the dusky pre-dawn light, muting the carnage somewhat. So complete was the destruction that he could only locate six bodies, Peewee, Ray, Aldo, Ricardo, Moose and Bucky. Of the other five—Reggie, Travis, Tommy, Vernon and Hal—he found no trace.

It was his last encounter with Bucky that would dominate his recollections of the grisly episode. The First Lieutenant was lying face down, just another anonymous soldier from the front page. Steve grabbed his shoulder pulling him onto his back. He gasped. It was clear from Bucky's pallor that he had bled out from his wounds. Drained of all color, his face was now that of a marble statue. But it was Bucky's staring eyes, locking Steve in their empty gaze that would remain imprinted on his mind.

He reached over and pressed closed Bucky's lids. The lifeless skin was cold and smooth like the marble it resembled. He thought of the fiancée in California, Mary Jo Smith, for whom he had no image, just a lasting sense of Bucky's quiet devotion to the girl. Tears welled up in his eyes. He thought of Angela, but quickly beat back her image, as he felt the urge to survive kick in. There's no time for that now, he thought. We gotta get the hell outta here before the dinks return. He scrambled back to Harrison, collecting stray ammo, a pack and several canteens along the way. There was no sign of the radio equipment. Casting one last look at the devastation, Steve and Harrison moved off into the brightening mist.

The two men crept slowly through dense underbrush on the lookout for the enemy and for anything that might indicate the presence of mines. Stripped of the security of a large group and without adequate equipment, each step they took was terrifying. Adrenalin coursed through their veins and the sweat poured off them. Capture or death seemed very real. It was only a matter of time.

They were traveling away from the rising sun toward Da Nang, or so they hoped, and the American installation there. But who really knew where they were? Dwelling on their dire circumstances wouldn't help matters, so Steve was careful to steer their terse conversation clear of the topic. Panic lay just beneath the surface and it took all his self-control to keep it in check. He knew it was worse for Harrison, whose whimpering convinced Steve it wouldn't take much to send him over the edge.

At night, they took turns sleeping, although sleep did not come easily to either of them now: too many horrors behind, too many dangers ahead. It was when they were on the cusp of sleep that they opened up to each other, partaking in the basic human need to connect. They told stories of their lives back home with Harrison talking about his family, the executive father, his older sister, Elise, and younger brother, Calvin, his girlfriends. Steve described life in Millmont, the closely-knit neighborhood, the football team. Harrison had played junior varsity at his prep school and was impressed that Steve was team captain.

They also reminisced about the other men, fondly, lightly, as if they were still alive; and brooded, as well, over the poor nameless LRRPs—they never even got to those bodies. In the moments before Company Equinox was hit, only three had been accounted for. Were the others taken prisoner?

Obsessively they rehashed the details. What the fuck had happened? They decided the company had fallen prey to guerillas using the missing LRRP unit as bait for more troops. Standing side by side out of the line of fire when the night exploded, their lives had been spared. But whether they were the lucky ones remained to be seen. For who knew what terrible fate awaited them?

When he knew Harrison was asleep, Steve closed his eyes and softly, tenderly summoned Angela from the depths of his mind. He saw her just as she'd looked last spring, in her prom dress of filmy gauze that had swirled around them like sea foam as they danced. What an image of perfection she had been that night. He remembered how everybody had stared, and how proud he felt to have her on his arm. It was a lasting image superseded only by one other—that of her silvern form at Christmastime, waiting for him in bed.

They awoke before dawn, and after inspecting Harrison's wound, set off wordlessly through the insect and pollen-filled air, stopping for a prolonged rest during the heat of the day. Picking up again in the late afternoon they trudged on into early evening matching their progress with the course of the sun.

They'd been parsing out the water carefully, three canteens worth, and a slim supply of C-rations they'd been able to collect from the site of the ambush: several packages of dried non-fat milk, which they poured in their mouths like Pixie Sticks followed by a chaser of water; a can each of fruit cocktail, some baked beans and Spam. Plus, a plastic bag of Bazooka, they'd scooped up from where it had landed several hours before, alone and eerily intact, even as its owner, Vernon was blown straight to eternity. How Vernon loved his Bazooka, they thought chewing a wad of his gum.

Now, sixty plus hours later, less than half a canteen of water remained, a growing worry as they were becoming rapidly dehydrated. They were on high alert for water, peering into the thick vegetation for the glint of a glassy pool or the neon green swatch of moss indicating an underlying spring, their ears constantly straining for sounds of gurgling.

At dawn on the third day, they each took a small swig before setting off. Judging by the lightness of the last canteen and the high-pitched sound the jostling water made within, they reckoned there was only a swallow remaining for each, which they agreed to save until their midday rest. Their situation was desperate now. The balmy pre-dawn temperatures quickly escalated, reaching almost unbearable heights by mid-morning, which the overhead canopy of leaves only modestly abated. And the day advanced ever bright, burning and cloudless. They had noted the distant crackle of machine gun fire the previous night, and fearful that enemy combatants were lurking nearby, had slowed their pace. It was the first sound of battle they'd heard since striking out alone together, a menacing reminder of their immediate peril, undercut only by thirst and fatigue.

They trudged along wearily all morning, pausing regularly to rest. Leaning against the hollow bole of a rubber tree, they mopped off their dripping faces. Finally, around noon they collapsed on the forest floor, each drawing a last swallow of tepid water from the canteen. Like some rare vintage wine, this final draught was slowly gulped down providing a wisp of relief to sandpaper throats.

It was curious how fate drew people together. The guys had shared a universal antipathy for Harrison, finding him an insufferable bore. And Steve's distaste for him had certainly sharpened after the episode with the VC corpse. But during three days together, Steve had come to respect Harrison, impressed by his stoicism, courage and grit. Common shareholders of profound loss, constant danger and uncertain future, these two survivors had bonded in an unlikely friendship.

In the late afternoon, Harrison took a turn leading the way. The vegetation had thinned out somewhat, which made the going easier. The sunlight was slanting at an angle through the undergrowth, infusing it with golden light. Thankfully, it would soon be time to quit for the night. Then, quite abruptly ahead, the thicket opened into a clearing that was airy and beckoning. Suddenly, Harrison let out a little squeal of delight.

He turned to Steve. "Hey, old buddy, I think we're saved. Look what's friggin' ahead." He pointed toward the ruins of a pagoda judging from what remained of its roofline, just visible through the foliage, maybe a hundred yards away. All but reclaimed by vines, the structure stood within what appeared to have once been a groomed expanse. But it was what stood at its center curiously free of encroaching growth that had seized Harrison's attention: the unmistakable stone surround of a well.

Harrison immediately dropped his gear and made a dash toward the font. Steve watched as his comrade emerged from the jungle shadows into the clearing. And, as Harrison burst from shade into sunlight, simultaneously, Steve saw, as if in slow motion, how when his foot hit the ground—his right foot, it was—the ground had exploded like a geyser beneath him, bursting upward, right through Harrison.

Later, Steve would marvel that the mine had not killed Harrison outright. That would have been better. Instead, it left him writhing on the ground, his cries shattering the silence. How could this be? One moment whole, the next moment, with one fatal misstep, his life seeping away. Steve had watched frozen in his tracks, as the scene unfolded. He hesitated only a second perhaps, before rushing to Harrison's side. Subsequently, he would recall how he sank to his knees beside the dying man, took his hand and told him he was going make it, Goddamn it. Everything would be all right. And how Harrison had stared back at him, eyes murky, face beaded with perspiration.

"Oh, man, it hurts bad," he sobbed. "Steve, you gotta help me. I'm too young to die." His sobbing intensified suddenly and he reached for Steve's hand. "Christ, I've never even been with a woman. I lied about all that. I'm a fucking virgin." His mouth quivered fitfully, like a little child's, then, he lapsed into incoherent, mumbling, a final lamentation as he moved beyond pain. He began to shake uncontrollably. He lasted only a few minutes more, before his eyelids fluttered and with a shudder he was gone. In shock, Steve remained motionless kneeling beside Harrison's body for several minutes, the swelling din of insects his only connection to the world around him. Then, the realization dawned on him. He was all alone now. Wailing, he fell upon the dead man.

At some point, he dragged Harrison's body into the shelter of the pagoda. Light from the setting sun filtered through broken rafters to fall onto the earthen floor. He moved Harrison across the space and laid him within a square of fading light. Then, he tore off a piece of his shirt and, dipping it into the spring, washed Harrison's face. Gently, he combed the boy's hair to one side with his fingers.

Afterwards, he went over to the well. Lying on his stomach, he greed-ily sucked water into his dry mouth, gulp after gulp, until his sides ached.

It was only when he stretched out alongside Harrison's body that he became aware of the peppering of automatic gunfire. He reached for his gun, placing additional rounds beside him. Then, overcome with exhaus-tion, he passed out, the gun lying across his midriff. He had become the lone sentinel guarding a dead man. One Harrison Henshaw III, felled by a Toe Popper somewhere in the badlands of Quang Tri Province.

CHAPTER SIX

*H*is bad arm was nudged again roughly. He noticed the pain wasn't as pronounced as before. It must be healing after all, Steve thought. The regular fare—a soggy bean cake he guessed—was pressed into his bound hands. He raised it to his mouth and bit off a chunk of the tasteless mound, allowing it to dissolve into mush before swallowing. He ate only to keep up strength. It was part of the routine now—another sort of duty. Sometimes, there was rice, a tin cupful, or fried squares flecked with brown matter, seaweed perhaps, gauging from its saltiness, something non-perishable and portable, ideal food for a tunnel dweller.

He was fed twice during waking hours which provided some structure to time: two bean cakes, four dipperfuls of water or so, describing the passage of a day, followed by a longer stretch that defined nighttime when he was left alone. It was a nocturnal netherworld down here. Only the faintest daylight from air holes in the ceiling penetrated the gloom. At night, the darkness was total, pierced only occasionally by the dart of a flickering torch passing along the adjoining corridor. Confined to an alcove, Steve had only a vague sense of the layout of this dim, dank place.

He remembered hazily the night of his capture, how he had remained awake inside the pagoda beside Harrison for what seemed like a long time.

But, he must have fallen asleep without realizing. It was the beam of a searchlight skimming over him, settling upon his sleeping form that woke him quite suddenly. Instinctively, he grabbed his machine gun and started firing into the menacing glare. He didn't remember being hit. But the peace that ensued remained crystal clear in his mind, as he felt himself borne away by a shimmering presence to a moonlit grove, or so it seemed. He believed that at that moment, close to death, his mother had come to him to lead him to this place of perfect bliss.

When he came to after he'd been captured, it seemed a horrible replay of that other ghastly awakening. This time, however, a sharp jabbing pain emanated from his right shoulder. He was lying on a straw mat spread over hard ground. His military uniform, boots and helmet were gone, in all probability, put back into service, the proud possession of a lucky VC guerilla. Instead, he was clad in a pair of crudely fashioned loose pants, shirtless with a thick bandage covering his wound. And there was something else he noted: for the first time in months, the air was cool. And it smelled musty too, much like the cellar back home, which had exposed earth walls. Processing this information, he suspected these were the notorious Vinh Moc tunnels the troops had heard about. In that case, he must be in North Vietnam.

The earlier gash on his cheekbone healed quickly, but his shoulder required ongoing attention. At first, he was tended by two men, one of whom held the arm motionless while the other cleaned and dressed the wound. Steve was able to mime that he was cold and they returned with a peasant tunic of coarse black cotton. As time passed, only one of the men continued to come, a small, glossy-haired fellow with the smooth, unlined face of a boy and soft feminine hands.

Maybe twice a day, the young man helped Steve to a nearby latrine, a crude hole dug in the ground covered with sapling lengths. An air hole above the latrine was largely ineffective in preventing the stench from wafting into the corridors.

In fitful sleep, Steve would see Harrison again poised to step into the clearing. Struggling to stop him, he'd scream, "No, Harrison, no!" and then watch helplessly as Harrison bounded towards the well. Or, he saw Marty once more, grotesquely twitching in the mud. Or, Bucky's vacant stare. And, in the misery of this subterranean hell, he doubted that he'd ever make it out alive.

Darkness was the enemy now. As it pressed against him, he felt the first tendrils of claustrophobia curl and tighten around his throat. In panic, he turned to Angela. Even now, in this godforsaken place he could conjure her up and take comfort in her otherworldly presence. Other times, he questioned if she had even existed. Then, he made himself concentrate so he might plainly see her gazing at him and hear again the caress of her voice. He recalled the soft touch of her skin beneath his fingertips. By God, she *was* real. At this sweet reaffirmation, his body would convulse with sobs.

And then he would retrieve her last letter from its hiding place under the mat, straining in the dim light to make out her script—though, by now, he knew it by heart. Again, as he recited the words, he heard her voice, soft and throaty in tandem with his own. The VC had taken all his personal effects, his dog tags and watch, the photo of Angela, and tried to take her letter. He had a faint recollection of snatching it back from them in his delirium and holding it tightly to his breast. Strangely, his captors had allowed him to keep it. Perhaps the dried apple blossoms falling free had something to do with it, conveying a universal message that penetrated their otherwise immovable armor.

Like Angela, he thought often of the passion they'd shared. He shut his eyes to recall the night at the seedy motel, forever more a precious sanctuary. Angela's lambent skin in the moonlight, the lack of hesitation, the raw hunger supplanting all else. And how the next morning she had kissed him softly awake. He had opened his eyes to see tears welling in hers. "How can I let you go?" she had asked, her voice breaking.

He remembered too the humorous aspects that threatened to turn the episode into a corny Doris Day movie: the disguise, the phony alibi, the motel clerk with his bad toupee. It was these memories that sustained him.

"Oh, Angela," he sighed.

Leaving her at the airport, looking so small and helpless had been one of the hardest things he'd ever done. How he longed to feel her arms around him again, to re-live that final kiss. He remembered pressing his forehead against the window as the plane took off, holding onto his final view of her, a speck of pink against the gray mass of the terminal until he couldn't see her anymore.

Now he wondered how he could have done it. What had possessed him? At the time it had seemed the right thing to do. He had been convinced of it. He remembered how upset she was when he told her his plans, how scared it made her. What was she feeling now?

Back home, 100 years ago now it seemed, the war had seemed black and white, and going into the army, a sure way to propel himself forward. The recruiter had painted such a rosy picture of things; it hadn't been until boot camp that reality set in. And then there'd been the months of warfare wherein he'd witnessed so much senseless bloodshed. It had been monumentally disillusioning.

A gnawing anxiety weighed on him. What if he had been reported dead? It stood to reason, they'd assume he was killed along with the rest. Poor Angela, he thought. But in the depths of despair, such concerns became irrelevant. "I'll probably die here anyway," he thought hopelessly. He prayed for rescue, envisioning an elite team storming the tunnels. But he also worried U.S. forces might bomb the tunnels. Certain death for those inside. Alone and stripped of any purpose but his own survival, he held on to the one thing he knew was true and good. "If I ever make it back, Angela," he vowed, "I'll never leave you again."

The last scabs from his shoulder finally flaked off and he could feel the smooth wide scar, tracing its boundaries with his fingers.

Not long after, the interrogations began. Two guards came and took him through a maze of winding passageways. The earth felt cool and smooth, packed hard by the compression of many feet. He was surprised they didn't bother to blindfold him and then wondered if this was an ominous sign. Along the way, they passed what Steve thought he recognized as a stash of American munitions and gear piled high in a corner. Looking vainly for signs of other POWs, he marveled at the number of people he saw along the way—women hovering over small mounds of embers, or sorting through foodstuffs, children at play in the corners—the murmur of myriad voices creating a continuous background babble. To his amazement, the tunnel appeared to house an entire bustling town reminding him of the ant farm he had as a kid with its complex network of passages. He thought of the fable about the industrious ant and saw a parallel to these crafty tunnel dwellers who had bested a formidable foe.

Finally, they reached a small brightly lit chamber. Steve squinted in the glare of two propane lanterns. They looked just like those from his Boy Scout trips to the Allegheny Mountains and wondered fleetingly if these ones came from Sears too. Three men dressed in standard black VC garb were already in the room when they entered. But there was something different—evidenced by the deferential manner of his escorts indicating these were not ordinary Viet Cong. The one in charge came over to Steve. He smiled slowly, revealing Chicklet teeth. Steve immediately thought of him as Alvin the chipmunk.

"Greetings, Prisoner Ryle," Alvin said in a nasal voice.

Steve started at hearing his name spoken in such good English. Alvin continued. "No, I am not telepathic. Just able to read U.S. army dog tag."

Alvin began to pace slowly back and forth.

"There has been notable rise in activity by U.S. army." He stopped and was standing in front of Steve, hands on his hips. "Why?"

"I have no clue." Steve replied.

Alvin regarded him coolly. "I do not believe you. You must know something about your army's operations."

"I'm sorry to disappoint you," Steve tried to explain. "But I'm only a private—a peon. I don't know squat."

"You must have information. The build-up is obvious." Alvin was visibly agitated.

"Maybe so, but I don't know anything about it. I just follow orders."

"I demand you tell me everything you know!" Alvin yelled.

Steve stared at him wordlessly. "I'm telling you I don't know anything." He repeated slowly. "I'm—"

Alvin cut him off. "So you refuse to cooperate?" He waited a beat and then barked something to the guards crouching in the corner. Jumping to their feet, they grabbed Steve by the arms and hauled him over to the table. Pushing him down onto it, they unbound his hands, snapping them into metal cuffs affixed to the table and then placed leg irons on his ankles. Alvin selected a long bamboo switch from a pile on the floor, swishing it through the air before handing it to one of his minions. Steve felt clammy sweat coat his palms. He'd heard about this form of torture before.

The first couple of swats to the soles of his feet, though painful, were bearable and he thought it wouldn't be so bad. But as blow after blow hit its mark, the pain grew worse. Soon, his flesh felt as if it was being seared with Napalm. After a few minutes, Alvin returned to pepper Steve with more questions. Dissatisfied with Steve's perceived lack of cooperation, he ordered the beating to continue until Steve finally blacked out.

There were more interrogations in the ensuing days and weeks. Try as he might, Steve could not convince Alvin of his lack of army intelligence. He began to think of himself as a handy punching bag on which his captors could take out their aggressions toward a greater foe. Alvin was always present at the beatings, but the supporting cast changed. There was no apparent schedule; at times they seemed a regular part of Steve's routine and, then, long stretches would follow when he was left utterly alone. He wondered if Alvin was away on some mission then, or whether it was just an elaborate plan to fuck with his mind.

But isolation remained the real torment and on some perverse level Steve found he almost preferred the torture to the endless hours of unbroken solitude. Any human contact, no matter how brutal, was better than none at all. To keep from going mad, Steve sorted through football plays, hummed favorite tunes and dwelled on memories of Angela.

He recalled how when he was first brought here, he had lain on his mat in agony. Perpetually thirsty, he would greedily gulp down the water brought him. The healing of his shoulder helped him gauge the amount of time he'd been here. A gaping wound at first; it was now a shiny scar. Three or four months must have elapsed since he was captured.

Could it really be September?

CHAPTER SEVEN

The cave-in occurred in the middle of the night, several hours after the day's final bean cake, when the tunnel's darkness was complete. At first, the approaching air raid sounded like a swarm of mosquitoes. Steve, kept awake by an infestation of lice in his scalp, picked out the sound and tracked it. Noting its steady rise in volume, he could barely contain his excitement. They're coming, he thought. Liberation was in sight. By escape or death.

In the brief flash as the shell hit, he watched earth and rubble pour into the tunnel like a swollen river. Choking and coughing, Steve stumbled through the dust-filled darkness, hands bound before him, tripping over people and debris. Chaos reigned in the ant farm now, as flashlights strobed about erratically and high-pitched voices within the agitated warren mingled with shrieks and the cries of babies. Reaching the site of the collapse, he saw escape was in reach. Adrenalin kicked in and the next moment he was scrambling over the dead and dying, hastily scaling a heap of dirt and rocks to emerge at the edge of the crater. Attaining solid ground, he was thrilled by the sensation of fresh air against his skin.

He immediately began to run, gritting his teeth against the pain in his feet and holding his hands in front of him like a cattle prod on a locomotive. The dark night that provided cover also obscured the lumpy mound in the path ahead. Steve fell upon the soft warm heap. He shuddered upon discovering himself in the embrace of a corpse, its garb drenched in warm blood. Then, the soldier in him kicked in. The terrain was too harsh and unforgiving for bare feet: Steve would need footwear if he had a prayer of escaping alive. He perused the body more closely. The man was wearing high-top sneakers: cheap Asian knock-offs of good old Chuck Taylors.

The task of removing the shoes with bound hands was difficult, but he finally succeeded. They looked small, but no matter, the toes could be cut out somehow. They had thick rubber soles; that's what counted. He eagerly pulled them on—his first footwear in many months. They pinched his toes like a son of a bitch, but they'd have to do for now. He laced them loosely and grabbed the small metal canister hanging from the man's waist, securing it around his own. He, then, pressed on full tilt for fifteen minutes or more, oblivious to the peril of land mines, intent only on disappearing into the jungle. When at last he felt he'd put enough distance between himself and his underground prison, he slowed his pace and turned his attention to freeing his hands. Finding a rock with a sharp edge, he began sawing through the stout rope until it broke apart and his hands were liberated at last. He stretched his arms raising them above his head for several minutes before letting them fall against his sides. How good it felt.

Next, he attacked the sneakers. The canvas was sturdy, and it took a good deal of effort to cut through it, but finally the threads began to fray, and Steve was able to tear the material open across the toe and around the front edge of the sole. He repeated the process with the other sneaker. Before putting them back on, he placed Angela's letter under an innersole.

It was time to inspect the contents of the canister he'd snagged. He couldn't believe his good luck. Inside, he discovered a small wealth of provisions all jumbled together: chunks of pickled egg and bean cake along with several lengths of dried mango, like shoe leather, within a loose matrix of cooked rice; sustenance enough to satisfy his shrunken stomach. He took a deep breath and started out through the dense rain forest, heading away from the rising sun. Unburdened by the heavy gear he'd carried as a soldier, he felt light, almost carefree.

At nightfall, he discovered a spring bubbling forth from the earth. After slaking his thirst and consuming a small ration of the rice mixture, he vigorously scrubbed his scalp to rid himself of lice; happily, his efforts seemed to work—the incessant itching abated. Then, dog-tired, he curled up on the soft earth beneath an aquilaria tree. He could hear the faint drone of planes and the dull drumming of distant gunfire, but he felt a renewed sense of optimism over his miraculous change in fortune.

After saturating his shirt in the spring and tanking up with water, Steve set off. He traveled several hours, breaking in the heat of the day to consume some rice and doze in the shadows, moving ahead thereafter until dusk when he scouted for a thicket in which to spend the night. He continued this routine the next day always on the alert for the enemy. At one point, he overheard voices and, peering through a gap in the foliage, his heart in his throat, saw a group of Viet Cong milling about a grassy clearing. In the background, he could make out the sluggish movement of a broad stroke of muddy water. They'd been briefed extensively on the geography of the region. This must be the Ben Hai that divided South and North Vietnam.

On its final mission, Company Equinox had been nearing the Demilitarized Zone that extended to the north and south of the Ben Hai River in a three-mile wide band. He reckoned he and Harrison were following a southerly course away from the DMZ, and the river. He knew the Vinh Moc tunnels lay to the north of the Ben Hai. Seeing the broad river before him, and observing the burning sun at his right shoulder as it journeyed westward, confirmed his suspicions that he'd been transported north across the river by his Viet Cong captors. His spirits sank for the DMZ was known to be heavily mined and crawling with guerrillas.

Moving just as Christensen had instructed, without footsteps, slowly and soundlessly, he stole through the underbrush, to skirt the enemy and head upriver in the dusky shadows. At a safe distance, he squatted and, opening the canister, finished the remaining morsels of food, smearing the last of the rice kernels onto a fingertip. Then, he flung the empty container into the bushes. Next, he removed his shoes and threaded their laces through his drawstring waist.

But what could be done about Angela's precious letter, which had seen him through so much? How could he safely transport it across the water? He couldn't bear the thought of losing it now.

An idea suddenly came to him. He broke off a length of pliable vine and fashioned a wreath of sorts for his head, which he lashed tightly together with a strip of cotton torn from his pant leg. He then wove the letter in and out among the rounds of vine and placed the primitive garland snugly on his head, realizing with delight he'd constructed a nifty bit of camouflage.

"Why, I must look like Jesus Christ himself in this get-up," he thought. "At least I'll scare the living daylights out of any VCs I run into. Send them straight back to the missionaries," he chuckled to himself.

When night fell, he crept to the water's edge and eased into the sheltering reeds in a single fluid movement. The thick mud oozed between his toes. He pushed off in the direction of the far shore, carving the water with a soundless breaststroke. He could feel the gentle thrust of the current pulling him. He counted each stroke, focusing on his goal to take his mind off the pain in his shoulder.

Upon reaching the far side, he crawled up the bank into the undergrowth where he untied his shoes from around his waist and removed his sopping clothing. Exhausted, he lay down, the crown of vines by his side, and slept.

When he awoke several hours later, it was still dark. He dressed and after a long drink of water, began following the river west. His goal was to reach one of the army bases that lay along the 17th parallel toward the Laotian border. Waking before dawn on the second day, he began his trek south away from the river.

The land was becoming hilly and the temperature dropped as he climbed. Weakened from lack of food, he moved slowly. Though he saw no sign of American occupation, he could hear rumbling ordinance in the distance. He had another close call when a band of a dozen or more VC guerrillas suddenly trotted into view along a ridge. Timing and luck were everything—his slowed pace, his frequent breaks had saved him. If he'd arrived a mere five minutes sooner, they'd have seen him.

Gradually, the thick vegetation gave way to an expanse of green resembling, Steve thought, the gentle hills of Pennsylvania. But the resemblance was deceptive, for it turned out to be a savanna of elephant grass—coarse, six-foot blades that ripped through his clothes and sliced at his skin, making for slow and painful progress. But there was no turning back and so he continued to traverse the harsh landscape, lured on by distant mist-covered hills.

The fever set in at some point during the night. Ill and dazed he couldn't be sure whether he was walking, or dreaming that he walked. With each step, the elephant grass jabbed at his exposed toes and hands, keeping him conscious and moving. Sometime in the pre-dawn hours, he finally left the savanna behind, staggering across red clay to begin his ascent into the foothills.

It was as he was stumbling through the mist, not knowing where he was or, by now, who he was, on the brink of giving up, that he came upon a rough track and, looking ahead to see where it led, first saw them.

Appearing suddenly out of nowhere, a pair of ponderous red stucco posts framing a decorative iron gate. They seemed so improbable, foreign and out of place. He blinked with disbelief, staring at them dumbfounded. This was not how he had imagined the gates of heaven to look, if that indeed was what they were. It was then that he noticed an ornate tile-plate bearing Western lettering on one gatepost. It swam before his eyes. He blinked again and lurching forward, managed to make out the inscription before he collapsed. VILLA INDOCHINE.

CHAPTER EIGHT

The soft whirring, as of angels' wings lured him upward from unconsciousness toward golden light. Even as he surfaced, he was filled with a sensation of peace pouring into him like a glorious elixir. He felt swaddled by the warmth of a greater being—a guardian angel whose wings beat softly above him. He was imbued with an overpowering sense of love, he smelled roses and felt his mother's lingering presence as if she had just left the room. His eyes flickered open, and he blinked against bright sun filtering through jalousies.

The room was sparsely furnished. Steve took in a caned armchair, shelf of books and most improbably, a Swiss cuckoo clock complete with chalet and pinecone weights. Most remarkable of all, he was in an honest-to-goodness bed made up with crisp white sheets. On the table beside him was Angela's battle-scarred letter, so he knew this wasn't a dream. A ceiling fan hummed overhead, the sound he recognized as the angels' wings he thought he'd heard. He picked out the glint of gold lettering on the books lining the shelf. Two titles jumped out at him: *A Child's Garden of Verses* and *The Jungle Book*. Steve's eyes widened in disbelief. Where the Heck was he?

He tried to make sense of the situation. It was all so improbable. What was he doing in this western style bedroom filled with English language books? He knew he was in Vietnam, Angela's letter on the bedside table told him that. But the months of captivity and the recent dangerous trek were so at odds with this cozy setting. He couldn't figure it out. Sensing he was safe, and too weak to investigate further, he fell back asleep.

When he awoke again, the light passing through the blinds had become muted, falling in stripes upon the saffron colored wall and on a man sitting across the room reading. He had a handsome face framed by chestnut hair, with high cheekbones, a finely chiseled nose and the complexion of one who has lived his life in the sun.

"So, you are finally awake," he said, looking up from his book. He rose to his feet and crossed the room to place his hand on Steve's forehead.

"Ah, you've cooled down quite a bit, I am pleased to say. You were burning up when we brought you in yesterday. Do you remember? Your eyes were open as we sponged you down." He formed his words carefully, speaking with a precise, clipped accent. "You must be thirsty. I will get water."

Returning a short while later with a celadon flask, he filled a tumbler and helping Steve to a sitting position, held the glass for him while he drank thirstily before he slumped back against the pillows.

"And how are these today?" he asked, lifting the coverlet to inspect Steve's swollen feet paved with blisters and crosshatched by cuts.

The man made sympathetic clucking noises at the sight of them. "Still pretty bad, I see, but better than before. My servant put aloe on them and will apply more later. You must be very hungry. Let me see about some sustenance for you."

The simple, clear broth the stranger brought tasted delicious. He fed it to Steve spoonful by spoonful, wiping his mouth every now and then with a linen napkin. "Now, you must rest again. I'll put the water here, just so. There's more in the *flaçon*. And, if you need anything in the night, a…*clochette*," he placed a small bell on the table by the bed. "And now, as we say, *dors bien*." He smoothed the covers and gave Steve a friendly pat on the arm before leaving the room.

As it turned out, Steve didn't need the bell. His screams woke the others. When the two men burst into the room, he was half out of the bed. "There, there," the man soothed after they had helped Steve back onto the mattress. "Shhh-shh. It was just a *cauchemar*—a nightmare. All is well, you are safe," he continued, blotting Steve's face with a damp cloth. "I will sit with you until you fall asleep."

Steve was already awake when the stranger returned the next morning. "Breakfast should be here presently." He took a seat. "*Alors,* I take it you're an American soldier, *hein?* And, from your attire, lately a prisoner." Steve didn't answer, still unsure what to make of it all.

"Allow me to introduce myself. I am Maurice de Vigny. It is mere chance we should meet. I have only just returned here myself—a fortnight ago, and will be here only a short while longer."

Steve stared at Maurice for some time before speaking. "My name's Steve Ryle," he extended a frail hand. "I'm a private in the U.S. army." He paused, "last thing I remember, I was stumbling through the jungle. And, then, I open my eyes to find myself in a bedroom right out of a movie set." He looked utterly baffled.

"And, Jesus, I'm *in* a Goddamn bed. What's going on anyway?" He began to laugh; it all seemed suddenly comical. "Is this heaven?"

Maurice chuckled. "No wonder you are confused," he said. "Let me explain. You are my guest at—my family's plantation. Duy Linh, my servant, found you outside the gates two days ago and summoned me. Together we brought you here." Maurice paused briefly before going on. "Now, perhaps you can tell me how you ended up outside my gates."

In a quavering voice Steve related the demise of Company Equinox, his imprisonment in the tunnels and eventual escape. Maurice had heard of such labyrinths extending several miles underground. Steve described his injury, the miracle white powder that hastened its healing. Maurice nodded, "Yannan Paiyao," he said. "Originally from Hunan Province in China, its critical ingredient, the herb tien chi ginseng, has been used for centuries in the Far East to treat traumatic injuries."

When Steve recounted swimming across the Ben Hai, Maurice shook his head. "It's quite a miracle, my friend, that you made it across the river alive. The border territory is heavily patrolled. You are very lucky indeed. I suspect the Ben Hai's where you contracted your dysentery."

Suddenly it occurred to Steve to ask the date. Maurice's reply was a shock. December 17th. So, he'd been held captive for eight months. Over two hundred days.

"I don't suppose you have a phone?" he asked thinking of Angela.

Maurice laughed. "Oh, no, I'm sorry. We used to have a radiophone, but that's long gone. I'm afraid all we have now is a short-wave transmitter.

I used it just this morning to alert the American authorities that you are here.

Steve felt both disappointment and relief. Part of him couldn't wait to hear Angela's voice, but he was also apprehensive. So much had happened to him. He knew the scars he bore were not just surface abrasions; more profound wounds maimed his spirit. How would Angela cope with this new Steve?

A rustle in the doorway announced the arrival of a slight man. He entered the room carrying a bamboo tray on which sat a covered china bowl.

Maurice gestured toward him. "Mr. Ryle, allow me to introduce Duy Linh, faithful major duomo of the Villa Indochine. It was he who discovered you. And Mr. Duy has brought you his famous *pho*. It will help you regain your strength. Merci, Monsieur Duy."

Aided by Maurice, Steve sat up supported by husk-filled pillows. Duy Linh set the tray before him and uncovered the bowl of steaming broth, garnished liberally with sweet potatoes, chickpeas, sliced egg, rice noodles and scallions. The piquant aroma of ginger filled the air and Steve suddenly felt very hungry.

He ate the soup slowly at first because it was so hot, sucking down the delicious spoonfuls, feeling his belly grow pleasantly warm. As he ate, he listened as Mr. de Vigny explained his mysterious presence in Vietnam.

"It is a long story and a bit sad, I'm afraid. But, first, you must agree to call me Maurice. 'Mr. de Vigny' is far too formal. Particularly, given the circumstances of your fateful arrival here, which, I feel, has bestowed upon us the immediate status of friends. You agree?" He arched an eyebrow and Steve nodded. "Well, then, Steve, let me say, the de Vigny association here in Khe Sanh Province goes back many years.

"My father, a botanist, first came here from France in the twenties, drawn to Southeast Asia, I suppose, first and foremost out of mere curiosity. The de Vignys had substantial holdings here dating back to the 19th century and since Papa's elder brother inherited the title and Château de Vigny, back in France, my father was left to deal with the family's more far-flung interests.

"From here, he traveled to Australia to see the flora of that great insular continent—and one flora in particular—my mother, Adelaide Eaton, whom he had fallen in love with after encountering her in Switzerland at the school his sister attended.

"They married and lived on the Eaton estate at first—a fascinating place for a botanist. But my father was an independent person. And so, he announced to my mother quite suddenly that they were to move to Indochine, or, Vietnam as you Americans call it, to take over the de Vigny coffee plantation.

"When my parents first arrived in Khe Sanh, the family compound was comprised only of a main pavilion and a few rough bamboo hootches. No de Vignys had lived here before, you see; the operation had always been run by an overseer.

"My mother kept an extensive journal detailing day-to-day life—quite a remarkable document. As a boy, she'd enthrall me with stories of their early years in the rainforest, which, in those days, was inhabited by an abundance of wildlife: elephants, gibbons—even tigers.

"Shortly after they established themselves here, work began on the plantation house itself," Maurice's sweeping gesture took in the heavily beamed ceiling above, the Audubon prints on the wall, the wide-planked wood floor.

"The plantation prospered and Papa spared no expense on the construction of his house. Tiles, exotic woods and ironwork were brought here from Hanoi, carpets from China and the furnishings and antiques imported from France.

"When I was born, the coffee plantation was at the height of its prosperity. Our beans were very much in demand. Why, Fauchon in Paris, couldn't keep them in stock. Other than the fact I had no brothers and sisters, this was a happy place to grow up—a very happy place. My playmates were the children of the local people here, the 'Bru'—my father's laborers.

"This, alas, is all that remains now of the great de Vigny plantation," he sighed, gesturing around the room. "It was another world in so many ways—a world of beauty and exotica and great luxury. I am sorry to see it go…" He paused before resuming.

"So, to answer your question, I am here, however briefly, because this is my home. This is my land. Or, perhaps given the current state of affairs, I should say, was." Maurice smiled gravely.

"That explains all those English books," Steve nodded toward the shelf, as he scooped the last of the noodles into his mouth.

"Ah, yes, those were my mother's favorites. She read them to me. This was my room, you see. I was sent away to boarding school in France when

I was 13, and my mother died but a few years later. Nothing much has changed since then. I'd come home every year to see Papa, but life here was too lonely for a young lad and given the onset of war with the Viet Minh—and, now, this latest debacle—it never made sense to be here long term. So, after I finished university in France, I went to Tullynally, my grandparents' place in Australia. That's my home."

There was a long pause. Then, Steve shot Maurice a puzzled look. "So, why are you here now?"

Maurice shrugged, a sadness in his eyes. "*Alors*, for some time, I've been scheming to remove Papa because of the increased hostilities in the region. The coffee operation closed down, let's see, maybe five years ago, and the laborers let go due to the growing conflict and problems of transporting the beans to the coast. I suppose if I'd been here to help out, we might have been able to keep things going a bit longer, but it was really only a matter of time...and my life is in Australia now. Linh has been my father's sole companion for the past few years." He pressed his fingers together, resting his chin on them, and was quiet for a moment.

"However," he began again, "Papa's deteriorating physical condition made his removal more pressing of late. He was a stubborn old man, insisting on remaining in his beloved Indochine to the end. When I learned he had recently taken a turn for the worse, I set evacuation plans in motion. I got here as quickly as I could, but, *tant pis,* he died the day before I arrived." His eyes shifted to the window. "I never had a chance to say good-bye."

"But we're in the middle of a war zone!" Steve protested. "How the hell did you get here?"

"Oh, it was a simple matter really. I was helicoptered in by your army." Maurice returned his gaze to Steve and smiled. "I can see how you might find this surprising—that the U.S. Army would assist a civilian in this way. But you see, my father was an ally of your country. Yes, he was a private citizen, but politically very powerful in Vietnam in a clandestine sort of way, and a loyal supporter of the cause of a free South Vietnam.

"Now that Papa is buried, all that is left to do is close up Villa Indochine and be on our way, Duy Linh and I.

"And a good thing as it happens," he lowered his voice. "I have reason to believe that very soon this area—while it's remained largely unaffected by the war up until now—will become extremely dangerous—in a matter of a few weeks, in fact."

He paused again then clasping his hands together, he abruptly changed the subject. His tone was bright now. "So, you have eaten well? Linh prepares a very fine pho. He has kept the kitchen garden going masterfully over the years. He is also an experienced keeper of poultry. It's these talents in husbandry that have sustained my father and Monsieur Duy all these years..." he hesitated, looking around the room, "in this splendid isolation."

Following the meal, Duy Linh helped Steve down the hall to the toilet. After relieving himself, he grasped the wall for support, and moved unsteadily to the sink. Washing his hands, he glanced up at his reflection and was startled to see enormous eyes staring back at him above hollow cheeks. His gaze travelled down to the sunken chest and distended belly below. His mind reeled at the emaciated old man he had become, a far cry from the gridiron star of just two years before. He felt he might collapse and called out to the servant for help.

The nightmares returned that night. Again, Maurice and Duy Linh hurried to Steve's bedside. Together the two men restrained him, Maurice's words were soothing, and Steve settled back in bed. "I just don't understand it. Sure, I had bad dreams in the tunnels, but nothing like this." Steve despaired.

"The mind is an amazing thing," Maurice observed. "Shutting down when necessary as a way of coping. You had enough to deal with just being in VC custody without reliving such trauma. Now, that you're safe, your mind can go back and begin to process it all. Revisiting these *memoires,* painful though they may be, is an important part of healing."

By next morning, Steve felt much stronger and welcomed Maurice's suggestion to take some air in the gardens. Duy Linh set up a teak planter's chair in the shade of a jambu tree. After helping Steve to his seat, he tucked a silk coverlet embroidered with flowers around him, and set a pot of aromatic jasmine tea on a ceramic garden stool. Cupping his hands around the thin-walled cup. Steve closed his eyes; his thoughts drifted to that other fragrant, primeval garden—the beloved apple orchard.

Word was received via Maurice's short wave radio that an evacuation helicopter was to arrive the following day to airlift them to Saigon. Steve was eager to get to a phone and call Angela. How happy she'd be to hear his voice, to learn he'd made it after all.

205

In preparation for departure, Maurice spent the afternoon packing away family papers and memorabilia and gathering together a few small treasures—his mother's journal and some old photographs to take with him. Larger items were placed in pantry cupboards and in the Vuitton trunks residing in the storeroom. Though Maurice had expressed pessimism over the fate of these items, Duy Linh's sense of protocol prevailed—window locks were rattled fast, shutters snapped closed and latched, and rattan shades unrolled with a ruffling sound. It was as if the residents were just leaving for their annual visit to France.

Maurice joined Steve for lunch on the terrace. That morning Duy Linh had wrung the necks of two chickens—no longer needed for eggs. "Tonight we will have a bit of a celebration," Maurice announced cheerfully. "Mr. Duy has a surprise in store for us—roast chicken—and I plan to raid Papa's wine cellar. He boasted a fine one once, as a matter of fact," he winked at Steve.

"So, you see, we'll have a little fun. It only seems fitting, our last night in this lovely place. We must bid the villa a proper adieu," he looked around wistfully. "I expect this will be the last time I see her. Please, by all means, have a look around if you feel up to it."

Offering his arm to Steve, Maurice escorted him down the steps to the garden. The morning mist had burned off. The Truong Son Mountains were boldly visible now, rising into the sky, a blue wall separating Vietnam from Cambodia. Although it was the winter season, the gardens were rich in flower and luxuriant plantings. There was a profusion of spidery white chrysanthemum blossoms, interspersed with lantana and coreopsis in shades of yellow and tangerine. Across the way, the rose bushes, though sparsely leafed, provided a gallant showing of winter blooms.

"So that's what I've been smelling all day: your roses," Steve remarked.

"Actually, no," said Maurice. "What you smell is the brazier of sandalwood on my father's grave. It's a lovely smell, no? It was my parents' wish to repose side-by-side at their beloved villa. Their graves are right over there by a pool of lotus." He gestured toward the shadows bordering the garden. "It's a very peaceful place. I know they are happy."

Steve dozed in the chair for most of the afternoon. When he finally got up, he made his way slowly to the terrace where the row of double French doors had been flung open to give the room one last airing. He could hear the soft billowing sound of dustsheets catching the air as Duy Linh spread them over the furniture. He peered into the room in time to see a sheet float over a faded needlepoint settee and watched as Mr. Duy systematically made his way around the room, covering the assemblage of de Vigny bergères, console tables and richly carved chests. Just as Steve entered the room, Mr. Duy was approaching a bow-fronted Chinese lacquer commode. The two men nodded to one another. Steve crossed the room and entered the hall.

As he moved along the corridor toward his room, he hesitated at the door leading into the library. It was a beautiful room, its walls the color of a millpond, and he was drawn inside. Handsome Oriental scrolls covered one wall, and above the fireplace hung a portrait of a man in a powdered wig and embroidered waistcoat. The other walls were lined with shelves of books, more than he'd seen anywhere, even the public library.

He walked over to the bookcases, his eyes skimming across row upon row of volumes: Maupassant, Voltaire, Beaumarchais, Baudelaire. All French, it would appear. His eyes wandered across the shelves. No, there were English works as well, he noticed, reading off the names silently to himself: Thackerey's *The Waverly Novels*, *The Complete Works of Shakespeare*, some Dickens, the collected poems of Wordsworth, Shelley and Byron, and, then, his eyes froze upon a single volume: *The Collected Poems of W.B. Yeats*. He felt his heart leap. W.B. Yeats. He was astounded. That book—here? He pulled it from the shelf and rifled through the pages until his eyes fell upon the poem, *their poem*. He could hear Angela's lilting voice reciting the words. Finding this link to her on the other side of the world sent chills up his spine and he began to sob.

When Maurice entered the library some time later, Steve was sitting in a campaign chair, the book open on his lap. His eyes were closed as he softly recited the poem. When he finished, Maurice cleared his throat. "Bravo, very nice," he said. "Quite the touching story of unrequited love—*n'est ce pas?* Yeats's life in a nutshell, *en réalité.*"

Steve's eyes opened with a start. He could feel his cheeks redden as he hastily closed the book. "So you know the poem?" he stammered.

Maurice crossed the room. "But, of course. It's a classic, *The Song of Wandering Aengus*, a staple of any well-rounded education." His eyes danced. Then, glancing at his watch, he placed his hand on Steve's shoulder. "It is already five o'clock, *mon ami*. I instructed Linh to draw you a bath at five-thirty. I thought we'd meet back here in the library at 6:30 if that suits you, *hein?*"

As promised, it was a festive evening at Villa Indochine. Duy Linh had lit a number of tin lanterns and candlelight flickered across the walls. Maurice produced two bottles of vintage Dom Pérignon from the cellar. A credit to its fastidious storage in a subterranean vault, the champagne was perfection—fully effervescent, crisp and heady. To Steve, who had never before tasted real champagne, it was just as Maurice said Dom Pérignon himself had described: "like drinking stars."

Just before they went in to dinner, Maurice crossed the room to the leaf-top desk, opening it to return with a package wrapped in rice paper. "*Alors*, here is a little present for you—the volume of Yeats's poetry that caught your fancy this afternoon—a parting token of Villa Indochine." He paused and, then, said sadly, almost as an afterthought, "I hold out little hope for this place, and it would please me for you to have a little piece of her."

It was like a dream, that evening, yet so very real—all those rich sensations, finely spiced chicken and vintage champagne, within the lavish surroundings of an enchanted arcadia against a backdrop of war and destruction. It was a fantastic chimera that on the morrow, as the chopper lifted, disappeared forever behind enveloping clouds.

PART FOUR

Worthington, Pennsylvania 1967

CHAPTER ONE

*A*nna broke the news to Tony after his weekly bowling game when she knew he'd be in a good mood. His demeanor instantly changed. He ran up the stairs and burst into Angela's room, his face purple with rage, Anna at his heels. "That fucking piece of shit—I'd kill him myself if he weren't already dead," he yelled pounding the wall with his fist.

Angela screamed, shielding her head protectively with her arms.

Anna had by now gotten hold of her husband and was shouting, "Stop it! Stop it! In the name of God, Tony! For Mercy's sake, your daughter's been through enough already." He wrenched free from her grip and stormed out of the room.

Anna embraced her sobbing daughter, "Oh, Angie Dear, please don't cry. We'll get through this somehow."

First thing the next morning Angela called Norma to let her know she was ready to come back to work.

"Are you sure, Honey? How 'bout we cut back your schedule to two afternoons a week for the time being—say, until you feel up to it," Norma suggested.

But Angela was desperate for distraction to ease her aching heart, and she needed money for the baby. She wanted to get back to the diner as quickly as possible; maybe Norma would even up her hours? "Please, Norma," she pleaded. "If I don't keep busy, I'll lose my mind."

"Poor thing," Norma shook her head sadly, addressing a man at the counter. "Those two were crazy in love. Never seen anything like it. And such a beautiful couple too. It's a damn shame."

Henry went directly over to Angela the next time he came in. He waited until she turned from wiping a table. "Angela, I just want to say how sorry I am about your loss," he said quietly.

"Thank you," she answered, eyes downcast. Kind words like these were likely to set her off crying, and she was determined to keep it together on the job. She collected herself and meeting his gaze, added, almost as an afterthought, "and thank you for the flowers."

"Please, don't mention it," he murmured. "It was a small gesture."

"Would you like your regular booth?" she asked, abruptly changing the subject.

"No, no, I can't stay. I have another engagement. I just dropped by to check on you."

She smiled faintly. "Well, I'm back," she said.

"I'm glad. Let me know if there's anything I can do, anything you need at all." He began to leave, then, hesitated, turning back to her." I lost my fiancée just a couple of months before our wedding, so I know what you're going through."

Indeed, in the weeks that followed, it was Henry who provided the most comfort. He sensed when she needed to talk and when she wanted to be left alone and, through it all, conveyed a sense of unwavering concern.

Toward the end of the month, Anna joined her at the kitchen table with a cup of coffee. "Angie, Honey, I met with Father Joe yesterday and he told me about a very nice place for girls in your condition. An old estate run by nuns. Near Harrisburg. There'll be other girls your own age there."

"You know how much I'll miss you, Sweetheart, but it's for the best. Father Joe said they'd have a place for you in a couple of weeks. They'll look after you until the baby comes. We'll pick you up at the hospital."

"And when we get back here, how do we explain the baby to everyone?" Angela looked anxious.

There was a long pause. "Honey," Anna said gently. "The baby isn't coming back here. There's a lovely family. Very affluent, I'm told, who are desperate for a child. They'll give your little one a loving home and a bright future." Anna rose and walked over to the coffee pot. "Such a load off our minds," she said, re-filling her cup.

Angela's face collapsed and she hunched over the table, her body shaking with sobs. "No, no. You can't make me give up Steve's baby," she wailed. Anna regarded her daughter in stony silence.

The D'Agneses remained adamant on the subject. It was the only solution. Once the baby was out of the equation, Angela could resume a normal, untarnished life.

But Angela was determined. There was no way she'd give up Steve's child. She knew she'd have to figure something out. Time was running out. They'd be packing her off to that home soon.

Facing the future alone was scary, but within her also glinted a thin interfacing of exhilaration for what lay ahead, forging a new life with this tangible link to Steve.

Henry didn't show up at Norma's for several days in the midst of this turmoil. His absence made Angela realize how much she had come to rely on his quiet strength. When he finally did appear, she couldn't help but bristle with annoyance. Where had he been? She decided to ignore him, busying herself with her other customers. After several minutes, Norma came over to her. "Angie, Mr. Worthington's been waiting for some time. Why haven't you taken his order?"

She looked over, pretending to notice him for the first time. "Well, he's just going to have to be patient. I've got my hands full here."

"Look Angie, he's a good customer and good for business." Norma intoned evenly. "So what if he likes you? There's no harm in that. I'll cover for you here while you take care of him." She said it kindly, but there was no mistaking the firmness in her voice.

Angela heaved a sigh and marched over to where Henry was sitting.

"So, what'll it be? Your usual?" She avoided his eyes as she busied herself retying her apron.

"Yes, thanks," he answered.

She returned some minutes later with coffee and an English muffin, placing them in front of him with a noticeable clatter.

"Angela, are you all right?" He looked up at her, concerned. "You seem a bit out of sorts."

"I'm fine," she replied tersely.

He drank the coffee and finished half the muffin. Without fully realizing it, Angela was keeping tabs on him out of the corner of her eye, as she attended to her other tables. Nevertheless, she didn't see him leave.

When she left an hour later, he was waiting for her outside. "Look, Angela, I'd like to talk with you. How about I drive you home?"

"Thanks, but I'd rather walk."

"Very well. Then, I'll walk with you. Would that be all right?" She shrugged.

They set off in silence until Henry finally ventured, "I don't know what's bothering you, but clearly something is. You know I'm a pretty good listener."

Angela sniffed dismissively.

"What's that supposed to mean?" he asked sharply.

"I just find that a little hard to believe. I mean you just disappear without so much as a word…"

"I was caught up in final negotiations for a new plant." He stopped in his tracks, grinning. "Why, Angela, I didn't know you cared."

"I don't. I mean I do—but not the way you think. You're my friend. Someone I can talk to. You seem to understand the way I feel better than anyone else. That's all."

"For a minute there, you were getting my hopes up, but, hey, I'm happy to be your friend," he said lightly. "Still, something else seems to be eating you. You know, it's true what they say, confiding in someone, makes you feel better." He paused, letting the sound of their footsteps fill the void.

"Whatever it is," he resumed, "it can't be that bad. And remember your secret's safe with me." His lighthearted words had a completely unexpected effect. Angela stopped walking. At first, he was bewildered, and, then, he could see she was crying. He turned back to her and placed his arms firmly around her shoulders. He tried to comfort her with reassuring words, but, mostly, he just held her and let her cry. Within Henry's strong arms, she felt protected and safe, her cheek pressed against his jacket. When she finally spoke, her words were muffled by soggy cashmere.

"I'm pregnant."

Henry didn't flinch, and she thought he hadn't heard her. But presently he asked, "Your boyfriend?" She nodded against his chest.

"Well, that's not the end of the world," he said brightly. "I thought it was much more serious than that." She lifted her head, an expression of surprise on her face. She had thought he'd be shocked or appalled or even disgusted, but he was none of these things. His manner toward her was completely unchanged.

"Look, Angela, there's no point your working yourself into a state over this. What's done is done."

"But my parents are going to send me away, and make me give the baby up. I just don't know what to do."

He pulled her close again until her sobbing subsided. Then stepping back and holding her at arm's length, he looked into her eyes and said: "I'll help you figure something out. I promise."

He took her arm. "Now, I'm going to take you home. I want you to get a good night's sleep and stop worrying, okay?" She nodded, comforted by his take-charge attitude.

The following Tuesday, Henry pulled into Norma's parking lot and switched off the ignition key. He leaned into the rear view mirror to smooth his hair, before opening the door to unfold his lanky frame. He buttoned his jacket and straightened his tie. It had been a long day already, a break-fast closing the annual directors' meeting of a Pittsburgh oil company. Then, there was the long drive home on the interstate. He could use a cup of coffee.

He entered the diner, pausing for a moment by the cashier's stand to peruse the room. Glancing at the clock he saw it was just before three o'clock, which explained the scarcity of customers. Paula was wiping off tables in the far corner, but Angela was nowhere in sight. Norma pushed through the kitchen swing doors and, seeing him, grabbed a menu. "Hey, there, Mr. Worthington, as you can see, you got the place to yourself," she slashed the air with the menu. "Sit wherever you like."

He took the nearby booth as she fetched coffee. As she set the cup before him, he, got right to the point. "I stopped by to see Angela. Is she around?"

Norma bought some time before answering, retrieving sugar and a stainless steel creamer from the next booth. "I'm afraid, you just missed her," she stated quietly. "She wasn't down on the schedule for today, but stopped by to pick up her paycheck."

"Then, I suppose I can catch her here tomorrow?"

"Well, actually, no. She gave notice yesterday. Said her aunt in Pittsburgh had a fall and needs a companion. I'm sorry to see her go, I told her, she's welcome back any time."

Henry's expression darkened. "Hmm, did she say when she'd be leaving?"

"Later today, I believe. The afternoon bus."

Henry rose like a shot, his coffee untouched. He slapped a five-dollar bill on the counter. "In that case, Norma, I have to run." He saluted her deferentially and was out the door. Norma smiled to herself.

Henry drove the speeding car through the winding streets, over the Lenape River to the Greyhound Depot. He hadn't been to the bus station since Lucinda and he picked up James, the Fresh Air Fund kid from Harlem, the summer he was ten.

The air was heavy with exhaust fumes and he could hear the rumble of an engine coming from the rear of the building. He pulled open the heavy glass door and scanned the room, knots of passengers, some traveling together, others alone, a mother with a squealing baby, a prim elderly woman wearing a hat and veil, handbag tightly clasped in her gloved hands, a scruffy man in flannel shirt and dark glasses. Everyday humanity.

Angela was nowhere to be seen.

Henry strode over to the counter. "What's the schedule for Pittsburgh?" he asked.

The clerk looked up from sorting through receipts. "Well, what bus did you have in mind? The 3:10 just pulled out," he said. Henry felt his heart sink. "The local that is, the express just got in from Philly. I'll be announcing it shortly."

Henry surveyed the room again. "Do you happen to have a passenger list," he inquired.

The clerk's eyes widened. "Nah, buddy," he scoffed. "This here's a bus company, not an airline."

Henry exhaled heavily. Damn, I missed her. He turned to go, his footstep leaden. Even as he grasped the door handle—he would think later how serendipitous the timing was, a mere second or two of delay changing the whole course of his life—his peripheral vision caught the slightest movement coming from the direction of the rest room, the sound of a door closing, the flash of corn silk hair. He turned around. And there she was. Angela. *His Angela*, he boldly thought. Seeing her there, before she saw him, he had a fleeting, precious moment all to himself in which to observe her just as she was. Beautiful, yes. But so much more. Her carriage, tall and straight and self-possessed, her quiet demeanor, suggested a grace

216

and nobility of character that was of the ages. It came to him in a flash. He knew what he must do.

"Angela," he moved toward her, arms outstretched, face a-beam. "There you are!" Flushed from the cover of drab surroundings, this radiant prize. Her eyes met his and she gasped. By then, he had reached her side and extended his hand toward her small plaid suitcase. "May I?" he asked.

"But, my bus, it's about to board," she stuttered.

"Angela, I need to talk to you."

"You don't understand." Her tone becoming strident. "I have to go. Now. This afternoon, before my parents find out and stop me." Tears began to pool in her eyes. She bit her lip and began slowly, "I've thought about this a lot. Believe me, I have." She formed her words with careful deliberation. "I can't and won't give my baby up. So I have to leave Worthington. I have no choice." She glanced around the room, pressing a hand against her mouth to suppress the sobs percolating within.

Henry placed his hand on her shoulder. "I understand, Angela. But don't worry about the bus. I can always drive you to Pittsburgh if need be. After we talk." Henry looped his arm through hers to guide her to his car.

She felt a wave of relief, as she sank into the passenger seat. She had an ally. Someone older and wiser who would know what to do.

"I told you the other day," Henry turned to face her, "I would help figure something out. Well, I've come up with a solution." He cleared his throat nervously then launched ahead.

"I think you know I care for you, although perhaps you don't realize quite how much." He pressed his hands together in front of him almost in prayer. "You gave me a real fright today, nearly walking out of my life like that. The prospect of losing you has given me new clarity."

He continued, his voice composed, resonant. "I realize this might seem overly hasty on my part, but Angela," his eyes latched onto hers, "I want to marry you and raise your child as my own."

Angela, dumbfounded, turned away. Of all the possibilities she had considered, this had never crossed her mind. Henry turned to her. "I assure you, I will always treat you with the utmost care and devotion. And, of course, you and the baby will never want for a thing." Sitting ramrod straight beside him, Angela's gaze was riveted to the dashboard in front of her.

He continued, his tone quiet, but firm: "The one condition I have is the child never knows the truth. It will bear my name and believe I am its father." He paused to allow his words to register. "Maybe it's my ego. You see, I had a severe case of mumps as a boy. The doctors said I could never father a child." Angela turned to face him again, her expression grave. "In any event, for a whole host of practical and emotional reasons this is my proviso."

"I understand you'll need some time to think about this," he continued, starting the car, "so how about we talk again next week?"

Filled with trepidation about Henry's proposal, Angela could think of nothing else. It was not merely a matter of the disparity between them: money, age, experience, but also that she didn't really know him. He was virtually a stranger.

Most troubling of all was the idea of depriving her child the knowledge of its true father—her beloved Steve. Ever since he'd died, she'd carried on imaginary conversations with their unborn child, describing the little quirks that were Steve's alone. To deny herself this comfort and her child its birthright seemed inconceivable. But she was desperate.

When she returned home from the bus depot and found her mother at the kitchen table weeping over her note, she knew in a flash what she must do. She would marry Henry to safeguard Steve's precious legacy and restore family harmony.

So it was that when Henry arrived at the diner at the appointed hour the following week, Angela, with pounding heart, crossed the parking lot to where the shiny convertible was waiting. Without hesitation, she blurted out the words: "I've thought it over, Henry, and my answer is, yes. I'll marry you."

A broad smile spread across his face. "Oh, Angela, that's terrific! I will speak to your father immediately."

Before she went to bed that night, she removed the ring Steve had given her and with tears streaming down her cheeks dropped it into her special candy tin. She sent a prayer up to heaven: "Oh, Steve, I hope you understand." As she lay in bed waiting for sleep, for the first time in a long time she was at peace. She hadn't quite realized until now how heavily her plight had weighed upon her. For the time being, she dismissed any apprehensions about marrying a man she didn't love. She trusted Henry. And for now, that was enough.

CHAPTER TWO

$\mathcal{A}$ weight had lifted from 310 Laburnum. That a family crisis had been averted with their daughter's reputation intact was an enormous relief for Anna and Tony; that Angela was marrying a Worthington willing to raise her child as his own, was a miracle.

Not long after, as Angela was heading upstairs after supper, her father called to her from the living room. She found him sitting on the sofa turning something over in his hands. He looked up as she approached and handed her what looked like a miniature deer antler.

"A *cornuto* from the old country. You put it on the crib," he explained. "Protects the baby from the evil eye."

She examined the coral twig. "Thank you, Poppa," she said solemnly. They had been tiptoeing around each other since the blow up. Angela knew this little peace offering was her father's way of making amends to her. A seemingly small gesture, it was huge coming from him, and Angela was touched.

Henry's mother, Lucinda Worthington, insisted on hosting the wedding ceremony: "it will be so much nicer and "intime" that way," she gushed at the lunch she invited Angela to at Belvoir on the heels of their engagement.

Angela had been exceedingly nervous about meeting Mrs. Worthington despite Henry's reassurances. "She's going to think I'm some slutty gold digger who's entrapped him," she worried, knowing Henry had told his mother she was pregnant. But her future mother-in-law gave no sign of any displeasure when she greeted Angela in Belvoir's front hall.

Lucinda was surprised he had gotten himself in such a pickle. But she was inclined to be forgiving given what he'd been through with Camilla. She wanted her son to be happy and it appeared that this girl made him so. It was curious he'd never mentioned her. Not once. "Well, still waters run deep," she thought to herself. Now seeing Angela with her own eyes, she understood. Henry had always been a connoisseur of beautiful things, and she could well imagine how he had become enchanted by her.

A man of simple pleasures fundamentally, Henry possessed a winning lack of pretension, largely attributable to the Spartan upbringing received at the hands of his mother. A product of an elite Maryland background, Lucinda claimed to have seen one too many children of affluence transformed into dissolute ne'er-do-wells, victims of too much money. She wanted to ensure that her only child was well rounded—a man of principle who would lead a productive life.

To that end, after the sudden death of Henry's father in a car accident, Lucinda made sure to avoid the usual American watering holes—Newport, Palm Beach and the like—preferring instead to travel abroad with her young son during school holidays. At first, they divided their summers between Switzerland and France, taking in the Alpine air before heading south for a month by the sea at Juan les Pins.

One summer, when Henry was twelve, they rented a farmhouse on the island of Corfu, and from there, made an extended tour of Greece. Then, for a series of summers thereafter, Lucinda engaged a villa on a slope overlooking Spoleto during the festival, allowing time for exploring the surrounding Umbrian countryside, its hill towns, Assisi and Orvieto. From these seminal experiences had sprung Henry's lifelong love of music, and all things Italian.

Although culturally rich, Henry would remember his childhood as a period of great loneliness. While he never lacked for company in the form of his ebullient mother, he longed for friends his own age. At 14, Henry was packed off to boarding school, an experience Lucinda regarded as essential, having graduated herself from Oldfields.

It was at St. Paul's that he first developed close friendships with his peers and was introduced to his lifelong passion: jazz. His philosophy teacher played the trumpet and offered to give Henry lessons. Lucinda was delighted by this unconventional pursuit, taking her son to Birdland and the Five Spot Café on weekends in New York.

By junior year, he had finally screwed up enough courage to invite Harriet Combs to be his date for Spring Weekend. A frequent guest at Belvoir thereafter, Harriet was an avid bridge player, which endeared her to Lucinda. In later years, Henry would remember those visits as one long drawn-out card game. Her talents at bridge aside, Harriet was plain and a little aloof. Eventually, even Lucinda found herself discouraging Henry from further pursuit.

At Yale, there had been the predictable series of dalliances with Henry squiring girls to debutante balls, Whiffenpoofs concerts and football games. New flames materialized at summer house parties and sailing on Martha's Vineyard, where, when Henry reached college age, Lucinda had broken down and bought a rambling cottage on the harbor in Edgartown. While Henry raced his sleek Herreshoff, *The Glass Slipper,* she spent long summer hours in the hammock among the lupine reading mysteries.

When he turned 21, Henry came into his inheritance. Lucinda watched from the sidelines as her son jetsetted around, confident that the values she'd instilled in him would serve as an anchor to windward. She knew in the end all would be well.

Henry thoroughly enjoyed these years of bachelorhood, happily playing the field. It wasn't until he met Camilla Stainbank at Harbour Island, the Christmas he turned 26, that marriage even crossed his mind. Following her tragic death soon after they became engaged, Henry disappeared from the social scene. Forswearing all the frivolous pleasures against which he had come to set his personal compass, he returned to Worthington to bury himself in work.

During the bleak period that followed, Henry kept largely to himself; women were the last thing on his mind. But, that all changed the moment he saw Angela. It happened when, by chance he entered Norma's Diner that fateful afternoon. Standing there jotting down an order in her pink uniform and smudged Keds, Angela's effect on him was immediate: a sudden burst of sunlight breaking through dense fog.

Today's luncheon at Belvoir was stiff to begin with; the air ruffling through open bay windows, and the sunlight dancing on the terrace beyond, the only reprieve. But as the meal proceeded, Lucinda became more animated, won over by Angela's quiet charm.

When they finished the last of the profiteroles, Lucinda turned to Angela. "Angela, Dear," she said brightly. "Come with me a moment. I'd like to have a word with you." Angela shot Henry a panicked look, but he just smiled and squeezed her hand.

Closing the library door behind her, Lucinda turned to face Angela. "Goodness, my dear, I'm not going to bite," she exclaimed with a fruity laugh. "I just want to have a little chat with you, get to know you a bit." She walked over to the window, moving the curtain to peer outside.

"Naturally, I was surprised to hear of your condition." She turned to regard Angela's rising color. "I mean, I hadn't expected Henry to-to…" She hesitated for a moment before continuing. "Well, these things do happen…"

"I confess, my dear, I find you rather a surprising choice for my son." She broke off, "oh dear, that didn't come out quite the way I meant," she apologized. "It's nothing personal, I assure you," she added quickly. "But, I think I can be frank with you, and I hope you can understand my qualms. You and my Henry come from such different backgrounds, it's going to be rather challenging bridging the gap." She fiddled absentmindedly with the curtain cord.

"However, in point of fact," she smiled at Angela, "my reservations are neither here nor there. The reality is my son loves you very much. I can see that. I want more than anything for him to be happy, particularly after all he's weathered, and so I am prepared to welcome you with open arms into our house and family. That's really all I want to say—except I'm delighted I'm going to have a grandchild—I hadn't thought it possible—but I am thrilled at the prospect I want you to know that, my dear."

Leaving Belvoir, Henry stopped the car near the end of the drive and withdrew a small leather box from his pocket. "I wanted to give this to you before lunch, so you'd know it wasn't a test." He smiled teasingly at her. "But it was in Mother's safe. I only just got it." She opened the box and gasped. A deep blue sapphire set between two large diamonds lay within. It flashed and sparkled with life.

"Do you like it?" he asked. "It was my grandmother's. The sapphire's quite striking don't you think?" He removed the ring from its velvet nest, and taking her left hand in his, slipped it onto her finger.

"Now, I must ask you officially." He took a deep breath. "Angela D'Agnese, will you do me the great honor of becoming my wife?" The surreal nature of this moment was not lost on her; she couldn't help thinking of Steve's ring, so simple by contrast, yet so precious, and of that other proposal only a few short months before. She forced her attention back to the present. Back to Henry.

With tears pricking her eyes, she murmured, "Yes."

She was hyper-aware of the ring. It felt so weighty, seeming to pull her hand down. She would have preferred to take it off, at least until she moved in with Henry. But Anna, afraid she'd lose it, urged her to keep it safely on her finger. And as the days passed, to Angela's surprise, she grew used to it and even came to like it, for it reminded her she was no longer a helpless victim of fate. She'd taken a brave step and was proceeding forward with her life.

Her grandparents, not understanding the situation, were upset there wasn't going to be a church wedding. Angela could hear her grandmother's voice, high and plaintive, complaining to her father in Italian. When things were finally explained to her, much to Angela's surprise she didn't utter a word of reproach, but soon the brightly colored yarn she favored was replaced with fine yellow wool, which she knitted on slender needles. She would nod and smile at Angela calling out, "Cara Angelina," as she passed by.

"I knew it!" crowed Norma when Angela told her the news. "I kept saying he was sweet on you."

"Just think, little Angela D'Agnese, living in that great big mansion, for Land's Sakes." She lifted her apron to dab her eyes. "Well, Honey, can you drop by and see old Norma one more time before you get hitched? How 'bout Friday afternoon?"

Norma swung open the door when Angela arrived at the diner Friday. "Surprise!" she cried. "Step right this way, little lady," she guided Angela toward the back where Gina and Suze waited at a booth gaily decorated with wedding bells, balloons and crepe paper.

The two friends watched Angela approach, each wondering to herself what it was that was so different about her now. In truth, it had been painful to spend time in her company in the aftermath of Steve's death. It was a relief to see her under entirely different circumstances.

There had been murmurings in the community, and plenty of raised eyebrows about her relationship with Henry. But her closest friends, knowing the depth of her anguish, how much she had loved Steve, understood. Henry Worthington offered an entirely different path from the one she'd been following with Steve. In marrying him, Angela could change the subject and embrace a new beginning.

Suze and Gina each noticed a luminous quality about Angela despite the rather remarkable lack of interest she now took in her appearance—baggy cardigans over drab shapeless dresses, causing a few in hindsight to speculate if there had been another reason for the hasty marriage.

"Aww, you guys," Angela looked from one to the other, her eyes shining. "Thank you!" She sat down and Norma squeezed in beside her. Paula appeared bearing a cake. "Hope you like caramel," Norma beamed.

Angela took a bite. "This is delicious," she declared.

There were murmurs of agreement. "I still can't get over it," Gina piped up, "you're getting married."

"Yeah, and to a Worthington, no less," Suze added.

Norma pushed the stack of presents toward Angela. "Now, Hon, you've got to open your presents before the blue hairs arrive for the Early Bird Special."

"Gifts? Wow." Angela began unwrapping her presents: a lacy wedding garter from Gina, Betty Crocker's *Cooking for Two* from Suze, a sachet from Paula, a crystal jam jar Charlene and Bev had bought together, and an electric percolator from Norma.

"It's Corning Ware," she said proudly.

"So when's the big day?" asked Gina.

"Yeah," added Suze excitedly."

Angela hesitated. "We've decided it's just going to be family," she said ignoring their fallen faces. She wished she could tell them the reason. She hated hurting their feelings.

"How about another piece of cake?" Norma offered cheerfully.

The morning of the wedding Angela dressed slowly, slipping the simple, yellow dress over her head. Clipping a barrette decorated with daisies into her hair, she glanced at herself in the mirror. It was all so unreal; she dared not allow her mind to drift beyond the rudiments of the day's schedule, to alight on the subject of her looming marriage.

Downstairs, she found her family assembled in the living room. Dressed in their Sunday best, they looked like they were going to a funeral. What would they think of Belvoir?

Anna sprang up from the sofa when Angela appeared. "Oh, Angie, how pretty you look." She was smiling broadly.

"Thanks, Ma," Angela kissed her.

"I guess we should be going," Angela's father said, consulting his watch.

John had brought down Angela's suitcases and placed them by the front door. It seemed incredible that she'd spent her entire life in this house, yet all she was taking with her could be contained in just two bags. The contents of her room upstairs remained, but she knew she wouldn't be back to claim any of her old things. They were vestiges of a past that would never fit into her new life.

John drove. Angela rode in the back between her mother and grandmother, her hands clasped in theirs. The two Tonys and Angela's grandfather followed in the second car.

Anna talked nervously the whole way, falling silent only when they turned into Belvoir's gates. Upon rounding a curve, the house became visible. John whistled and Angela's grandmother gasped, "Santa Maria! she exclaimed, peering through the window, "Che palazzo!"

Henry and Lucinda were waiting on the front steps; Henry, suave in a navy suit, his mother, tall and elegant in lavender. The D'Agneses got out of their cars and Henry made the introductions. Then, Lucinda ushered them all into the house. "Isn't this a joyous occasion?" she declared brightly, sensing the D'Agneses' unease. "I thought we'd have the ceremony in the drawing room. The light there at this time of day is so pleasant and it is spacious. Judge Goodwin is waiting for us there."

Turning to Angela, she said. "My dear, you look just lovely. That color is most becoming on you."

Henry had made his way to Angela's side and, placing his hand gently at the small of her back, he declared, "Hear, hear!" And, then, addressing his mother, he said, "I want to have a word with Angela before the ceremony. He shot an inquiring look at Mr. D'Agnese, "If I may?" Angela's father looked startled at being asked permission in Henry's house.

"Of course," he managed to stammer.

Henry guided Angela to the library. On the desk lay a nosegay of white and yellow roses.

"How beautiful," exclaimed Angela. "I completely forgot about a bouquet."

"Actually, I believe it's customary, for the groom to supply it," replied Henry, handing the flowers to her. She lifted them to her nose.

"I'm not clairvoyant, by the way," he said, indicating the yellow roses. "I called your mother and asked what you were wearing."

"Thank you," she said, pausing. "And, thank you, for making this all so easy for me and my family." Their eyes met.

"I have something else." He walked over to the desk and removing an oblong box from a pigeonhole.

"I want you to know that today you've made me the happiest man alive. I'd like you to wear these." He handed her the box. She opened it to reveal a string of creamy pearls.

"They're on the small size, but they're actually quite nice. You see they're real, not cultured, and perfectly matched in color and size—quite rare, really."

"They're beautiful," she said. She held them out to him. "Can you help me?"

He fastened them around her neck. "There," he said, admiring the effect of the pearls.

He then looked at her earnestly, and taking her hand, said, "Angela, I realize you don't yet feel the same way towards me as I do you." He paused looking down at his feet. "You've had a terrible time of it. I appreciate that and I want you to know we'll take our time getting to know each other. I love you enough to wait until you can return my affection." He squeezed her hand and smiled. "For now, I am content just to be with you."

Was there no end to this man's kindness, Angela wondered. She'd been dreading being alone with Henry; now she could relax and do her best to enjoy this bittersweet occasion. She embraced him warmly. "Thank you, Henry," she said.

The ceremony was brief. Afterwards, two maids passed champagne and Henry made a toast. When luncheon was announced, the group moved to the dining room where the table was set with spring flowers, gleaming silver and fine china. They dined on lobster Newberg accompanied by more champagne with a small, tiered wedding cake to follow.

After lunch, Henry pulled the car around front and opened the hood so Angela's brothers could examine the engine. When she emerged from the house, Tony Junior was sitting in the driver's seat, his left hand on the wheel, his right arm draped across the seat—a look of supreme satisfaction on his face. Catching sight of his new wife, Henry bounded up the steps to join her.

Angela kissed her parents goodbye and Henry shook their hands before descending the steps to the car. Reluctantly, Tony Junior got out, holding the door open for Henry. "Now I know just how James Bond feels—she's sure a beaut," he said, his eyes traveling up and down the length of the car.

Henry helped Angela in, shook her brothers' hands and got behind the wheel. The newlyweds waved a final farewell to the group, Henry tooted the horn, and the car proceeded slowly down the gravel drive.

It was Angela's first trip to New York City, and Henry delighted in showing her the sights. She had always dreamed of going there, but the little figurine of the Empire State Building on her bureau was the closest she'd ever come. She couldn't get over the tall buildings, the hustle and bustle and the great crowds of people. It was bigger and more exciting than she ever imagined.

Henry took her to Bergdorf Goodman their first morning and put her in the hands of a personal shopper, who helped her select a wardrobe of summer maternity wear: loose gossamer dresses that were flirty and chic, unlike anything she'd ever seen a pregnant woman wear. Though she swore she'd never put it on, Henry even insisted on buying a bathing suit. "You won't be able to resist the water in Eleuthera," he promised.

They dined at top restaurants and caught a performance of *Man of La Mancha* on Broadway, the hottest ticket in town. At the 21 Club, Angela was wide-eyed when Henry pointed out Jackie Kennedy at the next table. Her companion, Angela observed, was an older, rather homely man, a notorious Greek shipping magnate, Henry told her. The two seemed captivated by each other's company, and Angela had a hard time not staring. She felt an affinity for this woman, an icon of tragedy who appeared to have found happiness again after devastating loss.

Each night, they went to a different nightclub: Cafe Carlyle, the Persian Room and, once for a change of pace, a trendy discotheque in the East Village. Henry was in a celebratory mood, and delighted in squiring his beautiful young wife about town in her newly acquired finery. Most of the time, the city cast its spell on her and she was able to enjoy herself. Yet, there were moments of melancholia when she missed Steve, their simple devotion, and would catch her breath wondering if she'd ever get used to this glittering lifestyle.

Henry had been right about the water. Aquamarine at the shore, it gradually turned a more intense hue as it got deeper. Here and there among the reefs, turquoise pools appeared suspended against azure fields. The Triangle Bay Club was empty, it being the off-season, and Angela happily donned her swimsuit, spending hours swimming in the gentle sea. Afterwards, she would lie on the pink sand and snooze, a broad brimmed hat shielding her face, gradually turning golden brown in the sun.

Each day, Henry would play a round of golf or a spirited set of tennis with the pro, joining Angela on the beach afterwards. In the whirlwind visit to New York, and lazy days on Eleuthera, Angela discovered Henry was a wonderful companion, easy and fun to be with. Though anxious at first when their conversation lulled, she grew comfortable with the silences. She realized she didn't need to entertain Henry. He was content merely being in her presence, reading a book or writing letters.

In the evenings, they would sit on their verandah overlooking the ocean. Always at sunset, a breeze would pick up. Soft and fragrant, it caressed their skin as they walked along the hibiscus-bordered path to the dining room. At night, bands of moonlight filtered through the blinds onto the walls of their darkened bedroom and the palm fronds, stirred by trade winds, would crackle against the stucco walls. And, as the newlyweds lay together in a chaste embrace on the four-poster bed, Henry would speak of the love in his heart, a tremor in his voice.

But aside from a kiss, now and then, Henry was true to his word. Their conjugal interactions, whether in their elegant suite at the Carlyle or their bougainvillea-decked cottage on that Bahamian island, remained innocent and deferential. But the honeymoon cemented their relationship nonetheless, allowing them time to figure out how to fit together as a couple and for Angela to prepare for her new life as Mrs. Henry Clay Worthington, IV.

Back at Belvoir, reality set in. At first, Angela felt lonely and isolated. It didn't help that she never heard a peep out of anyone from her past. She figured they probably were intimidated about calling Belvoir, but it still hurt. She missed her family and the accustomed routine of her former life. She was, in effect, living with strangers whose handbook on life was completely different from the one she knew.

Every few days she would call home just to hear her mother's voice. Their conversations were stilted. Anna always seemed like she was in a hurry to get off the phone, as if perhaps she was taking up too much of Angela's time. Once or twice, Angela called in the evening to say hello to her father.

"Things haven't been the same without you around the place," he said gruffly.

As May turned to June, her belly grew big. It was thrilling to feel the baby move within her. She was awed when every now and then, a bulge would appear on her abdomen as a foot or elbow pushed against it.

Slowly, she settled in. Each morning after breakfast, she walked down the long drive to the gates with Henry's Springer Spaniel by her side. She'd spend the rest of the day by the pool, stretched out on a chaise longue buried in mysteries passed her way by Lucinda. She welcomed these distractions, which kept her from dwelling on the past and distracted her from apprehensions about childbirth.

Arrangements had been made to deliver the baby at the Magee-Womens Hospital of University of Pittsburgh Medical College. To limit speculation about Peyton's exact birth date, Henry reserved a suite for Angela and her mother at The William Penn Hotel. *Per* Doctor's orders, he said. "Angela apparently has developed gestational diabetes," he reported. With this white lie in place, it was easy to draw out their stay a month on either side of the delivery. He, of course, would be there for the birth and would visit as often as he could. Henry was glad that Anna could be there; it gave him peace of mind. For Anna, it was a dream vacation, a gesture that would forever endear Henry to her.

Peyton Randolph Worthington was born one afternoon in late September. The heat was oppressive when Angela checked into the hospital the day before. But an evening thunderstorm cleared up the humidity, and Peyton's birth day dawned cool and crystalline.

Despite the drawn-out labor, the baby was a tiny vision of perfection. No distortion to the perfectly formed face, with big liquid eyes and coy little smiles as she slept. In Angela's hospital room after pizza and champagne, Henry traced his forefinger across the newborn's cheek, remarking that her skin was so soft it was "like touching a cloud."

CHAPTER THREE

*A*ngela gazed down at the small bundle settled at her breast, its mouth tightly latched onto her nipple, one tiny hand spread atop the globe, gently pumping. How she enjoyed the profound intimacy that nursing provided, this time alone with the baby. She couldn't tell whether Margaret considered breast-feeding unseemly, or just resented the fact feedings were the exclusive domain of Angela for now. The housekeeper certainly relished all other baby chores—bathing, dressing, changing diapers. Peyton's arrival at Belvoir had added a lightness to her gait and unlocked her long silent singing voice, which was now heard crooning lullabies.

Finally, little Peyton nodded off, her mouth detaching itself, her hand motionless, as her head slipped to one side with a soft rumble of baby snore. The infant continued sucking at the air intermittently, milky dreams filling her head. Angela marveled yet again at the love she had for this little one. She stood and raising the baby to her shoulder crossed the room to the bassinet.

With the baby settled, she began rummaging through the closet looking for the tiny red velvet dress her parents had given Peyton to wear at the family Christmas party. Though rather too grown-up and bright for such a small baby, Angela decided she'd put her in it anyway. Her parents would be so pleased.

"Merry Christmas!" Angela and Henry cried in unison when Anna opened the door. All but ignoring the grown-ups, Anna swooped down on the woolly bundle in Angela's arms.

"Oh—just look at her," she exclaimed, pulling back the hood of Peyton's ivory bunting to reveal her rosy face. "How adorable. Let me hold her."

"Yes, Mama, of course. Let's just get her out of this thing."

Angela carried the baby over to the couch and, together, she and Anna removed Peyton's outerwear. She squirmed in protest, squeezing her eyes shut, rage turning her face deep red. Opening her mouth wide, she produced a piercing wail. Anna quickly took her from Angela, and began walking in circles around the room, gently bouncing her.

"There, there, sweet girl," she soothed. "You didn't like all that fussing, now did you? All nice and cozy you were—and we came along and ruffled your feathers. But, look, precious, you have on your lovely Christmas dress. Why, you're as pretty as a picture. Yes, you are. Just like a little Christmas angel," she cooed. Peyton had stopped crying and was staring at her grandmother intently. Angela was charmed watching their sweet pas de deux accompanied by the soft crooning of Andy Williams on the stereo.

The tree was in its usual place in front of the picture window where it could be seen from the street. It was the first year Angela hadn't helped hang the ornaments. She walked over to the crèche and fingered the papier-mâché figures—her grandmother's pride and joy. They didn't cheer her as before, but had the opposite effect, filling her with nostalgia. Just one year ago, this was her home. Now she was a guest.

And Steve... he'd been alive then, laughing at her side.

As her mind touched on these memories, her heart ached. Steve, oh, Steve. She could almost feel his presence here among them, as if he might just be in the other room. She blinked away tears. Through the fog of sorrow that descended on her, she heard her name and turned to see her mother with Peyton in her arms framed in the doorway. Seeing her daughter there Angela brightened. She closed the door on the past, forcing herself back into the present. Taking the baby from her mother, she kissed the soft little neck and carried her over to the tree. There was much to be thankful for in her new life.

"You seem pensive, my darling," Henry remarked, joining her.

"I was just reminiscing about the decorations," she said softly. "The ornaments are mostly Swedish, like this elf, but a cousin of Nonna's sent her the crèche from Naples many years ago. She's always been so proud of it."

"They're lovely," he said, kissing her cheek. "Can I get you some eggnog?"

They turned and went over to the card table where Angela's father had set out the punch bowl, punch glasses, a bottle of rum and a tin of nutmeg. Mr. D'Agnese came bustling over.

"Allow me," he said with a flourish. He ladled out eggnog, sprinkled a little nutmeg on top and handed it to Angela.

"Aren't you forgetting something?" asked Henry, indicating the rum.

Mr. D'Agnese looked at him, surprised. Angela could see a flicker of annoyance cross his face. It lasted only an instant and, then, an extraordinary thing happened, the irritation disappeared and his jovial expression returned.

Now as her father handed Henry the bottle, his tone was contrite. "Of course, I forgot. She's a married lady now."

Anna came over, camera in hand. "Tony, Honey, I want a picture of the four D'Agnese ladies: your mother, me, Angela and the baby, bless her little heart. Four generations. Isn't that something?"

Angela and Anna positioned themselves on either side of Nonna who held the baby tenderly in her arms and smiled a broad, toothless grin. Little Peyton was wide-eyed, looking up spellbound at her latest captor.

When Angela's brothers arrived, the family sat down to dinner. The dining room had been decorated with gold garlands and red bows. There was cannelloni and veal scaloppini along with a Swedish potato, anchovy and onion dish. Mr. D'Agnese poured red wine with a free hand, and the group soon became very jolly.

For dessert, they had rum cake in the living room. Angela's father put on Frank Sinatra and they chatted over coffee. Poppa and Nonna enjoyed a glass of grappa together before being escorted by their son to their bedroom in the new addition off the kitchen. Angela watched them, shuffling feebly down the hall together and thought what a touching picture they made, this elderly couple, arm in arm, great-grandparents to the child in the basket at her feet.

The boys excused themselves. They had plans to meet friends at Vinnie's for a holiday nightcap. And, in the commotion, Peyton, who had been sleeping soundly since before dinner, woke suddenly, hungry for a feeding. Angela retired upstairs to nurse the child.

Sitting in the armchair in her old room she gazed around at the contents: her collection of stuffed animals, the baby doll in worn seersucker perched on top of the bookshelf, the pink flowered piggy bank. And then she saw the prom picture. That enchanted night remained one of her most cherished memories. Her, beautiful dress, the gardenia on her wrist—she could smell its perfume even now—and Steve, her dashing prince, resplendent in evening serge.

Content as she was in her new life, a beautiful baby at her breast, seeing the lovers in the photo with their distinct aura of completeness, roused a stronghold of myriad feelings within her. She became painfully aware of the deficiency in her present circumstances. For in spite of all the material blessings, there was an unmistakable emptiness to her present existence. Poor as Steve and she were, they had had it all. Maybe it wasn't Belvoir and all that entailed, but it had been enough, everything they ever needed.

There was a timelessness of the moment captured in the photo that called her back to her former life. It was a potent reminder, after all, of what could have been—a whole other sort of wealth that had slipped through her fingers. She thought how eerily disconnected she felt from the figures in the photo. They were as strangers to her now. She couldn't bear to look at it any longer and turned away.

She could tell the room had been attended to recently as indicated by the placement of the embroidered baby pillow at the head of the bed. A christening present to Angela from her grandmother, it featured her name surrounded by flowers. She could not recall the last time she'd seen it; her mother must have squirreled it away years ago for safe-keeping. Her eyes glanced up to the wall at the framed piece of embroidery above the headboard—*Sov du lilla videung* from the Swedish lullaby Anna sang to her children at bedtime.

> A *little sunlight-prayer: Tiny wicker turning green.*
> *The sunlight's eye watches you.*
> *The sunlight's embrace cradles you.*

She gave Peyton an affectionate little squeeze thinking she would ask her mother for the hanging to put in the nursery at Belvoir.

When she returned to the living room, she signaled Henry it was time to go. As they said their goodbyes on the doorstep, the phone rang. "It must be Uncle Hans from St. Paul. I better answer. Merry Christmas!" Anna hurriedly kissed her daughter and ran toward the kitchen.

CHAPTER FOUR

*A*ngela reached for the folded newspaper at the far end of the banquette, crossed the kitchen and went up the back stairs. Once in her bedroom, she sank onto the window seat framed prettily by chintz swags that brushed her shoulder. She was grateful she had decided not to join Henry with his cousins in Sun Valley for their annual ski trip. With a heavy heart, she unfolded the newspaper. There it was in block letters: "Local Vietnam Hero: Alive!"

Her eyes alighted on the photo of Steve—his high school graduation picture. It was the same photo she'd kept in her wallet up until her wedding day.

Her heart convulsed looking at the photo. It was a handsome face—still the most beautiful she'd ever seen, that of the prince in her *Golden Book of Fairy Tales* with dancing eyes, easy smile and mane of golden hair.

The words swam before her eyes. "Native son, Stephen Ryle, reported killed, found alive! POW.... discovered in Khe Sahn Province...Australian businessman, Maurice de Vigny quoted as saying: 'Mr. Ryle was very, very ill.' Private Ryle is being held at an unspecified location in Saigon for de-briefing." But it was the last two sentences of the article that delivered the crushing blow: "Asked when he would be returning to the United States,

Private Ryle stated he is planning on moving to Australia to pursue a business venture with Mr. de Vigny."

Of course, she was ecstatic Steve was alive. How could she be otherwise? It was an unimaginably happy turn of events. But, she couldn't make sense of it. Why hadn't he called her immediately? It was so out of character, it took her breath away.

"Australia?" Angela repeated the word—his destination—slowly and incredulously. Who was this Mr. de Vigny, anyway? Why such a sudden, inexplicable hold over her Steve? She was seized with indignation. Moving on without so much as a backward glance. She shook her head in disbelief. Then, quite suddenly she was laughing bitterly: "But Angela, you're married to another man." Maybe so, but she knew this would never have kept her from running to Steve. Nothing would. Why hadn't he contacted her, she brooded. She began to doubt his love for her.

She snatched the newspaper from her lap and began ripping it apart, but meeting Steve's gaze, she instead dropped the paper and fell back against the cushions sobbing. When the tears ceased, she felt drained, but calmer. With a racing heart, she dialed Ryle's Auto Shop.

"Hello, Mr. Ryle?" she asked, her voice shaky. "It's Angela. I just heard the news. What a miracle—you must be over the moon."

There was a pause "Why, hello Angela. Yes, we're beside ourselves."

She took a deep breath and continued. "Of course. I am so happy for you and Carmel." She hesitated. "I also called to ask you how I can reach Steve."

There was a pause. "I'm sorry, I don't know." His tone was guarded.

"But I have to talk to him," she pleaded.

"Well, Angela, all I know is he says he's through with his life here; he wants to make a fresh start."

"But I love him," her voice broke.

There was silence at the other end. "I don't know what to say, Honey." He became choked up. "All his buddies killed and being a POW all those months...he's a changed man."

He cleared his throat. "Look, I'll give you Carmel's number. Maybe she can tell you how to get a hold of him."

Carmel was cool on the phone. "Yeah, I spoke to Stevie a few days ago. He didn't have a lot to say. Dad and I aren't too happy about this Australia idea, but there's nothing we can do. His mind's made up."

Later that night, Angela retrieved the newspaper from beside the window seat and carefully cut the article out with nail scissors, tears streaming down her cheeks. Her exotic new life and the arrival of little Peyton had been like balms to the blow suffered by Steve's death. But she was thrust back into deep grief once again: he was alive, but had chosen to turn his back on her. It was like acid poured into old wounds.

With Henry away, Angela retreated to her room to mourn her loss. But upon his return she made an effort to appear calm with a sleeping Peyton in her arms. Henry crossed the room to her side. He knelt before her, encircling her waist with his arms. "Are you alright?" he asked, not looking at her.

"Yes," she answered quietly, blinking back tears.

Over the course of the following year, while Angela never spoke his name and presented a serene exterior, inwardly she churned. In a desperate attempt to communicate, she sent Steve numerous letters. As the days turned into months however, with no word back, Angela recognized that he was lost to her.

Finally, she accepted that the dream was over; it was time to move forward with her own life. Having lost all she really wanted, she embraced her new existence, pushing Steve into the farthest reaches of her mind. She buried the "what-ifs" and "what-might-have-beens" and began to let Henry into her heart. And, watching her apple-cheeked baby grow into a dimpled, tow-headed toddler, the identity of the little girl as Steve Ryle's child became superseded by her status as Henry Clay Worthington's daughter.

CHAPTER FIVE

A formidable woman, Lucinda Worthington possessed good looks, wealth and intelligence. She had accepted Henry's marriage to Angela graciously. But she was not naïve, understanding that for a marriage between individuals from two such different worlds to succeed, common ground must be cultivated. She could see Angela possessed an inherent grace and was determined to build on it. And so Lucinda Worthington undertook the "finishing" of Angela, so as to transform her into an appropriate consort for her son.

"She's very young, Henry, and you have your entire lives ahead of you. Let me have her for a few months, and I will show her a bit of the world. I promise, you will never regret it."

She proposed an old-style grand tour that would vastly expand Angela's horizons "in a crash course sort of way," Lucinda gushed, acknowledging her own delight at the prospect of revisiting familiar old "friends," as she termed her favorite works of art. "As you know Henry Dear, it's important to have a solid foundation of culture. Angela will find this invaluable over the years."

Henry was quick to acquiesce, knowing once his mother got an idea in her head, there was little hope of dissuading her. He did insist that he be allowed to join them along the way. And so, it was set. Come spring, Lucinda and Angela, accompanied by baby Peyton and a nanny would embark for Europe.

On Easter Sunday, a couple of weeks prior to their departure, Angela joined her parents at church. It would be the last time they'd see each other until September. "Peyton's going to grow so much while you're away," Anna had protested when Angela told her about the trip.

"There you are, Honey!" Anna hissed, waving her gloves at Angela entering the vestibule with Peyton in her arms.

"And, just look at the doll baby in her very first Easter bonnet!" She squeezed Peyton's chin; she squirmed in response, arching her back against her mother.

Going down the aisle at the end of the service, Anna noticed with pride the appreciative stares cast in their direction. Several people even came up to them on the steps to admire the baby.

"Such beautiful dimples! And those sky blue eyes. My, she's a beauty?"

Angela was expected back at Belvoir for lunch. So while Tony walked her to her car, Anna went downstairs to the ladies room, still basking in the afterglow of having her daughter and granddaughter in church. The bathroom was empty. However, shortly after Anna closed the stall door, two women bustled in to occupy the neighboring cubicles.

"Did you see the baby?" Anna recognized the voice as that of the church secretary.

"I told you. She's the spitting image of you-know-who," the other woman exclaimed in a voice Anna didn't recognize.

"I know. I'd heard rumors. But had never laid eyes on her before today. The proof's in the pudding though."

"All I can say is they're sitting pretty now up there in that palace. Anna must be happy. Bet she's over there all the time." Anna was stung by this image of herself.

In rapid succession, the toilets flushed.

"Yeah, and it could have gone a whole other way. Being unmarried in that condition. And what I wonder is: does Steve Ryle know?"

Alone in her stall, Anna winced. How well she remembered the panic she felt when she discovered Angela was pregnant. Her mind then turned to that fateful phone call just before Christmas. Hearing Steve's voice on the other end was a shock, but it did not for one instant undermine her resolve. Sure, she was glad to learn he was alive. But she knew what she had to do. She had to protect her own. She knew poor. She'd done without her whole life. She thought of all the nice clothes, the nice things she could never afford. It would be different for Peyton and Angela.

"Angela's happily married," she had told him. She recalled his sharp intake of breath as soon as she'd spoken. She felt remorse knowing the pain inflicted by these words, but they had to be said. She wanted to make sure he'd be good and gone from her daughter's life. Angela had been through too much already. So, of course, had Steve. But that was not her concern. It was her daughter and granddaughter who mattered. The wife of Henry Worthington now, Anna knew Angela's future was secure and that she and Peyton were safe. And yet, she worried. What if someone contacted Steve about the baby that looked so much like him? She shuddered thinking of his returning to Millmont one day.

The speculation of these church-going women irked her. Any concerned mother would have done the same. But then a smile spread slowly across her face. It didn't matter what they said, neither one had a daughter installed at Belvoir.

Anna heard water running. "Steve? From what I hear Steve's in bad shape. But what about Mr. Worthington? You think she let him in on her little secret?"

"Who knows? She's either a really smooth operator or a heartless slut messing around with two different men. Poor Steve. I feel so bad for him." Fuming, it was all Anna could do to restrain herself from bursting out of the stall and confronting them.

"Well, I bet it won't last."

Footsteps, the whoosh of the door opening and closing and the women were gone, leaving Anna shaken, resolved to do whatever she could to uphold Angela and Henry's marriage.

CHAPTER SIX

*A*ccustomed to traveling in grand style, Lucinda liked to take her time, enjoying the journey as much as the destination. She regarded planes as uncivilized modern conveyances and avoided them at all costs. So she and her entourage took the sleeper to New York where they spent a week prior to their departure for Europe. While Peyton's nanny, Bridget, pushed her in her pram through Central Park, Lucinda took Angela under her wing, delighting in her role as tour guide.

In the evenings, they attended dinner parties in the apartments of Lucinda's well-heeled friends, or met for drinks at various clubs around town. Lucinda coached Angela to listen and not speak unless directly addressed. "There's no need for you to engage others in conversation at this point, my dear. At your age, you should watch and learn. I don't mean to be unkind, but nobody wants to hear a naïve, young girl prattle on. Once you get some experience, then, that's the time for you to join in. But you must always, always listen. And look people in the eye. There is nothing so irritating as an eye-wanderer. If you understand this basic rule, you will be an unqualified success."

As the S.S. France passed under the Verrazano Bridge, leaving New York Harbor behind, Angela felt as if she were crossing a line with the whole world opening up before her. The ocean breeze kissed her face and she sensed the promise that lay ahead.

Sleek and luxurious, the ocean liner was like a floating town with shops and restaurants, a movie theater, cabaret and pool. When Angela first walked into her stateroom, she didn't think she'd ever want to leave it to explore the rest of the ship. On the table beside the picture window was a large vase of red roses. The note read: "Until Venice! All my love, H."

Adjoining her stateroom was a smaller room with a single berth for Bridget and crib for Peyton. Lucinda's suite was on the other side. "Now, Lovey, for the next week, this is our little home away from home." She enthused to Angela. "The sitting room is for us all to enjoy."

Their fellow passengers in First Class kept mainly to themselves. Rumor had it there was a famous Italian film star on her way back from Hollywood, but they never saw her. Once or twice they spotted the honeymooning couple whose wedding reception had taken place on the ship prior to departure. Angela had caught sight of the bride as she went up on deck to throw her bouquet to the guests on the pier and was captivated by her bridal attire, a white satin mini dress and patent leather boots. "How vulgar," Lucinda hissed, as the bride ran giggling by.

Each morning at nine o'clock, Angela's steward, Michel, knocked at her door with a cheery, "Bonjour, Madame," bearing a tray of freshly squeezed orange juice, croissants and twin pots of steaming coffee and milk. Following breakfast, she walked around the deck with Peyton snug in her carriage. Once they completed their circuit and Bridget had taken the baby for her nap, Angela retreated to a deck chair where Andre, the deck steward magically appeared, a soft tartan blanket under his arm to tuck around her against the North Atlantic chill. He returned again at 11:30 with a steaming cup of beef bouillon, a signal it was time to think about going in to lunch. At the outset, Angela had worried about spending so much time with her intimidating mother-in-law, but had grown fond of Lucinda's entertaining company and relished their tête-à-têtes.

While Lucinda played bridge, Angela spent the balance of the afternoon, back on deck in the bracing air. She read, until lulled by the gentle rocking of ocean swells, she dozed off. Promptly at 4:00, Andre appeared again, this time with tea and biscuits, which Angela enjoyed before returning to her stateroom to play with Peyton. There was still plenty of time before dinner; Lucinda had made sure they were in the second seating. "All

civilized people eat after eight. Eating any earlier is a suburban innova-
tion," she opined.

The third evening out, Lucinda hosted a small cocktail party in her
stateroom. All the guests were assembled when the captain appeared in
his immaculate uniform. "Bon soir, Madame," he said, bending to kiss
Lucinda's hand. "The French Line is indeed honored to be graced by your
charming presence once again."

"Oh, Angela, there you are!" Lucinda beckoned to Angela. "Monsieur,
Le Capitaine, je voudrais vous presenter á ma belle fille," she smiled broadly.

"Enchanté, Madame," the captain bowed, casting an admiring eye on
Angela in pale pink organdy. Then, turning back to Lucinda, continued, "I
do hope you and your delightful daughter-in-law will join me for dinner
tomorrow night."

"We'd be delighted," Lucinda exclaimed. She then steered Angela
toward a younger couple. "Angela, Darling, I want to introduce you to
Gigi and Felix Van der Vere. A delightful couple who are returning to
Amsterdam after two years in New York."

Lucinda drifted away and Angela continued talking with the Van der
Veres—Gigi, pretty with lively eyes and throaty giggle, and Felix, debo-
nair and witty.

"You must join us later in the disco. It's a real scene," Gigi urged.

"Oh, I don't know..." replied Angela.

"A pretty girl like you should kick up her heels." Gigi exclaimed.
"You'll be the center of attention—all the men will want to dance with
you."

"I'm not sure my mother-in-law would approve," Angela conceded.

"Well, that's even better. Then, you'll have a really good time," she
laughed. "Don't you know that it's the forbidden pleasures that are the
sweetest." Her eyes twinkled.

When Angela and Lucinda arrived in the dining room later that evening, they saw a third place had been set at their table occupied by a dis-
tinguished looking man drinking a martini. Lucinda confused, turned to
the Maitre D'. "Oh, dear, I beg your pardon, there must be some mistake.
There's someone at our table."

"Oh, no, it's no mistake, Madame. Monsieur requested specifically to
sit with you."

"Well, I never," Lucinda muttered under her breath. "I guess there's nothing we can do about it now."

As they neared the table, the attractive middle-aged man jumped to his feet, bowed solicitously and clicked his heels together. "Good evening Madame, Mademoiselle. Jean-Louis Erlanger, at your service." He touched his lips to their outstretched hands. "I hope my presumption does not offend, but I could not let two such lovely ladies dine unaccompanied."

"Not at all. You are too kind to join me and my daughter-in-law," Lucinda responded pointedly.

"I have taken the liberty of ordering a bottle of champagne," he said. Lucinda looked surprised and, Angela noted, rather pleased.

As if on cue, a waiter appeared with a bottle of Pol Roger that he presented to Monsieur Erlanger for inspection. Another waiter placed flutes at their places. The bottle was opened with a soft "pop" and the champagne poured out. Jean-Louis raised his glass, "A votre santé." He winked. "To a splendid passage."

As dinner progressed through many courses, Jean-Louis proved an excellent companion, full of interesting and entertaining stories. A member of the French Resistance, he'd been with Hemingway when he "liberated" the Ritz Bar the day the Allies re-took Paris. By the time dessert arrived, he had managed to thoroughly charm Lucinda, so much so that when the time came to repair to the Fontainebleau Salon for coffee, she took his arm.

Throughout the crossing, and, indeed, during their trip on the Continent, there always seemed to be an abundance of men flocking around the two women, drawn by Lucinda's money and Angela's allure. While Lucinda clearly enjoyed the attention, she was intent on keeping these admirers at arm's length. To her, they were charming accompaniments to enliven social engagements, and no more.

After stops in London, Munich and Vienna, the Worthington ladies finally arrived in Venice where they were to spend a fortnight. Angela would never forget her first impressions of this glorious place, emerging from the train into bright sunshine to board a waiting water taxi. As they sped up the Grand Canal, she looked around in wonder at the floating city, the ornate bridges and fanciful architecture; its air, a pastiche of aromas, briny from the sea, and laced with notes of garlic and newly baked bread. When the boat slowed to approach the water gate at the Gritti Palace, Lucinda declared emphatically: "My, but it's marvelous being here again."

In the early mornings before Lucinda rose, Angela would push Peyton through the twisting streets to Piazza San Marco. Peyton loved to watch the pigeons rise and wheel around the square. The baby was an irresistible magnet to elderly Venetian women who cooed in delight as they passed by. Most days, Angela lingered over cappuccino and biscotti at Quadri with Peyton providing welcome protection from the Italian *ragazzi* who, nevertheless, shot admiring looks Angela's way.

On the day of Henry's arrival, Angela didn't deviate from her routine and so left word at the hotel for him to join her. It was a beautiful day; the piazza was drenched with bright morning sun. She kept an eye on the Sotoportego de l'Ascension on the western end of the piazza through which she knew Henry would come. She was anxious, wondering if it would be awkward seeing him again. There was so much she didn't know about Henry. She was aware his fiancé had had a thing for Venice and wondered how it would be for him to be here under such different circumstances.

She spotted him before he saw her. Tall and erect, he walked with an easy grace. How completely at home he seemed in this foreign place. As he neared, she noticed he carried a book casually under his arm and she wondered what it was. It could be anything; he was always surprising her. And it was then she realized how happy she was to see him.

His pace quickened, and a smile lit up his face as he caught sight of her. "How I've missed you, Darling," he said, embracing her. Holding her, his gaze shifted to Peyton who was fixated on the pigeons. Undoing her harness, he lifted her up and kissed her. She looked momentarily appalled, and then recognizing him, she cried out "Da-Da!" with delight.

He turned back to Angela, eyes sparkling, jigging Peyton in his arms. "I told Bridget to meet us here at noon so I can take you to lunch."

"I'm not sure I'm properly dressed," she looked down at her slacks.

"Harry's Bar won't turn away such a pretty face."

Feigning a headache, Lucinda retreated to her room that evening so Henry and Angela could enjoy a romantic dinner together. Henry hired a gondola to take them to an out of the way restaurant he knew. They sat on a jasmine-scented terrace overlooking a small canal and piazza beyond. As they dined on risotto dyed black by squid ink, Angela regaled Henry with stories of her adventures with Lucinda, their conversation punctuated by voices from the occasional passing boat below. Two troubadours sporting the striped shirts and straw hats of gondoliers arrived at their table to serenade Angela, casting soulful glances her way as they sang. Henry, laughing tossed them a 5,000 lire note. After sharing a decadent tiramisù, they rose and set off on a leisurely stroll back to the hotel.

That night, Angela finally gave herself to Henry. She was nervous at first. It was only her second time and with a man she wasn't in love with, but a romantic room in Venice, a handsome partner who knew how to please a woman, champagne, and music drifting up to their windows from the hotel restaurant did the trick. She found herself enjoying being naked with Henry, his weight pressed on her. She ran her fingers through his chest hair, felt his taut muscles rippling beneath his skin; smelled his sweat. She was excited by his deep kisses, his touch on her breasts. When he reached around to place a pillow under her hips, she wrapped her legs around him eager for him to take her. Afterwards, she slept like a baby. She'd been afraid her lost love would be a constant presence, but it was far easier than she had anticipated. Alone in bed with Henry, she was able to cordon Steve off for a time. It was only in the bathroom the next morning that she sat on the edge of the tub and wept.

After leaving Venice, they traveled to Portofino where they stayed in a hotel high above the Mediterranean before continuing on to Rome. In Paris, they checked into an elegant hotel in the 6th Arrondissement. "The Ritz has become much too flashy," Lucinda sniffed. "All those movie stars have just ruined the place."

Paris proved a potpourri of sights, smells and sounds. Of course, there was the art and history, but what Angela loved most was going to the open markets, seeing the neatly arranged produce, the fish and cheese. She never tired of observing the Parisians—the burly deliverymen whose voices would fill the street, the prim shopkeepers presiding hawk-eyed over their tidy dominions and the well-dressed professionals hurrying by on the side-walks. She acquired a taste for the distinctive smells, a blend of strong coffee, Gauloises cigarettes, diesel exhaust fumes, and every now and then a whiff of delicious perfume from a passing *elegante.* This mélange of aromas became so identified with the place that forever after if she caught any one of them again, it would immediately transport her back to that first visit to Paris.

Henry had spent a year after college working for a bank in the Place Vendôme and knew the city well. He delighted in exploring it with her, taking her to the Marché aux Puces where she bought an amber necklace and a little Meissen pug, and out-of-the-way districts, where tourists didn't go, to drink in authentic Parisian life. He spoke French fluently, though he kept complaining about how rusty he was. But to Angela he seemed to converse effortlessly with the locals.

In the afternoons, they strolled Peyton around the Luxembourg Gardens, charmed by its formal layout, the flowerbeds bisected by gravel paths and basins filled with hungry carp. They marveled at being in the very same environment depicted in the paintings they'd just seen at the Jeu de Paume along with the same cast of characters: nannies with their charges in tow, young couples, boys with model sailboats. Squinting her eyes, Angela saw the scene transform into a timeless image composed of dabs of color.

Lucinda insisted Angela accompany her to a private showing at Dior where she selected several items for herself and purchased a midnight blue evening gown for her daughter-in-law. "Goodness knows, my dear, it's an investment. Good design like this never goes out of style. Besides," she said squeezing Angela's arm, "it will make me feel less guilty about all the things I got."

Europe was a revelation to Angela. To the D'Agneses, "the old country" was backward, a place to be left behind. But Lucinda had shown her a world of wonders. At various points during the trip, whether from a gondola on the Grand Canal, a hotel terrace in the shadow of the Matterhorn, or a bench in Hyde Park, Angela would look up from her guidebook and gaze at her surroundings in awe.

Lucinda, who had always longed for a daughter, relished her role in Angela's transformation. She regarded the young girl as a *tabula rasa* on which to inscribe her hopes and dreams for future generations of Worthingtons. But even she couldn't have predicted how successful her efforts would be and how quickly Angela would rise to the challenges presented her. On the return voyage, Lucinda observed her daughter-in-law admiringly, across the table one evening, chatting gaily to her dinner companion, a pompous lawyer from New York. Whatever paltry common ground they had, Angela had clearly found, for he was chortling away, hanging on her every word and thoroughly enjoying himself. Lucinda sighed happily to herself. "Now, I know just how Henry Higgins feels!"

PART FIVE

Worthington, Pennsylvania 1987

CHAPTER ONE

*A*ngela awoke on the sofa her mind and body aching. Dreams of Steve, a decoupage of old memories pasted onto wild imaginings of their meeting again, had reeled through her head all night. Stiffly, she made her way out of the safety of the library to face the day and the future that lay ahead. Knowing Steve would soon be back in Worthington, Angela could think of little else. Emotions she thought resolved long ago were jostled to life. As Mr. Ryle's funeral drew near, after much deliberation, she decided she must go. She had to see Steve again. She wanted answers.

Arriving at the cemetery, she parked her car and, grabbing her sunglasses from the glove compartment, followed a couple over a rise to the gravesite. The priest was just taking his position beside the casket. The wind picked up. She shivered and reached for her collar, pulling it more tightly around her throat.

Steve was standing next to two women she assumed were Carmel and her daughter. She stole a couple of glances in his direction. She was rather taken aback at how familiar he was, even as she noted how changed. She couldn't put a finger on what was different other than a scar on his cheek. He was still handsome; ruggedness now supplanted boyish good looks, imparting the gravitas to his appearance that comes with maturity.

Angela's heart pounded. She was filled with misgivings. What was she doing there? What could they possibly have to say to each other after nearly twenty years? She considered leaving, but didn't want to draw attention to herself.

She allowed her eyes to wander about the gravesite. She took in the open grave, the earth piled beside it covered by a patch of neon Astroturf to protect the sensitivities of the bereaved. Her eyes rested on the coffin with its brass fittings and burnished wood. No expense had been spared.

She thought of Mr. Ryle and realized she didn't have a strong impression of the man who was her daughter's grandfather. She remembered him as quiet, not given to obvious displays of emotion. She recalled the toast he'd made at Steve's farewell party so many years ago. How proud he was of Steve—and how oblivious to the danger ahead. He was the one who drove her home from the Lenape Tavern that night. It was the longest amount of time they spent together. She heard again the skip in his voice when she called him upon hearing Steve was alive.

The priest concluded his benediction, and the casket was lowered slowly into the grave, the intense quiet broken only by the shuddering it made on reaching the bottom. Steve was the first to pitch a handful of dirt into the hole. It hit the casket with a clatter. Carmel and her daughter were next, Carmel lingering a moment to mouth a prayer. The others followed behind. Angela recognized Daisy Lombardo and May Shifflett in the crowd. Soft murmurings reached her ears: "…a wonderful father…pillar of the community…."

She recognized the heavy-set woman and bald man she'd followed as Marcia and Chuck Wright. After speaking to them for a few minutes, Steve turned to embrace his sister and niece.

The other mourners had moved off when Angela, taking a deep breath, advanced toward the lone figure by the grave. Now facing him, she cleared her voice to free the flow of words trapped within. "Hello, Steve," she said mechanically, her eyes moving downward from his face to study the wooden movement of her arm as she extended her hand in greeting. "I'm very sorry about your father."

He regarded her coolly. "Well, well, if it isn't Angela D'Agnese. Er-I mean Angela Worthington," he said. "Not in my wildest dreams would I have expected to see you here." He ignored her hand. Stung by his manner, Angela was about to say something, but Steve's attention had shifted to the grave. "Poor old Dad," he said. "Well, at least Ma and he are together again." Her gaze followed his, and she felt suddenly terribly out of place. She had come here to try and figure out what had happened. Looking at him now, so unfriendly and severe, she had her answer—there's nothing for me here, she thought, turning to leave.

"So, Angela, before you go, maybe you can clear something up for me. Something that's been bothering me all these years. I just want to know—was it the money?" She flinched, feeling anger rise within her. How dare he!

"Are you kidding me?" she replied icily. "You've got a lot of nerve. I mean, who ran off to Australia without so much as a word?" she exclaimed, her eyes flashing.

"Do you think there was anything left to come home to once I heard you were married?" he retorted. They glared at each other across an immeasurable void.

Shaking her head in disbelief, Angela broke the silence, her tone clipped and cold. "Contrary to what you might think, it wasn't about the money at all. When I heard you were dead, I was half out of my mind. Henry Worthington offered me salvation, and I leapt at it." She saw the coldness ebb from his eyes.

"Look, I'm sorry Angela," he relented. "Maybe we each did things we regret. In any event, I shouldn't have spoken to you that way. I guess it's the strain of being home after all these years—that and Dad's passing." He paused, his gaze fixed on the horizon.

"Anyway, it was a lifetime ago—ancient history, now. How about we agree to let bygones be bygones, okay?" Now it was he who extended a hand. "Friends?" he said, smiling encouragingly.

She nodded, taking his hand. "Thank you, Steve, I appreciate that." She turned to go.

"Say, how about I buy you a cup of coffee? Is Norma's still around?" he asked.

"I haven't been there in years, but it's still there, though it changed hands after Norma died," she answered. "But why not? I have some time to spare."

Driving to Norma's, Angela thought how ironic it was that they should be going to the diner that had figured so largely in their relationship.

"You look good, Angela." he said, when they were both settled in a booth and had ordered coffee. "Marriage to a Worthington must agree with you." He regretted the words as soon as they were out of his mouth

She shot him a look of annoyance and he quickly apologized. "I'm sorry, that was uncalled for, but, it's got to be interesting, to have lived on both sides of the tracks."

"It looks like you haven't done so bad yourself," she retorted, not entirely mollified.

He changed the subject. "So, I hear you have a kid." She willed herself to maintain her cool. Then, raising her eyes, she checked his face for deeper meaning, but his expression remained unchanged.

She knew she must be careful. Any misstep might give everything away and her loyalties were with Henry.

"Yes, I have a daughter, Peyton," she said, her words measured.

"Peyton? That's different. So, tell me about her."

Before she could answer, a man stopped beside their booth staring in disbelief. "Steve? Steve Ryle?" he asked.

"Hey, if it isn't Brian Wells," Steve exclaimed, jumping to his feet to embrace the fellow. Then, gesturing to his companion, "Do you know Angela D'Agnes-..." He caught himself, laughing. "I mean, Worthington?" Angela remembered that laugh. Its warmth stirred her. The men chatted back and forth compacting two decades into a sentence or two.

"He was a fullback," Steve said, taking his seat again. "A couple of years ahead of me. I can't believe how old he looks." He shook his head in disbelief.

"I guess we've all aged," Angela said, relieved the subject had shifted away from Peyton.

As the conversation continued, she noticed Steve pronounced certain words with a flat "a" sound and his speech was peppered with unusual turns of phrase. She looked at him across the table, revisiting those aspects that had held such attraction, and realized with relief her heart was not racing.

"I have to admit, when I think of Australia the things that come to mind are sheep, crocodiles and that famous opera house."

"Well, I don't know much about the opera house—and, not being Crocodile Dundee, I've only seen crocs in preserves. But sheep, now that's something I can tell you about." He grinned.

Angela felt her cheeks redden at the warmth of his smile and looked away. "You've lived there such a long time. Do you consider yourself Australian, now?"

Steve ran a hand through his hair, which was still thick and curly. "Of course, I'll always be an American. But Australia's my home now. The two countries have a lot in common, or I guess I should say, had—that sense of freedom and independence. I'm happy to say the pioneer determination is alive and well in Australia. Whereas here…it seems largely to have disappeared. In the States, people complain about government involvement, how it limits freedom and such, which, if you ask me, is a bunch of BS perpetuated by Big Business. In Australia, the original spirit of the country, what Maurice calls the *esprit de corps*, remains uncorrupted."

"Maurice?" she probed.

"Maurice de Vigny. He's my business partner and friend. He's the one who saved my life, back in Vietnam."

"Oh, yes, I remember reading about him." He looked at her quizzically. "In the paper. When you were found." She took a sip of coffee. "What a nightmare Vietnam must have been. I can' imagine." She ventured solemnly.

He nodded, staring into his coffee cup. "The worst part was seeing all my mates get killed. My entire platoon. Wiped out, except me and one other guy, that is. Incredible, right?" His eyes met hers. "Good, ordinary men, who made the ultimate sacrifice. And for what?" He shook his head.

"And the ones who made it back? Treated like fucking lepers. They stepped up to the plate when their country needed them, only to have the good old U,S of A turn its back on them afterwards.

"Look at Carmel's husband. He was there for two tours. All that gore he saw in the operating room must have got to him finally because he off-ed himself with a pistol after he'd been home a year."

"Oh my God," Angela gasped. "How horrible."

"Yeah, I know. It was rough on Carmel, but she made it through and is doing really well now.

"But this country's attitude to the returning Vietnam Vets was miserable. It's one of the reasons I didn't come back here. At least in Australia, I get respect for my military service." He took a swig of coffee. "But I don't want you to get the idea I spend my life obsessing about what's over and done with. Actually, living where I do—so far away, the past holds little relevance for me...I rarely think about it. I guess that's a sign I belong in Australia." He chuckled.

"On the plus side, I did track down the other guy who survived—Kevin Joyce. I wanted to try and see him, but he lives in Montana and couldn't come east. He did make me promise to go to the Vietnam Memorial before I head home."

They talked more about their lives, knitting together strands of information to complete the picture of the intervening years. Eventually they grew quiet as the background rattle of glasses, clink of china and snippets of conversation filled the silence. Somehow it felt right, lingering there wordlessly together in this place so full of memories. Finally, Angela's eyes drifted up to the clock.

"Oh, my goodness," she exclaimed. "It's quarter past four!" It seemed only a matter of minutes since they sat down, but nearly two hours had elapsed.

By now, the diner had emptied out. Their waitress, initially attentive, had long since retreated to her perch at the counter with a newspaper. From time to time, she glanced in their direction; but seeing them deep in conversation, returned to her reading.

"I'm sorry, Steve, but I really must get home. Henry..." Angela broke off; her husband's name seeming an awkward intrusion. "We have plans this evening," she finished, collecting her things.

"Well, Angela, it's been swell. I've often imagined what it would be like seeing you again."

"So, what's the verdict?" she asked boldly.

"It's different from what I expected. Less dramatic, I guess." He chuckled. "But, I have to say, all in all, it's been nice," he smiled, and together they rose to leave. Once outside, he walked her to her car. When they drew alongside, he said, almost shyly "I'm here for a few more days—going through Dad's things. Other than going to Chuck and Marcia's Saturday night, I have no plans. I don't suppose we could get together again before I leave? I'd sure appreciate the company."

As he spoke, she realized she too didn't want this to be their only encounter. Despite a twinge of uneasiness, she replied, "I'd like that, Steve."

They agreed to meet for lunch the following week, a plan Angela spent the whole drive home justifying. "What harm could it possibly do—it's just lunch with an old friend."

As she drove along, she was aware that her senses seemed curiously heightened. The air coming through her open window smelled sweet and the breeze that had seemed so cold in the cemetery earlier, now felt like a gentle caress against her cheek.

Her elevated mood carried her through the evening, "you were the belle of the ball tonight, Mrs. Worthington," Henry declared on the way home from dinner at the Hutchinsons. "I thought I'd never be able to pry you away from George Whitman—the old goat!"

"Oh, Henry, you're terrible. He's really quite sweet. But anyway, it wouldn't take much to outrun him," she said flashing him a mischievous smile.

Later, when Angela was flipping through a magazine in bed, Henry called out from the dressing room, "Oh, by the way, Dearest, it looks like I'll be in Chicago next week. Board meeting."

"Not again," she groaned putting down the magazine. "You were just there."

"Actually, Darling, it's been over a month." Watching her husband emerge from the bathroom, she was struck by how stooped his posture seemed. He ambled across the room and climbed into bed. "I'm afraid it can't be helped. Comes with the territory," he said, snuggling up to her.

"So how long will you be gone?"

"I leave Monday afternoon and will be away through the following weekend, I'm afraid."

"Gosh—so long?" She sighed, "Why do these meetings of yours have to take up an entire week?" Hearing about this business trip disturbed her equanimity. As long as her husband was in residence, ever solicitous and attentive and sturdy as a sea anchor, her predictable life would continue along as always.

"Well," he answered. "Ordinarily, I would come home Friday, but there's a board retreat scheduled for Saturday. I'm sorry, Sweetheart," he flashed her a contrite look. "But I'm certainly glad to hear you're going to miss me!" He added with a grin.

"I promise I'll make it up to you. For that matter, how about if we plan a getaway for later this month? Anywhere you choose. Paris? Or, maybe Eleuthera—for old times' sake? You decide." He kissed her forehead.

"It's okay, Henry. Come to think of it, the timing couldn't be better. Next weekend I'm meeting Peyton at the Homestead. Remember?"

CHAPTER TWO

ngela got to Norma's early and sat in a booth in back to wait for Steve. Ever since their meeting, she'd tried without success to put him out of her mind. In fact, he was all she could think of.

Now, as he entered the diner, her needling suspicions were confirmed as everything else—the turquoise upholstery, the shining chrome, the crowd of faces—all faded into the surrounding murkiness of inconsequential space, and she saw only him, moving toward her like a spot lit actor on a darkened stage. In an instant all became clear. He was central to her being; she had never stopped loving him.

"Hey, there, Angela," he said, joining her. "I'm not late, am I?" As he smiled, pleasing laugh lines crinkled around his eyes.

"Not at all. I got here early," she assured him, feeling that familiar giddiness of old ripple through her.

The waitress appeared. "How you folks doing today?" She asked amiably, handing them menus. "I'll be back in a jiff to take your order."

They perused the selection in silence. Far too agitated to eat anything, Angela decided on a bowl of soup. She put aside her menu, racking her mind for something to say. "So, I keep thinking," she began. "This must be so strange for you. Back in Millmont after all these years."

He nodded. "But in some ways, it's as if I never left—like being here with you at Norma's." She felt warmed by his words, though his tone was neutral.

"How are things going at your Dad's?"

"Oh, you know it's a combination of emotional and tedious." He fiddled with his glass making patterns with the water rings on the table. "Going through a lot of crap. But, also coming upon some treasures. Maybe, not in some people's books—I'm talking letters and photographs—but they're priceless to me."

Her heart went out to the motherless boy Steve had been, the traumatized soldier he'd become who in spite of it all, could remain so tenderhearted. She wanted nothing more than to take him in her arms and comfort him.

The food arrived. "Thanks, Darlin'," Steve grinned at the waitress. "Nothing like good old American fried chicken," he exclaimed, picking up a drumstick.

After barely touching her soup, Angela set down her spoon. "I don't know if this was such a good idea. Meeting like this."

Steve paused, fork in mid air. "Okay," he said slowly. "Would you like me to leave now—or can I finish my food first?"

"Don't you see how hard this is for me?" she asked, searching his face. "You were my soul mate..." She paused to gain control of her voice. "We never had a chance. You were ripped from me."

She looked outside where a couple was exchanging a kiss in the parking lot. "I finally succeeded in putting you out of my mind," she continued. "And then you come back...unearthing feelings I didn't know I still had." She shook her head. "I can only blame myself. I should never have tempted fate and gone to the funeral."

Several moments elapsed, then Steve said softly, "I don't know what to say Angela, other than I'm glad you still care. But, at the same time, I don't get it," he said, his voice hardening. "If what you say is true, this soul mate talk, why did you up and marry Henry Worthington so fast?"

Her eyes held his smoldering gaze for a long moment before she replied evenly, "Because I was pregnant."

"Well, that was quick work," he snorted. "I die," he made quote signs with his fingers. "You meet Mr. Deep Pockets whose shoulder you cry on. He knocks you up and, then, next thing we know: wedding bells!"

Angela waited for him to finish and then said quietly, "I got 'knocked up,' as you so delicately put it, *before* Henry—Do the math." She jumped to her feet and grabbing her coat, ran out of the diner.

She was fumbling for her keys when Steve caught up with her. He put his arms around her. She turned toward him, and he pulled her against his chest. His embrace tightened as he felt her body shake and heard her sob.

"Oh, Angie, if only I'd known," he said softly. "I would have moved heaven and earth to be with you."

He pulled away and cupping her face in his hands, he said, "Clearly we have lots to talk about. But not here, it's too public. How about my Dad's place?"

They drove to the Ryles' home in Steve's rental car, where Steve ushered her into the living room before making coffee. He brought her a mug, which she held with both hands.

"I was scared, at first," she began. "I didn't know how my family would react—especially my father. But thinking about you and knowing in my heart you'd take care of us—kept me going. Carrying your child and dreaming of our future made me so happy." She brushed a tear from her cheek. "I didn't tell anyone. Not Gina, not Suze. It was my secret, and I couldn't wait to share it with you."

She cast her eyes downward, as if addressing the floor, her voice hollow. "And, then, I heard you were dead and my world fell apart." Steve moved closer, putting his arm around her.

"It was easy to hide the pregnancy at first, but my mother figured it out. Eventually, I had to leave school."

"And your father?"

"As you can imagine, he was furious," Angela replied. "But, I actually welcomed his reaction. It took my mind off the pain of losing you.

"They were going to make me put the baby up for adoption, had already made the arrangements. I was desperate. I couldn't let that happen.

"Henry was a regular at Norma's, and always very nice to me. One day, I broke down and told him the whole story. I was so alone—he seemed my only friend—I couldn't be around the old crowd; it was too painful. Not long after, he asked me to marry him. I was in shock. But it seemed the only solution. His one stipulation was Peyton's paternity never be revealed." She watched the blue of Steve's eyes deepen. "You see, he can't father children himself." She looked into her mug. "I've kept my promise, that is, until today," she whispered.

Resting her forehead in her hand, she proceeded. "Henry is a good man. He's been a wonderful father to Peyton—the only father she's ever known, and I love him for that. I owe him so much. Actually, we both do." She looked at Steve gravely. "Henry stepped in and took charge of the situation. He saved Peyton." She sighed.

"By marrying him, I was able to keep her. But it was still very hard. A lot of people—your friends, for instance—think I threw you over for Henry's money. Just as you did."

Steve slipped off the couch and knelt before her. "Angela, if you only knew how this changes everything. Everything I came to believe all these years." He held her face in his hands. "I wrote you off long ago; turned my love to loathing. I thought I understood the situation. But now I realize I understand nothing—nothing, except this."

He leaned forward and kissed her. "If only your mother had told me when I called…but I suppose that's to be expected," he added sadly.

Angela pulled away from him abruptly, brushing away her tears. "What are you talking about?"

"When I called from Saigon." She stared at him incredulously.

"It was the first thing I did when I got there. Right before Christmas. That's when I found out you were married."

"What?" she cried. "Mama never told me!" Her mind reeled.

Steve sprang to his feet. "Jesus," he exhaled, pacing the floor in agitation. "Talk about star-crossed."

"But this wasn't some random outside force," Angela emphasized. "This was my own mother, taking matters into her own hands, playing God with us."

"Well, I think we know what her motivations were," he said bitterly. "Her daughter's hitched to a rich man—the bleedin' royalty of Worthington." He paused in front of Angela. "Think about it—the American Dream come true."

"But Mama knew what you meant to me," she protested. "Henry was nothing in comparison to that. To think, she sacrificed my happiness for money. I don't even know who she is."

266

He sighed heavily. "Well, clearly, your mother thought she knew a good thing when she saw it and didn't want to break you two up." He sat down beside her.

"It never occurred to me to question the situation. I believed your mother, and besides, I had nothing to offer. I certainly couldn't compete with Henry Worthington."

Angela placed her mug on the coffee table and folded her hands in her lap. "You know, I wrote you at your Aunt Deirdre's," she said quietly. "Carmel gave me her address. But you never responded."

"I threw them all away," he acknowledged. "You've got to understand how I felt. Thoroughly betrayed. All I wanted was to close the book on you."

They sat frozen in a silence broken only by the ticking of the kitchen clock. Then, as if following a preordained script, Steve reached for her hand, they rose from the couch and he led her upstairs. There was no hesitation, no restraint. Raw passion, denied so long, supplanted all else. They moved together, reveling in each other's touch. It didn't matter that they'd been together only once before. Having relived that sublime coupling time and again in the deep recesses of their minds, they knew each other by heart.

At last, in a sudden spiraling flare, he felt his essence exploding forth and her flesh tightening around him, a deep pulsing that merged seamlessly with his own ecstasy. When after several moments, Steve moved to disengage himself. Angela murmured a protest, clutching him to her. "No, please don't. Not yet," she whispered. "I want you inside me still." He laughed softly, kissing her forehead.

"My God, Angela, that was like a holy rite," he said stroking her cheek. "If you only knew, babe, how I've dreamed of this. All those nights I reached for you."

He rolled over onto his back and drew Angela to him so her head rested on his chest. "Sorry about the bed—I'm practically on top of you," he laughed.

"I like it, it's like we're one."

She reached over to finger first the pink scar bisecting his shoulder and then the one on his cheek.

"Souvenirs from the VC," he said smiling. Noting her furrowed brow, he added, "no big deal."

For the first time, she noticed her surroundings. They were in Steve's childhood bedroom. Framing the window were drapes in a busy pattern of trains, probably hung there by his mother when Steve was a small boy. Posters of the Lone Ranger, Johnny Unitas and the Beatles were stuck to the walls with masking tape. Over by the desk, in a neatly arranged group, Steve's football awards stood sentry beneath his high school diploma. Angela wondered if Mr. Ryle had come in here to dust them after he thought his boy had been killed, or if it was too painful for him to venture into this repository of all young Steve's hopes and dreams.

Suddenly, Steve started. "I must have nodded off," he said, kissing her. "So," he continued, nudging her playfully. "Tell me about our daughter."

"I have a picture in my purse downstairs."

"Can I see it?" he asked eagerly.

"Of course," Angela laughed.

He jumped up to retrieve the purse, handing it to Angela as he climbed back into bed.

Searching her wallet, she found the photo. "Prepare yourself," Angela warned, holding it to her chest, "she's all grown up." She handed Steve the photograph, curling up next to him and placing her head on his chest.

"Wow," he whispered, "she's beautiful."

Angela pondered what a profound moment this must be for Steve—this first glimpse of a child he hadn't known existed until a few hours before. Such an enormous piece of information to absorb. Yet what a pathetic crumb, one photograph. Thinking of the deprivation Steve had endured, she was filled with rage at her mother whose reckless actions had forever changed their destinies.

"She looks like you," she said simply.

"Knowing you and I have a child—that I'm a father…. It's a lot to digest."

Steve was quiet for a few moments. "Well, I reckon it's best to keep things as they are for the time being, but I would like to meet her someday."

Even as he spoke, a wild notion was beginning to form in Angela's mind and the suggestion slipped from her lips. Why couldn't he accompany her to the Homestead to meet Peyton? Steve leapt at this: a chance meeting—old friends who just happened to be in the same place…with Peyton never the wiser. Angela's heart soared at the prospect of seeing father and daughter together. Would there be an instant bond? She felt sure of it.

They talked on languorously, filling in the gaps of years spent apart, while basking in the seemingly impossible—that they were together again. And as the room darkened with the approach of evening, they made love again, a slow, savoring of one another before falling asleep in each other's arms.

When Angela opened her eyes she saw it was past 7:00. Margaret would be wondering where she was. She kissed Steve awake. They dressed and Steve drove her back to the diner to get her car.

Once at home, she was seized with a desire to find the little pearl ring Steve had given her so many years ago. She'd lost track of the quaint tin she'd put it in. She looked in all the likely places—the cedar chest under the bed, the sewing table, the closet—but it was nowhere to be found. Finally, it came to her that when the room had been re-papered, several boxes were taken to the attic. She ran up the stairs and found them. Rifling through the contents, she found the tin buried in the last box she checked. She held it in her hands for a moment looking at the bright poppies and violets. She thought of how much history it contained: such an ordinary receptacle, such priceless contents. She opened it, and there among the folded letters and yellowed clippings, was the diminutive silver apple of the moon, lodged quite incredibly, she noticed, within Steve's class ring. She extracted it and pressed the cool pearl to her lips.

Back in her room, she withdrew a fine gold chain from her jewelry box and slipping the ring on it, secured the clasp around her neck. The chain was long; the ring slipped between her breasts to rest close to her heart.

CHAPTER THREE

*T*hey decided to spend a romantic night together on the way to The Homestead. Angela was waiting for Steve at the 7-Eleven early Thursday morning when his cab arrived. "Hiya, beautiful," he greeted her. "Can you pop the trunk for me?"

He leaned into the window to kiss her. "Not here, Steve," she protested. "Someone might see us."

The boyish glint in his eyes seemed to whine back at her, "Okay, okay," but all he said was, "Can I get you a coffee for the road?"

He returned a few minutes later with two Styrofoam cups and "A honey bun for my honey bun," he teased. Angela started the car, eager to hit the open road and leave Worthington behind.

Steve unfolded the map. "So, we're headed to Hot Springs, Virginia— right? Let's see, I figure we'll pick up I-70 to 522 and head south toward Winchester. Somewhere below there," he poked the map with his finger, "There's the right little inn just waiting for us." He grinned.

It was a picture perfect day. The trees, though still mostly bare, showed evidence of new growth articulated as they were by a halo of bright green and clusters of tight, russet-hued buds. The wooded hills conveyed the texture of a stiff badger brush, with little flecks of color, tender green and pink, evident here and there in the distant thicket like daubs of paint applied by an artist.

As they drove, Angela became aware of the hint of magenta beading outlining the branches of redbud trees. "It's such a gorgeous day, we should have a picnic," she suggested. So when they switched drivers, they picked up sandwiches.

"This is like a dream. Together again" Steve reached over and squeezed her thigh.

Angela put a tape into the cassette player and the distinctive twang of Dire Straits filled the car. She shimmied deeper into her seat leaning her head against the headrest, her eyes on Steve. "Tell me more about Australia," she urged.

He glanced over at her, "Life Down Under? Where shall I begin?" He paused to collect his thoughts. "It took me awhile to get used to the place. Completely different topography, plants, animals, etcetera. I've grown accustomed to it now—but I still look around every once in awhile and am blown away by what I see." He described blast furnace heat in summer that turned the landscape tawny brown and unforgiving drought followed by torrential downpours that transformed dusty ground into thick mud.

He spoke of great flocks of budgerigars and kookaburras that would descend upon the land with raucous cries. When he got to the insects and reptiles, Angela shuddered, "I'd much rather hear about koalas and kangaroos," she said, watching the spring palette blur past her window.

Steve laughed. "Well, there're plenty of 'roos where I live at Tullynally, but koalas are rare."

"Tullynally? That's a funny name. Sounds like baby talk."

He chuckled. "Actually, it's named after an estate in Ireland. Maurice's great-grandfather came from a long line of drovers who worked on the place."

"Tell me about it," Angela prodded.

"Well, Tullynally's a sheep station in New South Wales, north west of Sydney."

"It's been in operation for over a century and is one of the most famous in Australia. At one point, it was one of the largest too—over two million acres."

Angela gasped. "That's unbelievable."

"In Australia enormous spreads aren't uncommon. Shoot, Anna Creek's six million acres." He glanced over at Angela. "Of course Tullynally's holdings have been substantially reduced over the years, but they're still considerable. I never saw the original house—it burned to the ground long before I got there, but I gather, it was quite the showplace.

"A fire—how terrible," she exclaimed.

He nodded, "yeah, fires are common. Part of the problem is the eucalyptus trees—they're loaded with oil and they're everywhere. All you need is a lightning strike and poof! And, drought and high temperatures only exacerbate the situation. Maybe you heard about the Ash Wednesday Fires a few years back? Seventy five people died and hundreds of homes were destroyed."

Angela's eyes widened.

"But it doesn't worry me. We take precautions—keep the land clear and the water cannons full."

Steve described how Maurice's great-grandfather arrived from Ireland in the 1840s to begin a new life as a sheep hand, and through hard work and a healthy dose of Irish luck was able to start an operation of his own, eventually building it into a small empire.

"It was love at first sight, or as Maurice says a *coup de foudre*." Steve was describing the meeting between Maurice's parents in Switzerland. "They saw each other across a crowded room, and that was it. Kind of like how I felt when I first laid eyes on you." He reached over to stroke her cheek.

"Anyway, they got married and moved to the family's coffee plantation in Vietnam. That's where I ended up. It was a miracle, really. If I hadn't happened on the Villa Indochine when I did, I would have surely died."

Steve explained how disorienting it had been waking up there the next day. "I thought I was dreaming. After everything I'd been through, it was surreal to find myself in that amazing place. Villa Indochine stays with me even now, though I was there only a couple of days. Seeing it fade into the distance that day as the helicopter took off was just so sad. We all knew it wouldn't survive the war."

He cleared his throat. "I couldn't wait to get to a phone. I was so excited to hear your voice again. Because of my circumstances, I was able to call you the very day I arrived in Saigon. As soon as I heard your mother's voice I knew something was wrong. She was cool, guarded." He looked over at Angela. "Hardly the reception I expected after all I'd been through. And then she said you were married. I was devastated. After I hung up, I kept hearing her voice telling me how happy you were." He was silent for a few minutes.

"The next week, I was supposed to meet up with Maurice," he continued. "But as soon as I was discharged I high-tailed it to the red-light district. That's where he found me, passed out in a back alley. He took me back to my quarters and ordered me to sober up and meet him at the Continental Palace the next night. It was over dinner that night that he proposed I come to Australia. I jumped at it. I was a broken man without a future."

"I owe Maurice a huge debt," Steve continued. Not only did he save my life, but he saved my sanity. You see, the war lived on in my head long after I left Vietnam. For years, I suffered from Post-Traumatic Stress. Maurice saw me through that ugly period, sitting up with me many a night."

"My life in Australia has been immensely rewarding. Maurice and I have been working side by side all these years to bring Tullynally back, returning sheep production to decent levels and planting a vineyard. We now have 150 acres planted with our very own hybrid that brings together a local grape with heirloom specimens from the de Vigny chateau in Bordeaux."

Sensing her unspoken curiosity about the nature of his relationship with Maurice, Steve explained, "He's the finest man I know. Like a brother to me—the brother I never had. It's true, at one time he hoped our friendship would blossom into something more. But that's not my thing. Let's just say we have mutual respect for each other's choices. In any event, it became moot about ten years ago when Maurice met the painter Simon Burgess at one of his art openings. Ever heard of him?" Steve looked at her for any sign of recognition.

"No, I haven't," Angela answered.

"Well he's a big deal over there. His paintings sell for hundreds of thousands. Anyway, the attraction was immediate. I knew as soon as I saw them together it was the real thing. Love is love, you know? And so, Simon moved to Tullynally. He's a great guy and while our living arrangement may strike some as rather unconventional—this straight guy living with a gay couple, it's really just normal life.

"As for me, I had a steady girlfriend for several years. A schoolteacher." He paused, his eyes scanning the countryside. "Yes, Ellie's a great girl. I even asked her to marry me, but in the end, I couldn't go through with it."

Angela turned to look at Steve, holding him with her brown-eyed gaze trying to fathom the unspoken emotions past actions conveyed. Then, steering the conversation in a different direction, she said, "I remember your speaking of an aunt in Australia. Do you ever see her?"

"Every chance I get. She and her family live in Queensland, about 1,500 miles away. No distance at all in Australia. I get a bush pilot friend of mine to fly me up there. I tell Aunt Dee I've dropped by for her famous porridge cake—tickles her to death." He laughed and shook his head. "She's like a second mother. I don't know what I'd do without her. So that's my story—not exactly what you'd expect from a Millmont kid, right?"

By now, they were traveling through the rolling countryside of Virginia's Piedmont. Here, the redbud had bloomed creating a glowing purple aura that seemed to hover over the trees, interspersed, every now and then, with splashes of white dogwood. Looking at the Blue Ridge forming a shimmering indigo wall against a brilliant sky, Angela wondered if this ancient range might not resemble that ethereal landscape of Khe Sanh Steve had described.

At the next rest area they pulled over. Angela retrieved a blanket from the back seat to spread on the ground. "What an extraordinary journey," she marveled, unwrapping the sandwiches. "Did you ever find out what happened to the plantation in Vietnam?"

"Villa Indochine? That entire area was carpet-bombed shortly after we left. Remember the Tet Offensive? It's a painful subject for Maurice. It was his childhood home, and his parents are buried there; understandably, he wants to remember the villa as it was."

Angela thought of Steve waking in that remarkable place, to the sound of the ceiling fan—the wings of an angel, he'd told her—his first thought had been he was in heaven. How exultant to realize he was alive and in that serene place after so many horrible months of war and imprisonment. Such sweet relief to know the nightmare was behind him, and the dream he shared with Angela but a phone call away. She could see him there in the gardens at Villa Indochine, brimming with hope.

CHAPTER FOUR

*T*he inn was at the end of a winding lane. Angela saw with some discomfort the ante-bellum house resembled Belvoir, though on a much smaller scale, and was relieved to find they were lodged in "the Dovecote," a renovated chicken coop out back. Whoever had done it showed both remarkable restraint and great panache. The room contained only a simple, king-sized bed and a copper slipper bathtub positioned directly before an expanse of window. The prospect—a hay field rimmed in hedgerows with mountains beyond—was a natural painting that changed with the seasons.

"Wow," Steve said, walking over to the window. "That's some view."

The girl who had brought them over from the main house smiled proudly. "*The Washington Post* did a story on country inns last fall, and this room was featured."

"And the tub," Steve continued, "it's enormous."

The girl laughed. "We get a lot of honeymooners." Steve caught Angela's eye and grinned at her.

"Oh yes, and there's a shower, sink and toilet in there," she gestured at a door in the corner.

Later at dinner, Steve reached across to take Angela's hand, "I don't mean to rush you, baby, but all I want to do is get you back in that room." A shiver of desire licked at her loins and she squeezed his hand in return.

On the lighted path to the room, Steve couldn't keep his hands off her and when they crossed the threshold, she pushed him away. "We have to slow down." She smiled slyly and whispered, "I want to take a bath with you."

He chuckled, "You do, do you?"

"Yes, and maybe, if you're a good boy, you can have your way with me there." She inclined her head towards the tub.

The bath filled quickly and in no time Steve was in it. He had lit candles and the room was bathed in soft, golden light. Angela, emerging from the bathroom, walked slowly across the room. When she was beside the tub she began to unbutton her blouse letting the silk flutter off her shoulders to the ground. She then undid her skirt and let that fall as well. Stepping out of it, she stood there in her favorite café au lait lace bra and panties. She met Steve's eye and biting her lip fetchingly, trailed her fingers over her breasts. Steve let out a long whistle. At this, she reached around and undid the bra, releasing her breasts. She then wriggled out of her panties and stepped into the tub. She stood in front of Steve. He pulled her to him. She loved the feel of his rough hands on her skin. It was sexy thinking of him sweating under the hot Australian sun laboring in manly pursuits. He began to explore her intimate terrain with his tongue delighting in the sweet nectar there. Angela moaned softly and arching her back, threaded her fingers through Steve's hair, gently pressing him to her. She squatted slightly into him, focusing on the intense pleasure building from the determined probing of his tongue. The pleasure was almost too much. Suddenly, a tremor shook her body. She gasped at the force of the orgasm, which lifted her up onto her tiptoes. Once it passed through her, she slipped down into the bath water next to Steve. Such sweetness. It was unreal.

She could feel his erect member brush her abdomen and she reached over to caress it. It was his turn now.

Grasping his penis firmly in her hands, she gently worked it as she might clay, stretching and pulling it, feeling it swell and grow further under her touch, and begin to dance above the bath water. She had not realized until now how much she hungered to take a man's cock, this man, her Steve's into her mouth.

She had been a novice until this very moment. But with Steve it became second nature, a driving, unstoppable force. She lowered her face slowly until she was trailing her tongue lightly around the moist head, lapping the sticky nectar onto her tongue, relishing the intense animal physicality of her actions. She, then, guided his penis into her mouth and began sucking more robustly until she felt its caress the back of her throat. In and out it plunged, her tongue swirling over it like fire. He was crying out now in ecstasy. This is what I've missed and craved all these years, she thought, swept away with passion. At the very cusp of coming, he pulled away and turned her so she faced the other way.

She grasped the sides of the tub while he took her from behind. The water splashed about wildly, sloshing over the sides as he plunged into her. She was crying out with pleasure, reveling in the deepness of penetration. When they both came, it seemed to go on and on, a giant surge of electricity that coursed through them.

Afterwards, as they mopped up the water, Steve was contrite, seeing Angela's bruised knees. "I hadn't even noticed," she confessed with a slight smile.

Later, lying in each other's arms in the immense bed, Steve reached over and fingered the pearl ring on its chain around her neck. He shot her a look of recognition. "I can't believe you held on to it all these years." His voice caught.

"Of course, I did! It's the silver apple of the moon you gave me."

He laughed. "I have to tell you that poem's been following me around. Even in Vietnam, it found me. Can you believe it? There was a volume of Yeats's poetry at the villa."

She gasped.

"It blew my mind, I can tell you. Maurice let me have it."

He lightly fingered her hair. "Did I mention I spend a lot of time writing these days." He grew serious. "And I have you to thank for it. You're the one who really turned me on to good writing."

"Really? You're a writer?" She was delighted.

"Yeah, it all started a few years back. We needed some press releases for the vineyard. It turned out I was quite good at it, and it led to other jobs. I was lucky because the editor of *The Sydney Morning Herald* bought a weekend place just down the road from us. We all hit it off, and when Mark learned about my little sideline, he threw me a couple of bones. One thing led to another and I ended up landing a steady gig writing book reviews. It's great; I get paid to read. Mostly bestsellers. You know: spy thrillers, family sagas, that kind of stuff. I'm actually considering writing one myself. I think I've got the formula down: boy meets girl, boy loses girl, but love prevails in the end. Sound familiar?" he teased.

After Steve fell asleep, Angela lay awake for some time, her head nestled within the arc of his shoulder. The intervening years had melted away, and it was if they'd never been apart. Happy though she'd been with Henry at Belvoir, Angela realized that world could never match the fulfillment she felt with this man, her Steve. That this perfect union was destined to end in just a few short days, with each returning to their respective lives in Australia and Belvoir, was unbearable.

"Love prevails in the end," she heard his voice again and as she lay there, feeling his warm flesh press and recede against her as he breathed, a determination built within her: there was only one thing to do. She must leave Henry. It was *their* turn now. She relaxed into the sleeping form of her lover and began to picture a future together in that wide-open land he described.

She was awakened by the first light of dawn glinting through the window. She gently shook Steve awake and as the sun began to flood the room, together they imagined the future they would share. There would be long rides to check on sheep, lambing season in the spring, the vineyard to tend. It would be a new life, a partnership in every sense of the word. How she would welcome that.

"What will Maurice say?" she wondered.

"Maurice will adore you," Steve declared.

One major obstacle remained: how to tell Henry about Steve. She felt a wave of guilt. It was the first time she had really thought of Henry since he left for his business trip. Telling him must be done gently and with supreme compassion. After all, she owed Henry—dear Henry so much. Secondarily, there was Peyton and the challenge of helping her understand. But then, of course, Peyton would have Henry, and he, her. In fact, the ordeal would unquestionably strengthen the close bond they already shared. At the thought of this, she instinctively suppressed that familiar feeling: odd one out, yet again.

"But we don't have to think about any of that now," she said, her lips planting a trail of kisses along Steve's neck. "It's something I must face alone after you've left."

CHAPTER FIVE

*B*ack on the road after breakfast, they continued through open farmland before turning onto the Goshen Pass where the road ran along the Maury River, swollen with winter melt-off.

They arrived at the Homestead mid-afternoon and, leaving their bags on a trolley with the bellboy, walked around the grounds. Spotting a path leading into the woods, they followed it up the hill to where a view opened up revealing the great hotel nestled within a verdant bowl framed by forests. Unfurled like a shining new canvas, the prospect before her enlivened Angela's imagination. She felt a sudden swell of giddiness at the thought of exotic places that lay tantalizingly ahead of her.

"What a lovely place," she sighed leaning into Steve. A gentle breeze ruffled the scarf at her neck and played with her hair. She closed her eyes and lifting her face skyward felt the sun penetrate her being, delighting in its warmth and the promise of the moment. The sudden piercing cry of a bird of prey stirred her. "What a magnificent sight: a raptor on the wing," Steve said pointing at the dark crimped shape soaring in the distance on an updraft, motionless. "Look at the size of that wingspan. An eagle, I do believe." The sweeping view, the surrounding wildness, the sense of freedom evoked by the lone great bird was exhilarating.

With some reluctance, they retraced their steps, descending through the woods to emerge into the open with the towering hotel looming just ahead. Hand-in-hand, they crossed the lawn to the verandah and took seats in the row of rocking chairs, briefly entertained by the commotion of arriving guests.

Stopping at the front desk afterwards for her key, Angela was handed a message from Henry. He'd called to send love to "his two girls." Angela felt her chest tighten. She folded the paper and shoved it deep into her pocket.

She told Peyton she'd be in the Great Hall. Angela found a secluded corner and settled herself in a loveseat. She loved the old world charm of the place and looked around the room with admiration, taking in the pairs of columns framing gracious alcoves, the chintz-covered armchairs and sofas arranged in pleasant groupings, the light shimmering through pink clerestory windows. A waiter approached to take her order.

"A cup of chamomile would be lovely. But that's all for now. I'm expecting my daughter to join me any minute; you can bring us the full high tea then."

The hall began to fill with a cheerful crowd. She suddenly glimpsed Peyton among the throng and setting down her cup, hurried over to greet her daughter.

"Peyton, Darling," she exclaimed, arms outstretched. "I'm so glad to see you." They hugged and then, Angela stepped back to admire her.

"Don't you look chic, Sweetie-pie. I love your leather mini. And there's the bag we got in New York. It's so good-looking." Peyton grinned.

Angela linked her arm through Peyton's. "I've already picked out a spot for us."

"Oh, good. I'm dying for a cup of tea," Peyton exclaimed.

They took their seats. "So, how was the drive, Sweetie? Angela prompted as the waiter set a laden tray before them.

"Oh, fine," Peyton replied. "It only took a couple of hours." She bit into a scone oozing with jam and cream. "M-m-m. This is delish." She licked the cream off her lips. "Did you make the appointments? The herbal wrap we talked about? And the pedicure?"

"We're all set." Angela took a sip of tea. "So, how are things at school?" She replaced the cup in the saucer.

"Much better. I didn't tell you that Charlie and I broke up just after Daddy's party. But we're back together now. I was actually thinking of canceling this weekend—no offense." She looked at her mother to gauge her reaction. "I haven't seen him for awhile and really miss him. I told him I'd head over to Charlottesville first thing Sunday so we could spend the day together. Hope that's okay."

Angela was glad to hear Peyton was still seeing Charlie. She liked him. Peyton chattered on about her plans to spend Easter at his family's in Richmond.

Emboldened by the light and pleasant nature of the present exchange with her daughter, and thinking of Steve upstairs waiting in his room, Angela was seized with a wild thought. Why not reveal Steve's identity to Peyton right now? "Peyton, Darling," she began, "I need to talk to you about something." She faltered, seeing Peyton's expression turn serious.

And then she continued speaking quickly: "Long ago, way before you were born there was a boy I loved very much and planned to marry. He was from Millmont, just like me—my high school sweetheart, in fact." She took a swallow of tea.

"He joined the army and was sent to Vietnam." She paused. "Then one day, I received the terrible news he'd been killed." She couldn't help it, her eyes began to well up and her voice broke, "I was devastated," she said hoarsely.

Peyton looked troubled seeing her mother so distressed. "Are you okay Mom?" she asked, concerned.

Angela nodded while dabbing at her eyes. "I'm sorry, Sweetheart," she said. "This is very emotional for me." She took a sip of water. "About that time, I met Daddy. He was wonderful—so supportive and comforting during that very sad time. We became friends and, well, eventually we got married."

"Yeah, Mom," Peyton nodded, now getting impatient, "so what's your point?"

"Well, you know the rest, Honey. We've lived a very happy life since then—the three of us." She bowed her head so her chin rested fleetingly upon clasped hands. "Well, it turns out the man I loved all those years ago wasn't killed. It was a terrible mistake." She inhaled deeply.

"And, I saw him again last week after all these years." Peyton's face had turned sheet-white and she looked horrified. Angela had to steel herself to continue. "As much as I love your father—and I do, Peyton, I realize I'm still very much in love with this man."

"Mom, I don't understand. What are you saying? You're not going to tell me you're thinking of leaving Daddy, are you?" Peyton asked, her voice becoming shrill.

"It may sound selfish to you—and maybe it is," Angela declared, "but I'm thinking of Steve too. He's suffered greatly and been deprived of so much. He deserves a chance at happiness."

By carefully evading her daughter's stricken look, Angela was able to deliver her earthshaking announcement.

"Peyton, he's here at the Homestead. Upstairs." And then, heedless of restraint, the dangerous words began to slip out. "You see, my darling, this man, Steve Ryle, is your real father—I was pregnant when I married Henry." Peyton was staring at her with disbelief. She jumped to her feet abruptly cutting her mother off.

"Is that why you invited me here—to tell me you're having an affair behind Daddy's back? And that you plan to leave him?" she stammered. "To think you, my mother, had the nerve to bring this man here, a total stranger you say is my father, so-so I could give you my blessing? Is that what you want?" Her eyes flashed as she quickly gathered up her things.

"Well, I'm sorry to mess up your plans, Mother Dearest, but I've got news for you: the last thing I'd do is stay here with you and your...your gigolo." Peyton glared at her mother. "You disgust me," she hissed. Angela watched in horror as Peyton stormed off, pushing past the other guests as she hurried toward the exit. She was overcome with stinging regret. What a fool she was. She saw clearly now how predictable Peyton's reaction was. Not only did she adore Henry, she would naturally feel loyal to him, the man she thought was her father. And aside from everything else, Angela realized guiltily, it was a cruel bombshell to drop on her daughter so suddenly. What sort of mother was she anyhow? Worst of all, she'd turned Peyton against Steve before she'd even had a chance to meet him. With all her heart Angela wished she could turn back the clock and start over.

Upstairs, she burst into tears. "I've ruined everything," she sobbed running into Steve's arms.

"Oh no, Angie, I don't believe that." He said when she told him what happened. "Nobody said this was going to be easy, and maybe sooner is better than later. At least, I'm still here to help you deal with the fallout."

Angela didn't want to leave the room, but Steve insisted they go downstairs for dinner.

Woody Pettus, the Homestead's Maitre D' led them past the dance floor crowded with couples swaying to the sensuous rhythm of *The Girl from Ipanema.*

Once seated, Steve reached for Angela's hand. "Okay, Love?" he asked.

She shook her head. "I can't stop thinking about the huge mess I made. I should have taken things more slowly...What an enormous shock for Peyton."

Steve lifted her hand to his lips. "Babe, everything will be all right. Peyton's almost a grown woman, after all; she'll come around in the end."

Angela sighed. "I hope so. Oh, if you'd only seen her. She was so angry." She took a sip of wine.

"Angie, listen to me. We'll work through this. It's only right that Peyton know the truth." His eyes searched hers. "It's her history, her reality. Eventually, she'll see that. "Look, we've weathered 20 years apart," Steve continued. "What's a few more months at this point?"

Angela nodded. "You're right. I'm just so sorry I botched things up— that you didn't have a chance to meet." She sighed. "And you know she'll call Henry." She felt terrible imagining this. Of course, she should be the one to break the news to her husband. He deserved that much.

Sitting here under the glint of crystal chandeliers, surrounded by couples in sleek evening attire, soothed by the band's sprightly cadences, it was inevitable that her mind would cast back to the birthday party where everything began; where the casual utterance of a name had caused her heart to be ripped open after so many years. With a pang, she recalled the look of delight on Henry's face as his beloved daughter approached with his cake. She had ruined things not only for Peyton, but for Henry, too. Her eyes met Steve's. Here was the sanctuary, the elixir of forgetfulness she needed. She could lose herself in those eyes.

Steve reached over and held Angela's hand. "I'm sorry it didn't go the way we hoped, Sweetheart."

They ordered dinner and as they ate Steve succeeded in shifting the conversation away from Peyton. The waiter arrived with dessert, placing the Homestead's signature "gold brick" before them. "So, how about a spin after this?" Steve's eyes twinkled. "It'll cheer you up."

A waltz had begun to play. Steve guided a reluctant Angela to the dance floor and began twirling her beneath the elegant domed ceiling. It was bliss being in the arms of the man she loved in this beautiful place. She felt cheered. She believed what he said. Everything would be all right. Her head resting on his shoulder as they danced, feeling the brush of his rough beard against her face, the caress of his hair, and encased within his scrubbed manly scent, her anxieties began to wane replaced by a giddiness at what lay ahead. Brightening, she leaned into him, pressing a kiss on his neck. *The End Makes All*, she murmured to herself.

They had just returned to their table when Woody came rushing up. "Mrs. Worthington?" he asked. Angela looked at him expectantly.

"I have an urgent message for you. I'm terribly sorry. There's been some kind of accident. You're to call home immediately."

CHAPTER SIX

*I*t was after midnight when they pulled up to the University of Virginia Hospital. Angela jumped out of the car and ran into the Emergency Room. "I need to find my daughter," she sobbed to the receptionist. "Peyton Worthington? She was in a car accident."

The woman handed her a clipboard. "If I could ask you to fill this out. I'll let them know you're here. In the meantime, you can take a seat." She gestured toward the waiting area.

"No. You don't understand," Angela said pushing the clipboard away. Her voice had risen to an hysterical pitch, "my daughter's been in a car crash. I'm told it's serious. I have to see her now."

"Okay, let me page Dr. Tobin."

Steve hurried though the glass doors to join her. "How is she? Have you heard anything?" Angela shook her head, her eyes brimming with tears.

"No. The doctor was just paged. Oh, Steve, it's all my fault," she wailed.

Clutching each other in the fluorescent glare, Steve's eyes rested on the wall clock, watching the second hand lurch forward from one tick to the next, feeling helpless and afraid. Finally, a man in surgical scrubs pushed through the double doors. "Mr. and Mrs. Worthington, I presume?" He extended his hand. "Dr. Tobin," he said.

"My daughter—is she going to be all right?" Angela asked.

The doctor herded them to a corner of the waiting area. "Your daughter's very lucky to be alive. Suffice it to say, if she hadn't been wearing a seat belt, she wouldn't be. As it is, she suffered a severe head injury and is in a coma. It's premature for me to say how long this will continue. With head injuries, the first 24 hours are crucial. Patients who exhibit signs of returning consciousness within this period stand a good chance of making a complete recovery.

"On the plus side, your daughter's CT scans look good. She will most likely have little, or no, recall of the accident or the events leading up to it—a blessing.

"As I said, it was very lucky your daughter was wearing her seat belt. But seat belts are not perfect and, in her case, on impact her seat belt restrained her with such force it caused rather significant internal injuries and substantial bleeding." He paused to take off his glasses and rub his eyes. "As to the head injury, the scans indicate a fracture along the western hemisphere. There's significant swelling so a shunt's been inserted to alleviate pressure on the brain.

"Normally in a case such as this where a minor is involved, we wait for parental permission before we undertake any invasive procedures, but the gravity of your daughter's condition necessitated an immediate blood transfusion, and indeed our most pressing concern right now is that she needs another one. As her parents, I'm sure you're aware individuals with O- blood can only receive O-." He looked from Steve to Angela. "At this point, we have depleted our supply. We have calls in to various blood banks and are waiting to hear back. As time is of the essence, if either of you are O-, it would be a Godsend."

Angela regarded the doctor with frightened eyes and shaking her head, whispered. "I have A blood…"

"O-? That's my blood type." Steve felt their eyes on him.

"Why, of course, you're the father." Dr. Tobin looked relieved.

While Steve was having his blood taken, Angela sat with Peyton, her daughter's limp hand clasped within her own. Her cheeks were wet with tears at the sight of her injured girl tethered to IV tubes, her head encased in bandages; she could find no way to circumvent the truth: it was she who had caused the accident. Carried away by her love for Steve and her zealousness, she'd thrown caution to the wind and her daughter had nearly died as a result.

Once Peyton received the blood transfusion, Angela called home. "Belvoir," Margaret answered on the first ring, her voice strained.

"It's me. Oh, don't cry, Margaret. We need to stay strong for Peyton." She paused to quell the tremor in her voice. "Any word from Mr. Worthington?"

She hung up the phone, bewildered. "Damn him!" In those first desperate moments at the Homestead, she had tried to reach Henry at the Drake only to learn he wasn't registered there. And hadn't been. Where was he? He'd told her that's where he'd be. How uncharacteristic of him not to let her know his plans had changed. But, she couldn't dwell on that now. She seated herself in the armchair in Peyton's room.

Unwinding the skein of Peyton's life, she considered once more how Peyton was the reason things had turned out the way they had. For if Angela hadn't been pregnant, she wouldn't have married Henry and when Steve was found alive she would have been free. And just as he'd said, *they'd have a bunch of kids, a nice big house* and live happily ever after. But Peyton's existence was the determining factor that had changed the course of her life. She shuddered thinking how in a flash it could all have been for naught.

According to the police report, fog had shrouded the road obscuring the wide turn at the crest of the mountain where Peyton lost control of her car. Skid marks told the story. She'd been driving too fast and finding her car heading off the road, she had overcompensated. The speeding car veered out of control and slammed into the concrete median with such force, it flipped over and slid 100 feet before coming to rest in a ditch. A truck driver radioed in the accident on his CB, and paramedics arrived at the scene within minutes to transport Peyton to the hospital.

The following morning, Dr. Tobin was cautiously optimistic. Peyton's condition seemed to be improving. Her blood pressure was normal, and she showed signs of returning consciousness. "Very encouraging. A testament to the human body's ability to heal," he said. Angela covered her face with her hands.

His voice softened, "Your daughter's stable now; you and your husband should get some rest. There's a Howard Johnson's just around the corner."

After the many hours spent in the hospital, the bright sunshine was disorienting. Drained from their ordeal, Angela and Steve walked to the hotel in silence. Once in the room, Steve took a shower while Angela called to give Margaret the good news. The housekeeper burst into tears when she heard. "You see, Margaret? Our prayers have been answered."

When asked if Henry had called, "No, not as yet," was Margaret's reply.

Angela sighed impatiently, thinking: this is unbelievable! "Okay, when he does call, tell him to get back to me right away, either at the hospital or at my room at the Howard Johnson's—that's where I am now." She was uneasy. To have completely lost track of Henry, and at a time when she needed him—when Peyton needed him—so desperately, was alarming. Something like this had never happened before. He'd left for Chicago on Monday. Where had he been during the intervening days?

Her mind began to race. Had she caught her husband in some kind of deception? "Darling, don't bother to try and reach me," he'd said. "I'll be hard to track down—in meetings the whole time. Leave it up to me to stay in touch." But, why, would he lie to her? What was he hiding?

As she put the puzzle pieces of recollection together, it slowly dawned on her. Henry was having an affair. This explained all the sorties to Chicago under the pretense of business. Were all those board meetings fabricated to disguise trysts with a mystery lover? That Henry had been unfaithful was wounding. But, her indignation began to subside as she realized the positive implications. Now, she had the perfect justification for her own actions.

Later that afternoon when she and Steve left the hospital, they felt as if an enormous weight had been lifted off their shoulders. Secure in the knowledge Peyton was out of danger, they strolled arm-in-arm past crowds of university students, fresh-faced boys with backpacks slung over their shoulders and pretty coeds in tight shirts and jeans sauntering along University Avenue.

Drawn to the sloping lawn framed by majestic magnolias, they crossed the street, passing fruit trees stippled with tight bunches of blossoms, and large sycamores hung with mottled bark, the color and thickness of elephant hide. They paused on the terrace encircling Thomas Jefferson's august Rotunda. Here, leaning on the balustrade, they peered into the cloister-like space below carpeted in myrtle. It was like being in a tree house, they thought, as they lingered in the twilight serenaded by a white throat. From here, they could see the hint of pavilion gardens. Standing in the quiet evening, suspended in time for a spell, they were captivated by the magic of the place, conscious on some level of the lasting import this memory would hold for them.

Forever after, Angela would remember that night in Charlottesville as a sort of benchmark of bittersweet perfection against which she would note the passage of the ensuing years.

Angela had been so frightened for Peyton, hardly able to take a breath, her body clenched in anxiety. Now, back in the hotel room, that fear turned to passion and they were soon naked. Trembling with desire, she reached for Steve, seized with the desire to grab hold of life in its most basic form. Her mouth was on his, kissing him hungrily. He responded with equal ardor, disentangling himself momentarily to switch off the lights, but Angela brushed his hand away. Leading him to the bed, she pushed him onto it, climbing on top to straddle him. She leaned down to nuzzle his neck, running her tongue along his skin. It tasted salty and she detected a musky note that excited her. She nipped him and he moaned, grabbing her hips and guiding her body on to his. Gasping softly, as he entered her, she gently gyrated to accommodate him. She'd been right to leave the lights on. It was thrilling watching pleasure flood his face. Her heart was bursting with love for him. "I love you Steve!" she cried. He stopped for a minute to whisper, "I love you too," pulling her down to kiss. They made love slowly and deliberately, their eyes locked, their bodies one. The sky was just beginning to lighten when they finally broke apart and slept.

CHAPTER SEVEN

"Good news!" the nurse greeted Angela the next morning when she stepped off the elevator. "Your daughter's been quite active; it looks like she may regain consciousness any time now. Oh, and by the way, your husband called, he'll be arriving later today."

Steve and Angela hurried to Peyton's room where they found Charlie Tazewell at her bedside. Momentarily caught off guard, Angela introduced Steve hastily as an old family friend.

With Henry's arrival now a reality, Angela thought about how she'd broach the subject of Steve with him. It was clear Peyton's recovery was destined to be a long one and it would take some time to extricate herself from her life in America and join Steve. However, she knew she had to act and make a clean breast of it. She could not live with deception, or succumb to playacting. Of course, she'd wait until after he saw Peyton. By then Steve would be in Washington where Angela planned to break away and join him prior to his departure for Australia. By then everything would be set.

Before he left, Steve went in to Peyton's room. He was still coming to grips with the fact this young woman was his daughter. Seeing beyond her bandages, he imagined her sparkling eyes, the same cornflower blue as his own, Angela said. He reached over to grasp his daughter's hand; her fingers were warm. She stirred and turned her face toward him. Her eyes fluttered open. He couldn't believe it. She blinked several times, then, met his gaze. Yes, he could see they were his. He held his breath as she slowly smiled at him and squeezed his hand. The connection he felt to her in that instant was thrilling, primal. Her eyes closed and fingers relaxed. He sat there for several minutes enchanted. Arriving in the room, Angela hesitated, moved by the sight of father and daughter.

"She opened her eyes and smiled at me as if to tell me she'll be okay," he whispered, his eyes shining. "All I could think of was my mother. How on her deathbed she said she was my *anamchara*. Well, Ma made her presence known this afternoon," he said quietly, eyes shifting to the movement of a cloud high in the sky outside the window. "I realize now I'm Peyton's *anamchara*." He turned back to his daughter, and bent to kiss her. "Good-bye, my dear child," he said softly.

Later that afternoon when Angela returned after dropping Steve at the train station, she took a seat in Peyton's room. If she could get beyond today, settle matters with Henry, she was convinced all would be well. Her new life, her true life, could begin. Gazing through the window at the hills, her thoughts were interrupted suddenly by Peyton's voice, child-like, tentative, "Ma-ma?" Angela turned to see her daughter, eyes wide open.

"Oh, my baby girl! Thank God, I've been so worried," she cried.

Peyton's voice was dreamy, her words came slowly. "I was sleeping just now when this strange man came to me and told me it was time to wake up—that I'd slept long enough. He seemed so familiar and so kind—and beautiful. Like an angel."

So, she'd seen him after all.

The door flung open and in rushed Henry. He ran to the bed. "My darling girl," he cried, his voice breaking. As he leaned over his daughter, Angela was struck by his pasty complexion and thinning hair.

Angela set off for Washington two days later. She found a parking space on the Mall and hurried along the gravel walkway. In the distance she could see the papery blossoms of the cherry trees along the tidal basin set off by the glint of dimpling water.

Then, there it was: imposing, moving, sacred: the monument that tabulated the true cost of the Vietnam War. On this sparkling April morning, it was crowded with families and veterans hovering over the expanse of polished granite etched with so many names. They shuffled past, hands reaching out every so often to run fingers along incised letters. Here and there, people held each other in shared grief.

It was Steve who spotted Angela first. He watched her for several minutes. Her sudden appearance was a salve—like the sun breaking through clouds. When he reached her side, he took her hands and kissed her lips. "My Angela," he said simply. "My glimmering girl." Then, he led her to the wall.

"I've found them all—every one of them." He smiled sadly. "I'm glad you're here with me," he said putting his arm around her. "Come on, I want you to meet someone." She shot him a puzzled look.

He guided her to the wall. "Angela, I want to introduce you to my friend, Martin Seamus O'Connor." His voice broke. She lifted her hand and ran her fingers along the grooves that formed Marty's name, feeling the cool stone beneath her fingertips. She noted her reflection in the polished surface, the union of past and present, living and dead. She remembered the name from Steve's letters, even after all these years. She looked at Steve. His cheeks shone with tears. She pulled him to her.

They drove to National Airport in silence. The specter of war, that great cruel force that had divided them, a weighty presence still. Angela looked out the window, concentrating on the eternity of the moment. Once Steve checked in, they found a quiet corner in which to wait. Angela felt a chill, recalling that other parting so long ago. "So, Angie, you haven't told me. How did it go with Henry?" Angela shook her head mutely.

He saw he must provide the words. "Not so great, I guess. Well, you've just got to be strong." He squeezed her hand and smiled.

"Oh, Steve, Steve, I can't come with you," Angela blurted out.

"I know, I know, Sweetheart, but don't be discouraged—a few months, even a year, that's no time at all after waiting twenty. Particularly, when we never even dreamed we'd be together again."

"No, Steve," she stuttered. "You don't understand. I didn't tell Henry."

Stunned, he looked at her. "What do you mean, you didn't tell him?" Angela was silent, her hands clasped so tightly together, her knuckles were white.

She took a deep breath. "Oh, Steve, Steve, my darling," she said softly. "I just learned Henry's very ill."

"I'm sorry to hear that, Angie," he said.

She spoke slowly, a tremor in her voice. "He has cancer—leukemia. He's been keeping it from me."" She buried her face in her hands. Steve put his arm around her, feeling her body shaking against his. "I can't abandon Henry now, not when he's so sick," she finally managed to say.

"Look Angela, I lost you once, I'm not going to lose you again," he declared.

She looked up at him, her eyes welling up, "Steve, you are my love— my life. This is not about you, about *us*." She searched his eyes before continuing. "Every fiber of my being aches to go with you. You know that. But what kind of person would I be if I did such a thing? How could I live with myself?"

She grabbed his arm. "I want to give you the best of me, not the worst. Leaving Henry now would be unconscionable. If I did such a thing, I fear it would corrupt me—it would corrupt us."

"So what's his prognosis?" demanded Steve.

"It's hard to say with leukemia. A lot depends on the individual, his immune system, his will to live." She sighed heavily. "Some patients survive a few months, some, much longer." She looked at Steve watching her words sink in.

"He's had it now for three years and has kept it to himself all that time—not wanting to worry me." She brushed away a tear. "You see, how decent he is."

"Yeah, well, what about me?" Steve flared. "God damn it, Angela, I've been denied so much: You, a daughter I didn't know about." He jumped to his feet. "When is it my turn?"

"You, of all people, must realize how hard this is for me," she exclaimed, reaching for his hand. "My heart is breaking." Her voice caught, and she paused to collect herself. "I feel such sadness about what happened. I don't know if I can ever speak to my mother again." She stifled a sob.

"It's so terribly unfair you're not a part of Peyton's life, nor she yours. But I don't know how to fix that right now. It's Peyton who's at the root of my decision. Can you imagine how she'd take my leaving when Henry has cancer? You know where last week's indiscretion of mine led... a car wreck that nearly killed her. Oh, Steve, *you* don't want us to take that risk again and jeopardize Peyton's—our child's wellbeing." She looked at him earnestly.

"Of course I yearn for the day when she can learn the truth about you—her wonderful father. The man I love." There was a tremor in her voice.

"Maybe I'm wrong," she continued quietly. "But I just don't see any other way—at least for now. When I consider all the circumstances, I realize I simply can't..." she paused mid-sentence as her eyes met Steve's. Then, taking a deep breath, she said quietly, "I won't leave Henry, not when his condition is so grave."

"Even if it means losing me?"

She looked at him dully. As Steve turned away, a little girl ran past them squealing, "Daddy, Daddy," into the arms of a soldier. His eyes briefly settled on an elderly couple across the way chatting companionably as they passed a chocolate bar between them. Angela and Steve's world might be collapsing, but the spectacle of everyday life continued around them.

His flight was announced. They had only a few minutes left. Finally, Steve reached for Angela's hand and held it tightly. When he next spoke, his voice was gentle.

"Right, well, I guess there's nothing more to say." Decorously, he lifted her hand to his lips, then, straightened abruptly, hoisting his rucksack over his shoulder.

"As I see it, Angela, there was a window of opportunity for us, but that window is closing now." He took a deep breath and slowly turned away.

Standing by the plate glass window, Angela rested her forehead against it, the tears spilling freely now. How could she let him go a second time? She watched as her lover emerged from the building onto the tarmac below. It was a scant run of images: his form vivid in the afternoon light, hesitating before crossing the pavement, the fleeting look he cast in her direction and that final view of him, ascending the stairs and disappearing into the plane.

EPILOGUE

Belvoir, 1997

From her window Angela could tell the reception was winding down. The band had played the last song. But the party atmosphere continued as the sound of voices, laughter and the clink of glasses reached her from the garden.

She was bathed in a warm afterglow as she reflected on the day's events. How pleased and proud Henry would have been. It was his kind of occasion, and it had gone off without a hitch. True, there had been a couple of tense moments: it was pouring rain when they woke up and the minister's car wouldn't start, but the sun came out and the best man volunteered to collect Reverend Farley. Even the ground had magically absorbed all the moisture so they could continue with the original plan of having the ceremony on the south lawn.

Peyton had made a beautiful bride, escorted down the aisle by her Uncle Tony to *The Prince of Denmark* trumpet voluntary. Angela dabbed away tears as she watched her precious girl marry her true love. Afterwards, everyone moved to the walled garden where the wedding party formed a receiving line and drinks were served.

Angela was on cloud nine greeting the guests. She kept glancing over at her daughter. So pretty! So happy! She couldn't get enough of her.

Now, looking back on the day, Angela reveled in so many wonderful images of Peyton, from picture-perfect bride to giddy newlywed, dancing barefoot with her handsome groom, her veil discarded, flowers in her hair.

Angela extended her arm across the bed to caress the empty space beside her as if to reach out to Henry to share this happy day. Their daughter was launched: a married woman with her own life to lead.

Lying there, Angela began to think about what she hadn't allowed herself to contemplate all during these last hectic days leading up to Peyton's wedding. Though she'd pushed it to a back corner, it had been in her mind all along, a tingling elation. The book. He'd sent the book. Yes, he'd sent it to Peyton, but he'd meant it for her.

She was filled with a sudden clarity. Tossing off the covers, she went to the window. She threw it open and leaned out. Lights twinkled from the tent and groups of stragglers lingered on the terrace below. The night air, redolent with the fragrance of lilacs from the bushes beneath her window, caressed her face.

"I must go to him!" she cried. And, then, in a spontaneous gesture she threw her arms outward toward the invisible thread connecting them. And from within her very core came the sweet certainty that Steve was waiting for her.

THE END

ACKNOWLEDGEMENTS

This book would not have been possible without the tireless efforts of Editors par excellence, Susan Langenkamp and Ted Corcoran, as well as that of the cadre of supportive friends who read the manuscript during various points of its execution: Sharon McSweeney, Margaret Hivnor, Melissa Knox-Raab, Sandra Mirkil, Sara Robinson, Colonel Richard G. Rounseville, Matilde Ventura Busana, Bill Pearson, Stephen Smith, Terri Beavers, and Amanda Stiff who re-lit the fire. Thanks also are due to Alida and Alexander Blundon for their help with the cover. Last, but certainly not least, abundant gratitude is extended to beloved late parents, who though departed, remain unfailing anamchairde to this day.

Made in the USA
San Bernardino, CA
04 June 2014